# Imprison the Sky

BOOKS BY A. C. GAUGHEN

*Scarlet*
*Lady Thief*
*Lion Heart*

———

*Reign the Earth*
*Imprison the Sky*

# Imprison the Sky

"Gaughen once again delivers vivid, complex characters, immersive worldbuilding, and a thrilling plot." —*Booklist*

"Gaughen weaves big concepts into the action-filled story. . . . Powerful young women who have hope and agency to change the world: What could be more timely?" —*Kirkus Reviews*

"Aspasia is a bold, complex heroine. . . . Readers new to the series will immediately seek out the previous volume." —*BCCB*

# Reign the Earth

"With a clever, strong-willed heroine, a downright terrifying villain, and complex relationships that leap off the page, *Reign the Earth* is the feminist fantasy I didn't know I needed." —**Erin Bowman**, author of *Vengeance Road*

★ "Gaughen delivers an emotionally resonant tale full of magic so powerful it can move the earth; rich writing and worldbuilding will appeal to readers seeking complex characters, palace intrigue, and weighty questions of power and loyalty." —*Publishers Weekly*, starred review

"A manifesto of female strength. . . . The readers who flock to this will find more than they expected, and Shalia's strength will give them something truly worth swooning over." —*Kirkus Reviews*

"A formidable heroine. . . . Fans of Chokshi's *The Star-Touched Queen* will appreciate Shalia's confidence, sense of agency, and ultimate defiance." —*BCCB*

# SCARLET

★ "A rip-roaring tale. . . . This has plenty for both the romantic
and the adventure lover. An affecting take on
an old story." —*Booklist*, starred review

"Gaughen creates a believable character in Scarlet,
a fierce but feeling heroine surviving in an inequitable
and unruly society." —*Publishers Weekly*

# LADY THIEF

"Filled with action, suspense, and a healthy dash of
passionate but controlled romance." —*SLJ*

"This series is not for the faint of heart. . . . Riveting." —*VOYA*

# LION HEART

"An even mix of heart-fluttering love scenes and gritty fight
sequences. Follow[s] in the tradition of Tamora Pierce's stories
of feisty, kickass heroines." —*Kirkus Reviews*

"Scarlet once again emerges as a complex, well-developed
protagonist. . . . A must-read series conclusion." —*SLJ*

# Imprison the Sky

## the elementae

## A. C. GAUGHEN

BLOOMSBURY
NEW YORK  LONDON  OXFORD  NEW DELHI  SYDNEY

BLOOMSBURY YA
Bloomsbury Publishing Inc., part of Bloomsbury Publishing Plc
1385 Broadway, New York, NY 10018

BLOOMSBURY and the Diana logo are trademarks of Bloomsbury Publishing Plc

First published in the United States of America in January 2019
by Bloomsbury YA
Paperback edition published in January 2020

Bloomsbury books may be purchased for business or promotional use. For information on
bulk purchases please contact Macmillan Corporate and Premium Sales Department at
specialmarkets@macmillan.com

ISBN 978-1-68119-116-4 (paperback)

The Library of Congress has cataloged the hardcover edition as follows:
Names: Gaughen, A. C., author.
Title: Imprison the sky / by A. C. Gaughen.
Description: New York : Bloomsbury, 2019. | Sequel to: Reign the earth.
Summary: Aspasia, eighteen, an Elementae who controls air, gets caught in
a battle between Cyrus, who forces her to capture slaves for market, and
a queen whose husband experiments on Elementae.
Identifiers: LCCN 2018010848 (print) • LCCN 2018018255 (e-book)
ISBN 978-1-68119-114-0 (hardcover) • ISBN 978-1-68119-115-7 (e-book)
Subjects: | CYAC: Fantasy. | Seafaring life—Fiction. | Slavery—Fiction. | Four elements
(philosophy)—Fiction. | Ability—Fiction.
Classification: LCC PZ7.G23176 Imp 2019 (print) | LCC PZ7.G23176 (e-book) |
DDC [Fic]—dc23
LC record available at https://lccn.loc.gov/2018010848

Book design by Kimi Weart
Typeset by Westchester Publishing Services
Printed and bound in the U.S.A. by Berryville Graphics Inc., Berryville, Virginia
2 4 6 8 10 9 7 5 3 1

All papers used by Bloomsbury Publishing Plc are natural, recyclable products made from
wood grown in well-managed forests. The manufacturing processes conform to the
environmental regulations of the country of origin.

To find out more about our authors and books visit www.bloomsbury.com
and sign up for our newsletters.

For my sister, Alisa,

You are not only one of the most strong, thoughtful, funny, and kind women I know, you're also so incredibly generous with your heart—I am so honored and grateful that I get to call you family. I love you.

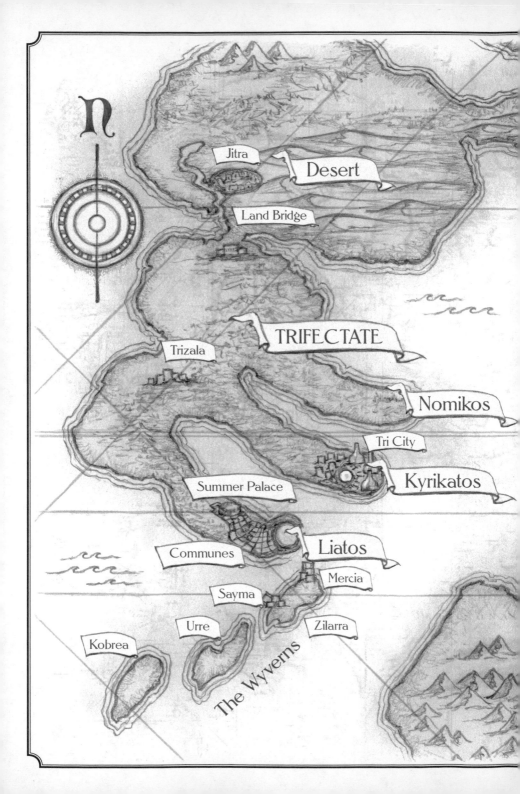

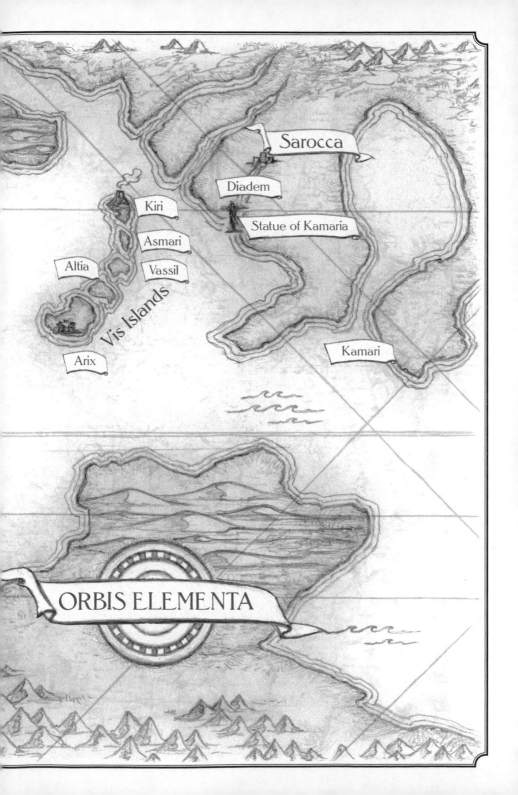

# A Black Circle

Pirates," I called. "Aim for the skies."

Behind me, Ori and Bast knew what that meant, and a heavy black sailcloth fell over the name *Ancora* carved into my stern. I reached out with my power, securing the lines on the bottom of the cloth to cleats on the side.

"Anika," I called.

"Right here, Captain," she said. She was ten and came up to my shoulder, but she was the only other air power I had on board, and I needed her help.

"Up," I told Anika.

She took a deep breath and held out her palms, and I put mine under them. I could feel the threads that united everything in the natural world, connecting my power to hers, to water, to earth, to fire. The threads trembled for me, waiting for a command from their captain the way everything else did.

I pushed, and the threads unfurled, splitting and multiplying to fasten to Anika's power and splice ours together. This wasn't something she could do on her own yet. Maybe ever.

The deck lurched, the bow lifting upward like we were cresting a tall wave. But we never came down, my power and Anika's pushing up on the sails, sliding under the hull, using the threads of the natural world to raise the ship up out of the water. I heard the telltale sound of water streaming off us as we left the ocean altogether.

*Flying.* The relentless tattoo of my heartbeat accelerated in triumph as we sailed higher, propelled by nothing but the will of two small girls, bending the natural world to our command.

Anika trembled with concentration, but the thrill of power rushed through my veins, feeding me, egging me on. *They'll be there*, I told myself. *This time, they'll be there.*

I wasn't sure if my brother and sister would be considered children still—Gryphon would be sixteen, and Pera would be fourteen. But it was a stone I hadn't turned yet, and that, more than anything, was why I was a damn fool for returning to Liatos.

"They nearly caught us last time," Navya reminded me, low in my ear.

"We're far enough away from the harbor," I countered. We were down the southern coast of Liatos, a few miles from the communes and the Oculus where I had almost lost a crewmate and the whole damn ship last time we were here.

"We're not losing anyone else," she said, and I wasn't sure if it was a promise or a question. I looked over at Ori, but he had been the first to vote for this plan. No one knew who I was searching for here, but we all knew Ori was hoping to find his twin sister, Dara, alive and well.

I couldn't imagine that an enemy Elementa had lasted very long in the hands of the Trifectate.

◆

Last time, it had been the moon that had given us away. We had already waited two days for a darker night, lurking outside the harbor where we couldn't be seen, but our supplies wouldn't have held out. We had to risk it or return to Cyrus empty handed, and we lost Dara and nearly our lives for that mistake.

Tonight, the sky was dark and clouded, the moon only a sliver behind the clouds, a strong easterly wind filling our sails. Perfect for my purposes.

The communes here sat higher up on the cliff, so there were no guards or protection from me. Guiding my ship, which had stopped dripping water, I went first for the enclosure that I'd heard was full of children.

They never used to guard their slaves at night, but I expected that might have changed after our last engagement, and I had to be prepared. I tightened my belt, heavy with crossbow bolts and a few knives. I looked at Bast, armed with several knives and a large sword on his hip.

"See you in the skies, Aspasia," Bast told me with a grin.

"See you in the skies," I responded. "Steady," I told Anika. She took a deep breath, and I eased my power away from hers. The ship trembled in the air but drew to a halt, the wood creaking as we held still, the air curling in circles around the hull to hold it aloft as the sails luffed gently without the forward propulsion.

I nodded to Bast, grabbed a long line, and jumped off the edge of the ship with him.

The air flew through my clothing and the long, heavy ropes of my hair as we fell. I was invincible, master of the sky and air, and none could dare defy me, hurt me, enslave me.

I looked over at Bast as I slowed our descent, and his smile was vicious and eager. Slaves no longer, here we became the masters.

We landed softly in one of the gray stone walled communes, each a large, dismal cell all its own, leaving the lines hanging behind us. No one knew we were here yet. I signaled Bast to stop, and I sent a gentle puff of air like an exhalation searching out through the enclosure, feeling along the threads into the dark building. There were long lines of beds with small bodies in them, and at the end of the room, a man sat upright, dozing but not fully asleep. Probably a guard.

I tested objects with my power—something round and hard on the floor was either a stone or a heavy pot, and I lifted it, sending it slamming into the guard's face. It landed and he fell as I walked into the room.

Pain would always precede my entrance, and it followed too in my wake, my ever-faithful shadow.

A few of the children heard the noise, waking but staying in their beds, staring at me, not knowing if this shape in the darkness was devil or savior.

I could take six. It was an impossible task, every time, and Bast made some of my decisions for me by plucking two children close to the door. Quickly, I stalked the length of the room, hoping, as always, that I'd see some kind of recognition in someone's face.

The truth was, I had no idea if I'd recognize my siblings if I ever found them. So I searched the only other way I knew how, and sent my power rushing through the room, feeling for the spark that would indicate another Elementa.

There wasn't any, and my heart sank, so I called, "We can take four more. Who's coming with us?"

There was a moment where no one moved. Then, like they agreed on it, several leaped from their beds. A boy pleaded with another boy not to leave, but he shook out of the other's grasp and came with me. Outside, the crew lowered the rowboat by ropes, and we stuffed it full of children. Six, but there was one more trying to climb in, so I took seven.

I pushed the boat up until my crew felt it, and then they hauled it by the lines, lifting the boat full of fear-faced children into the sky. Bast and I took the loose hanging lines, and I pointed toward the port wall.

Left wall. I hated that even the words changed when I was on land.

Bast took a rope and wound the line around his wrist, and I called the air to twine one around me as well. We started running at the wall, and I leveraged the air and the tension of the rope to swing us up and over, using the momentum to launch us into the next enclosure.

Bast and I landed quietly, letting go of the lines. He drew his sword, and I pushed back my leathers to expose the row of crossbow bolts at my waist.

I didn't need the bow. I was the bow.

There were two buildings in this larger enclosure, and my heart pounded with the unknown. We had up to six slots for men, and this was by far the more difficult part. "Quick and quiet," I reminded Bast in a whisper.

He licked his lips. "This one first?" he said, pointing his knife at the first building.

I sent my power searching out ahead of us, using where the air broke to sense walls, bars, beds, sleeping bodies that would feel a breeze on their faces. "Both are full of locked cages. No guards, but I imagine they're close."

He cast his watchful eyes around the enclosure. "Lead the way."

We moved forward quickly, going into the first building. Unlike when we raided the enclosures with the children, we had no expectations that these men would come easily.

Navya and Ori came in behind us, which meant that the rowboat was lowered down and ready to be filled. I searched with my eyes and power along the walls, finding a large ring of keys. As soon as the keys shivered in my hand, the men inside began to take notice.

"Who are you?"

"Someone's here!"

"We're going to be free!"

"You're not going to be free," I snarled. "But you will be taken out of here, if I like the look of you."

I stalked down the center aisle, flipping through the keys. I'd been through the communes enough to know roughly the kind of key that would open the doors, and I narrowed it down to three. Navya, Bast, and Ori flanked me as I found the first person I'd take—he was a large, scarred man who would fetch a fortune at the market.

"Open that door, little girl," he growled to me. "And see what's waiting if you think you can enslave me."

The lock clicked on the second key, and he charged the door as I stepped clear, pulling the keys away. I used my power to trip him, and it was all Bast and Ori needed to tie him with rope and blindfold him as Navya leaped over him to the next cell with me.

We had two more slaves secured when I heard an oily voice

from deeper in the building. "Might I volunteer? I could use a change of scenery."

With a chuckle, I went to the voice to find a lanky man leaning against his cell door. "A change of scenery," I repeated.

"Mm," he agreed. "The Trifectate is so dull this time of year."

His voice had a lilt to it that I couldn't quite place. "Very well," I said. "I'm still tying you up."

"Promises," he murmured. But when I opened the door, he turned around and presented his hands behind his back so we could bind him.

I had just finished tying a blindfold on him when I heard a brutal roar from outside. "Hells," I growled, dragging the volunteer with me as I ran to the doorway.

"Handled," Bast snapped, nodding to a slave who was slumped over in his seat.

Then an alarm bell started ringing hard and loud. "Faster!" I yelled at my crew.

Ori and Navya dashed back into the cells, and I looked around for the door to this enclosure. I found it, shoving the air against it hard to block it.

The ship above us jerked, and I could feel Anika's power waning.

"Bast—" I started, and he ran forward, jamming a knife into the ground in front of the door as bodies heaved against it.

"Hurry," I told him, and he nodded to me.

We ran back inside, and Ori and Navya had one more slave trussed and ready. "I've got it," Bast told me as Navya tossed him the keys.

"Get back to the boat as soon as you can," I ordered. "No one's getting left behind tonight."

I didn't wait to see their reaction. I went outside to the door, and my breath tangled in my chest.

The heavy, iron-reinforced door was starting to smoke, glowing red from the center where a black circle was developing.

The circle grew wider, and ash fell out of the door. In its place, I saw a young man standing there, his face sweaty and intense, his eyes finding mine as he continued to burn the door down.

Elementa.

No. The Trifectate did not *employ* Elementae—they killed them. Murdered them and made it a holy feast day.

But here was a young man using his power to burn through a door to get to me.

I glanced over my shoulder. Navya and Ori were crossing the enclosure with the last slave, and Bast jogged over to me with his sword drawn.

"Get on the boat!" I snarled. "I'll take care of myself."

He hesitated—he *hesitated*—and I nearly paid for it as an arrow flew out of the hot, ashen void in the door.

"Go!" I bellowed, and this time he obeyed. More arrows came at me, but I flung them away with my power, like swatting flies.

Then water came and cooled the ash, and four guards stepped carefully through the ruins of the door.

I backed up, but the guards didn't chase me.

Between the guards with their shiny steel were three people who didn't belong. They weren't in chains. They weren't in armor. One was a girl my own age. Another was a man. Another was a woman older than me.

The girl held up her hands, and the white stones in the enclosure started to rip up, tearing a straight line toward me.

There was no way in any number of hells that I would be captured again. Not by one of my own kind, for certain.

I whipped out a line to catch me, wrapping around my wrist and jerking me upward like I was flying. A trail of fire and a guttural yell followed me, but only me.

My crew and captives were halfway up to the ship, and I just needed to distract the Elementae a little longer.

Enough arrows were lying around now that I didn't even need to use up my bolts, and I picked up the discarded weapons with my power, hurling them at the guards faster and with more precision than a bowman. The guards broke formation to cover themselves, distracting their Elementae for precious seconds.

The rowboat inched higher.

A ball of water flew at me, tracking me better than I expected, and slammed me in the chest.

I was almost thirty feet in the air, and I fell. The water pressed hard on my body, not breaking, slamming me down to the earth.

But my power had always reacted to me. It listened to me, reacting first to my emotions and second to my conscious commands. So before my bones shattered against the white stone ground, my power stopped me, cushioning me and blasting the water off my chest.

Someone gasped, but I didn't have a moment to care. The line grabbed my wrist again, and using all the focus I could muster, I pushed the ship off hard in the air, flying high as the ship moved forward. I heard yelps from above, but my crew was used to this—they would recover.

A blast of fire nicked my ankle, but then I was out of range, trailing behind my ship as it raced full sail for the ocean.

I lowered the ship onto the surface of the ocean with a satisfying crash, dunking myself into the water behind it.

I let water fill my ears and used the sudden quiet to suck in a deep breath before my head went totally underwater.

The Trifectate had Elementae working for them. I'd heard for months now about the sick experiments going on in the Trifectate, which were terrifying enough. But if they were employing Elementae to fight for them, it meant I might not be able to return to those shores to find my family.

Damn it all.

I came back onto the surface, swimming to the side and calling a line to me. It pulled me up on the deck, and I watched my crew march about, practiced and efficient. Navya was at the wheel, and Anika was collapsed on the deck beside her, breathing slowly as Navya told her little sister to eat something to get her strength back. Navya called out to the riggers to trim the sails, and they scampered up the shrouds. Ori and Bast were belowdecks, no doubt securing our new cargo, and some of our littler ones were coiling ropes and securing the rowboat.

We were shipshape in no time, and I ducked belowdecks. "Is the cargo tucked in?" I asked Sophy, our cook, as I passed through the galley.

She looked up from where she was chopping carrots. "Quick work. I'll have a meal ready soon."

I opened the door at the end of the galley that led to our hold. Jogging down the stairs, I saw Ori and Bast working together to chain up the men first, two to a cell in our converted brig.

"He's a problem," Bast muttered to me, glancing at the big one with scars.

I sighed. "Figured he might be. There's always one, and he'll be worth the price."

Bast grimaced, but he led the cooperative volunteer down to the end of the row. The *Ancora* wasn't meant to be a slave ship—we didn't have a massive hold that held rows and rows of slaves, but we could carry up to about fifteen. Of course, almost half weren't going to make it to the slave markets at Sarocca.

"Make sure he's locked down," I warned Bast. The volunteer gave me an innocent look.

I nudged Ori's shoulder and took over his duties, wrestling back the men who tried to fight me, getting them into their chains as Ori gently herded the children into two cells without shackling them.

It had been seven years since I was taken from the communes, my home, sold by soldiers who wanted to line their own pockets by selling children they thought no one would miss in the chaos of the end of the war. Lined up on a gangplank, pushed forward and chained down with a hundred others in the fetid belly of a ship.

I couldn't stand to shackle the children. It was bad enough that we had to put them in the brig, but they needed time to adjust. It had taken two children throwing themselves overboard and one trying to burn down the ship from the galley to recognize that they wouldn't trust me until they were free and off the boat.

Freedom meant nothing until you could run with no one chasing you.

No matter what the reason, keeping them in the brig was cruel. My life had always been a careful balance between cruelty and hope.

By the time we were done, Sophy's meal was ready, and we went back to the galley, locking the hold behind us. "Ori, go get food. Bast, on deck," I told him, gesturing for him to follow me.

We got up to the deck, and I nodded Navya toward the galley. "Get some food," I ordered. "We'll be up here for a bit."

She agreed and went past us, and as I turned to Bast, he crossed his arms over his chest. "They have Elementae," he said, looking out over the water, keeping his voice quiet. "This changes things, Asp."

"I know," I told him.

"I'm not saying that we're not strong in other ways, but our edge is the Elementae in our crew. If we keep running up against these people, we are in serious trouble."

I glared at him. "I'm well aware," I grunted, trying to relax my jaw from its almost involuntary clench. "But I have yet to meet an air power that matches mine, in any event."

"Don't get cocky," he warned, smiling, but it grated.

"That wasn't what I wanted to discuss with you, Bast," I told him.

Maybe he moved back a little, or gave me a different look, but I felt the shift across the line that we continued to walk, from friends to captain and crew. "Yes, Captain?" he asked.

I pursed my lips, using my power to adjust the wheel slightly. "You hesitated," I accused, my eyes meeting his.

His nostrils flared. "When? I did not."

"When I told you to get on the boat. You hesitated."

"I'm not saying I did, but if I did, it would be because I wasn't planning on leaving you there to die. I thought we all agreed that shouldn't happen again."

"You are not the captain of this ship. In fact, that delay, that distraction almost got us both killed. Are you unable or unwilling to follow my orders?" I snapped as he opened his mouth to argue further.

It snapped shut, and he huffed a breath out through his nose. "No, Captain."

"Good. What happened to raise the alarm?"

Bast threw up his hands. "You're going to hold that against me? Be honest. This isn't about you being captain, it's about you punishing me because we're not together anymore."

I fought the desire to jam one of my crossbow bolts into my own eyeball. How could I be punishing him for a decision I made? He was the one who didn't agree with it, not me. That he kept bringing it up in childish ways made me happier and happier that I had. "Bast, you're my best sword, but something happened that I didn't see to alert the guards that we were there. You owe me an explanation, no matter what our history is."

"No, you owe me your trust. I've been sailing with you for four years, Asp. Longer than anyone else here. You can't trust that I would do everything possible to keep us safe? The guy fought me and I handled it, but he was *trying* to raise the alarm, as soon as he saw where we were taking him. I stopped him as quickly as I could." He shook his head. "You're being unfair and you know it."

"Thank you for the explanation. You're dismissed," I snapped. "Go get some food."

"Dammit, X!" he snapped.

"I'm not arguing about whether or not I'm being fair," I told him. "You can get food or you can stay here, but this conversation is done. Unless you really want me to sideline you for our next run."

He scoffed, crossing his arms again. "You'd never. You just said I'm your best sword."

"You are. And if I can't trust you, you're worthless."

It was too far, and I didn't like the shocked look on his face or the ugly feeling in my belly. But he looked away from me and muttered, "Yes, Captain," before turning and going belowdecks.

Growling with frustration, I climbed the shrouds up to the main yard, standing out on the edge of it, solid wood beneath my feet and the sail full and round beneath me. I held on to the line as I balanced, the deck and the problems with Bast far below me, nothing but the dark horizon ahead.

Somewhere in the distance, a weak flash signaled lightning that was too far away to cause concern, and I drank it in.

I walked out to the center of the yard where there were no lines to hang on to. I felt the ship buoy and fall beneath me, the wind coursing through me, supporting me, holding me.

I sent my power out over the waves, searching into the night to feel out dangers to my crew. It seemed like a ship in the port was gearing up to patrol the harbor, but it wouldn't be able to track us. We were already out of sight, and we were about to tack upwind and change course.

I closed my eyes, and air rushed over me, the ocean crashing against our hull, the distant cries of shorebirds punctuating the night. This was my domain, and I was the ultimate ruler of this stretch of ocean. No matter how false the feeling was, how deep the ache of depleted energy rattled in my bones, when I was out here I was free.

# Cursed Thing

Nearly two weeks later, I woke up falling. My back hit the edge of the wooden bed, the long way, right along my spine, and I cursed and sprawled onto the floor. My door opened with suspicious speed, and I saw Ori standing over me.

"I'm okay," I told him. He held out a hand and I took it, standing as the boat swayed beneath us. He glanced at the bed and I shrugged. He gave me a tiny smile. This was our half language, mine and Ori's—he hadn't spoken much since we lost his sister, Dara. Most of the rest of us assumed she was dead, and when her twin thought she died, something within him died too—perhaps his voice, or perhaps just any desire he had to talk.

I figured it was hard to speak when the person who understood you couldn't listen.

I pulled on my leathers to ward off the cold and went aboveboard.

As I hit the deck, the cold air rushed around me, greeting and rubbing like a cat desperate for attention. I flexed my hands, tugging on the threads as wind circled eagerly around me. I was almost at full strength after the communes, but it had taken a long while.

*Three hells.* Elementae were working for the Trifectate.

The memory stung me again. It was inconceivable.

My fingers curled into fists, and I reminded myself to find a new swear word—I didn't want to invoke the hells of a god I refused to believe in anymore. Every time my mind and my mouth betrayed my beliefs, it had the ashy taste of submission.

I went up to the quarterdeck where Anika stood, leaning weakly on the rail. She barely glanced at me before she obeyed my inevitable command and went belowdecks. I made my way to the wheel at the stern. "How was the night?" I asked Navya, looking out over the blue-gray morning calm.

"Sails," she told me, and with barely a thought, I took up where Anika left off, and the sails filled despite the nearly windless morning on the ocean. I watched the yellowed sailcloth fill with deep gulps of air, and then looked at Navya, who was watching where Anika had gone, ever the older sister. "It's not easy for her," she told me.

"I know."

"It's easier for you."

"It is. But unfortunately I can't do it all day and all night. Not much wind last night?"

"Will she learn?" Navya asked me. "Does she need more practice? Or will she never be like you?"

She didn't mean to accuse me of anything, but the morning and the edge of her voice, the need to protect her little sister, ground on me. "I don't know, Nav," I told her. "How could I know that?"

She squinted up at the sails. "I'm getting food. Ori?" she asked.

He nodded, and he walked along beside her as she followed her sister down belowdecks. Second in command in all things, Navya was the closest I had to a first mate, and I knew she'd make sure everyone—especially Arnav, her troublesome brother—had their orders before she slept for a few hours.

I sighed and let my power wrap around the wheel, stretching my control over the wind as if I were stretching muscles in my back. If I went too long without bending the wind to my will, I felt restless and caged and knotted inside myself.

The other members of the night watch waited for a replacement before heading down to get food from the galley and choosing a hammock in the hold, and for a sacred few moments, I was almost alone on the wide deck. I shut my eyes and rolled my neck, reaching out with my power.

Waves, clear and blue, churned themselves into foam against the hull, sweeping out in swirling bubbles behind us, turning the surface white.

Anika had taken us off the stream by accident—she couldn't feel it yet, but there was a certain way that air moved in the natural world. Some of it was cold and heavy, and some was warm and light. There was a wide band of steady, warm wind that we could slip into and follow, and the natural rhythms in my body always guided me back to it. I adjusted the wheel, pitching us toward it again.

Farther out, I felt the slide of something breaking the water, rubbing its long smooth body into the air. A whale, maybe—it felt huge. On the other edge, I could feel the piercing jabs of the port city of Diadem.

"Asp," I heard, but it was warped and far away.

It took a full long breath for me to pull back into myself, unsure how I had walked that wide outside my body. Bast stood before me, glowering right back at me, Ori by his shoulder holding breakfast for me and giving Bast a dark look.

Ori didn't look any other way at Bast since Dara was taken. It wasn't fair, the way Ori blamed him.

It should have been me he blamed.

Bast snapped his fingers in front of my face, and I slapped his hand away. "Rude," I told him.

"I called your name ten times," he said. He crossed his arms. "You can't do that, Asp. You can't just leave."

"I'm right here."

"You know what I mean," he said, his voice lower, his gaze flicking out over the crew. "You have to be more in control of your power."

It was one of those statements that amplified the cooling divide between us. I just shook my head at him; it wasn't worth fighting about. He had no idea what this power was. He couldn't, and I couldn't hold that against him, but I had no desire to explain.

"What's the problem, Bast?" I asked.

Ori handed me a biscuit and hard eggs and coffee, and I shoved the biscuit in the coffee to make it edible again. I missed soft, fresh bread and disliked the hardtack we resorted to a few days out of port. At least we had chickens. "Thank you, Ori."

Ori smiled at me and glared at Bast again before trotting down the stairs to the central part of the deck and climbing up the shrouds. Navya usually gave him a list of repairs that needed to be made, and he went about doing them in his quiet way.

Bast watched him go and stepped closer to me. I shifted,

putting the wooden plate I was balancing my breakfast on between us. "Will we make Diadem by nightfall?"

I took a deep breath and a bite of the slightly softened biscuit, measuring. "Just," I said.

"What will we do about Dara's spot?" he asked.

I squinted at him. He knew what we had to do about Dara's spot, but he couldn't be the one to suggest it, not the way things were going for him now. I lifted an eyebrow. "What do you reckon we do?" I asked, biting the biscuit again.

"You know what we have to do."

"What's that?" I asked around a mouthful.

He studied me for a long moment. "Is this you teasing me, X?" he asked.

I hated that he couldn't tell. I hated that the nickname I'd once enjoyed from him now just seemed to make me feel vulnerable—a reminder that he knew my secrets. I swallowed my food. "We need to replace her, Bast. But we also need to put it to vote, and you can't be the one to suggest it. I know."

"You don't have to come to see Cyrus," he said. "I can do it myself, if you want."

It was supposed to be a kindness—but was it still kind if it made me appear weaker? "No," I said flatly. "Take the wheel."

He drew a breath but didn't complain, and I glanced up at the sails. Closer to the stream, we were in more natural wind, and while I was awake and paying attention, the wind would always mind me. For the most part—it was like a child: when you didn't give it enough attention, sometimes its obedience would fray.

I swallowed my coffee and trotted down the steps, shelling the eggs as I went. I passed through the upper deck, walking the weather deck round the bow, checking the sails and the rigging and the placement of the crew, chucking the shells into the ocean, and biting into the eggs.

Before I went down, I looked up at Bast, at the stern of the boat, holding the wheel with two hands, his fingers tight around the handles.

There was a long time when looking at Bast gave me a warm, sinful feeling curling in my belly. He wasn't the first person I'd cared about like that, but it had lasted longer than with the other two crewmates. And Bast didn't have that piece of my heart that Tanta did, because she was the first person I'd ever kissed and touched and loved and lost.

The curl was still there, but its warmth had gone cold. There was something else too, something that scratched the back of my neck and threaded acid into my stomach.

That part was new. All the other crewmates had left me; I'd never had this, a slow disintegration of something that used to make me happy.

But I had never loved him, and he wanted me to.

I shook my head, looking away and ducking down below.

When I came into the galley, my hard glare sent everyone but Sophy up to the decks. Sophy doused the small flame we kept boxed in a sand pit and handed me the trencher full of eggs and biscuits. "Have they had water?" I asked.

"Yes, Captain," she said.

"We'll be in port by nightfall. You know what you need?"

"I'll have a list ready by then, Captain."

"Thanks, Soph," I told her. "We'll be having a vote in a few hours."

She took a basket of whatever was dirty and hauled it to the deck to clean. She was little, even for fifteen, and she'd been littler still when she started to cook for us, so I was always shocked by her ability to sling around heavy pots or armfuls of dishes. I used to have one of the boys help her, but she only got offended if I thought she couldn't handle something.

With a sigh, I pulled out my key from my belt and unlocked the door behind the galley. I turned down the narrow stair there, going farther below.

There weren't portholes down here; we were underwater, in the belly of the ship. We sprang little leaks often enough, but Ori was good about fixing them.

The man with the scars had been causing trouble for us all week, but it wasn't unusual. People fought harder when they saw a girl like me in charge. They fought doubly hard when you're a girl and barely eighteen, even if you looked the way I did.

I unlocked the first door, and the two men looked up from the benches. The scarred one was young, not even ten years older than I was, and I could never decide what was worse—taking men like him, who would be worked hard for the rest of their natural lives, or men like the older one beside him, who didn't have much of that life left and whose end I would probably hasten.

I didn't lie to myself—I was hastening both of their deaths. That was the one thing I was sure of.

But the younger ones definitely took longer to give up.

The scarred man stood and jerked on his chains when I opened the door, like he could burst out and free himself.

With a sigh, I told him, "Sit if you want food," and went to the old man beside him. I knelt before him, peeling the egg for him, and then peeling a second when he gently took the first from me. I pressed a biscuit into his hand.

"Thank you," he murmured.

"Don't thank her," growled the young one.

I looked at him. I was careful to crouch outside his range while I helped the old man.

"The funny thing is, you still believe you can be free," said our mysterious volunteer, his voice smug and knowing from deeper in the brig.

"Not everyone volunteered to be a slave," snapped the scarred fighter.

"I didn't volunteer," the other voice said lightly. "I chose my kind of slavery. That's the only choice you get."

"She's free," the fighter accused of me.

"Is she," was all the other voice said.

The fighter seemed to lose some of his fervor at this, and he sat down on the bench. Rather than come within his range, I tossed him two eggs and a biscuit.

Without missing a beat, he caught the biscuit and hurled it back at my face. It was so fast I didn't even think to stop it before it hit me, and he lunged up against his chains.

But I was still out of his reach, and now I was annoyed and he was out a biscuit. "What is your plan?" I snapped, touching my eyebrow, where it stung. Damned hard, terrible biscuits. "Knock me out with a biscuit? And then what? Get my keys, free yourself, and face down my entire crew and an ocean?"

"A crew of *children*," he sneered.

I shook my head, my powers itching at my hands, longing to show him just how powerful these children were, but I didn't ever show that to the cargo if I could avoid it.

Instead I just kicked the biscuit back his way, regretted giving him two eggs, and locked the door behind me.

I went down to the next cage, with two men we'd taken from the shipbuilders' camp. I gave these men three eggs apiece—they came to us broken and emaciated, and after weeks on the sea, they were rested and healing. Yes, I was giving them one kind of slavery instead of another, but at least I would keep them the best I could in between.

The last cage held the volunteer with his silky, knowing voice. He was probably a little older than the fighter, and after two weeks, I knew less about him—or why he wanted to come with us—than I had in the Bone Lands.

His head cocked to the side. "Biscuits again."

I tossed him his share as well. Of all the people currently in our hold, I watched him the closest. Maybe it was because he was here by choice, but I always had a suspicion that he could get out of here if he needed to. He caught his rations easily and gave me a sage nod.

"You're worse," the fighter growled as I passed by him again. His voice was dry and low, like the biscuit had sucked the spit out of him.

I pulled the volunteer's door shut and locked it.

"Worse than the Trifectate. Worse than whoever you're taking us to. You're worse than all of them. You're the most cursed thing I've ever met."

I scoffed, a wry smile on my mouth. "I'm the worst you've met?" I asked, shaking my head. "Lucky for you, then."

The other two cages, which were once full of children, were empty. At least that I could be proud of.

# Mothers Always Know

The sun was warm and full by the time the crew and ship were both settled enough that I could call a meeting.

Navya, Anika, and the night crew joined us, and I sat on the stairs, my elbows on my knees as Navya held her hands up.

"We'll make port in a few hours," she said, looking to Bast for confirmation. He nodded, crossing his arms. "We'll take a team to offload and restock, and everyone should be on the ship again by tomorrow morning," she said. She shouted names off, listing first the team that would be going and then the group that would stand watch. The watchers almost always had to be the Elementae—even with weapons and bad attitudes, there wasn't much a small hold of children could do if other traders decided they wanted our ship. Except, of course, if you could light them on fire or toss them in the ocean by looking at them.

She looked to me, and I held her gaze, trying to remind her that she was a great leader and if anyone could shepherd our crew through this vote, it was her. She sucked in a breath and faced the others. "We have to replace Dara," she said flatly. "Really we should try for two if we can; the crew was light even when she was here."

This wasn't a question, but people murmured among themselves, considering this.

"Votes to replace her with two," Navya called.

There were fifteen of us total, and six raised their hands. I kept my hand down—as captain, I was the only one without a vote.

"Replace her with one," Navya said.

Four.

"Not to replace her."

Three.

"Ori," I called softly, since he wasn't standing far from me, but it was loud enough to draw attention. "You have to vote."

He crossed his arms over his chest. Abstain.

"We replace her with two," Navya said. "In the usual way? Vote for yes," she called.

Thirteen hands rose. Ori crossed his arms over his chest.

"Then we'll divide the haul after the replacement," Navya announced. "Captain?" she asked, turning to me. "Anything else?"

"Is anyone leaving us in Diadem Port?" I asked. No matter how many times I asked this question, I couldn't stop my heart from stuttering in the gap, nervous and tight as I waited for their answer.

No one raised their hand. Ori crossed his arms on his chest again, beating his chest softly with his fists like he was a drum, or maybe he was reminding his heart to beat.

"Very well," I said. "We'll make port in a few hours. Everyone be ready."

◆

I didn't like land. I didn't think I was built for it; things felt far too solid there, too lawful and finite. On the water I was a ferry-man of sorts. A trader. On land, I knew the moral weight of what I did.

It wasn't unusual, then, to find tension curling inside me. Bast was watching me as if he wanted to argue about something, and I felt restless, too wide for my skin. So like the coward I'd some-how become, I didn't face any of it. I climbed the rigging and walked carefully out on the topsail yard, sitting on the wide beam that held up the sail.

It was easily my favorite place in the world.

As the day pressed on, I saw a smudge on the horizon, and I felt my stomach growing tight, then churning. Diadem Port came into view as the sun set behind us, and the first glimpse, as always, belonged to Kamaria.

She stood in stone, hundreds of feet in the air, guarding the entrance to the channel. Her arms were stretched wide, and her long hair was whipped around her and frozen in stone. Her eyes were covered, and I knew on that covering were the words: The Earth Will Crack Before Sarocca Falls.

She was the first queen of Sarocca, and legend had it she was a powerful earth element—she was the one who made the harbor to defend her country. As we passed by, I bowed my head to her, wondering if we were kindred in some way.

Diadem wasn't like any other port I knew. Instead of a wide, round harbor, it was a narrow slice, running up a tributary to the river. As you came up the channel, narrow spits of land to the left created little pocket harbors. It was a dangerous harbor for most boats; the narrowness made collisions more likely and required rowing a ship to mooring since sailors couldn't control where the wind would take them in a narrow lane.

Unless, of course, they could.

We went as far in as a ship like mine was able, hauling up a mooring buoy and securing it to the ship.

By the time the sails were furled and tied, the cargo had been loaded onto the upper deck and two longboats were coming out from shore to meet us, laden with Cyrus's dockworkers and henchmen. I saw Tommaso, Cyrus's head enforcer, standing in one, the gold thread in his robe glinting under the lantern swinging on a post in the boat.

We nodded once to each other across the water.

When the longboats came abreast of us, Tommaso's men came aboard to help us load down the boats with cargo and those of us going ashore. The human cargo was blindfolded and gagged, which some of them minded more than others. The one who threw a biscuit at me fought so much one of the men knocked him out, even knowing that would mean carrying him.

Navya was in charge while I was gone, and I gave her a solemn look as I climbed down the ladder to the longboats. Nothing about this situation was safe; nothing guaranteed this wouldn't be the trip when Cyrus decided I was worth more as a slave than a trader, and remembered she could just steal my cargo instead of paying for it.

It wasn't a possibility; it was an eventuality. One day, I'd get off this boat and I wouldn't ever return, and Navya knew it and I knew it.

Bast and Ori came with me, and I saw Arnav sulking beside Navya and Anika on the deck. He was a wildly untrained fire element, and it suited him. The middle of the three siblings, at twelve he was small but had so much anger balled up inside him he constantly craved the satisfaction of making others miserable. Usually that meant hitting things or picking fights. He wanted so badly to be the kind of enforcer that a man like Tommaso was, the kind of enforcer who would be sure I came back to the ship and made sure his sisters were safe and made sure no one hurt him, but he wasn't yet. And he would hate everyone and everything until he was.

At the dock, the others who needed to come ashore—like Sophy and a few crew to help her buy new food—split off. Tommaso and the rest of us hauled item after item into the waiting carts, throwing heavy cloth over all of it, including the people, as if it was that easy to just pretend they were *things*. As if hiding them would undo our sins.

I rode with Tommaso, Ori, and Bast in the other cart, and Tommaso tossed a heavy bag of coin to the port master. Cyrus always covered our mooring fees, and I was never sure if it was a favor or just a reminder that I was a dependent, like a child waiting for her mother to buy bread.

Cyrus's warehouse wasn't far. It was a huge stone building, an indication of how permanent this business was, how permanent Cyrus was—other traders fell prey to raiders and pirates, thieves who struck often and hard to steal cargo of all kinds, but especially slaves, and traders kept their operations mobile in response. Cyrus never hid. Cyrus had built such a strong empire that no thief would be able to break it down.

A huge wooden door hauled upward, pouring light out onto the street, and Tommaso led the carts inside. Someone came and took the horses, unhooking them and leading them out, and the business of unloading began. Everything went onto tables, parceled out by item and then amount, in neat stacks and rows, until we came to the human cargo. They were brought to wooden posts, their tied hands lashed to the post behind them.

Abla came out and began walking up and down the ranks, scratching out calculations on a sheet. "All in one piece?" she asked me off-handedly when she was a quarter way in.

"Me, or the cargo?" I asked.

She flicked her gaze to me. "I know the state of the cargo," she said, lifting a shoulder.

"I'm fine. Thanks for asking."

She made a soft grunting noise and made more marks.

The sound of a door drew my eye upward, and I saw Cyrus emerge from the ledger room and trot down the stairs, billows of thick, dark hair sweeping out behind her like a cape.

She came over to her sister, eyeing Abla's sheet. "Well?" she asked.

Abla waved her off, and Cyrus moved down the ranks, drinking in the treasures. She picked up the sack of black salt that came from the shores of Kiri and danced her fingers over the hammered gold bracelets from Liatos. She never could resist something shiny.

I had no idea how old Cyrus was—old enough to have a few strands of silver in her black hair, young enough that all her soft, round parts hadn't fallen any, which was clear in the close-fitting pants and shirt she favored—but her curiosity always made her seem younger. The world hadn't stopped interesting her yet, which always seemed bizarre.

Then she moved to the human cargo. She knew what her

buyers wanted, and she pinched their skin and pressed their teeth and examined their hands. She smiled, but her smile was razor sharp as she returned to me.

"No women, no children," she noted. "Always so strange that they never cross your path, hmm?"

I didn't react.

"Abla, give her the price so we can talk business," Cyrus ordered.

"Pearls or gold this time, Asp?" she asked.

"Depends on the price," I told her.

"Four hundred kings," she said. "So twenty-three pearls."

I crossed my arms and looked to Cyrus. "Try seven hundred kings," I told them. "We all know the value of the things I bring you."

Cyrus put a gold bracelet on. "We all know that you don't have a choice, Aspasia."

"You pay me less money and I can't bring you the same quality next time," I reminded her.

Cyrus looked to Abla.

"Six hundred, that's it," Abla said, raising her hand like I was assaulting her. "So thirty-four pearls."

"Thirty-five if you round up," I told her.

Her eyes narrowed. "Thirty-five if you round up."

"I'll take three hundred kings and eighteen pearls," I told her.

Abla opened her mouth to protest—probably my rounding up—but Cyrus waved once and Abla went off to get the money.

She handed me a small, light bag and a very heavy bag. I passed the kings to Bast to count, and I counted out the pearls.

I tugged off my coat and slung a bag across my body, filling it with the items when Bast was finished verifying. I put my coat on over it, hiding it from view and hands. "So," I said to Cyrus. "Let's talk."

Bast and Ori stayed downstairs, watching me. Cyrus led me up to her ledger room, a spare, empty space that betrayed nothing about her.

"I heard a story," she said, sitting at a chair behind a table. Cautiously, I settled against the wall inside the door, crossing my arms and keeping one eye on my crewmates through the warped pane of glass. "Someone broke into the Trifectate communes to steal laborers. They killed many, many soldiers. They suspect that it wasn't the first time."

"Was that the whole story?" I said. "It sounds boring." I kept my tone and body relaxed, but if she heard that much, she knew someone flew a ship into the communes.

Cyrus and I had never talked about my abilities. They surfaced after I went out on her ships, and my crew knew enough to be tight lipped about our powers. There were rumors about me, certainly, but Cyrus never asked me to confirm.

Now my power scraped at my neck, answering my emotions, my fear, my worry.

"Your value to me is extremely defined," she told me. "Whatever I earn from you in profit, less the cost of your ship, less the cost of you as a slave. If I suddenly think that your value as a slave goes up, or your profit goes down—you see the issue here."

I shook my head. "No, I don't think I do."

"Don't cost me more money, Aspasia. I don't care what you do to get your freight unless it's cutting into my business."

I shifted. "Is it?"

Her eyebrows lifted. "The Trifectate has been increasing their orders from across the sea. Every month, they buy more from me. They don't want people stolen from their shores."

My eyes narrowed. "You're supplying slaves to the communes?"

She laughed breezily. "No, darling girl. Slavery isn't legal in the Trifectate, remember?"

"Slavery isn't legal here," I reminded her.

She clucked her tongue. "Slavery isn't *illegal* in Sarocca. There's a difference."

"So you sell them slaves that aren't 'slaves,' " I said, rolling my eyes.

"No. I sell them Elementae to experiment on."

My stomach lurched and my power pulled so hard at the back of my neck that I winced. I stared at her for a long while, but each question I formed had an immediate, obvious answer.

*Why?* Money.

*How could you?* How is it different from other slaves?

*You know they're being tortured. Killed.* Cyrus didn't care. Why would she?

"So. You will not return to the communes this time. And even if you're tempted, I have it on good authority that every port has a damn good description of my ship and orders to obliterate you on sight. Do you understand me?"

My jaw tightened. I hated the Trifectate, and I always would, but the last time I had seen my family was in the communes. Returning there, like I had for years, was my best chance of finding them.

But I would never tell Cyrus that.

Unfortunately, I wasn't a good-enough liar to come up with a better excuse on the spot. "I do," I answered.

She leaned back. "Good. Now I need you to prove it. Next time you come into port, I need fifteen slaves to sell or I won't pay for a damn thing off your ship."

I sat up straighter. "Fifteen."

Her eyebrows lifted. "Business is picking up. The Saroccan king's new road has brought a whole new clientele to Diadem. I need pretty girls and strong children, Aspasia. I need to satisfy demand."

"No," I snarled. "You're telling me to stop doing risky things, but triple my usual haul?"

She turned the bracelet over on her wrist. "We both know you can do it. We both know you put so many more people on your boat than end up in my port."

My blood ran cold, but I fought to keep breathing, even as my power clawed at my skin, desperate to rise up and protect me.

"You think you can lie to me? Cheat me? You will make it right, Aspasia."

Fear and anger were making my skin tremble. "Or what?" I asked. "What if I don't? What if I just sail away and never return?"

"You don't want to honor your bargain?" she asked, sounding hurt, like a mother whose child said she didn't love her. She shook her head. "My sweet girl. You're a slave with a longer leash, Aspasia, but you're mine. You will always be mine. I never regretted our little deal, but if you run, there's nowhere you can go. You can't hide a face like yours, not from my spies. Not from me."

My scar usually made me feel fierce and powerful, like I had stolen something back from a world that had taken everything from me, but right then I hated it. Right then I would claw it off my face if I could.

She leaned back, propping her feet up on the desk. She looked at me, turning the bracelet over and over and over. "You know," she said, musing. "When I was a girl, I loved this boy. He used to whisper pretty things and give me pretty gifts. He kissed me and touched me and did all the delicious things I wasn't supposed to like. I was so thrilled with the secret of it—hiding it from my mother, letting her think I was pure and really I was a woman, a thing of sin and sensuality. And then he asked to marry me, and my mother told him—publicly, in front of our families—that he couldn't. Because I was filthy and ruined, and he couldn't have me because it wasn't proper."

My brow knotted at this strange insight into her life.

"You look confused," she observed.

I looked around the room like it might have a clue.

She sighed. "Children think they have their clever secrets. But mothers always know, Aspasia. I know exactly what you've been looking for."

This was the most important lie of all. My blood pounded in my veins, and I couldn't see straight, but I forced my breathing to be normal, my face to betray nothing. She didn't know. She couldn't know.

"What happens if I find it before you do?" she asked. "What happens if you're defying me when I do?"

*It.* She said *it*, not *them.* It could be a slip of the tongue— or it could be a guess, meant to make me betray some bit of information.

So I looked her in the eye and said, "I guess we'll just have to find out."

She bared her teeth in a savage grin and laughed, a throaty, pretty sound. "Yes!" she said. "That's what life is all about, my sweet girl. Discovery."

My stomach was tight and pushing high in my throat. A minute longer and I'd be sick. "Are we done here?" I asked her.

"Yes," she said. "Just remember, I don't like to be kept waiting."

As if I could forget. "I remember."

"Good," she said, standing. "Now let's go celebrate your triumphant return!"

She came and draped her arm around my waist, tugging me close to her. She walked out with me, smiling, and shouted to everyone below that it was time to celebrate.

She steered me down the stairs and out a door into the rapidly cooling night. I gulped the air, desperate for my stomach to settle and ease, pushing the fear out of my gut, praying for my power to settle down. My power was linked to my emotions, and it reacted the strongest, the most unpredictably, to my fear.

We walked down the smooth cobbled streets to the massive courtyard that was in the center of the city. It had a huge fountain pluming water into the sky, and already the night was heavy with laughter and spirits. Around the courtyard were brewhouses and liquor stills, competing for customers to crowd onto their low wooden benches by having women in bright dresses swing their hips and shout out front.

Cyrus moved us past all of this, going to the ornate old mansion that overlooked the courtyard. I didn't know the history of Sarocca well enough to know who'd lived there before Cyrus, but it was obvious it had been someone with old power and older money.

Now it was hers. Her throne of power, her den of sins.

The building had at least three floors that I knew of. The top floor was all bedrooms that smiling women would tug men to with a gentle but insistent hand. The second floor I didn't know much about; I guessed that it was Cyrus's private quarters with her sister, but I didn't know.

When we walked into the ground floor, we were assaulted first by the smell, then by the heat. No place in the world smelled like Cyrus's court, full of the rich and fragrant spices that were the profit of a booming trade business. A room of delicious food always welcomed guests, constantly refreshed by a team of women who weren't there for other pleasures.

My stomach growled; as little as I liked taking anything from Cyrus, she considered it insulting not to eat. The boys and I lurched toward the rich food, each filling a large wooden plate.

"I do love this," Bast crowed around a mouthful of something that looked like chocolate. He closed his eyes and swallowed deeply.

Even Ori was filling his plate with little trussed golden birds, roasted fruit, and fresh, hot, not-rock-hard bread.

By the time we sat down at the long table in the next room, armed men were pouring us goblets of wine and various patrons had noticed Cyrus, coming over to touch her hand or kiss her cheeks while she sat there watching us.

After a while, she waved, and one of the wine bearers stood near the entrance to the room, tapering off the stream of men. Cyrus leaned back, reclining and smiling at Bast as she popped tiny pieces of a hard cheese into her mouth. "So," she said, still looking at him. "Tell me a story, Bast."

Bast grinned under her attention, displaying a sly, self-satisfied smile that made him seem more charming than usual. He glanced at me, and I looked away. "Hmm, a story?" he said, drinking from his wine and then rubbing the rim of the goblet.

"A grand adventure," she demanded, drinking deeply and watching him.

Bast puffed up and stretched out, enjoying this role and the attention that came with it. He launched into a slightly taller tale of how we procured the salt from Kiri, and it made my skin prickle. Bast wasn't careful, and every word out of his mouth I feared would betray the real reason we'd been on the Vis Islands.

So I drank. I drank deeply until Cyrus led us over to a low, soft couch draped in an outrageous number of colors of silks. Abla joined us, and Tommaso, and after a while, we were laughing, swapping stories, sharing wounds. Bast got up to relieve himself, and Cyrus moved closer to me, stroking my hair back from my face.

"You've grown older, Aspasia," she whispered to me.

"I'm told that's the natural order of things," I drawled, looking into my shockingly empty cup.

"Just once more," she whispered. "Just once more, and I'll free you from your bargain. We'll be settled, and you can be free. You can even have my ship if you want it."

Acid and bitterness slid down my throat faster than the wine. "You'll never free me," I growled at her. "You have no reason to."

"I need you, Asp," she murmured, her lips hovering closer to my ear. "I need you. You're old enough now, you can come work for me, and we can rule the world together. Share the profits. Take the life you want."

My heart beat harder, a heavy, brutal throb inside my veins at her use of my old words.

"I just need to know you're loyal to me, Asp. I need to know that we can trust each other, the way I trust Abla. I need you to be my sister, my daughter. My blood."

But she knew I was lying to her. I didn't know how much she knew, but she knew something.

"I thought this was what you always wanted, pet. Money beyond imagining. Safety. Protection. I thought you wanted to be free."

I looked at her. "Will I be free?" I asked. "To buy and sell what I want? To go where I want? To never come back here if I choose?"

"It will be better than that," she said, smiling fondly. "I'll give you everything you want. I'll make your dreams come true, even the ones you don't think I know about. You'll have a mansion of your own. You'll never have to sell another slave if you choose. I know how you hate it. I just need you to prove your loyalty to me."

I licked my lips, looking at her. "Why do you make me do it if you know I hate it?" I asked her.

She stroked my cheek with a sweet smile. "Because I can."

Anger and hate twisted inside me, choking me. Before I knew what I was doing, I had pushed up from the couch, flipping the little table out of my way. The haze of the wine made my skin prickle and my face feel numb in the same dizzy moment.

One of the wine bearers grabbed my arm, shoving me against the wall and twisting it behind me. Too stunned to breathe, I gurgled against the wall.

"Oh, let her go," Cyrus breezed. "I'm sure I'll see you at the auction in the morning, right, pet?"

"Asp," Bast said sharply, coming back to the room as the man let me go.

"Stay," I snarled at him. I knew I was being mean, but it

felt like mercy that I didn't unleash the torrent of acid roiling inside me.

Ori caught my hand, and I wrenched away from him, storming out of the horrible palace until I hit cold air.

I gulped it down. I was shaking. Freedom. Freedom. Freedom. It tasted like ash, and then like ripe fruit, and then like ash again. I raked my nails over my scar, clawing at it, wanting it to be more ugly, more painful, more punishing.

I hated everything, especially myself.

# Crewmates

I climbed my way up the walls of the big, old temple, far more aided by my power than I would have been sober. Hidden on the roof, I didn't really sleep. I dozed, sometimes, but I startled at every noise below, and my bones didn't ease until the sun rose, throwing spears of punishing light.

My eyes burned and my head throbbed, and while the sharp, churning pain in my stomach was gone, in its place was the familiar ache.

I half climbed and half fell from my hiding place, stretching my sore limbs as I set off through the city, making my way back to the docks. The auction wasn't always held at Cyrus's warehouse—it used to move around much more often, but Cyrus had grown powerful, and she was keeping too many people far too rich for them to stop her now. So, in yet another brazen display, she held the auction on a barge in front of her warehouse. I think the original idea had been to stow the cargo and shove off if there was trouble, but she hadn't moved that vessel in years.

She was in a jeweled chair, wildly out of place up on the starkly functional dock above the barge. Abla was down with the slaves, running the auction as a group of five were brought out and given five minutes of public inspection before the bidding began.

I stood up on the dock as they started with the women. I crossed my arms and watched the gruesome spectacle, like I did every time. I made myself watch, and I made myself remember.

Something tapped my arm, and I jumped, seeing Ori holding bread to me. I took it and saw Bast bend over Cyrus's chair, going to kiss her. She waved him off before his lips met hers, but I still felt a shard of glass lodge somewhere in the back of my chest.

She'd slept with Bast. I knew enough about them both—especially him—to see that clearly. He would have never dared something so familiar if he didn't think he could.

She could have anyone, could make anyone with a pulse want her, and she had picked Bast. The only reason I could think of was because once he'd meant something to me.

Bast came over to us, red slightly coloring his cheeks from his dismissal. "Are y—"

"I think I'll stab you if I hear another sound out of your mouth," I growled at him. "So don't."

He smiled. "Oh, so you're jealous, hm?"

Ori cleared his throat and switched sides with me so he stepped between us.

A young woman cried out from the auction block, and my fingers dug into the soft bread. I couldn't tell whether she'd been bought or something else happened, but she was slumped against the pole, sobbing openly.

One of the handlers came up and cut her down, taking her away, and the sale moved on.

No one else seemed to care. Even Ori and Bast didn't flinch at this part; they didn't hate it the way I did.

I bit into the bread viciously, sad that the only thing I could tear apart with my teeth was food.

As much as I was here to purchase people—to *free* people—I also came to every damned auction because I had to. I *had* to stand there, to watch it happen, to remind myself every damned time of what I was doing. Of what I was contributing to, and of the fate that was lying in wait for me and everyone I cared about if I ever stopped.

I flinched as another woman screamed.

Thirty women were sold, most of them young, very few of them pretty or healthy, but that didn't affect their price. Most were broken and resigned, and one or two in the whole lot struggled against their fate.

*You still believe you can be free*, the oily volunteer had said. The thought made me shudder.

Like I had called him forward, the volunteer from the last run was in the first group of men brought out. He met my eyes and lifted his brows, and I felt Bast turn to look at me suspiciously.

I bowed my head, the only apology I could give him.

He gave me a small, knowing smile.

He and four others were tied to the center poles, and as the inspection began, someone spoke to the handlers and then to Abla. She spoke to the man for a few minutes and then waved him onward, noting things down on her ledger.

The handler moved forward, untying the volunteer, who didn't look even slightly surprised. I watched, grateful for something else to focus on. For Abla to sell him before the auction, his buyer had to have preempted with a huge sum.

The volunteer rubbed his wrists and followed the man who had purchased him off the barge. He came up the dock, and looking at me, he murmured something to the man beside him. The man stopped, and the volunteer came closer to me.

I bristled, but he smiled and bowed. "Thank you for a pleasant stay."

This seemed like a strange prelude if he was intending to attack me. "You're welcome?"

He glanced back at the man. "My employer would like to meet you."

My eyes flicked back to the auction. "Not now."

He followed my gaze, looking out at the auction he had escaped from unscathed. "Very well. Come to the fountain after your business is done."

I shook my head. "Nothing about that seems even a little tempting," I said.

He chuckled. "My employer would be very grateful. You know you have no sins to answer for on my account." His shoulders lifted. "There is no loss to me if you don't come. But I hope you do."

"Perhaps," I said.

He bowed again. "Thank you," he said. "Aspasia, isn't it? And my name is Favo."

I nodded to him and looked away.

Bast watched him go, crossing his arms and looking at me. "What was that?"

"As if I have any idea?" I said.

"What does he want with you at the fountain?"

"I don't know."

"You're not going."

I cringed hard as someone else cried out, this the stricken bellow of a grown man. I hated that Bast saw, and I hated that I could still react like that to the sound of someone having their hope beaten away.

Bast stepped to the side, just a little, turning slightly so that his arm was against me, his body a physical shield against the sound. His hand found mine, and we squeezed, vengefully, violently, weathering the storm of memory.

I had been here, just like he had.

Cut.

Bleeding.

Hurt.

Broken.

A crack rang out and a cry came after, like thunder following lightning. My forehead pushed on his shoulder. One of us was shaking—probably me.

I had to watch though. I owed it to the people I put in this market to know their suffering.

I loosed his hand, drawing a shaky breath and standing close to him, but not behind. Like a buttress, Ori pressed against my other side.

I counted thirty-seven men going through the ranks. There were fewer slaves on offer than usual, but the buyers were paying more than ever, bidding fast and hot. I looked at Cyrus and wondered if she was finding other ways to satisfy demands. I always suspected she did private sales of prime merchandise. She could probably limit the market like that, drive prices up for lesser goods . . .

Part of me was impressed at her business savvy. Part of me wanted to scratch at my scar until it hurt.

Then came the children. This was the difficult part, because I had to watch them all and see all of them at a glance, as they were brought up and once they were in the pen. Abla organized the auction by age, and that prevented siblings from going together on the block; more often than not there were siblings in the pen, and that meant I needed to figure out who belonged to whom, and do so as fast as I could.

Not to mention that I needed to know if any were Elementae.

We walked down to the barge, and while we moved, I felt the air, felt the wispy, fine fibers that ran through the air like thread and made it so I could control it. Those threads glittered and pulsed when I focused on them, and they always responded when another element was nearby.

The threads wove through the children as they were led into the pen, and I felt three sparks. Three elements.

We only had money and orders for two.

I watched them closely. Two of them stuck close by each other, and one withdrew into the center of the crowd. He had to be at least sixteen, teetering on the edge of being considered an adult, but he wasn't the largest boy there by any stretch.

The other two wrapped their arms around each other. They were two girls, one taller, one shorter, and if they weren't sisters, they knew each other and loved each other.

They had to be the ones we took.

Usually I felt good about this part—self-congratulatory, at the very least, that I was saving siblings from a life of horrible slavery, and girl siblings at that—but it wasn't sitting well today. My eyes kept darting to the boy. Something within me didn't want to leave him here.

But I never wanted to leave any of them here, least of all Elementae. Less so after Cyrus's revelation.

The youngest children went first, and my lip curled, looking at the people who bought them and wondering what they wanted a child slave for. They were cheaper, of course, and one day they would grow up to be full-sized slaves, but there were other reasons. Reasons that haunted me.

When the smaller girl was taken away from her sister, she screamed and screamed and screamed, and the older sister covered her mouth and cried.

One of the handlers slapped the young girl, and she stopped screaming as she was taken to the post. I went over to Abla.

"I'll take the crier," I told her.

Abla lifted an eyebrow. "Ninety kings."

"Seventy-five, don't gouge me," I snapped at her. She opened her mouth to counter again, and I said, "I'm buying another one too."

Her shoulder lifted. "Seventy-five."

She waved me toward the heavily fortified table where I was meant to pay, and a handler cut the girl down. Bast and Ori collected her without any direction from me, and I paid her value and went back to stand near Abla, ready to claim the other one as well.

I looked back at the pen. The remaining Elementa girl was

gripping the bars of the pen, stricken, but over her shoulder, whispering in her ear, calming her, was the boy.

Awareness prickled at the back of my neck. Something. Something. He was too calm, too composed, too alert. Everyone who went through the pens was either broken or fighting, and he was waiting. Poised to strike.

They both came up two lots later. The handlers pulled out five captives, and as the boy was drawn out, I heard a shriek.

No one else noticed it. Seagulls were shrieking and flapping everywhere this close to the water, and it was almost indistinguishable.

But I knew that sound. I knew I had heard it before. My head jerked up, and I saw a hawk wheeling, the seagulls giving him wide range.

I knew that bird. He had flown with us the night the queen of the Trifectate landed on my ship, the night I realized she was an Elementa just like I was, the night we lost Dara.

My skin went cold. It was some kind of a sign—this boy was coming with us. We would not lose another.

As they were being tied to the post, I saw someone else moving to Abla while I hesitated, and he pointed to the girl I wanted.

I shook my head, closing the gap between Abla and me. "Abla!" I started.

"Down!" one of the handlers growled, driving a heavy fist across the boy's face. He fell hard, but just as quickly sprang up, running at the handler. He was fighting the handlers? He didn't strike me as the foolhardy type.

But the large man who was trying to steal my girl was distracted, and I stepped in front of him.

"Two hundred twenty-five kings for the girl," I said quickly. Abla's eyebrows shot up—it was too much, but I couldn't risk the man paying more.

"Which girl?"

I pointed.

"I want her," the man said, realizing what was going on. "I'll pay two thirty."

I had no more kings. I looked desperately at the stage—I could give up my share of the pearls, but that was all I had.

The handler slammed another punch to the boy's face, and there was a horrible crack as he hit the stage, and blood sprayed out.

Abla didn't like blood.

"Put him down," snarled Abla. The boy was already flat on the ground—even if the boy didn't know what that meant, I did. Abla had just given the order to kill the boy, and it could tip the scales in my favor.

"Two hundred twenty-five kings, two pearls, and I'll put him down for you," I blurted before I knew what I was saying. "Save you the disposal costs."

The man huffed out a sound but didn't counter.

Abla waved me off, and I went to the money table, shaking. The handler shoved the boy toward Bast, which made him fall off the stage, his hands still tied behind his back as the handler cut down the other girl.

The other girl ran to the fallen boy and rolled him onto his back. He wasn't moving, and I came to them as well, kneeling down and slicing his bonds, willing him to be alive and be hale enough to walk.

The boy coughed, wiping blood from his face as he looked at the girl and then me. His eyes met mine for a long time, and I held out my hand to help him up.

He took it.

The girls grabbed each other, hugging tightly and crying, and I nudged everyone. We had to get off the barge and stop making a scene. Then we could figure out what in any number of hells was going on.

Bast and Ori helped the girls up the dock, but neither approached the boy. His eyes were fast, roving over us and the docks, thinking, planning, too tired or hurt to try to conceal it.

"You can run if you want," I told him softly. "Just wait until we're clear of the docks."

His head swung forward, and he didn't say anything to me, but he seemed slightly less frantic.

Usually we brought the new recruits to a brewhouse or something to be fed before making any decisions, but the boy was still bleeding and his clothes were torn and bloody too.

I took a moment to think, and then turned them down a narrow street that led away from the courtyard.

It wasn't a far walk. In a row of buildings all squished tightly together, we came to a little building painted blue that had a cracked wooden sign with a teacup on it.

We walked in the door. The shop was tiny, a purveyor of the teas that only a port town like Diadem had access to, and a dark-haired woman came out from the back.

Her face opened into a smile when she saw me. "Asp!" she cried, coming over to hug me.

I almost stopped her, stiffening when I realized her condition. "You're . . . ," I said dumbly.

"Having a baby is the common term," she said, turning from me to press a hand to Bast's cheek.

"Miss you, Anna," he said, stepping forward to kiss her cheek.

Her eyes moved over the others. "Come into the kitchen, I'll see to that," she said, looking at the boy in particular.

A fire roared in the kitchen, and she sat the three recruits down on a bench before it. I sat on the stone windowsill, and Ori sat in a chair by the door while Bast leaned against a table. When Anna went to fill a pot, Ori sprang up to take it from her at the same time that the boy did.

The boy was closer, and he took it, hooking it onto a stand in the fireplace.

"Thank you," Anna said warmly. "So—how new is this?"

"Just left the auction," I told her.

She put her hands on her hips. "Right. You'll want food, I imagine?"

The little girl agreed before her sister put her arm around her. Anna handed some bread and a chunk of cheese to Bast to cut, and Ori brought the food to them. When the boy took it, he turned around to look suspiciously at me.

"Asp, you're not going to say anything?" Anna prompted, gathering supplies to tend to the boy's wound.

I sighed, not leaving the windowsill. "You're free now," I told them, looking at my hands. "We didn't buy you to keep you as slaves. You're free now. But we know Diadem isn't the easiest city, and certainly not the place you're from. If you want, you are invited to come work on my ship as our crewmates. You'll share in the profits and leave when you wish, as long as it's at the end of a haul."

"This is a trick," the older girl said. "Why would you buy us if you didn't want us to be slaves? If we don't 'work' for you, we will be killed, is that it?"

"No," Anna said, settling onto the bench beside the boy. "I was part of Aspasia's crew for a year." She smiled. "My husband and I both."

"You should also know that I'm Elementae," I told them.

The boy's head swung to me, disturbing Anna's work, his gaze sharp and fierce and more than a little accusatory.

"E-Elementae?" the girl stammered. "We don't know what that is."

"You do," I told her. "You may not know it by that name, although I think you do." I looked at the fire, and the flames curled upward, dancing and twisting as I manipulated them with the wind. "I can't tell what element you are, but I know all three of you have one."

"A lot of the crew have powers," Bast said. "Not all. I don't. But it comes in handy."

"What happens if we say no?" the girl asked, her fingers digging into her little sister until the little girl tried to shake her off.

"Nothing," I told her. "I wish we could give you money to go live your own life, but we don't have more to spare. But you are free, and no one else can claim you as a slave." I lifted my shoulders. "But that is nearly impossible to enforce."

"What does it mean, leave at the end of a haul?" the boy asked.

"It can get dangerous, if we have taken on cargo of some kind and we lose people. You can leave at the beginning or end of a job, but we ask that you don't leave in the middle. If you must, though, that's not really up to me."

"What kind of cargo do you carry?" he asked, and there was something that struck me as threatening in his voice.

"All kinds," Bast said. "We're traders. Whatever we can get our hands on."

"You're the captain," he said, his eyes heavy on me.

"Yes," I said.

"What happened to your face?" he asked me, turning back to Anna as her fingers gently prompted his chin.

Anna sucked in a breath, stopping what she was doing. Bast's hand went to his knife handle, and Ori stood from where he'd sat, as if standing over this cocky boy would make him think better of asking questions about me.

"I cut myself," I told him.

His head cocked a little, but he nodded. "I'm Kairos," he said. "I'll join your crew."

# Spaces between the Elements

The girls took longer to decide, but eventually they joined us. The older girl was Linnea and the younger one was Thea, and I was eager for them to get on the boat. There was something wonderful that happened with my crew when new people came, because every single one of us had gone through what they had. Each crewmate remembered those feelings, sharp and never lost, and they went out of their way to make new people comfortable. Once the girls committed, I already could see Ori gravitating toward them, looking for someone to give care and affection to, to make him feel more human.

Kairos was edgier, and I could feel Bast taking an instant dislike to him. That didn't make anything easier, and it annoyed me. I found everything Bast did annoying, but still—this got in the way of things.

When we left Anna's, Kairos was all bandaged up, but he looked stronger than he had when we entered, and the more I watched him, the more I thought he was older, closer to my own age than sixteen. By Cyrus's standards, he never should have been classified as a child, but somehow he had hidden in the group.

I was beginning to think he was either fire or air; the two elements were close to each other, bordering each other, and my power liked his. The wind kept flicking around him like a puppy, feeling his energy, curious and interested.

As soon as we emerged, I heard the shrieking hawk's call again, and Kairos brightened. The bird swooped, but Kairos looked stunned when the bird landed on my shoulder, ruffling its beak into my hair even as its talons wedged vengefully into the leather covering my shoulders.

That night—the Tri Queen had mentioned something about the hawk belonging to her *brother*. Hadn't she?

"Well, hello, old friend," I said, rubbing his throat. He clicked at me, and it sounded gentle and fond.

"Osmost," Kairos called, and the bird hopped from my shoulder to his.

Kairos's eyes met mine, questioning, and I returned his inquiry—he had the same dark hair and eyes as the queen, the same desert skin, but the things that made her beautiful made him confrontationally handsome.

"You know my hawk," he said to me.

*I think I know* you, I thought. I grinned. "We have to return to the ship," I said to Bast and Ori, and they started shepherding the girls down the street.

Kairos's mouth tightened like he was fighting his need to say more. "You're a very strange girl," he told me, his brow furrowed.

It wasn't a question, and I didn't feel the need to react to it. "This way," I told him instead.

He fell into step beside me, and the bird took to the air. I watched his gait carefully. "I'm well enough," he told me, drawing my eyes up to his.

"Well enough on land isn't good for a ship," I told him. "You'll have a few days to rest when we set off. I'd let you have the cabin, but the girls will need it."

A stormy look crossed his face. "Why would the girls need the cabin?" he growled.

Outrage spun through me, but I tamped it out quick. It wasn't like I wasn't a monster—why shouldn't he suspect me of being one? All of us had been treated monstrously, and it left claw marks inside us.

I took a deep breath. "Because it's the only room that locks besides the brig," I told him, grinding the words out over my pride. "They won't have felt safe in a long while. I'd give that luxury to you if I could, but there's two of them."

"Oh," he said, bristling less. "Forgive me."

"You didn't say anything."

I felt his eyes on me, but I didn't look up. "I think you knew what I was thinking."

I crossed my arms. "You have every right to be suspicious. Were you with them long?"

He drew in a long breath, and it shuttered his eyes closed for a moment. I wondered if air tasted different when you were free. "Maybe a week? It's difficult to tell. They were on the ship before I was."

"There are questions I want to ask you when we're not

in public," I told him softly. "Maybe when we're not in Sarocca."

His jaunty, sly smile surprised me. "Yes, I know you do. I have many for you." He looked around. "Sarocca isn't safe?" he asked quietly.

"Nothing's safe," I said, harsher than I meant. "You should know that by now."

He stepped a little closer to me, but he didn't say anything as we walked back to the dock.

Sophy and the others who had gone to shore were all back before us, and though we always ran the risk that new recruits wouldn't join the crew, Sophy had prepared a small feast to welcome them, even making a cake in one of her little iron pots.

I took the boat out of the harbor with help from Ori and Navya, then I told them to go celebrate and I climbed the rigging to lounge between the mast and the yard as I took her out to open water. As the sun set, the wind got cold and bracing, and I reveled in it.

Kairos's bird swooped, dropping a half-eaten fish on the yard, raking out its guts with his beak and gulping it down.

"You need better manners," I told him, laughing.

He made a *cah-cah-cah* noise that almost sounded like he was laughing back, and he tossed a bit of the fish toward me.

"Very kind," I said. "But I wouldn't dream of depriving you."

"He doesn't do that," said a voice from below. I looked down and saw Kairos puzzling over the rigging. "Share food, I mean. Or talk to people who aren't me."

I snorted. "He's not talking."

"You know what I mean," he said, bracing his hands on his hips and looking up the long lines. "How is one supposed to get up there?"

"That's not a task for an injured duster," I told him, calling one of the lines over to me and climbing quickly down it.

"Duster?" he asked, squinting at me as I dropped the last few feet to the deck.

I slapped my hands together like I could brush off the rough feel of the rope. "Yeah," I said. "You're a desert boy, aren't you?"

"I'm a clansman," he said, insulted.

"That's what I mean," I told him, waving my hand. I went up the stair to the wheel, drawing in a long breath and sensing outward, feeling our course and if there were any ships nearby.

"So you have questions for me," he said, crossing his arms and leaning on the rail. Osmost shrieked before a splash of water, and he rose up again with another fish in his claws. Kairos watched him with a smile.

"You want to know how I know your bird," I told him.

"I want to know if you know me," he said, his eyes fixed on me.

The ship crested a wave, and for the moment in the lull between waves, it felt like we were hovering, still, frozen without the ocean below us.

"My sister told me about the communes," he said. "That was you, wasn't it?"

I kept my eyes on the sea, but I nodded.

"Thank you for what you did for her," he said.

His words felt like acid in my throat. "Stopping a terrible night from being more terrible doesn't make it a good night," I told him.

His eyebrows lifted.

I shook my head. "How are you here?" I said. "How were you being sold as a slave? I heard the queen was in hiding. Why aren't you with her?"

He didn't move much, but something about him seemed tense, coiled, dangerous. "Hiding," he ground out. "What do you mean?"

"Everyone heard that the desert broke faith with the Trifectate. They invaded, and the king feared for his wife's safety." I saw it then, how his fingers tightened so hard on his biceps he looked like he would tear through the material of his shirt.

"Oh yes," he snarled. "The god-king is so concerned for his wife."

"That's what they're saying," I told him. I shook my head. "No one believes it. Well, those who have a choice don't."

He looked surprised.

"But facts are usually buried somewhere in the muck of what the Trifectate says. Like that the queen isn't in the capital. And something happened with the desert."

"He murdered as many of my family and clan as he could," Kairos said sharply. "In front of us. When she was with his child. He tortured her for days."

"Because he thought she was a traitor?" I asked, my voice quiet.

"No," he said, and looked away from me.

"Because of her power," I said.

His eyes snapped back to mine, but he didn't say anything.

I shrugged. "In the communes, she was on the ship. Her guard told her to leap off, and I caught her so she didn't get hurt. I could feel it, when my power touched hers."

"It's not like Sarocca," he told me. "In the Trifectate, that power is incredibly dangerous."

I scoffed. "Sarocca's not better. People understand how powerful Elementae can be now, so either you wield your power or someone else does." My teeth ground together at the thought of Cyrus's new, booming business. "It's getting worse."

"Which is why you do what you do," he said.

He wasn't even close to me, but I pulled back anyway. "You have no idea what I do."

"No," he said thoughtfully. "I suppose I don't. But you think you know what I do."

I watched him, eager to capture his reaction. "I think you're connected to one of the elemental powers—fire or air by my guess."

He crossed his arms. "Connected."

I cocked my head at him, wondering how much he knew about his own power, or if he would show his own curiosity to me. "There are spaces between the elements, I think—there are many people who can't manipulate the element itself, but they have secondary abilities. Usually one or two of them. They work the same—they're grounded in an element, they're motivated by emotions, and you can practice and strengthen them. It's just another kind of Elementa."

"What do you mean, grounded in an element?" Kairos asked, his eyebrow lifting.

"Let's see—I've known a few different people with abilities like that. It varies. One girl could create frost, and then ice—she was grounded in water, but she couldn't manipulate all kinds of water. Another boy could create mud—he was between water and earth, but earth was definitely his stronger connection. Or someone who can create smoke—he's grounded in air."

"Why don't they have the full power?" he countered.

My shoulders lifted. "Do I look like a god? If I had those kinds of answers, I wouldn't be pulling you from a slave market," I told him.

If I were a god, I'd smite down anyone who dared violate, imprison, or harm those who were weaker or more vulnerable than them.

"Why do you think I have these abilities at all?" he asked.

I smirked. "I told you. I can feel it."

"So you could tell when we were at the auction. The girls have it too?"

"They have the potential for it, at least," I agreed.

"So you buy people with powers."

"Yes," I said, reacting more strongly than I should have to the sharpness in his tone. "For my own sick collection. Or so I can steal your powers and use them for myself. Or maybe I just kill you all."

"People do, you know," he said, his voice low. "Steal the powers."

I shook my head. "It's not possible."

"My sister saw it."

"Then she lied to you. Or she didn't know what she saw. Was this when she was being tortured?"

His eyes narrowed. "I've seen it too. Glimpses of it. The first one was a young girl with a fire power, but I think he's doing it to many others."

I felt the blood rush out of my head so fast I almost fell. "A girl," I breathed. Fire. What if it had been Dara?

"He drains the blood completely and channels it into someone else," Kairos said.

"You're talking about him, aren't you? The king who thinks he's a god?"

"Yes," he said, and his voice was flinty and low. His brother by marriage, I remembered.

My heart was pounding. "Don't mention that ever again. Please?" I said, my eyes skittering helplessly to the stair that led belowdecks. "Please don't."

He shook his head, a flicker of concern in his face. "I don't understand."

"You don't have to," I told him. "Just don't say anything about it again."

One hand lifted from his firmly crossed arms, and I didn't know if that was meant to show he didn't care, or he agreed, or he wouldn't promise anything.

Desperate to change the subject, I said, "Why did you rush the guards today? You're not a fool; you knew you couldn't have escaped that way. Unless you were planning to swim out."

"I can't swim," he said, raising his shoulders.

My eyes went wide. "What? You're on a boat. We'll have to teach you to swim."

He glanced cautiously at the water. "Very well."

"So why attack them?" My eyes skittered over him. "You didn't seem like you wanted them to kill you."

He drew in a breath. "People do that?" he asked.

"Use guards to kill themselves?" I shrugged. "I've seen it before."

He shook his head. "You were about to be outbid," he told me. "I knew I had to distract him somehow. It was the only thing I could think of."

Shame flushed my cheeks. "You knew I wanted to buy them."

He watched me, not reacting.

"Did you know I wasn't planning to buy you?"

His eyes dropped, but it was only a moment before he looked up again. "You did," he said. "That's all that matters."

"X," Bast called, coming up the staircase and looking at us. The name stung again, and I knew I should ask him to stop, but I didn't.

"Yeah," I said, clearing my throat.

"I think the girls are tired. I didn't know if you wanted to give them the room."

"Yeah," I said. "Come take the wheel." Bast jogged up the steps as I eased my power off the wheel, and I looked at Kairos. "You should rest. Heal up, so you can be of some use."

Without saying anything, Kairos turned to look at Osmost wheeling in the sky around the boat.

With a heavy sigh, I went belowdecks, going first to my cabin and lighting a candle so it wouldn't feel so dark and cold. I pulled out extra blankets, and went over to the intricately carved wooden box that usually sat on the shelf. I put it in the drawer where the blankets had been and shut it again.

Going to the kitchen, I hung back for a few minutes, looking at the girls. They were still pressed together, but they were smiling, color back in their cheeks, making them look pretty and very young. Ori was close to them, and the older girl was leaning toward him, trusting him. I hoped that stayed—Ori needed someone to care for, and I chafed when it was me.

Sophy was the first one to see me, and she stopped talking midsentence in a way that made me feel suddenly and irrevocably outside.

"Sorry," I said, then hated the need to apologize. "Give us a minute?"

Sophy and Ori and the few other crew members in the kitchen left, and the girls looked petrified.

I crouched down. I knew how much influence bodies wielded, and making myself smaller was an easy way to make them more comfortable. "I know you haven't been safe or alone for a long while," I told them, and Linnea swallowed nervously, her eyes meeting mine and sliding away again. "The captain's cabin is the only private room on the ship, and tradition is that new recruits get it to themselves for the first few nights. Just until you get on an even keel and know you can trust us."

Her eyes met mine for a few seconds, and I saw so many things there. Trust wasn't real to her right now, and I knew that. "Thank you," she said.

"I can show you where it is," I told her.

She was still wary as she stood, nudging her sister up with her. We walked through the main hold, and I showed her the hooks where only a few of the many hammocks were set up. "This is where everyone else sleeps," I told them.

Thea pushed one of the empty hammocks so it swung. "It looks like fun," she said.

"You can try it when you feel ready," I told them, looking more to Linnea. "Just let me know."

I opened the door to the cabin, and they walked in, finally separating to each look around. Linnea walked the perimeter, and I knew what she would look for—other doors, ways people could enter without her permission, things she couldn't control.

There weren't any.

"Here," I told her, handing her the key. "You can lock it behind me."

She took it, looking solemn and serious. "All the new recruits," she repeated, looking at the door.

"Kairos will sleep out in the main room," I told her. "I want at least two of you to feel comfortable."

"He protected us," she admitted. Her fingers curled around the key. Then her eyes met mine. "But he has secrets, you know."

I did my best not to glance at the drawer where I'd hidden the box. "I figure we all do."

She let out a breath, holding the key pressed against her body as if she could absorb it and always have the ability to lock or unlock what she needed to stay safe—chains, doors, hearts, memories.

"There are clothes in that chest," I said, pointing. "Mine and whatever else we've gathered. You're welcome to whatever you want."

"Thank you," Thea chirped, throwing herself on the bed. Linnea just looked down, holding the key tight.

"I'll see you in the morning," I told them. "We'll have a meeting tomorrow afternoon."

I left them alone, and the moment the door closed, I heard Linnea lock it.

Going for the main deck, I saw some of the others filing belowdecks and collapsing into their hammocks, but I wasn't ready to sleep yet. Nor were my duties done, of course.

I went to the main deck, and I saw Navya and her siblings. She was at the wheel with Bast, and Arnav and Anika were sitting cross-legged, chattering and rolling dice between them. Since they were usually fighting, this was a welcome change.

"Hey," Bast said, swinging under the railing to drop onto the lower deck beside me. He glanced up at Navya, but she was adjusting the wheel and watching her siblings.

"Hey," I returned, walking to the edge of the ship and looking up. No one was up in the lookout; it would be Arnav's turn soon, but I wasn't in a rush to have it manned.

"How are you?" he asked. He held some of the rigging, leaning his weight into it.

"What do you mean?" I asked, crossing my arms.

"Today," he said. "And last night."

"Yeah, you seemed really worried about me last night," I scoffed.

"Am I allowed to be?" he asked. I looked at him, and he pushed harder into the rigging, stretching to do it. "I don't know where we are, Asp. I feel like you hate me or don't trust me or something, and—it's just, we're all we've had for a really long time."

I sat on the rail, holding on to the rope even though the wind wouldn't let me fall.

"What did she say to you?" he asked.

"Nothing," I said, shaking my head.

"She was so mad at you," he said softly. He'd stepped closer to me. "I think that's why she wanted me. To hurt you. Which didn't even occur to me until this morning."

"What, you thought she loved you?" I snarled at him.

"Yeah," he said, shrugging his shoulders. "I thought it was about time someone did."

My eyes dropped to my feet. "That's not fair."

"I know," he said, stepping closer and tucking a thick, knotted rope of my hair behind my ear. "I'm sorry. I was just trying to say I know today was hard for you. I don't want to mean nothing to each other."

His hand lingered, touching my cheek, and for a long moment, something inside me ached. *I thought it was about time someone did.* I knew that feeling—and most days it felt strange and wrong that Bast and I couldn't just be that for each other by wanting it.

"Was it difficult for you?" I asked, swallowing. "The auction?"

He sighed, his rough fingertips brushing over my skin, right in front of my ear. "Thankfully, when I'm there all I think about now is the people we can save. The good we can do."

I searched his face, wondering if that's what I wanted. It sounded so much easier, to not feel the cry of another human like a physical blow. It also sounded like forgetting, like going numb, like falling so far under the waves there was no hope for air.

Could I continue to do my work if I stopped recognizing the damage it did?

His forehead grazed mine. "Do you remember last time we had a new recruit?"

My eyes darted to his. I did—we'd climbed up to the crow's nest to have some privacy, and after we were done, we'd slept in his hammock together, his arms around me all night. I'd slept deeply and well.

I nodded.

He smiled. "That was a perfect night."

My eyes drifted shut.

He kissed my forehead. "I just miss you, that's all," he said, stepping away. "I miss being allowed to care about you."

Then he went belowdecks, and the wind felt cold suddenly.

With a deep, heavy sigh, I finished my rounds of the ship. I saw Kairos sitting out on the bowsprit, Osmost hunkered down low behind him and looking like he was annoyed with his master.

I didn't disturb them, in part because I didn't know how to approach him, and standing there behind him made me feel more alone, more separate.

By the time I got back to the main deck, Arnav had made Anika cry, and I sent him up to the lookout and her up to the quarterdeck. There were a few other night positions—two people to patrol the decks and usually minor tasks like fixing rope—and they were all in order. I said good night to Navya and went belowdecks.

I stripped off my leathers, hanging them by a hammock toward the back. Bast raised his head from his hammock to look at me, and without a word, I went over to him and crawled carefully on top of him, sliding to his side in the hammock. He put his arm around my back, rubbing strong and slow.

My heart didn't feel the way I remembered, that giddy fizz of feeling him touch me. But I felt warm, and protected, and I could feel his heart beating in my ear. For right then, it was enough.

# A Sword and an Arrow

I never slept much, and though it felt nice to lie with someone else, warm and close, it made me dream of being buried alive, sand and dirt blocking the air from my lungs.

Waking up with a hard gasp made Bast's arms go tight around me. I fought him, yelping with a noise that made me sound wounded and small, and the hammock rocked hard.

"Asp," he hissed.

But I felt the motion of the hammock and flipped out of it, grabbing desperately for the ground and trying to breathe when I got there.

"Asp?" he said again.

I huffed out a breath. "Go back to sleep," I told him.

He made a resigned noise and probably did just that. I lay there, staring up at his back against the fabric. He held me when I wanted to go, and he let me go when I needed someone there.

That was enough to remind me that this had been a stupid decision.

After a minute I pushed off the ground, twisting the long ropes of my hair up and into a knot to get them off my sweating neck.

I went upstairs and let the cold wash over me. I'd left my leathers belowdecks, and I missed them suddenly.

"Want me to call Arnav down?" Navya asked from the quarterdeck.

I looked at her. She knew better than most of the crew just how little I slept, and she never pried or questioned me. Sometimes I wondered if I wanted her to—but I rather thought neither of us could bear being closer. She had enough people to love and worry after, and I already couldn't imagine the day when she left the crew. I wouldn't take it well.

"Sure," I said, looking up at the crow's nest.

"Arnav!" she shouted.

She frowned at the mast when there was no response from her little brother. She opened her mouth to shout again, but then he stood up, calling blearily back, "What? What happened?"

"Are you asleep?" she roared. "Get down here! If you can't stay awake you tell me. You don't just fall asleep. What if someone had been coming? What if we were about to be attacked?"

"Asp always knows when someone's coming," he yelled back as he threw his leg over. "It's a dumb job anyway. Everyone sleeps while they do it."

"You're not everyone," she told him. "I expect so much more of you. Start scrubbing."

"Navi!" he whined, climbing halfway down the rigging and dropping to the deck. "It's too cold to scrub. I'll do it tomorrow when it's sunny."

"No, you won't," she told him. "You'll do it right now."

"I don't want to!" he roared, and fire shot out from his hands.

Without thinking, I sent wind over, pushing the fire off the wood.

The fire was gone in a flash, and Arnav looked stunned.

"Scrubbing. Now," Navya told him.

"I can help if Aspasia is staying up," Anika volunteered.

"Shut up," Arnav muttered. "I don't need help."

Anika's mouth twisted a little, but she went and got the deck brushes while he lowered a pail into the ocean.

I climbed to the top yard of the front mast, stretching out and breathing, letting my power stretch. My eyes snagged on Kairos, still where I left him on the bowsprit. I wondered if I hadn't been asleep that long at all, and why a boy from the desert wanted to sit suspended above the water.

I stayed aloft through sunrise, and as long as I could. Navya caught my eye and saluted me as Bast came up and took the wheel, and I felt his eyes on me. The crew began to wake up, and my stomach growled and clenched.

I stood on the yard and stretched with a loud yawn. The ship was gliding over rougher water, and it felt like I was riding the back of an animal, guiding it as it pitched and rose with the waves.

I kicked my shoes off and gave them a gentle push to land on the deck. I saw a few of the crew dart their eyes up to me, but I didn't really care. I shucked my pants, letting the long, once-white shirt that was usually tucked into the pants hang loose.

Then I ran out the arm of the yard, and jumped.

I heard someone shout as I plummeted, diving deep into the water.

Ice closed in around me, and the heavy slam of being denied air made my power feel like it had snapped out of existence. I let the force of the fall push me low, and then I swam deeper, as low as I could go before my lungs started to burn, feeling like the threads of my power were all balled up inside my throat.

The water was dark. A few fish glimmered past me, catching the sun from above, but I couldn't see anything else. Closer to the Vis Islands the water became crystal clear, and no matter how deep I dove, I could always see the bottom, teeming with wildlife. This was a different blue, darker.

When I was desperate to take another breath, I kicked hard for the surface, pushing up and feeling the rush of belonging as soon as I crested the waves. I lay on my back, looking up at the sun in the clear sky.

Most of the crew had gathered over to the edge, and with a wave I took the wind from the sail to slow us to a halt. "Anyone else?" I called.

Arnav—who had spent barely an hour scrubbing before Navya sent him down to bed—whooped and leaped off the railing without any hesitation. A few of the others quickly followed, and a moment later Sophy came above deck and climbed down the ladder to the water.

Laughing, I swam over to Arnav and dunked him, and he kicked me under the water, sputtering and gasping as he surfaced. He vengefully slapped water at me and swam away.

"It's too cold!" Sophy called, clinging to the ladder. "I'll wait till it's sunnier out."

I let my head sink so cold salt water washed over me again. "If you like that sort of thing," I told her.

"Come on," she told me. "I'll make you some coffee while the brats play."

She got splashed for calling some of the younger ones brats, and screamed and scuttled up the ladder.

I called to a rope, and it swung out to me, wrapping around my wrist and drawing me out of the water by my power. For a moment I was sailing through the sky again, and it was the perfect balance to being crushed beneath the water a moment before.

Sophy got onto the deck at the same time I did, and I tried to wring my shirt out a little bit as she pulled on the overdress she had been wearing on top of a shirt similar to mine.

I felt eyes on me, and I looked up to see Bast running his gaze over my soaked body. His mouth quirked into a smile when I caught him, like I wouldn't mind him staring at me.

Which confused me.

I was dripping wet, and I gathered up my clothes and went down to the kitchen in search of the fire before Sophy. Kairos was there, looking into the fire, but something prickled at the back of my neck like I had just caught him doing something wrong.

My eyes drifted to the locked door, but the lock was still there.

"Morning," I said to him.

Maybe that was it. It wasn't until I addressed him that he looked up at me, and that was strange. That wasn't a natural thing to do—why hadn't he looked at me when I first came into the room?

Because he knew I was coming. And he'd stopped doing something else before I got there.

But now his eyes rushed over me before coming back up to my face. "Morning swim?" he asked.

"No, I'm just a sweaty sleeper," I told him.

His eyebrow lifted, and I came toward the fire, pulling the hot air from it and pushing it through my clothes. Because the room was small and there was only so much air, the fire flickered desperately, trying to lick the scraps of air left behind what I'd taken.

Air always seemed like an unlimited quantity to me, but the fire reminded me of the balance. For everything I did, there was always a cost.

I dropped my balled-up pants and shoes on the bench beside me and sat, suddenly aware of how bare my legs were.

"Sophy made biscuits," he said, holding the iron pan toward me.

I took one. She usually got butter when we were in port, so for a day or two we got fresh, soft biscuits instead of the brutal hard ones, and I scooped two out of the pan. There was honey and cheese too, and I was mashing all of this together when Sophy came down and clucked at me.

"I left out some bread for you last night," she told me. "I thought you might get hungry."

"I didn't think to look," I told her honestly. "But thank you."

She waved a hand. "I don't want to see that bird in here again, do you hear me?" she said, looking at Kairos.

He chuckled. "That's not something that I can control."

"Isn't he your bird?"

"Only in the same way that you're the captain's cook," he said, shrugging.

She narrowed her eyes at him. "Still."

"Coffee?" I said hopefully.

She pointed to a pot. "Make yourself useful," she told Kairos, handing him the stone pestle. She dumped a handful of the beans into the mortar bowl and showed him how to scrape them into a powder.

When the water in the pot began to boil, she tossed the ground beans in and let it all boil together for a few minutes more, and the rich smell filled the kitchen.

She waved at Kairos and he took the pot off the fire, and she ladled out two mugs for us both.

"So where do we go now?" Kairos asked.

"The closest thing we have to home," I told him. "Then off to trade again."

He looked into his cup, then rubbed his finger on his lip to take away the grit of the beans. "Will you go to the Trifectate?" he asked.

I glanced at Sophy, but she wasn't paying attention. "I wouldn't think you'd want to go there."

His shoulders lifted.

"Maybe," I said. "We usually do, but Cyrus doesn't want us to this time."

"Who is Cyrus?" he asked.

"She owns the ship," Sophy told him.

*She owns me,* was more to the heart of the matter.

"Have you seen the girls yet?" I asked her instead of saying it.

"The older one came and got food and went back to the cabin," she told me. "I don't think she slept much."

Even though I couldn't see the cabin, I glanced over my shoulder. "Do we need to worry about her?" I asked.

Sophy sighed, turning back to her work. "I worry about all of them, Captain."

I sighed too and put the mug down, and stood, shaking the pants out. Kairos's eyes watched me until I picked up the pants, and then his eyes dropped immediately, and a moment later he turned around.

I laughed, pulling the pants on and tucking my shirt into them. "It's difficult to be modest on a ship," I told his back.

"Yes, but it's not difficult to be respectful," he answered immediately.

My cheeks flushed a little at that. "Soph, we'll have a meeting at dusk," I told her. "Have you checked on the hold?"

I knew my wording was careful. It wasn't that Kairos couldn't know we traded slaves, but I didn't think he did yet, and I didn't want to broach the subject before I'd finished my damn coffee.

Her eyes flicked to Kairos. "I have. All's shipshape." Then she wedged her hands on her hips. "Coffee's not that bad, is it?" she asked Kairos.

I turned to look at him. He was squinting at the coffee, then blinking fast, wincing. His hand went to his temple as his eyes screwed shut. He jerked and dropped the coffee.

It hit the deck with a hard thud, and I slid closer to him on the bench.

"Kairos," I murmured, touching his shoulder. "Kairos, breathe. It's your power, right? Something to do with your power? This happens, just breathe." I rubbed his arms, trying to pull him back to me.

Sophy came forward and mopped up the coffee, putting the mug with the dirty dishes.

He huffed out a harsh breath. "Skies," he groaned. "I can't tell. Sometimes—sometimes it's like a dream, and it's putting my thoughts into something. Sometimes it's a vision, and it's what will come to pass."

*Vision*. That's his power? That was a new one for me.

"Hey," I said gently, rubbing his knees. "Keep breathing. If it's anything like mine, the breathing helps. Can you feel the threads? Do you know what I'm talking about?"

He winced, but it looked a little bit like a nod.

"Try stretching it, like you can pull it apart, make it slower. Try to feel it out."

He pressed his hand to his head. He drew in a slow breath. "He's going to hurt you, Aspasia. I see things with a sword, and an arrow, but the look on his face—" He winced again, pressing his fist to his temple.

My hands on him went still, and I looked to Sophy. She looked stricken, and I waved her upstairs. "Who, Kairos?"

"Bast," he said, and this stopped Sophy short.

I shook my head. "He's never hurt me. Not like that."

"He will." His eyes closed again. "Or maybe he's capable of it. Maybe he wants to. I don't know—that's less clear. I'll figure it out," he said. It sounded like a vow. "I promise. I'll figure it out."

"Sophy, go," I insisted, rubbing his knees again. She didn't hesitate, picking up her skirts and heading up to the top deck. "Kairos, don't strain. Whatever history Bast and I have, as long as he's on this ship he won't hurt me. Not like that."

"You keep saying that," Kairos said, breathing. "He's hurt you in other ways?"

He looked up and met my eyes, and I shrugged. "Sure," I said. "Your oldest friends usually know how to hurt you the worst."

"I have to be able to see them," he said, pressing his fingers into his temple, his voice low. "What's the point of this damned ability if I can't see them?"

"See who?" I asked, confused.

"The things I'm supposed to stop from happening," he told me. "If I can't see them, how can I stop them?"

My hands gripped his knees. Had he seen his family die, or his sister tortured? Had he felt it, without knowing how to stop it? "I don't know," I told him, moving my hands on his knees, not straying more than an inch for fear of crossing a line with him. His throat worked wildly, and he raised his arms to push his hands through his hair, holding his head as he hissed out a breath.

"So you can see the future."

His throat worked. "Pieces. Slivers. Even that I usually don't understand." He pushed his hands over his thighs until our fingers were dangerously close, then pulled back to do it again, like the tide. "I haven't . . . I haven't gotten a vision since."

"Since?" I prompted gently.

A choked noise came out of him, and his mouth pressed into a hard, flat line; his eyes squeezed shut, water pinching out at the edges.

"You don't have to tell me," I assured him. "You don't have to think about it."

He tilted his head back, leaning against the wooden wall. "I think about it every day. Every moment," he muttered to the woodwork.

"Me too," I told him. "We're all haunted here."

His chin bobbed and his fingertips covered the nails of my fingers, the slightest overlap. "What will you do about Bast?" he asked.

"Bast has a dark side—we all do—but I trust him." *Mostly.* "And as for your power, we can work on it. I can help you."

"No, you can't. Unless you're telling me you can see the future."

"No," I allowed. "But I've taught people to control fire, water, and earth. I had a girl who could talk to animals and a boy who was really disappointed to find all he could do was summon mud." He looked at me. "I helped them. I've been working with these powers for years."

He looked away again, staring at the ceiling. "I thought it was gone. I thought I'd gotten rid of it."

"Can't," I told him. "It's in your blood."

His fingertip pressed down on mine ever so slightly, but he didn't respond.

"You didn't sleep much," I guessed. "You should go sleep."

He shook his head.

"Kairos," I told him softly. "You're the one who's in pain right now."

"I can't sleep down here," he said. His eyes moved to the fire like it was the thing keeping him alive.

"You have to tell me why," I told him. "Or I can't help."

He didn't raise his head, so I watched his throat bob again. "The other ship," was all he said.

"What ship?" I said, and immediately realized what he meant. "Oh. The ship you were on before."

I stood, and he raised his head a little to look at me.

"Come on," I told him.

He took another breath before following along behind me.

I went up the stairs to the top deck, and once we hit the sunshine, I continued up the short stairs to the stern deck and led him to the very back of it. "Here," I said. "No one will disturb you, if the sun doesn't bother you. You can get under the cloth though."

He looked to where I was pointing over the rail, to the rowboat tied up and stored on a little ledge. "It's safe?" he asked.

"You won't fall in the water," I clarified.

Osmost dove in front of us, settling into the end of the boat and fluffing out his feathers before *cahk-cahk*ing at Kairos.

Kairos took another deep breath and swung his leg over, dropping down into the boat. It rocked only a little bit, and he braced himself. "I'll try," he said to me.

"All I ask."

"Thank you," he said. He took a breath like he wanted to say something else, but he closed his mouth and crouched into the boat, arranging himself and pulling the cloth over him.

I turned back to the ship, and saw Bast looking at me. Kairos's warning rang in my head, but there was nothing specific or damning in Kairos's words—and honestly, if it had crossed Bast's mind to hurt me, I could hardly blame him; I thought about murdering him roughly twice a day.

# Falling

After everyone got out of the water, I got us back on course as Navya called for a meeting.

We met before dusk, and I took my spot on the stairs as Navya stood at the rail on the quarterdeck.

"Linnea and Thea," I murmured to her.

"Ori?" she called. "Get the new girls?" He immediately ducked belowdecks.

A few minutes later, the girls came up. Sophy was right—Linnea didn't look very well at all.

"Captain?" Navya said. "What are our orders?"

"Cyrus wants fifteen," I said, and let that fall.

The crew looked to one another, murmuring and shaking heads, looking nervous and fearful. We'd never had that many on the ship—certainly not that many adult men. Fifteen men, if they overpowered us, could man the *Ancora* unaided.

"Fifteen what?" Kairos asked, his arms crossed, leaning against a railing. "What is it you trade, Captain?"

"Slaves," Navya answered. "We trade many things, but we need fifteen slaves."

Kairos's eye caught mine, his face hard and flat and unyielding.

Shame curled inside my stomach.

"We can't return to the Trifectate, which puts us in a difficult position. I think we should head down to the Wyverns," I said.

There was a small murmur, but many of the crew were looking at me blankly. "Where's that?" Arnav asked finally.

"South," I told him. "Three big islands with a very robust trade."

"Why haven't we gone before?" Sophy asked.

"It's farther," I said. "And dangerous. The Trifectate has been easier picking." And it was the last place I saw my family.

Bast scoffed, shaking his head at me.

"There's some rough sailing," I allowed, shooting a glare in his direction. "Particularly if we go all the way south. But I don't think we'll have to. I think we can get what we need from one of the northern islands."

"This is madness," Bast said. "Those mines are some of the most heavily fortified places I've ever heard of. I don't know if the element of surprise will be enough, X."

My shoulders lifted. "That's my recommendation."

"We could go all the way south," Bast offered.

I shook my head. "Slavery's not legal there."

Kairos frowned. "What does it matter if it's legal?"

I didn't explain. "If we want to fill this order, if we want to stay alive long enough to do it, we're going to have to go to the Wyverns."

"Suggest an alternate plan, Bast," Navya called. "You can't dissent without a viable option."

"Go back to the Trifectate," he said. "Stay away from the communes, and go to the hills on Liatos or something."

"No," I snapped back. "Cyrus said that the Trifectate has all its ports gunning for us hard."

"Then we fly inland," he said.

Anika made a noise of distress, but I snorted. "Says the boy who doesn't have to fly us."

His face flattened at this, and I knew I shouldn't have called him out on not having powers.

"You said *if*," Kairos called, his arms crossed, his face dark and unreadable.

I raised my eyebrows, not sure what he meant. Everyone looked to him.

"*If* you want to fill this order," he repeated. "Why do it at all?"

"Cyrus owns the *Ancora*," Navya said before I could answer. "We sail on it with a promise to bring her trade. We don't bring her what she wants, we lose the boat." Navya glanced at me. "The captain would have to answer for her disappointment."

"We fill the order," Bast snapped, turning his shoulder to Kairos. "That's obvious. *Where* is the question."

"Then we vote," Navya said. "Go to the Wyverns," she called.

There were eighteen of us now, and seventeen that had a vote. Bast crossed his arms with another noise of dissension, and a few people looked to him and didn't raise their hands.

Navya raised hers. Arnav, Ori, Sophy, Anika all raised their hands. Three more deckhands looked to Navya and raised theirs. Eight out of the seventeen.

Navya's mouth went thin. "Go back to the Trifectate," she called.

Bast and five others raised their hands.

"We all have to vote," I said, looking at Kairos and the girls. "You're a part of this crew, so you vote."

"You didn't."

"I can't," I said, shrugging. "I'm the captain." It was the familiar reasoning, but it was really that they had choices I didn't have, and I would do anything to keep it that way. "You have to vote."

"I'm not voting," Kairos said, shaking his head.

Navya's eyes darted to me, and Linnea and Thea looked at him.

"Little wonder you don't sleep at night, Captain," he sneered.

Linnea crossed her arms in front of Thea, holding her tight.

"Shut up," Arnav snarled, rushing ineffectually forward since about eight people stood between him and Kairos. "You shut up!"

"Arnav," Navya called gently.

He made it around to Kairos and pushed him, which again was ineffectual, since Kairos was leaning on the railing. He just looked at the younger boy. "You don't even realize what she's made you, boy."

"My name is Arnav," he yelled. "And I'll kill you if you talk to her like that."

"Arnav," I called, jumping up. The crew cleared a path for me to dart over to them, and I caught Arnav's arms from behind, holding him against my front. He didn't fight the hold. "Don't talk like that to your crewmates." My words were soft in his ear. "If you're my family, he's my family too."

"We all make a choice," Navya said, coming closer. "We have chosen to control our own fate. That's what this crew is."

"By taking away the choices of others," Kairos said, shaking his hand. "You were all slaves. How can you put someone else in chains?"

"You don't have to vote," I told him, my voice defeated. Navya looked at me, and Arnav craned his head up in my arms. I let go of his arms to squeeze his shoulders. "But if you don't vote, you have to get off the ship in the Vis Islands."

"Yeah," Arnav said, and I rolled my eyes at Arnav's bravado above his head.

"We'll go to the Wyverns," Linnea said immediately.

"You both must vote," Navya said.

"Wyverns," Thea said.

"Why can't he abstain?" Sophy asked. "You let Ori abstain."

"About replacing his sister," I snapped at her. "He shouldn't have to vote on that."

"He can't abstain for his first vote," Bast said. "Not about something like this. If he's not with us, he's a liability."

"Then you're a liability," Sophy returned hotly. "You didn't agree with the plan that has the majority now."

"I won't question the captain once the plan has been made," he said. "Just like she wouldn't blink if my plan won."

"Like hell," Sophy muttered.

"You tell me, Kairos," I said, looking back at him. "Tell me you still want to be here if you don't want to do what we do."

"No," he said easily. "I don't want to be here."

It hurt. "Then we'll leave you in the Vis Islands. I'm sorry this didn't work." I nodded once, squeezing Arnav again before letting him go. The crew was quiet as I moved back to the steps and sat.

"We'll be in the Vis Islands tomorrow," Navya announced.

"We'll take a day there. Anyone who wishes to sail with us should be on the ship by sunrise the next day."

"Does anyone else wish to leave the ship in the islands?" I asked. Everyone else stayed silent.

"Very well," Navya said. "Back to your posts."

Kairos remained still, waiting while everyone shot him glares as they returned to work. Some muttered insults in his direction, but I couldn't hear the words.

Bast came over to me. "I don't know about this, Asp," he said.

"Him or the plan?" I asked.

"The plan," he said, making a sour face. "I'm glad he's going. I didn't like him the moment you bought him. Which you never explained, by the way."

I rubbed my face. "She was going to kill him. It came out of my share," I assured him.

"Ingrate," he growled in Kairos's direction.

"Stop," I told him. "Can you blame him?"

"He's making it seem like we're something we're not," Bast said. "We're not bad people."

"Yes," I said. "We are. Or maybe I am." My head was hurting, and I dug my fingers into my temples. "There's no other plan, Bast, and we already voted. I don't know what you want me to say."

"You left pretty quickly last night," he said, dropping his voice and coming closer to me.

The feeling of breathing hard, my pulse racing with imagined fear from my dreams, needing space but also needing *someone*, rolled through me again. Feeling helpless on the floorboards beneath his hammock and not knowing how to connect to my old friend anymore.

"You'll be more at ease when we can be back in your cabin," he said. "I missed sleeping in there."

"We?" I asked, looking up at him.

His shoulders lifted.

"I thought you wanted to be in my life," I said. "Or allowed to care about me. Did that mean . . . together?"

"Well, I thought last night—"

"No," I told him, standing. "You said all those things and I thought it meant we could be friends."

"Friends who sleep on top of each other?" he asked, like I was stupid. "I said those things because I love you, Aspasia. I know you know that."

"I don't know that," I told him, lowering my voice as I glanced around. "What was supposed to give me that impression? You sleeping with Cyrus?"

"That's low," he grunted.

"Of *you*," I returned.

"You were the one who didn't want to be with me, Asp. Do you remember that?"

I drew a breath. "I've never changed my mind about that, Bast. Not once. I thought I was clear about that; I didn't mean for last night to change anything."

"Well, it definitely changed how clear things look," he told me. He shook his head. "You still want me, Asp. You can't deny that."

"I don't want to keep hurting you, Bast," I told him. "I don't want to be with you. But I miss what our friendship was before all of this."

"All of this," he scoffed. "You mean being in love, Aspasia."

Except I hadn't ever felt that way, and I hadn't ever said those words to him. But he had loved me—it just wasn't how I wanted to be loved, and that, more than anything, was why I told him I didn't want to be with him.

"I need to go look after some things, Bast," I told him. "Navya's watching the wheel for you."

"Fine," he muttered, pushing past me to go up the stairs.

I went down belowdecks to the kitchen and the locked door. I unlocked it, opening the door and pulling it shut behind me. The air was hot, and I descended the short stair, turning left where the brig was right, to the fortified room that was just beneath the bunk room. All our treasure was down there, including mine. Any of the others who wanted to keep their share in here could, but no one else did right now. It was usually a good indication of how much trust there was at the moment on the ship.

I entered, then shut and locked the door behind me, crossing the mostly empty room.

I opened the small chest that was mine, sitting on the floor to open it and go through my funds. I wasn't rich. I had money that I kept stored on the islands, but I also kept the shares of a few hauls with me when we sailed, just in case.

There was coin and a few pearls loose in the bottom, and two bags, one black and one red. I turned the box around, using the lid as a tray, and opened the two pouches, using the bags to keep the amounts separate.

In the black bag, there were seventeen pearls. I carefully arranged them in rows as I counted them, touching each one. Each one was a life I had saved, free and clear. It was someone who had started in slavery and would never return there, the balance that was left after accounting for my misdeeds.

The red bag was far heavier. It contained eighty-three pearls, and I did the same thing, carefully arranging them, touching them, remembering the souls that I had ferried across from one enslavement to another.

With a heavy sigh, I took five pearls from the black bag and held them, letting them tuck into the dips between my fingers. Five more slaves that I had delivered to Cyrus's hands.

I picked up three pearls from the ones in my hand. Kairos, Linnea, and Thea.

I put three back in the black bag, and two went on to the red bag. Fifteen lives I had saved; eighty-five that I had condemned.

More than that, there were only fifteen pearls left, and I had fifteen slots that Cyrus wanted filled. It wasn't enough that my pile of sins, my literal debt, had grown astronomically over the years. Now the small profit, the small amount of lives that I could successfully claim, would be wiped away.

My scar burned, and I tamped down the bile rising in my throat. I put the pearls back in the bags, back in the chest, and I looked to my money.

I couldn't make a policy of it, but I didn't want to leave Kairos with nothing on an island that he wasn't familiar with. That wasn't his home, and he needed to get to his sister and whatever was left of his family.

I had six pearls, and another fifty kings. I halved the kings and took two pearls, filling a small leather sack with them and separating it out. It would be more than enough for passage and to keep himself fed and free on the way.

Tucking the bag under my arm, I locked up my things and unlocked the door to let myself out of the room. I gasped and dropped the bag to see Kairos standing there.

The bag never touched the ground. My power caught it, and I leaned down and picked it up, tucking it under my arm again as a fearful warning ran down my spine. "Kairos," I said, turning my back to him slowly so I could lock the door again.

"You have to stop this, Aspasia," he told me, his voice a growl. "I know you think you're doing something good, and you are in many ways, helping those children. But you're damning them in the process. You're making children buy and sell slaves. What kind of monster does that?"

I turned back to him, pocketing the key, trying to keep space between us in the narrow hallway. "I don't think I'm doing something good," I told him. "I know exactly how evil I am. But for them, what's better? I don't know another way to help them be free and get back to their families. Ultimately, the sin is mine, not theirs."

"Why?" he asked. "Because they don't go to the auction? There's no difference between you all."

"There is," I insisted.

He stepped forward, crowding against me. "Is that what you say to yourself when you murder? When you tear families apart? When you leave a baby to die because his mother will fetch a high price?"

I couldn't help shuddering hard, and pain made my eyes prick. "Is that what you saw?" I asked, heartbroken. "Did that happen?"

He stepped away from me. "Don't do that. This isn't about me. You have a slippery habit of flipping the conversation, Captain."

"I don't kill people," I told him.

"You do," he said. "Even if you're not the one killing that child, you're helping a system that doesn't care about human life to continue. You're allowing men who do to exist."

I felt tears stinging in my eyes. "I know that."

"You care about people," he said, his voice losing its fury. "Deeply. Even I can see that. I don't understand why you do this, Aspasia. How you can turn away from the suffering of some, but not others."

"Because there are shades of horrible," I told him. "If I'm supplying the trade, there's one less slot for a captain like that."

"That's not good enough," he told me.

"Kairos," I said, sniffing hard to keep the tears back. "I know intimately how unforgivable the things I've done are. But you're leaving. So I don't need them recounted by you before you go."

"I don't understand!" he yelled. I jumped, and a tear fell. I pushed it away quickly. "Great Skies, you can't be a slave trader and cry about it, Aspasia! If you feel like you're doing wrong, just stop it. Don't do it."

But it was never that simple. *What happens if I find it before you do?* Cyrus had asked. *What happens if you're defying me when I do?* If I could do this one thing, I could have this ship for myself. I could sail the world over looking for my brother and sister, and she couldn't say anything about it. I could free as many children as I could buy or steal, and no one would end up a slave like I had.

Clearing my throat, I told him, "You don't have to understand. As soon as we make land, you can leave, and that's all there is to say about it."

His jaw worked. "I've been seeing flashes. Not visions, but glimpses. Feelings. There is an awful reckoning coming for you."

Meeting his eyes, I looked up at him. "Finally."

This seemed to startle him into a moment of silence, and I ran up the stairs. Sophy was there, and her mouth opened. "Lock it when he comes up," I told her.

She just nodded.

When Anika came up for the night, I sent her back down below, even as Navya rolled her eyes at me. Instead, I climbed up to the yard and called my power hard.

I couldn't make any of this damn situation easier, but I could always count on the wind. It came flooding to me, my loyal follower, rushing along the threads of the natural world and making them spark with energy.

There was a fine line between calling a storm and calling the wind—to do the former, I had to manipulate the air high above, pulling it down, mixing cold and warm, heavy and light, until the natural world was so tied in knots that a storm came to my hand.

Calling the wind was different. It was closer, easier, a happy puppy that wagged its tail for my delight. Even so, the wind demanded balance in all things, and if I used wind here, the recoil in the skies would call up a storm a day or two behind me.

But for now the skies were clear, the wind was strong, and the only precipitation came from the frantic sea spray as we crested the waves. Even Osmost tucked in his feathers and stayed on deck on his master's shoulder. Kairos watched me, judging me, and I felt his rebukes—all too true—burn through my chest. Part of me wanted to rush to Bast, to his arms, feel his kiss and let him remind me that he didn't think we were monsters.

A bigger part of me hated that Bast couldn't see how awful

this was, and resented him for choosing to be here when he could leave.

Sweat trickled down my neck, between my shoulders, a strange kind of relief on my salted skin. I knew I shouldn't push so hard; I'd be weak and exhausted when I got us home, but I couldn't stop. It was that or scratch my scar until it bled rivers down my face and made every smile hurt the way it should.

We made the islands just before dawn, sailing past Arix Island, the first in the archipelago, as Altia and then Vassil came into view. I could see the austere slopes of Kiri in the distance, barely a shadow in the blue light before the sun broke.

I stumbled down from the yard, losing my footing and grip more than once.

"Aspasia," Navya said, worried. "I can get Anika."

"For what?" Kairos asked, coming to us as I climbed up to the quarterdeck. I felt dizzy, the world pitching around me with more than the rock of the boat.

"I'm fine," I told her. Pulling open the flap of my leather coat, I tugged out the bag I'd shoved into the too-small pocket and tossed it at Kairos. "Here," I told him. He caught it against his chest, not opening it as he looked at me.

I felt Navya's shocked eyes on me.

"I won't take your charity," he told me, pushing the bag away from him. "And certainly not your money won from blood."

"It's tradition," I lied. "You get your purchase price back when you leave."

"I won't—" he started as Navya also began to speak, but I cut them off, seeing the rocks ahead that signaled the place I usually started the ascent.

"Hold on!" I shouted.

Kairos turned, looking over the bow as we were heading straight for a visible patch of rocks that lay in front of the sheer rock faces of Altia.

"Captain!" Navya shouted. "You need Anik—"

But the boat had already started to tilt, the bow lifting in the air. I did it carefully, not wanting to raise it too high too fast and risk pitching everyone out of their beds. Instead, I leaned the boat to the side, keeling as we rose with a shower of water streaming off our hull.

The strain was glorious, feeling the threads stretch and pull taut and respond to me as air pushed upward through the sails, under the hull, eddying to create an updraft that the whole ship sailed on, leaving the water and flying through the air.

Osmost trilled out his delight as he caught the same wind, flying upward beside us.

"You're going to kill us!" Kairos bellowed at me.

The boat curled, missing the cliffs and sailing tilted on an axis, easing up and around, going swift and sure as we rose in the sky, circling the high cliff that spindled into a towering point of rock.

No matter how many times we had done this together, it was stunning. Sun was breaking onto the high cliffs, illuminating the other Vis Islands beyond Altia, even making Kiri's dark peaks look lush and inviting. Light glittered in the stream of droplets that was still dripping from our hull as wind rippled across the deck, filling the sails, pushing us forward.

The crew wasn't impervious to this effect, and everyone stood clustered on the rails as we watched our village grow closer.

"All hands to your stations!" Navya cried, slapping one hand on the rail. "Prepare the lines! Prepare to land!"

Jolted into activity, the crew rushed to follow orders. Only

Kairos, Linnea, and Thea remained on the rails, watching in wonder as we continued to fly. I didn't call them away, but let them appreciate my glory.

As we grew closer, it was clear that the peak that had looked so tiny from below wasn't; it was wide and flat, wide enough to hold the boat on the grassy platform that created a dry dock for us.

My hands were shaking, and I stretched them out so I could hold the boat more easily.

It didn't help. "Captain!" I heard from behind me, but I couldn't turn and risk losing what precious little remained of my focus.

We faltered in the air, and suddenly the gravity of just how tired and worn I was after days of not sleeping and hours of pushing myself struck me. I didn't even know what would happen if I couldn't handle the boat—we were hundreds of feet in the air, with nothing but a field of sharp rocks below us.

Fear curled into my power, and the boat slipped down a few feet. I heard someone shout.

"Anika!" I called, my voice breaking.

She appeared before me, her small face pale and eyes wide, but she held out her arms, mirroring my posture.

I pulled in a deep breath, letting it out as I wove our power together and guided the ship toward our spot, the dry dock formed from earth and stone. As soon as it touched the soft grass, the crew threw lines over the edge, tying the boat down to the various anchors we'd built to protect the ship over the years.

Anika's hands dropped, and I felt the strange, foreign sensation of falling.

# Stay Together

When I woke, for once the moving shapes I saw were of fire. I was lying on a hearth, with blankets heaped on me making me sweat, and every inch of my body ached as I started to move. "Oh balls," I groaned.

"*Fool*," I heard from behind me. I turned a little to find Charly with her hands on her hips, directing that to me.

Sophy's older sister looked remarkably similar to her in that moment. I started to sit up, then sighed and decided against it.

"You absolute fool," she accused me again, stomping over to me, the noise made much more impactful by her wooden leg. "Using your power like that? What were you thinking? Don't you remember the last time?"

"Yes," I told her. "I just haven't been sleeping. I didn't realize it was bad until it was."

"You could have *killed* them, do you know that?" she told me, her voice more worried than angry suddenly.

The weight of that slid into my stomach along with all the other rocks I'd been swallowing lately. "I'm sorry, Charly."

"You were ice cold," she told me, turning away.

That explained the blankets, at least. I pulled them off, folding them onto a chair near the fire before I started to ease myself up again.

She was staring into a soup pot, her mouth tight and drawn in like a purse string.

"I'm sorry, Charly," I told her again.

"I thought you were dead," she said bitterly into the soup.

I hugged her from behind. "But I'm not."

She turned and hugged me properly, kissing my head in a way that reminded me of the little I remembered of my own mother. "Don't ever be, Aspasia. Agreed?"

"Yes," I agreed, but it was a foolish thing to promise.

"It's bad enough that I can't be out there with you. Don't make it worse."

"You're needed here anyway," I told her, reluctantly pulling away from her. "How are the last ones we brought?"

She stirred the soup, then rapped the wooden spoon on the edge of the pot. "They're adjusting." She put her hands on her hips. "You remember the little girl with the burn on her cheek?" she said, looking at me grimly. I nodded, like I remembered, but I didn't. We took the slaves too quickly, and I usually spent as little time as I could with them until we set them free on Altia.

Even then, anyone who I had freed from slavery never really liked to see me. I didn't blame them. "What about her?" I asked, crossing my arms and leaning on the counter.

"She was taken with her family from Kyrikatos. Which means that the damn Tri King is throwing anyone he wishes into slavery."

A cold pain knifed into my gut. "She was with her family in the communes?"

Charly shook her head. "Taken there with them. Split up. She knows for sure her mother's dead. She thinks her father was brought to the shipyard."

Which was a death sentence all its own. The men who worked in the massive, stories-deep shipbuilders' camp lasted less than a year. Which meant that this was most likely the safest place for the girl. Familyless, but free.

"But yes, they're all coming along." With a sigh, she waved her spoon at the back door. "You better go tell them you're awake. And that dinner's soon."

"Who?" I questioned.

I opened the door. Arnav was leaning against it, Anika curled up in his arms. Ori was beside them.

"Hey," I said softly, leaning down to touch Anika's cheek and ruffle Arnav's hair.

He jerked away, glaring savagely at me.

I looked at Ori, who clasped my hand in a tight grip. "Arnav," I told him, looking back to him. "I'm okay. I'm sorry if I scared you."

He pinched Anika to make her jump out of his arms. "I wasn't scared," he snapped, standing up as soon as he could.

He stalked off, and even though the motion screamed down my back, I went after him. "Hey!" I shouted. "Arnav!"

"Just leave if you want to leave!" he shrieked at me. "I don't care! I won't even notice!"

"Leave?" I asked.

"Dying's the same damn thing!" he cursed.

"I'm not leaving you," I told him. "Not ever. Not until you want to leave me and go live a happy life off the ship."

"I won't ever leave the ship," he told me, but he stopped running away from me.

"Then we'll always be crew," I told him. "And crew is family, right?"

He turned, his arms stubborn across his chest, and I pretended I didn't see the tears on his face. "I don't want you to leave," he told me.

I put my arms around him, and his hug back to me was fierce and hard. "I'm okay," I assured him again. "Or I will be once Charly feeds me."

"What happened?" he asked. "Why did you collapse like that?"

I knelt down in front of him. "I don't really know what happened. I collapsed? Then what?"

"You weren't moving. Your skin was cold. That traitor hurt you, didn't he?" Arnav snarled.

"No," I told him. "He didn't have anything to do with it. I think I just ran out of power."

"Why did you run out? You never run out."

"I was tired," I told him. "It's happened before."

He considered this. "You haven't been sleeping much," he said. "I can take more hours at night. I'm sorry if I haven't been working like you want me to."

My heart ached. "You're a great worker, Arnav. But come on— you left your sister and Ori and perfectly good soup. Where's Navya?"

"She had to go do stuff with the house before we leave again."

I turned, like maybe I would see her in the far field where her little stone and lumber house stood. Many of our families had homes on the island, protected by the ones like Charly who stayed behind.

"I can carry it over," he volunteered. "The soup."

"Thanks," I said. "Ask Charly if she needs help, though."

I swept Anika up as we passed her. She snugged tight against me for a few long minutes before she broke away to hold tight to my hand. Ori was already helping Charly.

Charly gave them all instructions, and she led the way out of the big kitchen to the front hall. It was a huge house, and it only got bigger as we kept adding on to it.

The burble of voices was loud even before we opened the door, and it swamped us. People swarmed forward to help Charly and the others, taking her food to the big fireplace and hooking it onto a stand. Two other tables were filled with food.

There were more tables since our last big dinner, and the people at them had changed shape. Most of them gathered around Charly, but only a few knew me well enough to come up to me. Instead, I always felt like I made them uneasy—maybe because of my scar, or because if I brought them here, I could take them away.

I found Sophy and Bast sitting together, and I went and sat with them. Sophy leaped up and hugged me as soon as I sat. "Oh, you had us worried," she told me.

"I'm fine," I told her, waving her off. "I'm always fine."

"Glad to hear it," Bast said, bumping my shoulder.

We fell quiet as we watched the others. There were maybe a hundred people in our little village now. I'd taken 131 people from slavery and either brought them here, set them free in other places, or hired them onto the crew. In this room, there were people from every country I knew of, with skin tones and hair colors like an ever-shifting quilt of color and cultures. There were even some in the village who had come between visits from my ship, and Charly tended to keep a watchful eye on those most of all. It was a long walk down the island, but we kept a few boats hidden so we could get off island and trade as needed. I wondered if we'd have to build onto the main house again—I'd have to leave money for that. Food and trees for lumber were easy enough to find, but anything needing metal—like nails, unfortunately— required money and trade.

I saw with interest that one of the older ones had a baby now. I didn't even realize she'd been with child—maybe she just hadn't come to the dinners much. I doubted they lived in the main house.

Villagers brought dishes to the tables until they buckled under the weight, and people were going up in waves. Charly brought me over some soup and sat beside Sophy, chattering about everything that had happened in the week or so we'd been gone.

I ate it, more hungry than usual as I watched the group. I noticed when the door opened and Kairos came in, glancing around to gain his bearings before going to the food and piling a high plate. He came over to our table, sitting beside Charly.

"This soup looks wonderful," he told her. "Thank you for inviting me to this."

"Everyone's invited," Sophy said.

"Especially you," Charly said, patting his hand.

My eyebrows rose.

"He's the one who carried you all the way to me," she explained. Kairos met my eyes for a moment before returning to his food.

"Thank you," I said. There were other questions, like how he knew where to go, but I didn't ask them.

"So what is this place?" he asked.

"Charly runs it," I told him as Charly opened her mouth.

"Me?" she asked, confused.

"Don't you?" I asked her.

"Well, sure, I keep it running, but that's not really important."

"Of course it's important," Kairos said. "Are all these children islanders? They don't look like the Vis that I've met."

"They're not the Vis people," Charly said, looking to me, unsure. "There are some Vis on other islands—mostly Kiri. I hear there's more of them in Sarocca than here. Everyone went into hiding after . . . that mess, and the islands were abandoned."

"I didn't think there were any left," he said. "Someone I know will be very relieved to hear that." He looked thoughtful, then ate some of his food. "So where did all these children come from, if not here?"

"You didn't have to bring me here," I said, changing the subject. "You could have just been on your way."

"On his way?" Charly said, horrified. "It's a three-day hike down to the water. How do you propose he get anywhere from there?"

"He could hire out one of the boats," I countered. "He has money for it."

Bast's attention shot to Kairos, and suddenly I regretted keeping one secret to betray another. "How does he have money for that?" Bast asked me.

"What is it you don't want me to know about these children?" Kairos asked.

"She's just being modest," Charly said, frowning at me.

"Modest?" Kairos scoffed.

But Sophy was wise to it. "Come on, Charly. Asp doesn't want him to know because he's already made up his mind that he's not one of us. If he's decided that, we don't have to trust him with our secrets."

Charly's confusion turned to Kairos now. "Why don't you want to join the crew? Didn't you just join up in Sarocca?" she asked. "You weren't with them last time."

Kairos hesitated. "I just didn't realize the kind of business they were in," he said carefully.

"What do you mean?" she said, sounding distressed. "Be plain about it."

"I won't force people into slavery," he said, raising his chin. "I'm not going to be part of this. It's wrong."

To my surprise, Charly laughed. She patted his back, and he bristled a little. "Good," she said. "Good. If you can turn your eyes away from the lives in this room, then good," she said. "You're not strong enough for what they do."

His eyes narrowed. "I don't understand."

"This is what we do," Bast said sharply. "We steal slaves and we resell the men, but we bring women and children here, where they can't be found again. Where they can be free. Occasionally, we buy new people from the market for the crew, and we free them too."

"You're displacing people from their homes," he said, but the fury was gone from his voice.

"Not yet," Sophy said. "We take slaves from other places—like the communes—so we can at least free women and children before we send the men elsewhere."

"Aspasia built this house," Charly said. "And funds it. She keeps it running so all these children have a home. If they want to leave, we all do what we can to send them back to their families. If they have them still."

"Most don't," Sophy said, squeezing her sister.

"But you still enslave men," Kairos said.

"Yes," I said, thinking of the all-too-heavy red pouch of pearls. "That's the only way I can keep it running. But this is the biggest secret we all keep, Kairos. You can't tell anyone once you leave. You have to promise."

"What do the Elementae have to do with this?" he demanded, not satisfied yet.

Sophy lifted a shoulder. "We try to buy Elementae when we can for crew. It's the only way we can crew a ship with children."

I gestured around the room. "Usually it takes until you're between eight and twelve for powers to appear," I told him. "So the children we save without knowing if they'll become Elementae. Some have. Some haven't."

"He still has to promise," Sophy insisted. "Not to tell."

He looked at me, his face still glowering and confused. "I promise."

I stood from the bench, clearing my throat. "Did Charly already give you a bed? There must be some free."

"She did," he said, watching me.

"Good," I said.

"I think he should apologize," Bast said as I turned to go. "Before we leave. He should apologize for the things he said to you."

The boys looked at each other, and I felt tension bristle across the table.

"He wasn't wrong," I told Bast. "Why should this place change any of his thoughts? He shouldn't want to apologize, and I damn well don't want to hear it. So stop stirring up trouble."

Bast looked stung.

"I'm glad I met you, Kairos," I said. "Please get safely back to your family. That's all that matters."

His throat worked, and he nodded mutely.

I took my bowl away and brought it into the kitchen. I left it there, going up the back stairs to the two rooms above the kitchen.

When we'd all needed a home so desperately, I'd built the kitchen with enough space for everyone to lie down to sleep. The bedrooms above had come next. I went over to the left first, pulling out my keys and unlocking the door.

It was untouched. There were two beds in there, and I'd stuffed them full of bedding that was almost certainly moldered by now. I'd thought then that if I just made them a home, Gryphon and Pera would just appear, falling magically into my grasp.

Over the years, I'd filled it with various treasures that my brother and sister would like—a pewter dragon figure for my brother and a little book of rhymes for my sister. The last I'd seen them had been seven years ago, the day we'd all been taken to the communes and split up.

It was stupid. This whole thing was stupid, but I'd made the room to look like their shared room in our tiny house in Liatos and filled it with things they liked back then. I couldn't imagine Pera—who would be fourteen now, if she was still alive—still liked rhymes. Gryphon would be sixteen.

I wondered if they had powers, like I did. Not all siblings did— Nayva had nothing to speak of and Arnav and Anika both did.

It crossed my mind every time I searched for a kid at auction that maybe that would be how I found my family.

And now Cyrus was selling Elementae to the Trifectate to be tortured and killed. What if she had sold them?

Their toys sat in dust on the tables, and it made me feel empty and broken.

I had never committed a child to slavery. Could I start now? Was this empty room—the chance to keep sailing, keep searching for my family—worth sentencing a child to that fate? Could I possibly fill Cyrus's order the way she wanted?

If the answer was no, there were limited options for me. She could take the ship. She could take my freedom.

She could take my life.

I had to acknowledge that there were several possibilities that involved me never setting foot on the *Ancora* again, and if that were true, never returning to Altia. Or at least, not for many years.

I had built a home for my siblings that they would never see, but I had to make sure the people who did live here would be protected.

I went to my room across the hall. I pulled out fresh clothes from the chest by my bed, noting the small vial of blue liquid that Charly had left there for me. Taking the clothes and a piece of soap, I went back down the stairs, through the kitchen, and out to the back.

The night was cooling off quickly, and I followed the stone path down to the lake. It was right at the edge of the little plateau that our village was built on, and the frequent rain on the island kept it fresh and full before it trickled down the edge to feed the stream that ran down from our perch.

There were new houses. I saw Navya's, which she had been working on building for her siblings, and a new, small house that was only just being framed. I saw the small field of crops that we all helped tend, and the pen of chickens and livestock that we slowly developed. Pride pulled my spine taller—we had made something here. A tiny protected home for those who didn't have one left in the world.

The feeling in me changed as I thought of someone finding them here, disturbing the peace that had taken so long to build.

I walked around to the far side of the lake, hoping to find space where I wouldn't be bothered. I certainly wasn't all that shy about my body—it wasn't something I knew to care much about after years of living on a ship with boys and girls alike—but I just didn't want to talk to people.

Shucking off my clothes on the bank, I dove into the warm water, taking the soap to my body and my hair, scrubbing at the knotted strands and trying to soak the salt out of my skin. After a while I lay on my back in the water, staring up at the cloudless sky, a bright moon, and impossibly gorgeous stars that I couldn't see in places like Diadem.

Our village was probably my favorite place in the world, but it still didn't feel like home to me. Nothing did, and nothing would, I suspected, until I found my brother and sister and brought them here, safe from the people who would hurt them. Protected. Defended.

*I'm trusting you, Aspasia*, my father had told me. He'd had worry in his eyes, and I'd wondered in the years between then and now if he'd known he wasn't coming back to us. *I'm trusting you to take care of your brother and sister. Do whatever you have to, but stay together.*

I had vowed to do so, but my promise hadn't lasted a week before we were all split up. Two weeks later, I was taken away in the night by the soldiers and placed on a ship bound for Sarocca.

I pulled myself out of the water to dry on the shore, cold and shivery in the moonlight. My hair was the worst of it—it could soak up so much water that it would take hours to dry on its own. I put my shirt on and blew air through the strands, holding it off my neck and back so it didn't soak my shirt. My arms ached when it was done, but at least I was dry and clean in a way I would never hope to be while I was at sea.

When I walked back, I heard water sloshing and moving, and I saw a dark shape catch the moonlight in the water. It was Kairos, and I wondered if his preference for respect meant that I should announce myself.

"You're welcome to join me," he called. "But I do know you're there."

I crossed my arms and came forward, sitting on a log someone had put by the edge. I brought my knees up, holding them to me. He was only a head and shoulders above the dark water, but it made his eyes glow with light.

"You should have told me everything," he said.

I scoffed. "Like hell I should. You don't deserve to know everything."

"You're not very good at defending yourself," he told me.

"Sure I am."

"I accused you of many things, and it turns out none of them are as simple as I assumed. Which you could have thrown right back in my face if you wanted."

I shrugged. "You shouldn't kid yourself, Kairos. I've done some good things, but you weren't wrong when you said I'm a monster.

I am. I've had to be. And if it came to getting what I want, I would kill anyone. I would take anyone away from their family. I would enslave anyone." Even as I said it, I wasn't sure. That would mean selling children—a real, finite act that crossed every line I'd ever drawn—to keep myself in a position to maybe find my brother and sister.

"But that raises the very interesting question of what you want, Aspasia. Because it's not money, I know that by now."

"Do you?" I questioned.

"Sure. You give it away too easily—it's not precious to you. I know you don't give their purchase price to people when they leave. You're not the best liar."

I scoffed. "You can see the future, so you're a little harder to lie to."

"Not my point," he said. "Is that soap you have?"

I pitched it to him, and it splashed into the water. He grabbed it, scrubbing his body and hair and giving me the unabashed chance to watch his hands move over his skin. I would never deny that he was very, very handsome.

He caught me looking and grinned.

I smiled right back.

"I'm not leaving the ship," he announced. "I'll be on it in the morning."

I sat up straighter. "Really? Why?"

"Many reasons," he said. "But first because I have felt more often than I care to admit like I don't understand what's going on here, and I'm not satisfied with that. I like truly knowing things."

That seemed dangerous. "I'm not some puzzle for you to unlock," I told him.

"It's not just you. It's this whole life of yours. I think I'm here for a reason, and I don't think my purpose has ended yet. Fate is still moving her pieces around us."

His words made something shiver inside me. "Do you believe that?" I asked. "Fate?"

He dunked under, rinsing his body and head. He came back up with a splutter. "Turn around," he said. "So I can get out."

I opened my mouth for some clever remark but thought better of it and turned, tugging my knees back up with a sigh.

"Yes," he said after a long moment, during which I heard water streaming off him as he came out of the water. "I believe in fate."

"Only for the good things," I clarified, pressing my chin into my knee. "Like that you'll see your family again, or that you deserved to be freed from slavery. Right?"

"No," he said. "Well, I hope not. Those seem more to me like hope than fate. But no, I think there's something turning in the world, and we can't stop it. I think that's why I get visions— fate is moving pieces around an invisible board, and I am granted a window into that."

"Have you been getting any more visions?" I asked.

"No," he said. "But you said something about teaching me."

He touched my back, and I looked up at him, his shirt damp and sticking to him, his pants dark on his legs. I stood, and our chests were close together, and for a moment, our faces were inches apart.

It was strange. On a boat, everything was tight and close, but this was different. This was a wholly separate kind of close, breathing the same air, daring the other to look away. I was aware then that I wanted him—to kiss him, or touch him, see what his skin felt like. See what happened when I kissed his neck. Find out what he would do with his hands.

It seemed easy to guess that he felt at least a shade of the same curiosity and interest—he wasn't looking away, wasn't moving away.

"I did," I said, smiling thoughtfully at him.

He smiled back. "I've known two very powerful Elementae," he told me. "But I'd never felt anything like that, your flying the ship to get up here."

A self-satisfied pleasure bubbled up in me. "Not in the desert anymore," I told him archly.

"No," he said. "But can you imagine what you could do with a ship on a dune? It would change everything."

Desire snaked through me; I could picture it. The hot, dry sun beating down as I rode the sand like an ocean, flying across the stark landscape.

"How did you come to know so much about your power?" he asked.

"Practice," I said, blinking the vision away. "And trying to help lots of other kids with theirs."

He nodded, and it brought our faces closer together. I could feel his breath mix with mine. I could kiss him, right now. I think he'd want it. I think I'd enjoy it, tasting a kiss from the boy who so recently thought I was a monster.

An ache rolled in the muscles between my shoulders. Not tonight, not now, maybe not ever—I knew what it felt like to be powerless, and as his captain, as a woman who had purchased his *life* from the auction block not long before, taking that step would be crossing a line right now.

"I need to get back," I told him, stepping away. "But I suppose I'll see you on the ship."

"I'll walk you," he said, falling in step beside me like nothing had happened. Well, nothing *had* happened.

"Are you sure?" I said, not about him walking me. "You have a family to get back to. It sounds like they need you very much."

"They do," he said, his voice soft. "And I need them. But it's not that simple, is it? Several days to get down the cliffs, several days to get a boat. Several more days to make it back to the Trifectate, and even then, I don't know where they are. They could be anywhere."

"You don't know where they would go?"

His jaw went tense and bumpy. "My sister's protected by the Resistance now. It's possible they would go to the desert, maybe, but she wouldn't stay there. Shalia has the heir to the Bone Lands in her belly and the commander of the Trifectate at her side—she's never been a woman to sit still and wait for her brothers to return. She's in the Bone Lands, and I have no idea how to go about finding her."

"So you're just giving up," I accused.

He shook his head. "No. Something makes me believe that I can help them most by being here right now. I can't explain it—I haven't had a vision, I don't know for sure. But I feel it—you will lead me to her. Her and my brother both."

I sighed. "Be careful with that," I told him. "What if it turns out that it's the opposite? Can you live with yourself if you find out they needed you and you weren't there?"

His laugh was low and bitter. "They did need me," he said. "I wasn't there. So that's what I'm trying to figure out."

"You mentioned something about that before," I started carefully. "What happened?"

"I had a vision," he said simply, "and I couldn't figure out what it meant until my family was bleeding at my feet."

Without thinking, I held my dirty clothes with one hand and pushed the other into his, squeezing.

He turned and gave me a faint, sweet smile. "You have the strangest ways about you, Aspasia."

I started to pull my hand away, but his fingers threaded through mine and held my hand tight.

"It's easy enough to guess that something happened with your family," he said, his voice a low, private whisper. "Your siblings, maybe? When you're ready, you can tell me."

"What makes you say that?" I asked.

He chuckled. "First, the way your hand just went tense. Second, it's in every inch of this place. In what you do. You're desperate to keep families together as much as you can. I'm guessing because you had one once, and don't anymore."

"Of course I had a family," I said, harsh. I pulled my apparently traitorous hand away from his. "We all did. But the easiest way to break people is to splinter them away from the people who make them strong. So it's my story and a hundred other people's. It doesn't mean I have some deep, dark secret to hide."

His eyes narrowed on me in a way that saw everything. "I think it does."

"Well, I suppose you can think what you want. More importantly, are you any good with a weapon?" I asked.

"A weapon?" he repeated.

"Yes," I said as we came near the big house. "It's fine. We'll work on training you. I'd like you to be able to handle yourself before we get to the Wyverns."

"How long is the sail there?" he asked.

"A little more than a week with my boat," I told him, shrugging. "So you'll have some time to learn."

He gave me one of his unnerving smiles. "I'm sure I'll pick it up."

"Good. I'll see you in the morning." I gestured to the flashes of light I saw past the corner of the kitchen. "I'm sure some of the crew have set up a bonfire by now." A laugh rose up, calling us over.

"You're not going," he observed as I turned toward the kitchen door.

I saw Charly sitting by the embers of the fire, waiting for me, and I shook my head. "I need sleep," I told him.

"I'll see you on the ship," he said.

I walked inside the house, going over to the low-banked fire and sitting on the hearth. Charly smiled at me. "So," she said knowingly.

"My money's in the roof," I told her. "Do you already know that? If you go up to the ridge, there are coins and pearls hidden all the way along there."

She opened her mouth with a scowl.

"I trust you," I told her quickly. "I know you'll only take what you need. And it won't be easy to get it without my power, but you'll manage. Ladders, I imagine, and one of the boys you trust."

"Aspasia," she said.

"It's important," I continued. "You need money to keep this place going. To keep it protected from anyone who could hurt us."

"You're coming back," she told me fiercely.

"Should I?" I asked, my voice rough, looking at the fire instead of her face. "If I do what she wants, I'll cross a line I can't come back from. But it will let me keep this place running, keep giving kids work, keep giving kids choices that I don't have. Which is more important—this, or the rules?"

"To not trade women and children, you mean?" she asked. I looked at her, and she shrugged. "Sophy mentioned there was a big order. It's not difficult to make the connection." She sighed. "I can't make that decision for you. You know that. But if it meant protecting Sophy, I'd do it."

My mouth opened. "You're that sure."

"I am," she said. "That's why I thank the gods that I'm not the captain, Asp. Most of us would crumble under such decisions. We don't have your strength."

Slowly, my head shook. "The price for what I do is rising. Fast. I don't know what will happen next time I go back to port."

"If it goes south, then we'll all come for you," she promised.

I felt tears pushing in my eyes. "I don't want that."

"You don't deserve this," she told me, her voice hushed and quiet.

"I've been living on stolen time," I reminded her. "It had to end sometime." With a sigh I stood, leaning over her to kiss her cheek.

She stood and clutched me to her, hugging me hard.

"I left you a draft," she told me. "Be strong. Stay strong."

I nodded against her neck and pulled away.

I went upstairs where it was dark and lightless. It wasn't that I could see in the dark, it was just that my power was still active, feeling ahead for me, so I knew what was there even without seeing. I went over to the bed and drank Charly's sleeping draft down without another thought.

# The Tri Queen

We had said sunrise, but I woke up well after the sun. It wasn't a good sleep—I felt sluggish and drugged, like some giant squid in the dreamworld was still wrapping its tentacles around me.

I stumbled downstairs to find Charly loading Bast and Ori down with big baskets of food covered with oilcloth to take up to the ship in the sheets of pouring rain that had cropped up overnight, following in the wake of my power.

They all looked over to me, and I waved Bast and Ori off into the rain. Charly handed me a cup of coffee and told the boys, "Tell Sophy *exactly* what I've told you!"

"Yes, Charly," Bast said. Ori smiled, and Charly pressed a fond hand to his cheek.

They headed off, and I shrugged awkwardly into my leathers with one hand as I tried to drink the coffee. "I told them to take their time because you weren't up yet," she reported. "Everyone's been fed a good breakfast. Saved you some. You slept?" she asked, pulling the cloth off a plate by the fire.

I pried open the roll to shove the soft eggs and cheese and pota-toes into it. "Thank you, Charly," I told her, kissing her cheek.

"When will I see you again?" she asked.

"Two weeks, at the earliest."

"Very well. Mind Sophy, will you? She and I had a bit of a falling-out last night."

I stopped. "You did? What about?"

"Mihal," she said, huffing out a frustrated breath.

"Mihal?" Mihal was an older boy—a man now, I supposed—one of the first we'd dropped here. He was a year or two older than I was, and one of the biggest helps—constructing almost all the buildings for us. "That reminds me," I said, tugging out a small purse of kings. "I'm sure we'll be needing more space soon, won't we?"

She took it. "Depending on who you bring back, for sure. But Sophy and Mihal—well, I found them together and I got into a bit of a rage about it."

I laughed at that. "How 'together'?"

She flushed and slapped a cloth at me. "Kissing, young cap-tain, they were *kissing*. She just seems very young, and it seems terribly unfair to go off to sea the very next day."

There was a happy bubble in my heart. We'd had so many girls who had been hurt, really hurt, by men in the world. The idea that the world had changed so much that Sophy kissing a boy seemed somehow illicit—that was *glorious*.

Charly, however, was very unhappy with my reaction. "You won't take it seriously at all, will you? Always flouncing around with Bast, you are."

I scrunched up my nose. "I'm not sure we ever *flounced*, to be fair. But even if we did, we certainly don't flounce anymore," I told her, then sighed.

"The way he was speaking of you last night, he didn't seem to think that at all," she said.

I rubbed at the weariness and tension in my neck. "I know. How do I explain this to him, Charly? He doesn't understand."

She leaned onto the stool by the fire, stretching out her bad leg. "He's always been in love with you, Asp. I know you know that."

I put the coffee down and crossed my arms. "He slept with Cyrus," I told her. "He can't love me too much."

"You really don't see it?" she said softly. "Asp, you know more of his history than anyone. How badly he was treated. He tries, but deep down he is a very broken little boy who is all too fast growing up into a very broken man."

"It's not an excuse," I told her, shaking my head. "We all have brutal pasts. We all put our faith in this family."

"But we're not all in love with someone who doesn't love us back. I'm just saying it's hard for anyone to cope with, but it's harder still because you're his superior. There has to be some part of him that knows if you're not in love with him, he has to leave the ship—to leave the only family he's ever had, the only place he's been safe."

I caught my breath. "I would never make him leave."

"No," she agreed. "But how could he stay?"

I took a deep, too-hot drink of the coffee, and it stung the whole way down. "Dammit, Charly." I sighed.

"Let's be honest," she said, wedging herself up again. She patted my cheek. "I don't stay off the ship because of my leg. I stay off because you can't stand someone who's right as often as I am."

"There's a difference between being right and thinking you're right," I reminded her. I kissed her cheek before taking a final swallow of coffee and heading for the door, biting into my stuffed roll. "You're a better cook than your sister!" I shouted over my shoulder.

"Obviously," I heard her mutter as I shut the door behind me.

For most people, it was a rather long climb up the rope ladder to get back to the deck of the ship, but I just grabbed ahold of it and let my power drag me along with the ladder, rain soaking deliciously through my clothes, even though my leathers wouldn't appreciate the damp. I landed on the ship, coiling the line and finding Navya in view. "Am I the last?" I asked her, shucking my heavy hair away from my face.

"Everyone's accounted for," she said, blinking against the onslaught. "Including one we weren't counting on."

I followed her gaze to Kairos, who was helping some of the others with the rigging. He lifted his chin when our eyes met, with a cocky little smile. "Good," I said, turning back to Navya.

"Are you strong enough for this?" she asked me.

I grinned at her. "We'll find out. Crew, untie us and let's get under way!"

As soon as the riggers stepped clear of the sails, I started to luff them out with my power as others scrambled to draw in the anchoring lines. There was a brisk wind with the driving rain, and I grinned up at the gray-black billows of clouds, appreciating their assistance as rain spattered on my face.

I stretched my arms, waiting for the all clear. When Navya gave it to me, I pushed the wind hard into the sails and the ship skidded forward over the grass. I drew a deep breath, steadying us, and pushed harder.

The ship slid forward on the wet grass, hitting the open air and dropping a few feet before rushing forward with another push of my power. We curled back around Altia's high cliffs, turning out past the grand water temple on Arix, a huge network of white buildings growing like frozen waves out of green grass, before we gently landed on the stormy, gray-blue ocean.

The crew cheered when we hit the water, and I smiled. "Now," I said, turning to Navya, who had taken the wheel. "We have a lot to do before we get to the Wyverns. Most importantly, Anika and I need to be as strong as possible. Beyond that, the rest of us—even Sophy and the littler ones—need to be ready for one hell of a fight that I hope we never see."

She nodded. "Very well. We should probably start with the new recruits—figure out where their skills lie." She glanced around. "After the rain stops, at least."

"See it done," I agreed.

"Additionally, we need to talk about our reserves, and what we'll trade in the Wyverns," she said. "Assuming that's the plan."

And what a terrible plan it was. "Yes, we'll have to. I don't think we can risk taking the ship to the Trifectate right now."

Her shoulders lifted. "Could be good. New items."

"I don't like not knowing how Cyrus will like something," I admitted. "Too much of the price hangs on her whims."

"As does your life, doesn't it?" she asked.

Unease churned in my stomach. "Yes. Which is another thing we should talk about."

"What do you mean?" she asked, stepping closer.

I glanced around. "When we return to Diadem, you have to keep the crew safe. There's a good chance I won't be coming back to the ship."

Her eyes were heavy on me for a long time, but there was a reason I was telling her and not Bast or Ori or Sophy. "I know what to do."

"I know you do," I told her. "But I want you to think about what else we need. If I'm gone, and you're captain, who needs to learn what."

She tightened her grip on the wheel. "I'll consider it."

"Thank you," I told her.

Less than an hour later, the rain had eased off and Navya had our weapons unloaded from the hold. She slung a sword low over her hips, and her short dark hair was pinned back. Linnea, Thea, and Kairos were all lined up on the deck with most of the crew gathered round to watch. I went up on the yard, watching where they couldn't watch me back.

"Hold it like this," Navya corrected Linnea, which I thought was probably a fair assessment of her skills already. She moved her fingers around the sword grip.

"It's heavy," Linnea complained.

"And sharp," Navya said. "Try swinging it a little."

Navya stepped clear and Linnea did, feeling the weight, easing the sword in figure eights in front of her.

"Bast," Navya called, waving him over. "Raise your sword," she instructed. He did, and stayed still.

"Try hitting him," Navya said to Linnea.

"My *sword*, please," Bast clarified.

Navya snorted.

Linnea swung it. It hit his sword with a strangled clang that made Osmost shriek, and Linnea dropped the sword with a yelp.

To my surprise, before Navya even directed her to it, she crouched down and picked it up, trying again.

She was by no means a natural, but she seemed to like the idea of having a weapon in her hand, and that was good enough for me. Navya spent a while more, teaching her some basic forms before Linnea's arm got tired.

Then Navya moved on to Thea, giving her a knife to practice with. She told her, "The most important thing is to hold on to it," then added, "and push as hard as you can."

Anika volunteered to show her, and the two girls ran off to the stern deck together. Linnea looked lost.

"Your turn, Kairos," Navya said. "Do you have any experience with a sword?"

He unsheathed one, looking at it. "Not as such," he said, the careful phrasing of which caught my interest.

"We'll go slow," she said. "Try to take my sword away from me."

He cast the sheath aside. He crouched down a little, raising his sword and giving her a nod like he was the one controlling the fight.

Navya waited for him to advance, but he stayed still and ready, watching her carefully in a way that lifted the hairs on the back of my neck. When Navya stepped forward, he diverted to the side, making her chase him before she even attempted a first blow.

She frowned.

When she lunged for him, he darted away so quickly that their swords came nowhere near connecting. He drew her forward, going backward up the stairs to the quarterdeck as she followed, and I climbed into the rigging to watch them.

She swung again, a side blow, and again he slid out of her path entirely—he might as well have not had the sword. She was getting annoyed, and she tried again, and again, never making contact.

"The point is to engage," she told Kairos.

"I believe the point is to keep the sword away from my insides," he returned.

"You were instructed—" she said, swinging her sword again.

This time metal whispered along metal, and Kairos did some strange roll of his hand that popped the sword right out of Navya's. She halted with a gasp as it flew up and he caught it in his free hand.

"How did you do that?" she asked, awestruck. "That was amazing!"

He grinned at her. "Mostly by distracting you."

"Can you show me?" she asked.

He laughed and agreed.

"Bet you can't take my sword," Bast said, stepping forward.

"I'm a better swordsman than you," Navya reminded him.

He shrugged. "It's a trick. It won't work if I know what he's doing. Being able to distract someone isn't the same as fighting."

Kairos hadn't lost his grin, but he did start to ease back, assessing the room he had to fight. He tossed Navya's sword back to her. "No, it isn't," he agreed. "So you want me to take your sword? Or you want to fight me?"

Bast swung his sword lazily so it whistled through the air. "I want to know what would happen if someone boarded this ship who wanted you dead."

Kairos shrugged. "I don't think you want that."

I hadn't moved down the shrouds or done anything to draw his attention, but Bast looked up at me for the briefest of moments. Kairos turned to follow his gaze, and his grin just got wider as he turned back to Bast.

"Oh," Kairos said with a chuckle.

Blood rushed into my face, uncomfortable under my scar, and Bast yelled, lunging forward to swing hard at Kairos. Kairos ducked and darted away, and Bast chased him, swinging again so Kairos deflected it with his sword and a bright, ringing clash of metal.

Bast gained speed, parrying back and forth, side to side, meeting Kairos's sword every time, but even I could tell it was Bast who looked off balance, not Kairos. When Bast swung wide, Kairos dodged the blow altogether and sprang past Bast, making him spin.

Kairos moved lightning quick, and Bast took a moment to track him, following his movements and meeting his pace. Kairos controlled the fight.

Bast made two fast swings before taking a deep lunge, but Kairos saw it coming and moved. Totally losing his center, Bast tripped, falling forward.

I gasped as the crew went still. Bast's sword went out to the side, so I knew he hadn't impaled anything but his pride.

I leaped down to the deck as Bast pushed himself up, blood staining his teeth as he lunged at Kairos again.

"Enough!" I yelled.

"We're not done," Bast snarled in a spray of bloody spittle.

I rolled my eyes. "Bast, clean yourself up." Someone passed him a rag, and he wiped at his mouth, then spat on the deck. "So," I said, climbing the stairs to the quarterdeck and looking at Kairos. "Is it fair to say you're comfortable and accomplished with a blade?"

His eyes glittered, and I wondered if even that was the whole truth—either this boy had very good fighting skills or he wanted me to think he did.

"Something like that," he agreed.

Osmost shrieked overhead, and it sounded downright gleeful.

"A good fighter isn't the same as a good teacher," I said, willing myself not to look at Bast. "Have you ever taught someone?"

The cocky glitter dulled from his eyes, but the smile didn't move. "Yes," he said.

"You can start with me," Navya volunteered.

"What about you?" Kairos asked, his eyes on me.

I smiled. "I don't use a sword."

He raised his blade slowly toward my neck. "What if someone came after you with one?"

The lines on the ship came alive, snaking around his body, constricting his arm until he dropped the sword and pulling him hard against the wheel so his head craned back and his throat was exposed. One of the crossbow bolts from my belt flew up, twirling to stay aloft, pressing lightly into the pulse at his throat.

Several of the crew chuckled at this, and I came over to him, patting his cheek as he huffed for breath against his bonds. "Not really something I worry about," I said, releasing him.

"Maybe you should," he said, rubbing his arms where the rope had scraped him. "You never know when you'll be in a fight you don't expect."

I shook my head. "I'm far more worried about the things I let hurt me than the things I'd never see coming. Navya," I called. She stepped in, sword ready, and Kairos shook his head at me.

I jogged lightly down the quarterdeck steps, and Linnea moved closer to me, her face pale and hollow looking. She touched my arm, and immediately seemed to regret the contact. "Your power," she said softly. "Can you teach me that?"

"Depends," I said. "What's your power?"

She shook her head, and I paused, looking around. I motioned for her to go up to the bow while the others let out a cheer for something Navya did against Kairos. As far from the others as we could get, I lifted myself to sit on the rail. "Do you know what your power is?" I asked again gently.

She shivered. "I don't know," she said. "It doesn't—I'm not like you."

"Air?" I asked.

"Strong," she whispered.

"I wasn't at first," I admitted. "It took me a long time to control it the way I do. Now the sea and I—we get along, somehow. It works."

She shook her head, digging her fingernails into the wooden rail until her pink skin went white.

"You've felt your power, though, yes?" I asked her.

She nodded.

"What happened?"

"Only a few times," she said. "When I think about things that happened."

She didn't have to tell me they were bad things. I had taken enough young, pretty girls away from the auction that even if I could never really know her story, I thought I probably knew her fears. "What did your power do?"

"The ground shakes," she said, flicking her eyes up at me and down again.

She probably didn't know why, but the feel of the wood—pierced with iron nails, rich with the feel of minerals and soil—was reassuring, especially this far out into the ocean. "You're probably an earth element," I told her.

"Can you control earth?" she asked.

"No," I said. Before she could pull away, I quickly added, "But you can. The elemental powers—they're all connected to our emotions. The more you practice, the easier it is to separate it from emotion, but even then, emotion will take over if you let it." I tapped my fingers on the rail, thinking. "The difficult part is we don't have a whole lot of earth to practice with at sea. Oh," I realized, smiling, "unless Sophy lets us use her pots. That might be a great place to start."

"Pots?" she asked.

"Iron," I told her. "It comes from the earth; I'm sure you'd be able to control that."

Her breath sucked in. "You've met others with this power?" she asked.

I shook my head. "There's much I understand about the powers, and much I don't, but everyone I've ever met who can control air started to do so around the same time as I did, almost four years ago. I think water was the first. Fire powers started occurring about two years ago, and the earth was more recent. So I've never met anyone else with power over earth, but I wouldn't be surprised if it starts becoming more common."

"You believe that Thea has this power too, don't you?" she asked me.

"*A* power, yes. Maybe not yours. It's rare for siblings to have the same element, but often they all have power. Not all—Arnav and Anika, Navya's siblings, both have powers, and she doesn't," I explained. "Some have pieces of a power, like Kairos. And that can still be very powerful. But how old is Thea? Eleven?"

"Ten," she told me.

I squinted, thinking of all the kids I'd had onboard with powers. "If she hasn't felt it yet, she may be coming into it soon."

I winced; I felt something, like someone was scratching the shoulder of my powers.

Shaking my head, I continued, "I believe later today or tomorrow Navya will want those with powers practicing as well. Can we practice then?"

Worriedly, she followed my gaze out over the water. "All right," she said.

With a deep breath, I stepped up onto the rail and went out to the bowsprit. Osmost came, giving short, high shrieks in warning at me.

"I know," I snapped as he spread his wings, falling until he could land on my shoulder. I wasn't wearing my leathers, and his claws bit deep, but I liked the sharpness of the pain.

"Linnea?" I called, turning. She had started to walk away, but she stopped. "Tell Navya to batten the hatches. I think we have a problem."

I didn't mean it to frighten her, but the girl looked spooked anyway and ran off to do my bidding. Not long after, Bast, Kairos, and Anika came over, standing on the deck behind the bowsprit. Osmost yelled in my ear, and Kairos stepped up behind me as the wind started to rise.

"What is it?" he shouted, his clothes starting to whip around his body.

"There's a ship up ahead," I said, rolling my shoulders to get the warning ache out of my muscles. "The air does not like whatever is on it. It doesn't want me to take us near there."

"The wind warns you?" he asked, his words blowing away from him.

I scowled. "The wind is a very chatty bastard, usually!"

"What do you need, Asp?" Bast yelled.

I heard Anika's high voice, but I couldn't hear what she said. I was tempted to call her up with me, but while she was getting better at working the wind, she couldn't do this.

"Belowdecks!" I shouted back.

I didn't look back to see if they obeyed me. Instead, I looked up to the gray, rolling clouds above me.

As a child, I never really thought about how far away clouds were. They seemed to hover right above me, just out of reach, like I could grab them if I jumped high enough or tried hard enough. Once I grew with my power, I knew how high they were, and how much effort it took to call a storm to me where the air was thin and distant and the clouds wanted to be commanded by no thing on earth.

I could see the sails on the horizon. They looked dark, patched with deep green, and I knew those sails—it was the *Mycara*, a ship full of pirate traders with a reputation for violence. A shudder ran through me, and I felt it echo too long in my tired bones.

I turned to Kairos and Bast. "I'm still not strong enough," I told them. "I can't get a storm between us. Pulling up the wind will help them as much as us."

"Should I get Anika?" Bast asked.

"No," I said, gritting my teeth. "Bast, go. Tell the others to get the little ones belowdecks. Kairos, arm the rest. I'll do as much as I can, but we're about to engage."

They both obeyed, leaving me alone on the bowsprit.

The *Mycara* was closer now, and I sucked in a breath, trying to draw steel down my spine. For all the hells in the world, the *Mycara* was the last ship I wanted to tussle with.

"X," I heard, and I turned to see Bast standing there. I growled out a sigh and hopped off the bowsprit. "We're locked down."

"Good."

He nodded grimly. "Maybe he isn't looking to fight." We shared a disbelieving glance. "Well, at least the new kid isn't bad with a sword."

My eyebrows lifted. "I didn't think you were ready to admit that."

He grunted. "He's good. I don't mind it when we're fighting the same enemy."

I looked over his face. "You don't trust him."

Bast's jaw rolled. "I think he came on this ship with an agenda. I can't help feeling like you're getting played here."

"That's fair. But for now, I trust him," I said.

Bast stepped closer to me, drawing my eyes up. "You trust everyone, Asp. That's nice for you, but it makes me play the villain so you don't end up dead."

I snorted. "I do not trust everyone."

"You do. It's the most dangerous quality about you."

Shaking my head, I crossed my arms and turned away from him. "I'll try to keep us far enough away that they can't board us easily. I should be able to manage that."

"Good. Afterward, you need to rest. We can sail the normal way until you're at full strength."

I dismissed this with a wave, looking over the crew. The older ones were manning their stations with weapons, while Anika hid up in the crow's nest with Fisk, one of our youngest who could— with very little control—manipulate water.

My heart started the heavy thrum and beat of battle, and I walked out to the very tip of the bow, the boat crashing onto waves beneath me. I felt a shadow on me, and I turned to see Kairos turning a sword in each hand, stretching.

Lightning crackled up in the clouds.

Threads tugged through my power at the crack of the lightning, and I glanced up, shocked. The threads led straight back to Kairos. The lightning was reacting to him.

We were getting closer to the *Mycara*, coming up alongside her as Bast manned the wheel. I could see the grimy figures dotting the deck, staring us down.

Then one of the sailors ran to the stern of the boat, and just as we were coming into range, they dropped a white flag.

"Asp!" Bast called from the wheel.

"I see it!" I yelled back.

"What does that mean?" Kairos asked behind me.

I turned to him, scowling. "It means they don't want to fight us. But knowing Skiver, he's up to something else."

"If they don't want to fight, can't we just sail on by?"

"Yes," I said. "And we will."

I had no sooner said the words than I heard a heavy splash, and I looked over to see a boat in the water, with Skiver and two of his men rowing toward us.

"All the damn-blasted hells," I growled, jumping down from the bowsprit. "Kairos, tell Linnea that unfortunately, I have to take my cabin back. Looks like Skiver's feeling chatty."

Kairos's eyes tried to stop me. "You're not talking to that man alone."

I pushed past him. "Still the captain, duster. Go do as I asked."

I didn't bother watching to see if he obeyed; there were far more pressing problems. Instead, I went to the starboard rail, watching Skiver come close. His men had swords, but no arrows or long-range weapons. "What do you think you're doing, Skiver?" I shouted.

"I have a proposition for you," he shouted back. "Coming to discuss it."

"I have neither the time nor the inclination," I told him.

"She said you'd say that," Skiver yelled. "Cyrus says we should be friends, you and I."

My hackles rose and my skin crawled, mostly because I knew then what Skiver knew the second he saw my sails—if he invoked her name, I'd have to let him on and hear him out, and whatever came next, I knew I wasn't going to like it.

His boat was almost to us. "Permission to come aboard?" he called.

My nails dug into the wood of the rails. "Permission granted," I growled back.

I strode over to Sophy, on deck with a sword at the ready, and took her knife, jamming it in the waist of my pants. "Go belowdecks," I murmured. "Keep the little ones out of sight until they're gone."

She disappeared down the stairs. I turned to Navya, snapping my fingers at Bast to come closer. "Nav, I want you on deck. Get Ori to guard the hold," I ordered. "Bast, on deck, and Kairos will wait outside my door."

"I'll wait—" Bast started.

"No," I said. "Skiver's got two guards, and Kairos can take them both. You and Nav need to hold off the rest of his ship if necessary. Understood?"

Navya and Bast looked at each other, then me. "Yes, Captain," they said together. Kairos appeared from belowdecks, and Navya went to him as I turned to meet Skiver, coming up over the edge.

The man repulsed me. He had a long, rough, scrabbled beard knotted into braids like tongues hanging from his chin, and his brown skin looked so worn and beaten by the sun and the drink that I couldn't tell how old he really was. His eyes were rimmed with red, and he was always panting, his breath scraping over his lips and teeth like he was stealing it from the world. He was bald, save for the black ink staining his skull in warped designs that I didn't recognize.

"Captain Aspasia," he said, his mouth twisting into something like a smile. He inclined his head to me. "Your crew is looking as . . . fresh as ever."

"Is this a public or a private conversation?" I asked.

He chuckled. "I'd prefer private," he said.

"Come with me," I said, leading him down the stairs. I glanced to Kairos, waiting with his arms over his chest at the start of the hallway to my cabin. He handed me the key, then folded his arms again and watched us as the captain and his two men followed me down.

I opened the door and gestured him inside, but stopped the others. "Your men will stay out here," I said.

Skiver sneered, but nodded to them after a long moment. I shut the door on them, leaving it unlocked as I turned to Skiver.

He surveyed the room, looking over my desk first, which had nothing on it thanks to there having been guests in the room, then went over to the cot, picking up a dress that Linnea must have left there. He held it up, chuckling and looking over to me like he was picturing me in it. A surly pirate in a frilly gown.

I crossed my arms, leaning against the door. "I'm waiting, Skiver."

"I saw you on the docks the other day," he told me. "Didn't even say hello to me."

"Didn't see you."

"Well, Cyrus and I got to talking about you afterward. Long conversation, you know how she is. She has a theory about you."

Panic curled in my throat, but I didn't say anything, didn't move, just watched him and waited.

"She thinks you're a witch," he said, his eyes gleaming at me. "She thinks the wind bends to your will."

The panic was dripping into my stomach as visions of getting sold to a quaesitor and taken back to the thrice-damned Trifectate ripped through my mind.

He studied me for long moments. "Or if not, you're the luckiest damn sailor I've ever seen."

"Thanks," I said. "Why are you here?"

"A few reasons," he said, shrugging.

I curled my fingers tighter on my arms.

"Cyrus wants you to hurry up," he said. "She thought I would have run across you a day or two ago. Where do you go when you leave Diadem?"

I didn't break his seedy, leering gaze. "I always give my crew a rest after a score."

"She told me that if you take too long, I'll get a reward for dragging you back."

There was a metallic noise, and I couldn't tell if the sound was real or in my memory, the rattle of chains, the unforgiving click of manacles, the jangle of keys that held my fate but didn't belong to me.

"Yes," he hissed, leaning closer to my face. "That catches your interest, doesn't it?"

"She gave me no timeline. You can tell her I'll return when I have what she needs."

"I think I'll follow you, just to be certain."

I huffed out a breath. "Really. Your crew would be content to play nanny to my ship?"

"There are other options," he offered.

"You have yet to present me with anything that seems like a legitimate threat, much less an option," I told him.

"Have you heard about the *Tri Queen*?" he asked.

I froze, willing Kairos not to come bursting through the door. "No," I said.

"It's a ship. Full of gold," he said, and my heart started beating again. "The Trifectate asked for aid from Sarocca, and they got it. Now every pirate on the sea is out to get the gold, and Cyrus wants you to help me."

"I only take orders from Cyrus," I told him. "She gave me a very specific order. So I'm not inclined to believe you."

His lips curled back. "Don't be so insolent with me, girl. I could snap my fingers and Cyrus would deliver you to me with a pretty bow around your neck. This is a mutually beneficial deal. You think your crew wants to pass up that gold?"

"What makes you think I could help you find it?"

"I have good information on where she is," he said. "But every pirate on this ocean is looking for that frigate. With a little luck—or a little witchcraft—we could easily be the first."

"No," I said, and watched as the word caused his fists to ball and his mouth to sputter and open. "If Cyrus wanted me to do something else, she would have given you papers indicating such, with the code that I would expect from her. So I'm guessing you did ask for me, and she told you to shove your bowsprit someplace unpleasant." I slid my hand over the knife hilt. "So at the risk of repeating her words, I think we're done here."

He strode closer to me, and I stayed still against the wall, my knife tight in my fingers as he leaned closer, his fetid breath fogging over me. "I know what you are," he growled. "You think you can cut your face and make a deal and that makes some kind of difference, but it doesn't. You're a slave and you'll always be a slave. So delay, Captain. Take so much as an uncharted tack from your course and you will know what it's like to have me as your master."

My stomach curled and clenched from more than just the smell of him. Cyrus told him I was a slave? It was stupid—I didn't love Cyrus, I didn't trust her, and yet that stung like a betrayal.

"Maybe," I said. "But for now, I still have the immense pleasure of telling you no." With my spare hand, I reached out to the door I hadn't strayed from and opened it.

Skiver's eyes darted over, and I knew without looking that Kairos was hulking near, enough of a threat to give Skiver pause.

"My friend can escort you off the ship," I told Skiver, and Kairos stepped in. Rather than looking like some snarling dog, Kairos was grinning his maddening, knowing smile, and it seemed to disturb Skiver and his men just as much as it did me.

"With pleasure," Kairos said, gesturing for the men to move, and then for Skiver to pass him.

He reached for the door and paused, his eyes waiting for mine to rest on him. When they did, I saw the smile gone, and he gave me a slow and careful nod. Checking. Assuring.

The sick feeling of helplessness was a snake around my throat, wending and winding tighter and tighter, and I didn't—I couldn't—show that to him. Not now, not when I needed to reassure him, not the other way around.

I was the thrice-damned *captain.*

I scowled back, pushing away from the wall as he shut the door behind him. I felt my stomach churn, all the reactions and anger I'd held back rushing to the surface. Bracing against the wall, I waited until I couldn't hear their steps anymore to hammer my fists against the door, then slam the key in the lock and turn it.

Damn them. Damn those first cruel men who stole me from my siblings and *sold* me, damn Cyrus for buying me, damn Cyrus for not trusting me to be her perfect little villain.

I damned them all until my fists were raw.

Heaving with breath, I reached out with my power, threading it through the gap in the door, the windows, sighing and letting

it break away from my body to reach out. I felt the threads warp-
ing around Skiver, and I could track him, walking over the deck
and slowly lowering himself over the side.

When the small boat left our ship, I let my power go. I could
feel Anika, anxiously urging the sails to fill, and I went over to
the cot, curled on the bed, and let each of Skiver's words and
threats slice over my skin like a knife.

It was too much. I'd used too much power again, and the words
I'd swallowed were too heavy in my stomach. Tucking my body
against the wall, I fell asleep.

# Hope Was Ash

When I came abovedeck again, it was nighttime. Navya was at the wheel, and I knew from the noise as I'd passed the galley that most of the crew were eating their supper.

Navya's mouth set into a hard line when she saw me. "No," she said immediately. "Bast said we're sailing the regular way."

"My way is our regular way," I reminded her. "It will take us twice as long."

"Don't care," she said. "The Wyverns will be enough of a problem with you at full strength, much less anything but."

"Well, what the hell am I supposed to do, then?" I growled.

She leveled a glare at me that was usually reserved for Arnav. "Rest."

Shaking my head, I made for the rigging, but the second my hand touched the rope, she called out, "No. Not there."

"Why not?" I yelled.

Her eyes lifted up to the sails. "I don't know if you can even stop yourself from using your power when you're up there, Asp.

Sophy's serving dinner; go get something to eat. Count your coins, if it makes you feel better."

Scowling, I obeyed her, going belowdecks, edging toward the kitchen where laughter and love were rolling out like warmth from the fire.

"You don't like your crew."

It was Kairos, his voice low in my ear. New heat rushed through me, but I said, "I love my crew."

"But you don't like to be with them."

My arms curled around myself with a heavy sigh. "The moment I join them—things change. They're never like this when I'm with them."

His breath tickled my neck, and for a horrible moment, it took me back to Skiver and the sick feeling of helplessness he left in his wake.

I stepped away from Kairos, rubbing my neck as I turned to him. "Stop," I said, and it sounded too plaintive to my ears.

His eyes saw too much, and he just watched me. "Forgive me," he said.

I shook my head with a rough, bone-deep sigh, keeping my arms around me and going into the kitchen. Sophy saw me and called out, and everyone stopped talking. Ori scooted closer to Linnea to give me a place to sit, and some of the others who had finished said they were due up on deck.

Sophy spooned out some stew, and Bast's eyes were heavy on me. His gaze flickered over as Kairos came in and sat down with us around the fire, but then returned to me. "What did Skiver want from you?" Bast asked.

*Me*, I wanted to say, but the truth tangled in my throat. "Sarocca and the Trifectate are ferrying gold between them. Everyone is losing their collective mind over robbing the ship, including Skiver."

"And he wants our help?"

"I said no," I clarified.

Bast waited a moment too long to nod in agreement, and I saw the shine in his eyes, the greed that touched everyone at the thought of a life-changing amount of gold. But I still had to return to Cyrus, so maybe it was selfish to have made that choice for the rest of my crew. If we went after the gold, they'd be rich, but I'd be dead.

Maybe that's what I was afraid of. In that situation, maybe they'd choose the gold.

"How long until we make the Wyverns?" Sophy asked.

"Little more than a week, depending on how long I'm not allowed to help for," I grunted, my gaze slicing over to Bast.

"Not long," he said. "I don't want to overtax Anika either. Remember, you couldn't call up that storm today, X."

"I hate it when you call her X," Sophy said suddenly, her mouth twisting around the words. "It's mean."

"It's not mean," Bast said, frowning. "She knows why I call her that."

"Aye, I do too, because of her scar," Sophy said, pointing a wooden spoon at him. "None of us like to be reminded of our pasts. Specially our past hurts."

"She doesn't mind, do you, Asp?" Bast asked, looking to me.

I pressed my lips together, meeting his gaze and not saying anything.

His face fell a little, and it felt like I was telling him I didn't want to be with him all over again.

Then he huffed out a breath, shaking his head like he wasn't a bit surprised. "Consider me corrected, Sophy," he said, his voice empty of bravado.

Bast stood up and tossed his bowl in the basin with a clatter, and we all watched him leave. Ori patted my arm, going up and following him.

Linnea stood too. "Thank you for letting my sister and me use the cabin," she said.

"You'll be comfortable in the main quarters? You can have it back if you need it."

"We'll be fine," she said. Then she followed the others.

Sophy clucked her tongue, turning around to the basin. "Sorry, Asp. I didn't mean to ruin dinner."

"I know," I told her. "You didn't do anything wrong."

With a sigh, she heaved the heavy basin of dishes up. Kairos jumped to his feet to help her, but she waved him off. "Sit, eat," she ordered.

He looked at me and the now-empty kitchen with raised eyebrows. "If you wanted to get me alone, you could have just asked," he teased.

The ship pitched a little, and I stood up, kicking the sand in the pit over the fire to douse it. I held on to my stew and turned. "Come on," I told him.

I led him through the belly of the ship to my cabin. I shut the door behind us, lit two of the hanging lanterns that swayed with the motion of the ship, and rummaged in one of the drawers until I found a bottle of a bitter Saroccan liquor. I tossed it to him and sat down on the floor in front of my cot, leaning my back against it and digging into my food.

He stood, looking at me with the same bemused expression he had in the kitchen.

"Sit," I said. "Open that up."

"You like giving orders," he noticed with a grin, but he did what I asked, sitting close enough so that I could reach out and touch him if I wanted. He pulled the cork out of the bottle and sniffed it.

"Skies," he sputtered. "That is . . . something."

I smiled. "I know," I said. "It's this awful liquor they make from malt wine, and it's so bad they put berries in to flavor it."

He tried a swig of it and coughed hard. "Charming," he wheezed, passing it to me.

I took a slow drink, but a deep one nonetheless.

He laughed, watching me drink it. "I guess sailors get their reputation for good reason," he said.

I closed my eyes for a moment before opening them and passing the bottle to him. "I like the way it burns going down. Anything that helps you make terrible decisions during and makes you feel so horrible the day after should be a little more upfront about its nature, don't you think?"

He just chuckled and shook his head, putting the bottle between us. "So why did you bring me here?" he asked.

The liquor burned in my chest, and I shrugged. "I didn't want to eat dinner alone. And I wondered what you heard today."

He made a low rumbling noise in his chest, taking another drink. He grinned around another cough. "That really is foul stuff."

My mouth tugged up. "Skiver or the liquor?"

"Both," he allowed. "I heard him mention the *Tri Queen*," he said, looking down and away from me. "And talk about your scar. And Cyrus."

"He meant the ship," I told him. "Not your sister."

He didn't look at me, examining the bottle instead.

"Very well," I said, taking the bottle from him and drinking. "Ask me your questions."

He lifted his head, watching me wipe a drop of liquor from my lip, and asked, "Tell me about your scar."

I smiled. "You asked it differently the first time."

"I figure that was the wrong question. Maybe this one you'll answer." He tilted his head. "But it's true, isn't it? That you cut yourself."

I leaned my head back on the cot. "If I answer you, I have to explain about Cyrus too."

"Very well."

"It's not that easy," I told him softly. "If you know these things, you're involved. It makes it harder to walk away, and you need to walk away, don't you?"

He didn't speak, so I lifted my head to look at him. His elbow rested on the cot, turned so that he could watch me, his finger rubbing idly over his top lip. "I'm with you for now," he said. "If you want to tell me the story, I'd like to hear it."

"I came to Cyrus on a ship like this," I told him. "Or maybe closer to what you were on. Big hold. Lots of people chained to the floor. Filthy and full of disease, mostly because there weren't enough men to check on us often, so most people just relieved themselves where they sat. I was lucky to make the trip alive."

*Lucky.* It was a disgusting word for having survived that. The memory of it washed over me like hot acid, mirrored by the burn inside my chest.

"We were brought to Cyrus to be sold. Poked and prodded,

told our lives had a price. But when they got to me, I'd been able to free my hands from the ropes, and I stole Tommaso's knife. Everyone jumped back, thinking I'd use it on them, but I cut this into my face before anyone could stop me." I touched my tongue against the rough bunch of scar tissue inside my mouth, the center of the X where I'd cut straight through my cheek. "Cyrus told everyone to get back and came to me. She asked why I had done it. I told her it was my body, and I would mark it as I saw fit to remind whoever bought me that it didn't belong to them.

"She knelt down to me. Blood was everywhere, and she touched my cheek. She told me later it didn't matter—she could have sold me just as easily scarred and ugly as whole and pretty. But in that moment, she asked me instead why I did it. The truth was, I needed to be the one in control. I needed to be the one *taking*. So I told her I would take the life I wanted, and if I couldn't do that, I would take my life."

The words, that long-ago promise, fell between us. I wondered if he knew what it was like, to have the kind of sadness yawning in your chest that makes death seem like a wise and welcome option.

My eyes flicked to him. Of course he did. In death, he would see his whole family again.

"She let you go?" he asked. His eyes moved to mine, capturing me.

"No," I said softly. "Skiver wasn't wrong when he called me a slave. We made a bargain, that I could work off my price with her as a trader. I worked on another ship until the captain of this ship was killed, and she made me captain of the *Ancora*."

"When did this happen?" he asked. He was leaning toward me now, and his hand came closer to touch the scar.

"I was eleven when I made the deal," I told him. "Fifteen when I was made captain."

"So young," he said, watching me.

I laughed. "I think she expected me to die."

He shook his head slowly. "Why didn't you run? Just take the ship and run."

"Run where?" I asked, thinking of empty beds and the dark night I had last seen my family. My voice went rough. "Run to what?"

"Freedom. Safety."

*As if there is such a thing.*

"I have my reasons. This work . . . it's not the best answer, and I know that. It's not solving everything, but there are a lot of people who aren't slaves because of what I've done." I thought of the black and red bags, the former ever lighter and the latter ever heavier, waiting for the deposits this next run would offer. "It's racking up so many debts on my soul I can hardly stand the weight. But it's something. A tiny match in the dark."

"You know it's different this time, don't you? When you return to her, you're covered in blood. When you return to Sarocca, she'll break you," he told me. "I've seen it."

"You had a vision?" I asked, turning to him.

He took a deep breath, his chest rising and falling. "A long flash. That was it."

I moved away from the cot so I could face him completely, folding my legs under me. "We can work with that. Do you feel the threads?" I asked.

He put the bottle aside and mirrored my posture. "Yes, but just barely. Shalia described it like fabric, but to me it feels like a spiderweb. I touch it and it crumbles."

"You're not concentrating," I tell him, taking his hands.

I gasped at the skin-to-skin contact. He was definitely grounded in air—my power could feel his, almost like I could touch his. "You . . . ," he said, awed, looking around him like he could see the threads. Maybe he could. "It's like you electrified them."

I could feel the electricity he spoke of, but that was entirely his doing, buried somewhere in his power, this fascinating tie to lightning. "Close your eyes. Are the threads stronger?"

He obeyed me. "Yes. Much."

"So how does your power work? How do you summon visions?"

"I don't, usually."

"Can you feel the threads when you get the visions?"

He drew in a slow breath, thinking. "Yes. It feels like jaws snapping shut. Like something folding in on itself."

*Interesting.* "Try folding the threads."

"How?"

"It's easier if you use your hands to start with. And if you can harness whatever emotion makes you most powerful."

He opened his eyes. "I have no idea what that means."

"The powers change the more you use them," I explained. "I've practiced with mine so much and so often I usually don't even think to use it—it just immediately responds to whatever I'm feeling. It can even react to my dreams." Or nightmares, but that wasn't relevant.

"Really?"

I nodded. "I have had many bruises on my backside from that."

He looked curiously toward my rear end, but I slapped his hand lightly. "For you, you're learning how to use it. These powers, for whatever reason, are linked to our emotions. They strike to the core of who we are, so to use it, you have to harness it through your emotions until it becomes second nature."

"So there's an emotion that makes me powerful?"

I shrugged. "It's different for everyone. Anger is pretty common. So is love, if you're into that sort of thing. They're easy emotions."

"What's yours?" he asked.

I felt the immediate desire to open my mouth and tell him the truth, but it was too personal. "I barely remember," I lied.

He narrowed his eyes with a smile. "Do I need to remind you you're a terrible liar?"

"No," I said. "You're a good fighter, right?"

His eyebrow lifted. "I am an excellent fighter."

I scoffed. "Well. When you're fighting, what do you feel? Anger? Heat?"

His brow furrowed. "I never fight angry. It clouds your mind."

"Then what?"

He took a breath. "If I'm being honest, I feel confident. Calm. I know I can beat anyone if I don't lose my temper. If I don't let my emotions get the better of me." He met my gaze. "But you're telling me to do the opposite."

"No," I said, shaking my head. "You're thinking of negative emotions—rage, hate, anger. But trust and belief—those are powerful emotions."

"Is belief an emotion?" he asked skeptically.

"Isn't it? Don't you feel that, when you're so sure of yourself?"

His throat worked. "I suppose so."

"So trust. Fold the threads."

He closed his eyes, and I closed mine too, catching my breath as his hands shifted, never breaking contact but flipping so his hands were on top, pressing my palms down to his knees. His fingertips moved absently over my palms, and the tiny action made my body rush with awareness.

He drew in a sharp breath, and I opened my eyes. His eyes were closed, but his eyeballs moved frantically under his lids, left to right and back again. "What are you seeing?" I asked softly.

He didn't answer. He wasn't in distress, so I didn't break the contact, but I watched him, wondering how I could protect him from whatever he was seeing. I couldn't think of anything to do, so I sat there, watching. Staying with him.

His hands curled and he sucked in a deep breath when his eyes opened. Panting, he collapsed forward, and I caught his head with my shoulder. "Whoa," I said. "You're safe. I'm here."

His hands pressed into my knees as he tried to pull in an even breath. "Skies," he moaned.

"You saw something?"

He nodded his head against my shoulder, and he pulled back, slumping down against the side of the cot. His forehead was damp with sweat, and he looked dazed. When his eyes focused on me, I knew he'd seen something with me in it.

"You can't go back to Cyrus, Asp. When you do, you're bleeding, and someone else is with you. I can't see who it is, but I think Cyrus kills them. To hurt you." He looked at me like this has already happened. "Why didn't you use your power? Why didn't you fight her?"

I rubbed his knee. "I don't know. It hasn't happened yet."

His eyes were on my face again. "Don't go back there."

"I can't run from her," I told him. Not yet. "And making me

bleed won't break me." He opened his mouth to protest again, but I didn't want to hear it. "Speaking of not fighting back, how did you come to be on that ship? You're essentially a prince. How did you become a slave?"

His eyes drifted shut, and he leaned back on the cot. I took the moment to appreciate him—the position made his jaw look huge and powerful, his neck corded and bumpy, his shoulders broad beneath it. "I fell," he said simply.

My eyes dragged back to his face. "Fell."

"I was taking tremendous pleasure in rendering the Tri King's face to a pulp, and I fell. Off a cliff. I think a rock hit me, and the next thing I knew for sure, I was half in the water, on a bank near where the river met the ocean. Bleeding. I found a little fishing village and they took me in, but I was ill for days. When I finally thought I was getting stronger, the village was raided. I managed to kill about ten men before they took me."

"Of course you did." I snorted. "Was it for your family?" I asked. "That you were beating the king?"

His lip lifted slightly in a snarl. "He has committed so many sins against my kin and me that I can hardly say which one that was for."

"Kings are all useless," I told him.

"I don't believe that," he said, shaking his head. "My father is as close to a king as my people have. He's a good man, and a very good leader." His eyes shut, and he flinched like a physical pain struck him. "*Was*," he murmured.

I wanted to ask about his father—he never said so specifically, but I imagined his use of "was" meant his father died with the others—but it felt too close, like it would only be a question or two from asking about my father. Or worse, a question or two away from me caring too much about him. "Well, then kings are all useless on the sea," I told him. "The sea doesn't give any number of damns about your station or rank or wealth. She bows to no man."

"She does a very pleasant bow to the beach," he said.

"Sure. Unless she's using her teeth to make the waves rake the earth away."

"Any number of damns," he repeated thoughtfully. "The Tri Prince always used to say three hells and thrice damned and all that. Same thing?"

"Opposite thing," I grunted. "I will not claim that as my religion. Not now, nor ever."

"Hmm," he mused. "So I'm guessing that means you came from the Trifectate."

I took the bottle and drank, not answering him.

He chuckled a little. "So. Did you ever like Bast calling you X?" he asked.

My lips quirked, but it wasn't a real smile. "Usually I'm very proud of this scar. It's more than a reminder—it's what defines me. I liked that he could see that about me."

"No," he said, his voice suddenly soft. "That doesn't define you."

I looked at him, and his eyes snapped with the same electricity that I was sure he could call down from the skies. "Sure it does."

"You want to see yourself as some vicious thing that would claw her way to freedom, but you have that chance and you don't take it. You don't really want it, not as much as you want something else. I can't help but think it has something to do with your family, but let's just say I believe you, that you're risking your life and safety every day to protect women and children you don't know from the fate you suffered. To me, that means you're defined by this overwhelming sense of hope to keep fighting this unrelenting tide. Not by your scar."

I kept my eyes on his as I drew in a slow, steady breath that made my heart pound. He could see that? Truth be told, I was both things—I was a violent, brutal girl who would do anything to survive, but my power came from hope. That was my most powerful emotion; it was the thing that made me strong and unbreakable.

It usually left me feeling foolish and young, but I could never ignore that hope was the guiding force in my life. Hope for my family, my friends. Hope for safety and home. Was that what love was supposed to be, choosing a person who brought out the part of you that you liked best? For that slow, steady breath, I could imagine the future spinning out, and I could envision the possibility of seeing myself through Kairos's eyes.

I looked away. "Hope is a cruel thing," I told him honestly. Hope gave me power, but it was also to blame for every pain I'd ever felt.

"I know," he said, his voice still hushed and soft.

"Tell me about your family," I said. "Tell me what you're going back to."

"Half of what I had," he said. "Less than."

"You can't look at it like that," I told him. "You said they didn't all die, did they?"

"My sister survived," he said. "My oldest brother wasn't near when it happened." His face suddenly tightened, and I saw water shine at the edge of his eyes. "My sister's baby survived. I have to get back to her before I'm an uncle."

"How far along is she?"

"Three months or so when I left, to the best of my knowledge. Maybe four or five now?"

"Do they know you're alive?" I asked.

His face turned to me, and the water was thicker, brighter. "No." He sniffed, looking up. "She lied for you, you know."

"For me?" I asked, confused.

"She made it on deck of the ship, didn't she? She told her husband that she didn't know who attacked the Trifectate because she never got on board."

Warmth rushed down my spine. Kindness from anyone was always unexpected, but kindness from a stranger who owed me less than nothing seemed bigger than most. "She made it on board." I took a deep breath. I didn't want to ask this question—I didn't want to know the answer. But I had to. As captain, as the one person who should have fought for Dara, I had to. "You mentioned before . . . there was a girl who was captured. She had the ability to control fire. Was she . . . we lost one of us that night that I met your sister. Her name was Dara."

His eyes lingered on me for a long time. "What do you want to know?"

"You know of her."

"Yes," he said.

"She's Ori's sister," I admitted.

His eyes were heavy and dark now. "She was," he told me.

I curled my knees up, fighting the sudden wave of nausea that washed over me. "What happened?"

"There are two different ways to explain this," he said. "I know that they caught a girl from the ship; my sister told me her name was Dara, and I knew from things here and there that she was taken away. That's what I know from other people. But my sister . . ." His jaw rolled and he shook his head sharply. He sucked in a breath through his nose before continuing. "The Tri King tortured my sister. Along with others with powers, to study them. When we broke her out, we found bodies. When I touched the one who most looked like she could still be alive, I saw her. Here. On this boat. When I came here, I knew who she had to be."

"She looked alive," I repeated, my voice rough.

He looked at me, his eyes wet. "She wasn't, Asp."

The nausea settled like a weight in my stomach, turning into something worse. I ducked my head into my knees, trying not to move, desperately wishing his eyes away from me as horrible tears rushed out of me, stealing my breath, making me shake.

I knew she had died. I saw Ori's face—the way he stopped talking—he could tell. I was sure of it. But like that—to first think she was safe, to think she missed a horrible death, and to then be tortured. Alone. Without her crew around her. Without her crew coming to find her.

Why hadn't we gone after her? Why didn't I save her?

The moment that question pounded in my mind, I felt Kairos wrap his arms around me, pulling my tight, balled-up body against his. I thought of going to tell Ori about his sister, and something within me shattered, breaking open and flooding wide.

I couldn't stop crying. Hope was ash.

# A Terrible Dream

He smelled like the sun. I wasn't sure what it was, or how it was possible, but his scent was like sun-soaked earth, even all the way out at sea. At some point Kairos had brought me to the bed, and we'd fallen asleep, me curled so tight against him that my small fists were clawing into his shirt. When I woke, the smell of his skin was so foreign, so out of place, that I didn't want to move or release him. I just stayed there, close and warm.

When he woke up, he stirred a little, tucking his head closer to mine and running his hand up and down my spine. "Morning," he murmured.

"Hey," I whispered.

"Feeling better?" he asked.

I sighed, pushing my head against his chest. "No," I said softly. "Because now I have to go tell Ori what you told me."

"It should come from me," he said.

"No," I said, pulling away. "I'm his friend. She was my responsibility, and I didn't go back for her."

He swallowed. "I was there. Besides, I know what he's feeling right now. It needs to be me."

"How would you have felt if some stranger told you about your family? He deserves to find out from a friend. I'll tell him to talk to you after." Kairos opened his mouth again, but I stopped him. "Don't argue," I said.

"You and your orders," he murmured, brushing a kiss over my forehead. "You don't have to hoard all the difficult things, you know."

"It's just coincidence that the right thing is usually also the difficult thing," I said.

"Says the slave trader," he said.

I tucked closer against him, burrowing into his arms and ignoring his comment. "Maybe this resting thing isn't so bad."

He chuckled, and as the noise rumbled in his chest I felt it all over, and his arms tightened on me, holding me close.

We stayed like that for a while longer, dozing, talking softly, letting the sun move through the portholes and skate over us. When we finally broke apart, Kairos kissed my cheek and went on deck, and I stared at the bed, confused. There had been a few crewmates that I'd enjoyed secret, thrilling touches with, but there had only been two people I'd really cared about. With Bast, it had taken a long time before we had gotten to that place, where we were comfortable just being together without trying to make it about something else. It was only when we were exhausted, when we'd discovered every inch of the other person's body, that we relaxed into this.

Tanta and I hadn't ever really had this—we'd been friends first, friends always, and then we were together before I was captain. We never had time or a place to be calm and close together, just touching each other's skin because it was nice to be near each other.

I wasn't sure whether Kairos and I would ever move toward the feverish heat to touch each other, but it was strange that we had somehow fallen into this ease with each other when I hadn't known him for a full week yet. Stranger still, I liked it.

Any appreciation of that, however, died when I left the cabin. I went up on deck, and it was a day of bright sun and hot wind, warm even without my leathers, my shirt flapping around me.

"Navya," I called, walking up to the wheel.

"Elementae practice," she told me, waving over the deck. "But I'm trying to keep it short; it's a good day for deck scrubbing."

A ball of flame burst from Arnav's hands that made the others jump back, and Anika had her hands up, shaping it, keeping the flame contained with the wind.

I saw a small pot rush through the air and followed it to Linnea's hands. She looked stunned and dropped it. After a moment, she held out her hand again and it leaped up into her grasp.

It was good to have an earth element. That could come in handy, especially in the Wyvern mines.

Then again, an uncontrolled earth element in a mine could be awful.

"Good," I told Navya. "Have you seen Ori?"

She looked around, then pointed to Fisk and Thea, where Ori was sitting on the rail and watching over them, a broad, proud smile on his face when I felt like I hadn't seen him smile in weeks.

Of course, I was about to take that away from him.

Fisk was only nine years old, and the youngest person I had ever trained with powers. He was pulling water up out of the ocean, splashing it at Thea, who was watching him intently.

Maybe she was a water element. They were always useful to have on board.

We had two more Elementae; there was Addy, a thirteen-year-old girl with long black hair and another water power, and Copper, a fourteen-year-old boy with pale skin who had the unusual ability to create and control smoke. Like Kairos, he was one of the people whose powers lay somewhere on the fringes and often showed up in one or more ways. Copper had been a problem for his first year on the ship. He was—as ever—trying to show Arnav a few things, but the boys didn't get on. They should have—they were close in age and both of their gifts were rooted in fire, but Copper had grown already and was brawny and a foot taller than Arnav. More than that, he had excellent control of his power.

The biggest surprise, however, was Kairos. He was talking to Arnav, and though Arnav's face was twisted in a mulish scowl, he seemed to be listening, and he reached again, drawing a thin, careful line of fire.

Kairos patted his back, and looked to me.

It was an easy, if cowardly, decision to talk to Kairos for a moment while I gathered my courage to ruin Ori's day.

"So confident in your own powers you're teaching Arnav?" I asked.

His grin lost nothing. "I didn't know teaching and learning happened independently of each other."

"Asp, watch this!" Arnav told me, drawing slow circles with the line of fire in the air.

I crossed my arms. "You learned how to do that today?" I asked him.

He lifted a shoulder. "A lot happens while you're asleep."

Kairos chuckled at this.

"Arnav, that's really good." My eyebrows lifted, and I motioned him toward Copper. "Why don't you teach Copper how to do that with smoke?"

Arnav's eyes lit with a wicked glint, and he grinned. Copper looked a little nervous.

Kairos looked toward Ori, then gave me a small nod of encouragement.

With a ragged sigh, I went over to the two small ones and Ori. He smiled at me, and it made my chest hurt.

"Ori," I said. "Can we talk?"

He jumped off the rail, skirting the kids as he came to walk beside me up to the stern deck, where we were as alone as we would get. He raised his palm, almost like he was about to touch my elbow, but he didn't, and I took that to mean he was ready to hear what I had to say.

At least, he thought he was ready to hear it. I leaned against the stern rail, looking out at our wake. "How's Linnea?" I asked.

A flush rose in his cheeks, but he shrugged, a hint of a smile on his mouth.

I licked my lips, hoisting myself onto the rail. "I have no idea how to tell you this, Ori," I admitted.

He looked up at me and patted his hand on my knee. *Comforting* me.

It made my tears start all over again, but I tried to ignore them as best I could. "Kairos was in the communes after we left," I told him, struggling to keep my voice even. "He said that they caught Dara." I stared down at the deck, and my tears fell onto the wood.

I didn't look at him, but he moved, and I knew it was hope, lacing itself around his spine, telling him to ignore everything he knew and feared for the past weeks. Making it all disappear like waking from a terrible dream.

I gripped his arm, willing it to stop, not wanting to see as he dared hope his sister was still alive. "But the king took her some-place else. To use her powers. And she died there."

His arm wrenched away from me, but I held fast, not letting him go even as he yanked me off the railing.

"Ori!" I cried.

He pulled away again, hard, frantic, and crashed his arm down on mine to break the hold. His breath was rushing high and fast, making tortured noises.

Then he opened his mouth, clawing at his tongue, digging his nails into it like he was trying to tear it out.

"Ori, stop!" I ordered, throwing myself at him. He shoved me away but I came back, trapping his arms down and using the wind to help. It was then that he broke, and he started crying so hard that we fell to the deck.

He pulled away from me, curling into a ball, and I sighed, sitting in front of him with one hand on his foot. "I'm here," I told him, tears rushing down my face. "I'm not going anywhere."

I turned to see Bast, Navya, Kairos, and some of the others edging up the stairs, watching us, but I waved them away with a harsh glare, trying to give him a moment to grieve.

Navya was the first to turn away and herd the others back, and I huddled closer to Ori, my hand never leaving his foot.

It was a long while before he was calm and I could suggest he consider talking to Kairos, and it went quickly from an idea he didn't want to hear to something he seemed utterly desperate for.

So I called Kairos and waited while he came forward, mimicking my pose and sitting in front of Ori. I moved away, climbing the rigging before anyone could tell me not to. I climbed to the highest sail of the tallest mast, holding the mast above the small weather flag and standing on the yard.

I had no intention of losing another crew member. Ever.

The next morning, there was a pall over the whole crew. The wind was low and almost still, and I itched to use my power. I could have pushed us onward, but I remembered my promise to rest, and after a particularly intense weapons practice, I nudged Kairos toward the rail.

"Can anyone tell me," I asked loudly, "what the one thing any sailor worth her salt has to know how to do?"

"Sail!" Arnav shouted eagerly.

I sighed. "Yes, well, other than that."

"Aspasia," Kairos warned.

"Swim!" Fisk yelled.

"That's the one," I said, and gave Kairos a wicked grin as I pushed him hard, sending him sprawling against the railing before he flipped backward over it with a strangled cry.

I kicked off my boots and stripped my pants off, leaving just the long white shirt as I jumped up onto the rail and dove in after him.

Kairos hadn't come up from beneath the waves, so I let myself slide deep into the water until I saw him, hanging there, pawing wildly at the water without moving up.

I clasped him around his chest and kicked upward, and he broke the surface with a desperate gasp of air, struggling against me and spluttering curses.

Laughing, I held him tight. "Kick," I told him. "Kick your legs slowly. Then move your arms in the water, almost like they're oars, but move them back and forth," I told him.

He was still gasping for breath and shuddering a little, and I looked up to see everyone hanging over the rail.

"Isn't anyone else coming in?" I shouted.

"You're the worst person ever," Kairos sputtered at me.

"Keep that up and I'll swim off," I teased him. "Try to get into a rhythm. I'm going to let go—it will be easier without me hanging on."

His eyes widened and he sucked in a breath but didn't object, and when I swam back he bobbed down a bit, but kicked himself higher.

"This is treading water," I told him. "Do you want to try to move yet?"

A wave splashed over us as he tried to answer, and then another as some of the others jumped in the water. I turned to watch them, and when I looked back at Kairos, his head was underwater.

I pulled him up, and he gulped for breath. "The idea is to stay above the water," I told him. "Have you ever seen a dog swim?"

"Oh yes, with all the dogs and bodies of water we *don't have* in the desert," he snapped at me.

"Don't be a brat," I told him. "Keep kicking your legs, but

instead of waving your arms back and forth, paddle your hands to the front like you're scooping water."

He tried, and was so stiff in his back and shoulders that he didn't really go anywhere and looked utterly foolish.

I smiled, but Arnav laughed. "You're a terrible swimmer," he told Kairos. "Really, really awful."

"Thanks, Arnav," Kairos snapped.

I put my hand on Kairos's arm. "Relax a little," I said. "Take deep breaths. It's okay if your face gets in the water, just don't let your mouth and nose go under when you're trying to take a breath."

He tried to ease up a little, and he moved forward a bit, still awkwardly keeping his chin above water. I lay on my back, swimming lazily so I could watch him.

"Why can't I do that?" Kairos asked.

"Swim on your back?" I said. "Try it."

It took him an uncoordinated moment to turn in the water, but when he did he seemed a little more relaxed, and keeping his head out of the water was easier. "It's going in my ears," he said.

"That's okay. Let them go under, and you can hear the water talk to you," I told him, flipping onto my stomach so I could keep an eye on him.

He seemed to like this, paddling aimlessly with his ears underwater, and I followed him as he swam blindly up toward the bow, luxuriating in the sunlight. He took broader strokes and deeper breaths, and after a while, he raised his head, looking at me with a smile. "I can swim," he announced proudly.

"Still poorly," I reminded him.

He glanced around, and I noticed we were on the other side

of the boat from everyone else. He grinned and came closer to me, but the wicked glint in his eye was ruined by his sloppy swimming, and I laughed, diving under the water.

I turned to watch as he followed me with purpose before he seemed to realize he was deep beneath the water, sucked in some kind of breath through his nose, and ended up jerking back with his mouth open. I rolled my eyes, swimming up to catch him and pull him to the surface. He coughed and gasped and clung to me, and I pulled us back to the boat, laughing hard. "It's nice to know you're not good at everything," I told him as I brought him to the ladder.

"I'm good at everything I spend an incredible amount of time practicing," he told me.

Holding the ladder, I moved closer to him with a sly smile. "I suppose I'll just have to spend an incredible amount of time teaching you to swim," I told him.

Our bodies were soaked, and the parts of me that were above the surface should have been frozen, but there was an exciting heat twisting between him and me. My leg grazed his in the water, and his eyes dropped to my mouth.

I swayed forward, feeling his breath on my wet skin, but with a laugh I pushed away from the ladder, sliding back through the water.

He grinned at me. "Trying to motivate me?" he asked.

"Yes," I replied, grinning back at him.

He pushed off the ladder too, a twisted grimace on his face as water flooded up over his chest and chin. He grunted, paddling awkwardly, and I laughed again. "I will figure this out, and one day you'll be very sorry," he promised.

I let him catch up to me, and I put my hand on his chest, running a fingertip over a line in his neck. "Will I?" I murmured.

His hands touched my sides, but to do that he stopped swimming, and I barely got a chance to howl out a laugh as we fell beneath the waves. He started to panic, but I touched his cheek, and for a long moment, our eyes met underwater as we sank down. My fingers inched forward and touched his lips, and the dark centers of his eyes widened like he was trying to drink me in.

But then he looked up like he'd never see the surface again, and I wrapped my arms around him and kicked.

He copied me, his arms strong around me, binding us together in the shifting light filtered through the water.

When we broke the surface, the spell shattered, and he gulped in a breath, gasping hard and leaning his head against my shoulder. "Skies," he sputtered.

My nose grazed over the skin on his neck. "Did I nearly kill you?" I asked.

His fingers tightened on my skin under the water. "I think I nearly let you," he said.

Fisk and Arnav shrieked around the bow, splashing water, and I pulled Kairos back to the ladder, reluctantly tugging out of his arms. "Good first lesson," I told him, and didn't wait for his response before diving deep under the water, ignoring the places my skin still tingled with his touch.

# Serobini

After a few more days, we left the warm waters far off the southern coasts of the Trifectate. The air was still warm and dry, but my power could sense the distant chill in the wind. The northernmost of the Wyverns was so hot it was damn near tropical, but the southernmost had parts that were covered in snow year-round.

It took us eight days in total to reach the Wyverns since I was eager to make up for lost time once I was rested. There were three major islands, each nearly as big as the Trifectate if you mashed their lands into the same shape. Zilarra was the first island, with its main port at the northern tip of the island. It would be the first thing we sailed past, but I had every intention of going right on by. There was a bustling market there, but as the easily accessible port, it was lousy with lazy traders and legitimate businessmen, and I had no use for paying higher prices for lower quality. It took us another day, but I led the boat down to the port of Sayma.

This port was smaller. It stood at the mouth of a river but had only a small allowance for the ocean-faring vessels; the most it could safely hold was about six. Which kept prices high, but it also kept quality exceptionally high. Unfortunately, this was also the slave market with the greatest reputation in the world.

We took up a mooring, and Navya shouted out orders to the rest of the crew. We planned on being here a few days, so the first group was sent off to get supplies; when they returned others would be allowed to go for pleasure in shifts, and Sophy would make the final trip for still more supplies and perishables.

In that time, I would hopefully have discovered where their secret mines were and how to easily fly over, steal slaves, and leave.

Simple.

It was hot enough that I didn't want to wear my leathers, but I didn't like feeling so exposed with my bag slung across my shoulders. I didn't have all our gold in there—Navya, Ori, and Bast were all entrusted to buy goods as well and had a cache on their persons—but still. The best way I knew not to get robbed was never to leave anything vulnerable.

Kairos was strapping on a sword belt when we were about to board the rowboat to shore. "It's not your turn to leave," Navya told him. "We go by seniority."

"I'm coming with you three," he told her.

She looked at me, but I shook my head. "Captain says no," she told him.

"Captain can speak for herself. You'll need my help."

"No, we won't. This is the easy part," I told him. "Stay here, wait for your turn to go ashore."

Bast chuckled, and Kairos raised his eyebrows. "As you wish, Captain."

We boarded the rowboat with Fisk and Arnav at the oars, and

I stood tall in the boat as we made our way to the main docks. When we arrived, I waited, watching until Fisk and Arnav were well on their way back to the ship to leave.

"What are we looking for?" Navya asked as we walked down the dock. The wooden planks quickly changed to massive stone walkways thick with people as we headed for the central market.

"Any metals or jewelry should be well priced here," I told her. "Ori, pay special attention to that—I know you're excellent with shiny objects." He grinned at me. "Navya and Bast, you know what gets a good price, and of course, anything new and exciting that will interest Cyrus. Buy what you can and get back to the boat with it. I have some contacts here; I'll try to find some information to point us in a good direction."

Bast looked at me with a warning. "You have to admit when you're in over your head, Asp."

"I'm not," I told him, turning away to lead us. "We'll find a way. We always do."

"Not in an unfamiliar place. Not when you don't even know where the mine is." Bast grunted. "Dammit, Ori, don't elbow me. I can tell her when she's being an ass."

"I'm still the captain," I snapped. We passed a shop, one of the open buildings that defined the start of the market, and out front there were four chained slaves blinking against the hot sun. I turned away.

"Why don't we just take them from the market?" Navya asked, her voice a hushed whisper after we passed.

"We might," I told her. "But they won't keep them here at night. I imagine they're under lock and key. At a mine, you work them hard enough and guard the enclosure and you don't need to worry about them at night."

She lifted a shoulder, looking away.

The thoroughfare opened up past the shop; the market was a huge circle, bound off by two circles of columns, one inside the other. Buildings created the outer border, and within the columns, there were two neat circles of stalls that opened up and closed each day. Cloths of every color were spread between the columns to keep the punishing sun away, and they cast the whole place in an ever-shifting tumble of brightly colored light.

"Be back to the docks before dark," I told them, pointing them in one direction while I went in the other.

I gripped my bag, holding it tight to my hip as I shifted through the throngs of people. My hackles were up—everything felt like a threat, like danger, like I shouldn't be here right now. I couldn't tell if it was the wind warning me, or if it was just my looming lack of faith that I could complete this order at all.

I made my way slowly to the back of the market. I hadn't been here in a year, but the last I'd seen Sayma's port, one of my crew had left the ship to make her life here. She was from here originally, and she'd found her mother still alive and well. She gained a position in one of the bigger market shops, and she was happy. Hopefully a year hadn't changed so much.

The shop was owned by a wealthy cloth merchant, and bolts of bold, bright silks fluttered in the breeze as I approached the shop.

"Beautiful," said a girl, noting my interest and hooking a long, brightly woven scarf around my shoulders. "So beautiful on you! You must have it."

"I'll take it," I told her. "And four more in other colors, please."

She brightened like the gold I was about to hand her was

glinting in her eyes. "Yes, yes, of course. You shall have it, *maisa*," she told me.

"I'm not a maisa," I told her, probably too sharply, but it was the respectful term for a wealthy slaver in the Wyverns. "But I do have an extra coin for you if you could find Zelia for me."

She frowned. "Is that a person?" she asked.

"She worked here," I told her, my heart sinking.

"Oh," she said. "I have only been here a few weeks. Come inside, I will ask someone who has been here longer."

I pushed through the drapes of cloth to a clean, orderly shop. There was a very short, very round girl with dark hair carefully folding cloth, and she looked up at the girl, and then me.

"Maisa, welcome," she said, then looked to her compatriot hopefully.

"She wants five scarves," she told her quickly. "She was asking for a girl named Zella."

"Zelia," I corrected, and the girl bowed apologetically before she went to collect the scarves. "I remember you. You were here a year ago."

The round girl smiled. "I've been here longer than that," she told me, in a fond, easy way that made me think she wasn't treated poorly. "But Zelia didn't stay long. She caught the eye of a nice young man, and they live down the coast last I heard."

My heart sank. It was entirely possible this trip was doomed. "Thank you." The other girl held out the scarves and told me the price, and I gave it to her plus an extra coin for both of them. The Saroccan king was much more valuable than the Trifectate tri-kings or the Wyvern silver ingots, and the girls treated me like a princess when they saw it.

I left, wandering until I found a rickety stall that served cups of a sweetened kind of coffee, and I bought a roll with meat cooked inside it, thinking as I downed the drink.

There was a small statue of a woman with big, wide hips and rings and rings of golden necklaces covering her breasts. She held her hands aloft, above huddled figures of men kneeling at her feet. I always liked this goddess—the people in the Wyverns believed in twin goddesses, sisters of wisdom and chaos, and this was Serobini, the embodiment of chaos. She reigned over the markets, feeding on the chance, the change, the unpredictability that they brought every day. Chaotic, and female, and holy for being so.

She was also a favorite of Cyrus, and the comparison stung the joy out of the thought.

"Aspasia."

My head turned sharply, and it was like I had conjured the goddess of chaos into life. There was a tall girl in front of me, a silk cloth clinging to her hips and nothing but heaps of bronze necklaces to cover her above that. Her eyes were lined with a thin line of bright white that made her eyes look unnaturally huge against pale gold skin that reminded me of sun rays.

For long moments, I just stared at her. Then she smiled her crooked smile, and I suddenly saw the girl I had known beneath it all. "Tanta," I realized, stunned. I shook my head. "What in all the hells are you doing here?"

She moved closer to me, her smile never faltering as her eyes ran over my face, memorizing me. She came close enough that I could feel her breath on my lips, and I held mine. "You asked about Zelia at that shop," she said. "I went in just after you and they told me. I knew it was you." She drew in a slow breath, her eyelids fluttering closed, and she pressed her lips to mine.

The kiss was brief and chaste, but I still felt heat rush into my face and the lovely, familiar tug of the love I'd always had for her wrap around me like something warm and comforting. "Come," she said. "We have so much to discuss."

Yes—that was clear. I had last seen her in the Trifectate with her savings in hand when she said she was leaving the ship to make a life there. She wasn't the first person I'd said good-bye to, and she wouldn't be the last, but Tanta was the first person I loved who had left me, and every time I was in the Trifectate, part of me still looked for her.

I'd been looking on the wrong shore.

She tugged my hand, not waiting for an answer as she brought me out of the market, going to a conveyance that had no real walls, just elaborately carved panels that let the air rush through, with two horses and two large men to guide it.

"All done?" one man asked her, bowing.

"My plans have changed," she told them with authority. "Take us back, please."

The other man bowed also, opening up the door to reveal two cushioned seats. Tanta tugged me inside, bringing us to lounge on one small seat rather than two. Nearly nose to nose, she grinned at me. "You must tell me everything."

"Me?" I asked. "I haven't seen you in three years, and that was in the Trifectate."

She rolled her eyes. "Who likes that hideous place? No one. The king started burning people with abilities, and so I left. I found a ship to Sayma, and I fell in love. And as you can see, I'm kept very, very well."

"Where are we going?" I asked her.

"I can't ruin the surprise. It is too grand!" she said. "Can you even believe how lucky I am? Can you even believe that the dirty, hardscrabble girl scrubbing deck would be this a few years later?" she asked, waving her hand slowly down her body. Her necklaces were shifting, and the curve of her breast was becoming more obvious.

"Maybe I should be sitting over there," I said, gesturing to the other seat. "Especially if you're in love."

"Oh, it isn't the same," she told me. "You and I—we were girls together, doing things all girls should do. There will always be love between us, but that doesn't mean that we're still *in* love. You know—you must have fallen in love a hundred times by now."

I laughed. "Hardly."

"Once?" she asked, looking horrified. "Did I break your heart forever? Did you never get over me?" The horror had changed to something closer to thrilled.

I laughed again. "No, Tanta. You didn't break my heart to start with, much less forever."

She made a face. "Well, that's just rude."

I sighed. "I wanted to be in love once. It just wasn't what I thought it would be. It certainly wasn't what *he* thought it would be."

"He," she repeated, waggling her brows. "So I'm your only lady love."

She was teasing me, but I searched her face. "So far," I said.

"We'll get back to the he," she said, giggling. "Another crewmate, I assume." She gasped. "You are still captain, aren't you?"

I smiled. "Yes. And yes, another crewmate."

"Did you break his heart?"

I looked down. "He thinks I did. It wasn't that different from us, you know—we were friends for the longest time, and then something happened. Unlike you, he just thought that it meant everything."

Her nose wrinkled. "It means nothing until you both agree it means something," she told me. "That wasn't fair of him."

"That's what I thought too," I told her.

"Did I know him?"

It took me a minute to think, to go back through the tangled threads of history to figure out when she left and he came. "You met, actually. He came on board about a month before you left."

She gasped. "Oh! It's that Smash boy, isn't it? No—Bash!"

I laughed. "Bast. But yes."

She shook her head. "I never liked him. He cleaved a little too hard to you, much too fast."

Had he? We'd become fast friends, but honestly, I always thought part of that had been because Tanta left, not something that happened before. "Well, that's as close as I've come to it."

She searched my face with a mischievous look in her eye. "No, that isn't the end of the story. There's someone else. Someone you like," she told me. Her eyes flared. "Or someone you're lusting for, at least."

I tried to fight off a smile. "Someone I'm deciding if I like," I told her.

"Boy or girl?"

*Man* was my immediate response, and I felt heat rush to my face at the thought. "Boy."

She grabbed my hands. "I must meet him. I have to approve!"

I laughed. "Tanta, why don't you tell me where we're going?"

She looked out the grates, and I followed her gaze. We were on a road out of town, and electric blue water the color of her silk skirt bordered us on one side. "We're almost there," she told me slyly.

I straightened, looking around as much as I could through the carvings of the moving carriage. I could see the silver-plated walls glinting in the sun up ahead, and I knew enough about the Wyverns to know that only a royal was allowed to use metals this way—and only a royal had the silver to use.

Whipping my face back to Tanta, I gasped, but she just laughed, petting my arm. "We're going to have the most wonderful time!"

Sure enough, the silver gates opened into the courtyard of the royal palace. One of the royal palaces, I should say—from what I heard there were at least three per island, all the better to keep the three phaedrae from dealing with one another.

Tanta happily flounced out of the carriage as soon as the guards opened the door, and I held my bag tight as I followed her. The whole courtyard was a stunning mosaic of tiny tiles of glass and stone, but Tanta didn't seem to care at all as she caught my arm and dragged me inside.

There were two large stone buildings, but she brought me straight down a long hallway of open arches to a pair of massive silver doors. The guards silently opened them for Tanta, who let go of me to bounce into the room.

I stopped. I had heard of this place, but I never knew which palace it was in or if it was even real. The room's floor was covered in a mosaic—unlike the one outside, this was made of silver, gold, emeralds, rubies, and other jewels I couldn't even name. The metals were soft and worn down around the hard, unyielding pride of the gems; the whole room sparkled with daunting wealth and the sunlight pouring in from large windows above.

"Aspasia," Tanta snapped, like she had said my name already. I raised my head, and dropped to my knees in what I hoped I was correctly remembering was the Wyverni custom.

"Captain Aspasia of the *Ancora*," Tanta said proudly. "I am honored to introduce you to the High Phaedra of Zilarra, second in line to the Wyvern throne."

I wasn't sure if I was supposed to, but I raised my head to see a very amused and unbelievably stunning woman, dressed in some kind of delicate pale blue dress with cascading layers of necklaces, her skin so smooth and dark she shone like one of the jewels around her. She watched me, lounging in a jeweled throne with Tanta perched on the arm. "Welcome," she told me. She tugged Tanta to her, pulling her mouth to hers for a kiss. "My love, let's go to the garden—this room can be a little overwhelming."

Tanta smiled and stood, and the phaedra followed, watching Tanta fondly. I trailed behind them, dazzled as the sunlight struck their necklaces and glittered. Out here I could see that the phaedra had necklaces of silver, not bronze like Tanta, and many more of them, the fine chains artfully layered. Her dark hair was bound up, with more pieces and bits of silver keeping it there.

The garden itself was shaded by high-flown carvings, similar to the carriage, looming over us and casting us in precarious shade, making the whole place seem like I was gazing through a gossamer cloth into a dream. There were people, still as stone, all in the same white cloth, evenly spaced at columns throughout the garden, and I wondered if they were slaves.

I wondered if I could steal from Tanta. More than that, I

wondered if it was even possible—Tanta knew what I did, and she'd be able to spot my game pretty far away.

There was a large area around a fountain where the carvings were more solid and the shade was more complete, and the phaedra chose a long, white couch to lie upon. Tanta sat by her feet, calling to one of the motionless figures. The man peeled away from the column, kneeling to her as she asked for food and drink, then spirited away through the garden.

"I always wondered if we would meet," the phaedra said, and the weight of her full attention was intense. Of all the powerful people I'd met, most could do this—when they truly looked at you, you were suddenly visible, like a shaft of light was on your face. When they looked away, they took the light with them.

With Cyrus, I had been trained to recognize that as a dangerous feeling. I wasn't sure if this woman's attention was equally as life threatening.

"Tanta doesn't speak of you often," she said, and I saw Tanta duck her head. "But when she does, it's fondly. I think you helped her survive a difficult time in her life."

My throat felt dry and rough. "She helped me too." There were some days when I knew I would never have made it through those years without her. There were other days when I felt the power in my hands now and thought that was enough to rewrite my past vulnerabilities.

"So tell me," she said, smiling. "When did you first know you had the ability to control the air?"

Every muscle in my body went tense, but Tanta jumped up, coming to grasp my hand and sit with me. "I told her," she said. "But it's safe. I swear it."

"It's true," she said gently. "I know of your gifts, and Tanta's ability to manipulate water. I am so very curious about it all—when did it begin?"

Tanta knew these answers, and either she had told them already and the phaedra wanted to see if I would lie to her, or she hadn't, and I shouldn't tell her either. "A few years ago," I said vaguely. "While I was on board the *Wanderer*."

"The ship you two met on," she said, smiling like she was putting a puzzle together. "Your ship now is the *Ancora*?"

"Yes."

"Very interesting," the phaedra said, smiling as three servants set out trays brimming with food and drink on low tables. I thought of Cyrus again, and how her continuous banquet seemed to be some kind of devil's bargain to trick me into staying there.

Tanta poured me some of the prized sweet coffee, and I took it in good faith.

"So what of you?" I asked, sipping the hot drink. "How did you two meet?"

"I hired her," the phaedra said fondly.

I looked to Tanta. "To do what?"

She opened her mouth, but the phaedra spoke. "To assist with our mining process here. Tanta's ability to move water was invaluable."

This brought many questions to mind, but they were all for Tanta, in private. Did this mean she was just another version of a slave?

"I'd like to ask you—" the phaedra started, but a cry that dissolved quickly into a laugh cut through her. She sat up straight, alert, and relaxed only when two children came into view, chasing each other through the garden.

Tanta smiled, calling them over to us, and one barreled

forward to throw herself into Tanta's arms. The smaller one moved more carefully, climbing the three shallow stairs bent forward at the waist, gripping the next stair with his hands as he wedged himself up.

He tottered over to the phaedra, and she swung him up to sit comfortably in her lap. He sank into her, bringing his thumb—which I could only imagine was fairly dirty—up to suck on.

It was shockingly . . . domestic.

"Aspasia, please meet the Lower Phaedrae of Zilarra, Ibal and Izar," she said, bouncing the girl in her lap when she said Ibal.

Ibal had pale skin and bright golden curls, and Izar had olive skin that looked far closer to mine—they looked like they were neither related to each other nor to the phaedra.

"Your children?" I asked.

The phaedra gave me a motherly smile. "You seem confused."

"I would never assume to know Wyverni ways enough to be confused," I denied.

"We do not believe that royalty should be an accident of birth," she told me. "I chose my children, just as I was chosen."

I nodded, unsure if I was supposed to be interacting with the children.

"I was about to ask you a question," the phaedra said, rubbing the little boy's hair back from his face. "I've had many Elementae in my household over the past few years, but I've never met someone who can control earth. I always thought it simply wasn't possible—we consider the earth to be holy here, and it made sense to me that She could not be moved by mortal hands. But now I hear that people have seen a reemergence of this element."

I watched her steadily. "I've heard the same."

"I'm hopeful," she told me. "If I could find people with such gifts, it would change the nature of mining in Zilarra, if not all of the Wyverns."

A warning streaked through the muscles on my neck and back, but I wasn't sure if it was the wind or my own fear. "You're looking for Elementae slaves," I clarified, keeping my voice even. Mentioning the mines was more of a lead than I hoped for, and I had to keep my emotions in check to follow it. "You think I can help?"

"Not *slaves*," she said. "As I said, the earth is a holy thing to me. It follows, then, that anyone who can control such an element—or any element—is a thing worthy of praise. To put such a person in chains would be . . ." She shuddered instead of finishing the sentence.

*All people*, I wanted to correct her. All people should not be in chains; all people should be praised.

"No," she continued. "I'm interested in paying someone very, very well to do this work."

"I might know someone in Sarocca who would be interested," I told her. "But I would have to see the mines first. I would like to know what you would have them do before I send them to you."

Her gaze narrowed a little as she appraised me. I stared back; I knew the power of not blinking first. "Very well," she told me. "Tomorrow. We will meet you at the docks at first light."

# The Language of Hope

I left Tanta in her cushioned palace without a moment to speak to her alone. The carriage brought me back to the docks well after dark.

"Take you to yer boat for a tithe," called a voice from beyond the weak light of the dock lanterns.

"No thanks," I replied, walking to the end of the dock and stretching my power out over the water. I felt my way along the ship until I found the bell near the ship's wheel, and I shoved it a little. Navya or Bast would hear it and send someone out for me.

I sat at the end of the dock, letting my eyes adjust to the darkness. Dark was never fully dark, or black—it was layered shades of blue, dark and light, washing together. No matter how far I sailed, once my eyes adjusted to another sky, a new, delicately shaded world was unveiled like there were always things lurking that we couldn't see until we learned how to see them.

Soon enough I saw a little boat coming through the darkness, and I was amused to see Kairos at the oars, his face twisting with concentration as his body rolled with the motion of rowing.

"Did you piss off Navya?" I asked, swinging my legs over the water as he came closer.

"Volunteered," he said, easing back to grin up at me as the boat floated closer. I stepped easily into it as it slid beneath my feet, sinking down into the seat in front of him.

"I take it you didn't make it to shore today," I said with a smile.

"I did not," he agreed. "It seems I'm on the low end of your hierarchy."

"You're new," I told him. "You should be."

"And how was your day, Captain?"

I leaned back, searching the sky and the clouded-over stars. "Exceptionally strange, actually."

"How so?" he asked, heaving the words out as he hauled the oars back.

"Chased one ghost and found another," I told him. "And possibly a way into the mines tomorrow."

"Well, that sounds promising."

"Confusing," I told him. "I distrust things that play perfectly into my subversive desires."

He chuckled at that. "Does this mean I get to come tomorrow?"

He was the best fighter I currently had on my crew. "Yes," I decided. "I think it does."

"You could push this boat with nothing but your power, couldn't you?" he asked on another hard pull.

I grinned. "Absolutely."

He chuckled. "Thanks for the assistance, then."

"It will help you build muscle," I teased.

He grinned. "My muscles are just fine, and you know it."

I laughed, fighting a smile. "Well, you still can't swim."

He huffed. "I have yet to drown; I think that's in my favor."

A thought of the two of us, treading water and panting for breath, our faces close enough to feel breath on damp skin, passed through my mind. "You need more practice."

Maybe mind reading was another power of his, because he looked at me like he knew what I was thinking, and he smiled, and his gaze on me felt warm and interested. "I'll hold you to it."

"Have you practiced today? With your visions?"

He nodded. "Trying. It's easier when you're around, but it also means that you usually dominate the visions. I could reliably call up a vision of my sister, but it was brief."

"What do you see?"

"I'm hugging her. On board a ship."

My eyebrows rose. "Will that happen?"

He sighed. "I don't know. When it's something I *want* to happen, I can't really tell the difference."

I considered this. "You said visions, plural. Have you had other visions of me lately?"

He grinned at me, that bright, confident grin, and I knew he had.

"Are you going to tell me about them?" I demanded.

"Absolutely not," he said, glancing over his shoulder to measure the distance to the boat.

"That hardly seems fair," I protested.

"My power, not yours," he told me, guiding us against the boat.

"Coming aboard!" I shouted, and a moment later two ropes

were tossed down. We tied them to the ends of the boat and climbed up the ladder while the others pulled the boat out of the water, just by a few feet to keep it available but prevent it from drifting off.

"Navya and Bast, my cabin for reports," I told them. "And someone tell Sophy I want to see her too!" I started heading below and noticed Kairos was not behind me. "Do I have to order you to follow me?" I snapped. "Come on!"

He shook his head with a smile, but obeyed.

Navya and Bast accompanied us down, and once I lit a candle in my cabin, I noticed Bast, his arms crossed over his chest, giving Kairos a glare out of the side of his eye.

"So," I said, pulling out an old map of the Wyverns and spreading it on my desk. "We've been invited to tour the mines tomorrow."

Bast whistled. "How on earth did you manage that?"

I sighed. "An old crewmate made an introduction to the phaedra," I told him.

He looked to Navya. "What's that?" he asked her.

"A Wyverni princess," Kairos volunteered.

Bast glared at him full on. "How would you know that?"

*Because his sister's a queen*, I wanted to answer. "More specifically, the phaedrae each rule an island," I told them, pointing to Zilarra. "So this phaedra runs all the mines here. She says she wants to hire an earth element to streamline the mining process for her."

"You're selling Linnea?" Sophy growled, opening the door without knocking.

"Welcome," I drawled. "No, Sophy, I'm not selling Linnea. I

told the phaedra I would make a connection to someone I knew in Sarocca—if I approved of the conditions of the mine. She does not and will never know of Linnea or her powers."

Sophy came farther into the room, scowling. "Well, that makes more sense," she grumbled.

"Yes," I told her. "And we should be able to figure out if it's even possible for us to fly the ship to the mine, and if so, how to steal slaves."

"Didn't you say this is a friend of your friend?" Kairos asked.

I rubbed my forehead, then sharply put my hand down because I hardly wanted them to see me worry. "Yes."

"So you're going to steal from her? Royalty, no less."

I looked at the map. "I haven't completely decided yet. There are a lot of things to be considered."

"Why don't you just buy them? You don't steal jewels and whatever else you sell to Cyrus," Kairos protested.

"Do we really have to waste time with landlegs's questions?" Bast grunted.

"*Landlegs?*" Kairos repeated, then looked at his own legs. "How is that even an insult?" He squinted. "How is that even a word?"

"It means you're not used to the sea," Navya told him. "And buying slaves just puts more money in the pockets of slavers, which Asp won't do."

"Except Cyrus," Kairos clarified. "You'll put plenty of money in her hand."

That had a surprising sting to it, considering I had told him how our arrangement worked, how little choice I had. I shot him a look that, judging from his slightly fallen face in reaction, was probably more full of hurt than I meant.

"What's the plan?" Bast snapped, glaring at Kairos again.

"She comes to get us at the dock at dawn," I told them. "Navya, I need you to make sure the ship is secure tomorrow. I don't want any Elementae going ashore in case this is some kind of a trick to steal our people. Bast, I want you to take those without powers to shore to finish up as much of our business as you can. Hopefully we'll have another day here, but if this goes poorly and we need to move fast, I don't want to be forced to stop in the Wyverns again before we head back home. I want you to coordinate with Sophy to make sure we're covered for supplies. Understood?"

Sophy and Navya nodded firmly, but Bast's brows drew tight together. "You can't go alone," he told me. "If you suspect any kind of a trick, it's not a good idea."

"I'm aware," I said, meeting his eyes coolly.

His eyes shifted from me to Kairos, and instead of the burst of anger I expected, he just shook his head with a chuckle that sounded like a sneer. "Of course. You're taking him with you."

"I am pretty handy in a fight," Kairos said lightly.

"You've lost your damn mind," Bast told me, leaning forward like this was a private talk between us and not in front of three other people. "You're trusting the wrong people, Asp. And it's going to get you killed."

I didn't flinch away from him. "Navya knows what to do if that happens," I told him.

"Get out," he said, and for a moment I thought he was talking to me. But then he swung his head around and shouted it again at the others. "*Get out!*"

I could feel more than see Kairos coiling like a snake as Bast's voice rose, but it was Navya who called Kai's name, nudging him toward the door. Kairos went, and I didn't need to look at him to know that just like with Skiver, he'd be right outside my door.

"Bast," I said with a sigh, shaking my head.

"Are you sleeping with him?" Bast asked.

"Yes," I lied. Bast choked on his own words, nearly turning purple as rage filled him. "There," I told him. "Does that feel better? Is that what you want, to obsess over whatever I'm doing with another crew member?"

"Does that mean you're not?" he demanded.

I crossed my arms, leaning against the wall. "Bast, stop acting like this is about him. It's not. It's about you and me."

"You're damn right it is," he snapped. "I *hate* him, and I hate that I hate him. When was the last time we had someone on board that I could actually stand to learn something from? I see how you are with him, and he hasn't earned your trust. And I hate that he has it. I hate that you're giving it away to him when I had to earn it." He shook his head. "No. I hate that you're giving it to him when I've lost it somehow."

"You didn't lose my trust," I told him softly. *Though keep this up and we'll see.* "Or my friendship."

He looked up at me and his face wasn't angry. It was hurt and raw and fighting something back that was so close to the surface he was shaking a little. "You're the only one I trust, Asp. You know that. You're the only one."

I swallowed. Bast's past was dark, I knew that. His own mother, the person who was supposed to love him most, sold him into this life. He had his reasons not to trust people, but it wasn't fair of him to ask *me* not to trust.

His hand was a fist on the table, and I covered it with my

fingers. "I know, Bast. We're in this together. We always have been."

He gave a ragged sigh. "I'm frustrated, Asp. We lost something and I don't even know how it happened, and I went from feeling like your partner to feeling like just another crewmate, and I need more for my life than this."

My chest felt tight. "You're thinking about leaving," I realized, and Charly's warnings rushed through my mind again.

"I don't want to," he said. Then he shook his head. "Maybe I do."

I had said half good-byes to everyone in my mind except Bast. He liked this life, and he didn't have ties anywhere. It wasn't that I thought we would sail together for life, but I just hadn't been prepared for him to leave. For being the only one tied to this ship like an anchor.

"Don't say that just to say it," I told him, my voice hushed. "If you mean it, say it. If you don't, don't you dare manipulate me."

"I want to have more control," he said.

I watched him. "That makes sense."

"You say you trust me, but I'm not even your second in command," he reminded me. That had always bothered him, and I didn't have the stones to look at his face when he said it. "Cyrus offered me a ship. I'm thinking about it."

My stomach tightened and twisted. He would *choose* this life? He owed Cyrus nothing, and though I'm sure she promised him everything, he would choose this life.

"Well," I said, my voice coming out rough and gravelly. "Let me know when you make a decision."

"There could be two of us," he said. "Think of the protection you'd have with another boat at your stern. Think of the people who we could free from this life."

But Bast was too easily tempted. It was a nice idea, but too soon he would want to fill Cyrus's orders as she demanded, let her fill his palm with gold. He would become like all the others, and forget the life he had come from to buy the ability to never be vulnerable again.

In his eyes, a captain didn't have to trust. A captain need only command, and trust became a thing that was given to you, laid at your feet like a gift.

I shook my head. "I can't help you with that decision, Bast."

He lifted a shoulder. "I just want you to be careful with this guy."

"Noted," I told him. I bit my lip and looked up, trying to acknowledge that at least he thought he was doing the right thing. Maybe it was the right thing—for him. "Thank you for telling me about the ship."

He stepped nearer to me, kissing my cheek over my crossed arms, and I resented it, like he was using our past closeness to force me to see things his way now.

He left the cabin without another word, leaving the door open. I knew Kairos, if not Navya as well, was in the passageway.

I didn't care. From the drawer I had hidden it in, I pulled out the carved box and opened it up. These were my treasures, and even looking at them made me feel better. More human.

"What's that?" I heard softly from behind me.

Kairos came into the room; I heard his steps creaking ever so slightly on the floor. I brought the box to the cot, needing suddenly to share this with someone. It helped a little that it was someone like him, who felt slavery like a glancing blow; unlike Bast, it had never sunk its dark claws into him. Kairos, at his heart, was still good.

Folding my legs under me, I pulled my treasures out of the box slowly. First there was a doll, made from gathered-up lengths of discarded thread, bound together and shaped, with buttons sewn on for eyes. He laughed as I handed it to him and sat on the bed, the box and its contents between us. "Catryn had something like this," he told me. "It was torn tent cloth instead of thread, but it looked much the same."

I touched the ragged edge of the cloth. "The girl who owned this was from a cloth-making commune in Liatos, in the Trifectate," I told him. "Is Catryn—?"

"My baby sister," he said, his voice rough and low.

He ran his finger over the eyes gently, but I picked up another of my treasures, a broken piece of tile with an incredibly detailed, tiny painting on it. It was of a house and a blue sky and green grass with white flowers.

"That was from a little boy," I explained. "His mother made that for him. He hadn't seen her in a long while."

There was a folded, worn piece of paper, and I handed it to him. He opened it, reading, "There's a day that comes when all the gray stops looking the same, and I find beauty in the tiny variations of sky to stone to salt. I don't know whether that is salvation, or damnation."

He looked up at me, confused, his throat bobbing. "Who was this from?"

My shoulders lifted. "I'm not sure. It was left in the hold after we off-loaded people."

"All of this . . . ," he realized. "It's from slaves."

I nodded, my throat feeling tight.

"Why do you keep it?"

"Because," I told him, "it's hope. And freedom."

He flipped the paper over cautiously. "How so?" he asked.

My shoulders lifted. "You would think that when you're broken, and beaten within an inch of your life, and hopeless, there's no place for beautiful things. For painting, and carving, and toys, and poems. You would think that you could break a whole group of people and take that away from them." I shook my head. "But you can't. I've never come across people who aren't finding ways to create something joyful, no matter how limited their materials, or how little time they have." I sighed. "Even when they have no tools, and no materials, they sing. Art is the language of hope."

Lastly, I took out the small carved wooden horse from the bottom of the box. Part of the horse's flank had sheared off because it was the wrong grain of wood to have been carved like that, just a scrap that was the only thing my father could keep once he was taken into the communes. Kairos touched it reverently, and his fingertip traced the letter *A* on the horse's neck. If he knew this was mine, the only thing I had of my family, he didn't say so, or question me.

"I know it's complicated," I said softly, my throat rough. "But don't throw it in my face that I still serve Cyrus. That I give her money and keep her powerful."

He sighed, looking at my treasures. "You talk to me about my strongest emotion, but this is yours, isn't it?" he said gently. "Hope. This is what you hold on to, what gets you through every battle."

I took the horse back from him, clutching it, not answering. I couldn't answer him.

"Why won't you admit that?" he said softly.

"I'm a pirate slave-trading airship captain. What right do I have to hope for anything?" I growled, but it sounded weak.

"Who are you looking for, Aspasia?" he asked, his voice incredibly low, impossibly soft. "Is your family still out there? Does Cyrus have them?"

I looked up to him, my heart fierce. "I will never tell you that," I promised him. "I will never tell anyone, as long as it can be used against me."

He drew in a slow, careful breath, as if more might startle me into silence. "I won't make you."

I placed the things in the box and put it back on the shelf where I could see it. When I turned to him, he was still on my bed, watching me.

I knelt in front of him on the bed. His eyes were soft and warm, full of steadiness that slowly, slowly called my heart into a strong, even beat. My breath drew in and went out, unhurried.

I leaned forward, grazing his mouth with my lips. His lips curled against mine, and I shifted a little. He chased me, his mouth pressing a gentle kiss against my lower lip.

I pulled away, shaking my head. "Kairos," I said softly. "There are ships where currying favor with the captain is how you survive. I may give a lot of orders, but if you want this—you and me—it has to be your choice."

His thumb touched the very edge of my face, touching the little hairs there. "If anyone doesn't have a choice on this ship, Aspasia, it's you."

I met his eyes, resolute. "You know what I mean. Cyrus, she uses her power to get whatever she wants from people. I'm not like that. You know that, don't you?"

"I know. And this is my choice," he assured me, his thumb dragging down to my jaw, the pads of his fingers following in its wake. "Am I yours?"

I thought of Bast, his warning and our history, and Tanta, and I considered Kairos, this brave heart in front of me. Yes, I wanted him. Yes, I wanted him to want me. "Yes," I whispered.

His hand slid over my neck, his mouth opening to mine. His tongue moved, and I felt heat burst behind my eyes, arcing down my neck and spine like I had swallowed a thunderbolt. My hands came up too, digging into his hair, roving over his shoulders and neck.

It wasn't the most comfortable position to kiss someone in, and he seemed to recognize this. His arm slid around my back, tugging me up and over until we landed, side by side, on the bed. His hand stroked up and down my spine as our mouths twisted and moved, and I couldn't believe how aware of my skin I felt—like I was burning, or crackling. Every other time I had done this, it was such a rush—every breath and touch demanded more, and faster, and closer. But with Kairos, I liked the slow drag of his fingers on my back, and I liked the engulfing sensations of kissing him. If all we ever did was kiss, I was perfectly happy with that. Which was very new.

I traced the tiny hairs on the back of his neck that grew softer and disappeared under his shirt, worrying each one with my fingertips as we shifted, first a little this way so I was on my back and he was leaning against me, then slowly moving the other way, so I was nearly on top of him.

Slow, decadent, sweet kisses made heat bloom in my stomach and skin and toes. I loved the soft, rumbling noises he made against my mouth, and each time I heard a new one I wanted to make it happen again.

When I broke from his mouth to sigh and press my lips against his neck, tasting the skin there, his fingers curled into my shoulders, pulling me close. He moved, pressing me on my back again so he could kiss my neck, my cheek, my nose.

I laughed, and he smiled at me. Even that caused a strange sensation in me. I couldn't remember ever having laughed with someone during a moment like this. He kissed the corner of my smile, and I shivered.

"I like when you smile," he whispered against my mouth.

"I like how you show your appreciation," I said softly.

The laughter was still bubbling inside me when he kissed me again, digging his fingers through my knotted hair, twining it around his hands to keep my face close to his.

Sophy's dinner bell rang distantly through the door, and it still took us several moments to stop kissing. When our mouths moved apart, we eased onto the pillow, looking at each other. He stroked slowly along my jawline, skirting the edges of my scar without touching it. His eyes were bright and warm, and I didn't want to move. I liked seeing his face when he was looking at me.

"We should go to dinner," he murmured.

I smiled. "You should come back here after dinner."

He kissed the tip of my nose again, and I smiled. "As you command, Captain."

He kept his hands on mine as we got up from the bed, which didn't feel like helping me up as much as it did a desire to keep us attached. He caught my face, gave me another quick kiss before he let me go, and left the room while I took a long moment to breathe.

It was probably a terrible idea, and I knew it would end—either with him leaving to rejoin his family or with me finally reckoning with my fate—but there was a kind of comfort in that. We could only mean so much to each other, and there was no time for it to be totally ruined like it was with Bast.

It was a beautiful night, and instead of serving in shifts belowdecks, Sophy hauled the stew up onto the top deck. Fisk and Addy were both fiddlers, and once they finished eating, they started playing tunes.

It was barely seconds before the little ones started dancing, mostly just jumping and kicking their legs a little, but Arnav knew how to dance properly. To my surprise, he asked Thea to dance with a tomato-red face, and she shyly accepted. Navya danced with Anika, and I clapped along.

"Come on," Bast said, coming up beside me and holding out his hand. "We're still friends, aren't we?"

There had been so many times when Bast and I had danced on this deck, more often as friends than not, and I wanted to believe it was just that simple. I took his hand and gave a yelp as he swung me around.

We leaped and jumped, stomping our feet, and when we barely slowed down Ori caught me, spinning me fast away from Bast and making me laugh. When I stopped reeling, I saw a happy smile on his sad face, and it made my chest crack like a chick bursting out of an egg.

He was a sloppy dancer, rocking us side to side as we wheeled around the deck, and we stopped as Sophy took to the dance floor, lifting her skirts so we could see her feet, stomping and tapping so fast it was blinding and we all had to watch and clap along.

When she stopped, I saw Ori catch Linnea with much more shy intent, and the chick inside my chest cracked off another piece of shell.

Addy stopped with a flourish, and we all paused as she looked to Fisk, pushing him forward, encouraging him.

He cleared his throat and looked at her, then at the crew, and she started playing a fast, fun tune.

*Ain't no better life, better life*
*Than a crewmate on* Ancora
*Ain't no better life, better life*
*It's the ship that I adore-ah*

I leaned my head back and howled with delighted laughter and clapped my hands to the tune as hard as I could. Fisk was proud of himself now, tapping his foot as the rest of us clapped.

*Ya sleep all day, ya work all night*
*When you're working on* Ancora
*But if you delay, you'll get a fight*
*From the captain of* Ancora

People turned to me and roared at this, and I just laughed happily along.

*We've got some secrets we won't tell*
*'Bout the powers of* Ancora

*Water, wind, earth, and flames as well*
*All to protect our* Ancora

*Ain't no better life, better life*
*Than a crewmate on* Ancora
*Ain't no better life, better life*
*It's the ship that I adore-ah*

When he finished the verse, he took up his fiddle again, and the rest of the crew began shouting out this chorus, dancing up a storm. I stepped back, little by little, until I was against the rail of the ship, and I sat on it with a sigh. I was itching to go up to the yard, but it felt so wrong to want to be alone when my crew was enjoying themselves.

My eyes searched out Kairos. He sat on the top step of the stair leading up to the stern, his arms propped up on his knees, and in the lamplight on the deck, he looked . . . heartbroken.

I couldn't help myself. I got off the rail and went over to him, sitting beside him on the step. "Tell me," I said. "It will help."

"Tell you what?" he asked, turning to look at me, his eyes catching on my lips.

But this conversation wasn't about that. "Whatever it is about this that reminds you of home."

He sighed, tugging my hand and interlacing our fingers. "Everything," he said softly.

I pulled my hand away from his, and he met my eyes. "Come to the cabin," I said softly.

He drew in a breath and nodded, and I went belowdecks before him, but it was only minutes later that he came into the cabin behind me, putting his arms around my waist, and I turned, hugging him.

He was hurting, and I knew it, and it felt far more important in that moment to hold on to him than it did to kiss him and return to the blissful bubble we'd been wrapped inside before. So I tugged him to the bed, and I wrapped myself around him, holding him tight as he breathed against my skin, murmuring soft comforts in his ear.

He held on to me just as tight, and before long, he was asleep in my arms. It took me longer to fall asleep, watching him, trying to sort out the strange new feelings in my chest.

# Seven Percent

Kairos was calling my name before I woke up. Very gently, very softly, just below my ear, and I nuzzled against his face.

"It's time to go," he told me.

With a heavy sigh, I looked up. The sky through the porthole was midnight black with an edge of blue at the horizon. He kissed my cheek as he pulled away from me, letting cold creep between us.

I sat up from the bed, pushing my knotted strands of hair off my face. I strapped on my belt and looked at him. "Do you have whatever weapons you need?"

His eyebrows rose. "Will they let me take them?"

"I'd conceal a knife or two," I advised.

He shook his head. "The mine will have heavily armed guards. If anyone there has a sword, I can take it from them."

I stopped. "Really?"

He lifted his shoulder.

"Keep talking like that and I'll have to keep you around."

We went up to the deck, and Arnav was asleep near the wheel, where Navya stood as night watch. She gently shook her brother. "Arnav, take the captain to shore."

"By myself?" he complained, rubbing his face.

"You can do it," she told him.

He didn't like this, but he grimaced and stood, stretching out. It was always shocking to me the way boys grew—just all of a sudden, their legs and arms looked like they'd been stretched overnight. Arnav was getting hints of that, and I ruffled his hair as he came over to us and helped lower the boat back into the water.

Kairos manned the oars with him on the way there, and Arnav looked between us. "Want me to go with you?" he asked me gravely. "We still don't know if we can trust this one."

I snorted, but Kairos indignantly protested, "And I thought we bonded."

"You're good with powers and swords and stuff," Arnav allowed, shrugging. "But you're not family yet."

"Well, I'm working on it. I have to prove my worth somehow, don't I?" Kairos asked.

"I can go if you want me to," Arnav told me seriously.

"Thank you," I said, just as grave. "But someone needs to defend the ship."

He thought about this. "Yeah, I know."

Kairos winked at me as they pulled back the oars together, and it wasn't long until we were at the shore. A baker was loading fresh breads onto a small boat to tempt anyone in the harbor. I tossed a coin at him, and he caught it.

"How much will that buy me?" I asked.

"Three loaves," he said.

I nodded, and he passed them back over. I brought them to

Arnav. "Save some for the rest of the ship!" I told him when he bit into a loaf.

"That must be it," Kairos said, pointing forward.

I turned and saw a conveyance that was like the one from the day before, but larger, gilded with silver.

"Think so," I said, starting toward it. "How much do you know about the Wyverni?"

"Not much," he said. "Three sisters. One queen. Only women inherit, and I know like the clans, they don't necessarily equate royalty with bloodlines. All their money is in slaves, precious metals, and gems."

I shrugged. "Well, that's more than I knew yesterday."

"Also—aren't they a little mystic? I remember something about them treating the Vis Islanders like gods."

But that hardly meant they were trustworthy. "Something like that."

"If they want an earth power—"

"Stop talking," I ordered him, holding up my hand as we neared the carriage. A guard opened the door, and Tanta leaned forward to smile brightly at us and wave.

Before that moment, I hadn't thought of the implications of Tanta and Kairos being in a single small space together, and I wondered if I would get through this day without both knowing what the other meant to me.

Tanta seemed to instantly change her mind about staying in the carriage, and she leaped out with a happy laugh, bounding up to us. She threw her arms around my neck and kissed me, just as she had done in the market the day before, and I felt a blush rising on my cheeks.

She let me go, and I touched my mouth as I saw a stunned

grin on Kairos's face. "Hello," he greeted her as she turned to him, giving her a very formal-looking bow.

She gasped. "Oh, with a bow like that, you must be a clansman," she said, and he straightened with a genuine, warm smile.

"I am," he said.

"Of course you are—goodness, look how handsome you are. I'm Tanta," she said, and took his hand, tugging him forward. "My phaedra, wait until you see him!"

I heard a muffled—but far more dignified—snort from inside the carriage, and I trailed behind them as Kairos smiled at me over his shoulder.

They climbed up into the carriage, and I heard the phaedra say, "Indeed, very handsome."

Within the confines of the carriage, Kairos got down onto one knee, bowing forward over it to the phaedra. "High Phaedra," he greeted her softly. "We are most honored."

"What is your name?" she asked, and he rose up, looking to me and offering me a hand into the carriage. For some reason, I took it, liking the moment of innocent heat of fingers on skin.

"I'm Kairos d'Dragyn," he told her, bowing his head when he couldn't physically bow around me.

"Captain, your friend has much better manners than you do," the phaedra said as I got into the carriage and bowed to her as well.

I froze. "Forgive me, Phaedra," I said. "I hope I haven't offended."

"No," she said, smiling at me. "But you are broadcloth, and he is silk. He was meant to be a courtier." She waved me back, and I sat on the seat beside Kairos, our thighs touching.

Kairos smiled, delighted by this. "Don't worry, Captain, both have their necessary purposes. Silk never fares well on the sea."

The phaedra laughed at this, charmed, and I couldn't help

smiling as well. All hells, the man could turn the head of anyone if he wished.

"I'm so happy you could both join us this morning," the phaedra said. "We have a long ride, I'm afraid, to the mine, so I hope you'll be comfortable." She motioned to Tanta, who unfolded a table from the side of the carriage and laid an impressive feast of food upon it. "Eat. Ease yourself. We shall have a chance to chat."

Kairos didn't hesitate. "I don't know about you, but I am quite fascinated by that greeting. How do you know the captain, Tanta?"

"We are the oldest of friends," she told him, but I noticed she touched her lover's knee when she said it, and I wondered if perhaps she should not have been so free with her affection.

"After all, what is a kiss between friends," he said with a laugh.

Tanta's smile turned sultry. "Oh, clansman, that wasn't a kiss," she told him.

This made the phaedra laugh, and I smiled, incredibly uncomfortable. "How long were you and the captain together?" Kairos asked.

"We sailed for almost three years together," she told him, not taking his bait at another meaning of "together."

"Hmm," he said, smiling. "So you must know all the good secrets."

"She usually does," the phaedra said.

Tanta beamed at this. "Well, a girl does what she must."

"Then please, tell me everything I need to know about the Wyverns," Kairos asked, his gaze shrewd on her. "I've never been here before."

"There are three islands," she said. "Zilarra, Urre, and Kobrea. Nearly in a straight line, with the Trifectate to the northwest, and to the south—"

"I don't think that's what he means, my love," the phaedra said, watching us. "Is it?"

He grinned. "I like the question because it changes based on the listener. What do you believe I need to know about the Wyverns, Phaedra?"

"We serve old gods," she said. "Our ways are older still. Like the mines we cull, our resources are rooted deep in the earth. Like the mountains that protect the mines, we stretch to the sky. We honor our world in a way that most of the places you've seen do not, and we have long been richly rewarded for it." She shook her head. "Places like the Trifectate believe that man can meddle in the ways of gods; they believe that calling a thing by another name will make it true, and that breaking a temple will also eradicate the spirit that once was housed there. The world is not so fickle."

"Certainly," he said warmly, but I wondered if he agreed, or if it was meant to mislead.

"I'm surprised that you worship earth, and yet you mine metal," I said tentatively. I didn't like to ask such questions about people's religions, but it seemed important—if she would truly treat an earth element well was, after all, the "reason" for my presence. "It seems like a god might object to the earth being used in such a manner."

She shook her head. "No. We eat plants, we hunt animals—the earth provides, and we are nourished. Besides, do you know what a wyvern is?" she asked.

I looked at Kairos, then back to the phaedra. "An island," I said, sensing that wasn't the correct answer.

She smiled. "The islands are named for a kind of lizard," she said. "With claws, and wings like an eagle. They're cave dwellers, and it's said that they protected the islands' inhabitants when they first lived here, but when people stopped honoring them the way they should, the wyverns went to the mountains to hide themselves. The people who would become my ancestors went in search of them and found ore instead. It is thought that at the bottom of the mine, the wyverns still sleep."

"My people have many such stories," Kairos said fondly. "Supposedly there is a dragon beneath the sands, which is why they shift so often. My family is named for it."

The phaedra beamed at this. "I can hardly say if such things are true, but it's nice to come from something, isn't it?"

He nodded. "To have history. If you have a legacy, it makes me believe you might have a destiny."

"Quite," she said. "So tell me how you came to be with the captain," she said to him. "You don't strike me as a sailor."

He made a face. "They call me landlegs," he confided.

Tanta laughed, and the phaedra looked at her. Tanta shrugged. "Well, I can just imagine him in a storm," she told her lover.

"Please, you were no better," I told them. "Tanta would hide below in bad weather. Couldn't be counted on for a thing."

"I could, I just didn't want to," she clarified. "One of my first storms I saw our friend fall when her leg was caught in a rope. Her leg had to be cut off," she said with a shiver. "It seemed prudent to stay out of the ocean's way."

I shuddered to remember that storm when Charly lost her leg—that was before we'd found Sophy too, and Charly fought like hell to stay on the seas until we'd found her sister in the Saroccan markets.

Kairos raised his hands. "I will be happy to be called landlegs as long as it's plural," he amended. He shook his head at the phaedra. "I've only been with the captain a short while. We joined up in Sarocca," he said.

I couldn't tell him, but I was incredibly grateful for Kairos's instincts right then, saying "joined up" instead of "purchased" or "freed." It wasn't that she couldn't know how our ship worked, I just couldn't think of a reason why she needed to know, and in my mind knowledge like that had to be earned.

The phaedra kept peppering us with questions, and Kairos answered, managing to do so in a way that never seemed defensive or like he was avoiding giving her information. I barely spoke, watching their exchanges, watching Tanta. She seemed totally at ease, and if this was some kind of a trap, I would have expected her to give me a clue.

Unless, of course, she was helping the phaedra trap me. It had been a long while since I'd known her—was that even possible?

We were going up into the mountains, away from the shore, and more than an hour into the ride, I despaired of being able to bring my ship up here. It was far, and high, and I couldn't keep the ship aloft for more than an hour. Maybe with Anika, and Kairos—but then how in any number of hells was I supposed to get the ship out again?

"You've been very quiet," the phaedra noticed, looking at me. The carriage was slowing down, pitching up, and climbing.

"Well, as you noticed, I don't have the best manners," I reminded her. "Seems smarter to keep from offending people."

"Hm," she said. "Well, we have almost arrived—any moment now we will be passing through the gate."

The carriage stopped for a moment, and looking out the

window, all I could see was green. Lush layers of green every-where, like we were in a jungle.

The carriage started again, and the phaedra said, "Now, don't panic," just as the whole carriage was plunged into darkness.

My fingers curled instinctively into Kairos's knee, and he tugged my hand off him, gripping my fingers instead. I found myself tapping his fingers, even and slow, just to make sure he was still there beside me. "Where are we?" I asked.

"The entrance to the mine is at the end of a very long tunnel," the phaedra explained. "Otherwise the roads make it fairly obvious where all the expensive things are hidden."

I wondered if she meant the gold or the slaves.

It took me a long moment to realize that Kairos was tapping back, his fingers trembling a little. I remembered what he told me, about being belowdecks on the ship that had captured him, and I wondered if he was feeling that again. Carefully, infinitesimally, I sent air over him, like I was brushing his face, like my fingers were on his skin.

There was a noise low in his throat, and I knew he felt it.

At the first hint of light, I reluctantly took my hand from his. Tanta would see it and instantly know too much about him, about us, and while that wasn't the worst thing in the world, it wasn't ideal either.

Light broke open on us, and I blinked as the carriage slowed. Moments later the door opened, and I waited dutifully as the phaedra was the first to get out, then Tanta, then Kairos. He caught my hand as I got out, another excuse, another moment, and I couldn't look at him.

The mine was not what I expected. The jungle was all around

us, but we were standing in a cleared patch of earth. In uneven, concentric circles, wide ledges winded down into the ground. At each level, people stood on the steps, hacking at the ground with pickaxes, tossing chunks of earth into various bins behind them. Between the bins, overseers roved, big men with belts heavy with whips and knives, all their tools of incentive for slaves who weren't cooperative.

We skirted around the edge of the top of the mine to a series of large buildings fitted against the mountain, and as we did, the phaedra began to proudly explain her work. "This is our mine," she told us, waving her hand. "One of them, at least. The ground is rich here, and while the primary veins that we pursue are of silver, they lead us to considerable amounts of gold and copper bound up with them. This kind of depth mining has been very lucrative for us; as Tanta knows, we also have sluice mines, but those don't yield nearly what these do."

"What is sluice mining?" I asked.

"Gold can often be found in loose sediment here," Tanta said. "So if you run water through it, you can easily separate the gold from the other rock."

"So this is what you did here originally?" I asked her.

She nodded. "The mine is really very productive."

My eyes roved over the men with whips. I couldn't see a single man using them, but still—the worst part of slavery wasn't getting hit. It was the threat of it, a sword always pressed against your throat, and knowing that nothing but the whims of another person kept you from death.

"An Elementa would never be treated as a slave," the phaedra told me, following my eyes. "If I were to have an Elementa assist in our mining, she would have a percentage of our profits—whatever we pull from the earth would, in part, be hers. As it should be." I drew my eyes forward, but the phaedra still watched me. "Your eyes do not believe me," she noticed. "Why do you fear I would treat an Elementa as a slave?"

"It is the practice in many places. Elementae are killed in the Trifectate. In Sarocca, they're supposed to be free, but such powers attract the notice of powerful people who would prefer to take than to earn."

Her warm eyes moved from me to Tanta, and Tanta looked down, keeping her eyes and her secrets away from her lover. She had laughed it off earlier, but I could only imagine what had happened in the Trifectate for her to leave so quickly.

"It is not so here," the phaedra said. Even though I wanted to believe her, did it matter? There were *hundreds* of slaves here. Why should abilities keep one person safe and the lack of such doom another?

She brought us into one of the buildings, and I expected it to be dark, but it was bright, with huge open arches at the back that let in light and air while still protecting from the elements. There were many people at the long tables, eating food despite the odd hour.

"Our slaves work for the sunlight hours each day," the phaedra said. "During that time they are allowed two meals and rest breaks, at their discretion. Once the day is done, everyone eats a third meal together."

I noticed a man with a whip beside another without one, and I asked, "The overseers eat here also?"

"Yes. The facility is strongly guarded, and deeply hidden in the dangerous jungle. We don't have issues with slaves running away, so we've never had the need to place distrust between such groups."

"Besides," Tanta added, "the overseers are slaves also. Those that perform well are rewarded."

I looked to the phaedra for confirmation of this, and she lifted a shoulder. "I've never known slavery. It seems wrong for someone who has never felt a whip to administer the use of it, doesn't it?"

I felt heat flush my face, and I struggled to contain myself. *Wrong?* Wrong was putting the life of one slave in the hands of another and acting like it washed your conscience of responsibility. Wrong was not paying workers when you could clearly afford to. Wrong—it was *all* wrong.

The words would betray too much about what I did, about the disagreements I had with my own profession. Instead I made some kind of grunted, strangled noise of assent.

She took us to the sleeping accommodations, and then we had a meal in the hall, with the slaves and overseers around us. The food was delicious—perhaps not as rich as her typical fare, but certainly fit for the phaedra's consumption.

After lunch, the phaedra excused herself to go speak to whoever ran the mine, and I gripped Tanta's hand, pulling her close. "You worked for her?" I asked her. "Is she truthful about all of this?"

"Yes," Tanta said. "Not everyone who has so much power abuses it."

"She still keeps slaves. Hundreds of slaves. That is still an abuse of power, Tanta," I returned, my words sharp.

"And you still trade them," she snapped. "Now you tell me— are you being honest with her, or are you here to rob us? Because honestly, I can't tell anymore."

"I do know an earth element," I told her.

Her eyes narrowed. "That's not a full answer."

"No, it isn't," I said, meeting her gaze.

"What's to stop me from telling her all the little details about your trade?" she hissed at me.

I raised an eyebrow. "Love and loyalty?"

"I was rather thinking there would be a number involved," she told me.

My eyebrows rose. "So it's okay if I'm here to steal from your lover, as long as you get a cut?"

A dark shadow passed over her face that made her ugly for a moment. "This is the best situation I've ever had, but that doesn't mean it's permanent. It doesn't mean I'm safe. You know that— we're never safe."

I watched her for a long moment.

"Company," Kairos warned.

"I'm not going to rob her," I promised. Tanta gave me a look, and I added, "But I'll give you five percent if I do."

"Seven percent," she insisted, just as the phaedra reappeared.

"Well," the phaedra said. "My business here is done. Are there more questions you have for me, Captain, or are you satisfied?"

"Quite satisfied," I told her. "Thank you for your hospitality."

"I hope you'll feel comfortable recommending your friend to us," she said.

"When I return to Sarocca, I will tell him what I've seen," I said. "Beyond that, it is his decision."

She nodded. "That is all I can ask." With a smile, she led us to the carriage, and on the ride back, I stayed silent as Kairos filled the gap with his pleasant chatter. I watched the jungle recede to the city, and my mouth tasted like ash.

I couldn't—physically or morally—steal from the phaedra or Tanta.

Which meant I had no plan.

Again.

The phaedra left us where she had picked us up, and Tanta promised to come meet me the next morning to say our proper goodbyes. I waited until the carriage had gone, looking out over the water at the lowering sun.

Kairos watched me. "We're not going back yet?" he asked.

I sighed. "I don't know what to tell them when we do."

"We're not going through with the plan."

"No," I agreed. "It's a bad plan, in many ways. Primarily that it can't actually work. The mines are too far inland, I don't really know where they are because of that tunnel, and I don't think I can steal from Tanta."

His shoulders lifted. "Maybe it's time to run. Maybe you just take the ship and the crew and we head far away from Sarocca."

"Skiver will come after us," I pointed out.

His eyes glittered. "You're faster than Skiver."

"We need to go home," I told him. "I can't tear families apart with no notice. I can't man the ship without them. I can't be that close to Saroccan waters without tremendous risk."

"Then we'll buy the slaves," he said. "It's not nice, but it's an option."

My gut churned. It felt wrong. "No," I said softly. "We'll just go back. I always knew she was going to punish me for filling the order my way rather than hers, so this will just be a little worse."

"And what if she kills you?"

My eyes moved to his as all the things I knew he didn't want to hear rushed through my head. *It won't matter. I'm prepared to die, and the ship is prepared to go on without me.*

But he had lost enough, and I lied to him instead. "She won't kill me."

"Aspasia," he said, his voice soft and pained.

I sighed raggedly. "What, Kairos? Being protective is damn useless if there is something you just can't avoid."

"Then give me a way to take her leverage from her," he told me, his voice steely.

I frowned. "What do you mean?"

"You are one of the most powerful people I've ever met. You could level her whole damn warehouse with a thought. So if she's punishing you, you're letting her. And I know it's because of your family, or something to do with that. Things you won't tell me, and I don't want to make you. But don't ask me to let you suffer—maybe even let you die—when I am powerful too. I can take her leverage away, and you can tell her to shove her punishment right where it belongs," he told me, his eyes fierce, his body leaning close to me.

I drew in a breath, wanting to tell him about my siblings. Wanting to explain that I would spend my entire life bleeding if it meant finding them one day and reuniting us like I'd been able to do for so many others. I needed the ship to stay on the water, and I needed to stay on the water to be able to keep searching.

But if that were true, wouldn't I just buy the slaves? Did I want to protect my soul more than I wanted to stay on the water?

Or was it a relief to think I might finally get the punishment I so richly deserved?

"I know," he said, even though I hadn't said any of that. "There are things you can't tell me. Or won't. Or don't want to. But don't tell me there aren't other ways to solve your problem. There are. There always are."

He was so close that I pressed my forehead to his for a moment. The gentle contact felt like relief, and we both sighed. "I'll think about it, all right?"

His hands rested on my hips. Our eyes were open, just staring at each other for a long moment. "For what it's worth, I think you're doing the right thing. Here," he clarified.

I smiled, pulling away from him. It was sundown, and there would be crew that knew to come back to the docks now, and I didn't want anyone to see us being so close. "That assumes there is a right thing."

We walked down the dock in silence. A moment later, Sophy and Bast appeared, loaded with supplies, and we took some off their hands as Fisk and Copper showed up with the rowboat.

"Do we want to know how it went?" Sophy asked.

"Wait till we're back on the ship," Bast warned her.

When we made it on deck, I called Navya and Bast down to my cabin. I turned around, planning to tell Kairos to join us, but I didn't see him and decided against provoking Bast for what Kairos already knew.

In my cabin, I explained to them most of what had happened, and the impossibility of stealing from the phaedra.

They both rocked back, looking crestfallen. Navya raised her eyes to me. "What do we do, Captain?"

Sometimes I hated that they looked to me for answers. I was no older or wiser than they were. Other than the scar on my face, I wasn't even sure there was much reason I was captain over them. "We'll head back," I told them, my voice inescapably grim. "And we'll disappoint Cyrus."

Bast opened his mouth, but a knock sounded on the door. "Come in," I called out, assuming it was Kairos.

But Linnea opened the door, her chin high and even a little haughty, color on her cheeks. "Were you even going to tell me?" she asked.

I looked at the two others in my cabin. "Tell you what?"

"That some princess will pay me large sums of money to use my power?" she asked. "Kairos said it's a portion of whatever is taken from the mines."

"Yes," I said. "But Linnea, she's still a slaver. I have no guarantee that you won't be mistreated, or that you'll be truly free. The deal seemed far too good to be true."

"There is never a guarantee that I will not be mistreated," she snarled. "You would prevent me from earning enough money to keep my sister and me safe and well fed. How could you do that?"

"You barely know how to use your power," I told her sternly. "Honestly, I didn't take it seriously as an offer. I was trying to get into their mines."

"Yes," she said. "To steal. Because that's what you do. You'd rather have me be a thief and a slaver myself than rich and free and off this boat."

"It's a *ship*," I protested, but I was overtaken by Bast saying,

"That's enough, Linnea. You chose to stay and voted on the plan, same as the rest of us."

She crossed her arms. "I want to go. And I want you to use whatever influence you have to make sure that my sister stays with me. Forever. If I'm truly free on this boat, you'll let me."

"We'll be shorthanded again," Navya pointed out.

"I don't care," Linnea said.

"It's her choice," I said, grinding my teeth. "Tomorrow morning, I will take you to the phaedra, Linnea." I glared at her, a different kind of protective anger rising in me. "But you have to be the one to tell Ori tonight."

This caught her off guard, and color flushed over her face. "Agreed." She started to close the door and looked at me. "Thank you," she said crisply.

I nodded once.

She shut the door, and I pushed my hair back, wrenching it into a knot of twisted strands. "Tomorrow get everyone ashore who hasn't been off the boat."

"What are we going to do about the slaves?" Bast demanded. "We can't go back empty handed."

*We.* What, did he fear my failure would impact his captaincy? "I'll come up with another plan," I told him. His mouth opened, and I held up a palm. "Which we will bring to a vote. Now leave me, please," I told them.

Navya went to obey. Bast hesitated, and as the need to punch him in his face rose in my gut, Navya tugged him out of the room.

The door didn't shut behind them, and I heard Kairos's voice a moment later, saying, "Aspasia," softly.

I slammed the door in his face.

# Words Aren't Enough

I didn't sleep. I stayed in my cabin, endlessly weighing my options. Trading Linnea could work for us—I was certain I could make a deal to benefit us. The phaedra would give me whatever I wanted for a power such as hers.

But what did I want? To continue sailing, to maybe even be free, and yet cross the one line I never had? Or to maintain this one, flimsy boundary and face down the most powerful slaver in Sarocca?

When the sun rose, hot and lacking answers, I searched for Ori. I found him with Linnea, up on the deck, huddled close together by the stern like they had been talking all night.

I hated her. How could she leave him? How could she not see how monumental his trust and affection were?

When they saw me, they stood, hand in hand, and Linnea kissed his cheek before letting his hand go and walking past me. I glared at her.

Ori's mouth twisted, and I stepped closer to him, grabbing him in a hug before I knew what I was doing. He hugged me back, fierce and tight, shaking a little in my arms. "Let me go, Aspasia," he whispered softly.

I jerked away from him, shocked by the request and the sound of his voice. "Did I hurt you?" I asked.

But there were tears on his face. "Let me go with her," he said, his words slow and careful. "I will stay here if you want me to. I will stay with you if you need me."

I felt like every solid thing beneath my feet was gone, and there was just water, a place where the wind and the air couldn't reach me. "Leave," I said softly.

I looked at his face. We were his family, but we were a family that had failed him. We had lost his sister, and now all he saw was the empty space where she was supposed to be. Until Linnea made him smile again.

"You barely know her," I protested.

His shoulders just lifted and fell, and I wondered how I would feel if someone said the same about Kairos. It hadn't been long, and yet—yet.

Tears fell down my cheeks, because I knew what I had to tell him. I knew that if he stayed on board, he'd never be more than a broken half of a set, and if he went with Linnea—even if they weren't even a couple, even in love, he would be a person in a different story.

So I hugged him again and whispered, "Of course you can go. I wouldn't ever deny you a damn thing, Ori."

He held tight onto me, and he let me cry on him, and in that moment, I knew my decision had been made.

It wasn't long after when we got in the rowboat with Thea, Linnea, and Ori, Fisk manning the oars for us. Kairos watched us get in the boat with crossed arms and a scowl, but he didn't ask to go. Maybe he knew the future well enough to know I would have never agreed.

The whole crew lined up on the deck to say good-bye to our mates, and my stomach felt hollow, my heart broken. It was good, I decided. It was good that Ori was leaving us too. He should never have to feel this weight crushing his chest as person after person was chipped away from him. Dara was enough.

At the dock, Tanta's face turned curious when she saw my company. "Your retinue seems to be growing by the day," she told me, her eyebrows raised in delicate interest.

"I have a deal to make with your phaedra," I told her. "I have an earth element that would like to work with her."

"Two," Ori said.

I tried to disguise my shock, and I failed badly. He looked sheepish and shrugged his shoulders. "I didn't know for a long while," he said, looking at me. "When I did—I didn't want it."

"Guards," Tanta said with a smile. "Please fetch us a larger carriage."

The guards ran to do her bidding, and I couldn't help but stare at Ori. So many secrets, and so many hurts—no wonder he had kept silent for so long.

The carriage came faster than I thought it would, and we bundled inside. Tanta chattered happily about this turn of events, but I wasn't listening to her. I didn't care.

We were brought to the silver palace, and the phaedra received us in the garden with her children playing around her. "So," the phaedra said after Tanta explained why we were there. "You were keeping things from me."

I lifted an eyebrow. "I keep things from everyone," I told her. "But the decision was always theirs."

"You will negotiate terms, I take it?" she said.

"Yes," I said. "For both of them."

"What of the little one?"

Linnea clutched her sister, but I didn't react. "That is a stipulation," I told her. "She will be taken care of as part of Linnea's contract, and she will never be separated from her sister."

"Linnea will be free to support her as she chooses," the phaedra agreed. "I would never need to put that in a contract."

"She needs that in a contract," I told her.

The phaedra nodded once.

"So we will discuss the terms of their employment with you, and also the recompense made to the *Ancora*," I continued.

"Recompense?" the phaedra repeated.

"Yes," I told her, my gaze unflinching as I met her eyes. "We are losing three crew members in the middle of a run. We need certain considerations to be made to us. Additionally, there is a fee for having sourced such powerful people for you."

"A fee," she repeated, smiling.

"Yes," I told her. "As you said yourself, these people are invaluable to you. Forgive me, but I do intend to put a value on it."

"What are these fees and compensations?" she asked.

My heart thundered as I kept my eyes cool. I had to make the decision, irrevocably, to obey Cyrus and buy my freedom and condemn women and children to slavery. Keep fighting and searching.

Or give it all up. Risk the consequences, risk my life, and disappoint Cyrus.

"Twenty-five slaves," I said. "Hearty men in good health. That will serve as compensation. Five hundred pearls for the fee."

Her lips pursed. "Pearls are more precious here than they are in Sarocca," she said. "But emeralds are more precious there than they are here. One pound of emeralds."

"Cut emeralds or raw?" I asked.

"Raw."

"Cut, and I will agree."

Her eyes narrowed at me. "Very well. Agreed. But I cannot do twenty-five men. It is impossible. Ten, perhaps."

"Twenty."

She swallowed deeply like she was weighing the price in her head, but I was offering her something truly without price, and she knew that. I could be demanding so much more. "Fifteen. We truly do not have the available inventory for more."

*Inventory.* "Agreed," I said, keeping a snarl off my face.

"You can select them at the market."

I waved my hand. "No need. I trust your judgment."

She smiled. "Thank you. I will have them delivered to your ship by sundown, and my guards will take you to select the jewels. Now, on to the terms of their employment."

"Yesterday you offered a percentage of all ore taken from the mine. What percentage?"

"One percent," she said. "In a good day, we mine a hundred pounds of different ores. They would have a pound of that. Each." She looked over to the Elementae in question. "That is without their assistance."

"One percent for one year," I told her. "The earth element is young for both of them, if not for the world at large, and they are both still training. After one year, two percent each."

"Very fair," she agreed.

"Their meals, accommodations, and all reasonable living expenses will never be taken from this percentage," I told her. I had seen "salaries" devolve into slavery by such agreements.

She gave no indication that was her plan. "Of course."

"Naturally, this agreement assumes that they will be able to leave at any time, at their own will, and you will not impede their exit."

She thought for a moment. "I would like some notice so I can adequately adjust my operation. One month," she said.

"One week."

"Two."

I looked to them, and Ori nodded. "Agreed," I said.

"Any other stipulations?" she asked.

Again, my eyes moved to them, and this time it was Linnea who shook her head.

"No," I relayed.

The phaedra squinted at me, thoughtful. "Very well. Once I have proof of their powers, we will have an agreement."

I had warned them to expect this. "Do you have anything in particular that you would like them to do?" I asked.

"To be very honest, I'm not sure what they can do," she told me.

I took one of the silver cups, and I put it at the edge of the table. "Like we practiced, Linnea," I told her.

She gently pushed Thea away from her a pace, and held out her hand. The cup flew across the air to Linnea's palm, and the phaedra clapped.

Ori drew a breath and held his hand out, and rather than the cup flying from her hand to his, the silver plating came off the cup, leaving an earthen cup in Linnea's hand and a nugget of silver in his.

The phaedra stood, rushing over to him. "You can separate the metal out?" she asked.

Ori's eyes flicked nervously over to me, but he nodded.

"If you both can do that, I will start you at two percent," she promised. "That will change everything."

"I'm still learning," Linnea admitted softly.

Inspired, the phaedra went back to the table, taking off her rings and tossing the contents out of small wooden boxes, salt and fruits spilling over the table. She sheltered her work with her body and hid a ring under each box.

"Can you tell which has silver and which has gold?" the phaedra asked, stepping away.

Ori frowned, rubbing the chunk in his hand. He licked his lips and looked at Linnea, then back. "The first box is silver," he told us. "It's difficult to be sure about the gold without getting to know it first."

Linnea was concentrating. "But it has a stone in it. Doesn't it?"

The phaedra stared at them. "Together, we will change the fate of the Wyverns," she told them. "Thank you. I am deeply honored by your gifts. Please, come and eat with me. Relax. Unless you need to return to your ship, you can stay here tonight and we will take you to the mines tomorrow."

They came and sat on the long couch beside me, Ori's fingers threading through Linnea's.

I drew a breath. "I should go," I said, standing. The phaedra stood with me, and I met her eyes, hesitating. "I don't trust people willingly," I told her. "But I'm trusting you to do right by these people. At the risk of threatening your royal personage, I will come back and find them, and if you have deceived me, I will rectify the situation."

She stepped forward and hugged me. "Your people are your heart," she told me. "As are mine. I will treat them like my own."

My eyes were burning with tears, and her hugging me didn't help. I pulled away, and I came and kissed Tanta's cheek. "I can't stay, Tanta," I told her, before she even asked. "I have to go."

She kissed my cheek back, and even that small contact felt like a spike. I needed venom and pain, not kindness. I needed something to justify how hurt and heartbroken I felt.

Thea ran over and hugged me, and Linnea came closer. "I never trusted you," she told me, her eyes on the ground. "But you— what you did—you never—" She halted, and her hand went to her mouth. I saw a tear fall onto the ground, and sharp claws raked through my belly.

"Don't," I grunted. "You deserve to hate the world for what it's done to you. I'm no better."

She looked up at me, her mouth tight and pained, and tears in tracks on her face. "Yes, you are," she said.

I glanced at Ori, but I just couldn't. I pried Thea away from me, made some kind of choked good-bye, and nearly ran through the garden.

I knew Ori was following me. He didn't catch me until we were in the outer courtyard, where the carriage stood to take me back alone, and he grabbed my elbow, hauling me back against him to hug him tight.

We gripped each other so tight it did actually hurt, and this made the tears run out of me. I felt his wet face on my neck, and his chest shuddered against mine.

"This is why I couldn't speak," he said. "Words aren't enough."

"But you know, don't you?" I told him. "I would die for you. If she hurts you, I will burn down all three islands to get you out of here. You will never be a slave again."

"Because you freed me," he said. "Because *you* freed me."

Horribly, truly freeing someone meant watching them leave me.

He let me go for a second, then changed his mind and hugged me again. "Don't be her slave forever," he told me.

I let him go, my face hot and slick with tears, and all I could feel as I stepped into the carriage was hurt and young and terribly alone.

The phaedra sent one of her servants with me, and the guards brought me to another heavily guarded fortress that was much more practical and fortified. The buildings were huge but undecorated, and I walked into a warehouse not unlike Cyrus's. There were long, empty tables, and the servant called to someone who brought out a heavy chest, placing it on a table beside a scale.

"You may select your jewels," the servant said, while another person went off at a whispered command.

I pored over them. I knew a little about emeralds—the larger ones were fabulously expensive, but the smaller ones were easier to sell. There weren't many people with the means to buy one the size of a child's fist, and these were not the ones on offer anyway. I found two the size of a robin's egg, and those were valuable enough. I sifted through the rest, finding shiny chunks with good color that would delight Cyrus.

If I showed them to her. It might be wiser to keep these as they were and spread them through the crew, or save them for purchasing new crewmates.

As I waited for them to pack the emeralds for me, the servant was given a small wooden box, and he came over to me, bowing with his hands out. "A gift," he said. "The phaedra is most grateful to you."

I took the box, opening the lid. There was a jewel inside, squarish and mounted on a fine silver chain. It was totally clear and transparent, but it glittered like light was trapped inside it.

"What is this?" I asked.

"It's a diamond," he told me. "And one of the phaedra's greatest treasures."

Which probably translated into something I couldn't sell. But still, I recognized the generosity of giving up something that meant so much, and I bowed back to him. "Please tell her how honored I am at her gift."

He bowed.

I took the emeralds, and the carriage brought me back to the docks. I wanted to go back to the market, to do anything to buy some time to myself before I had to go back to the boat and face everyone else, be a captain instead of a girl who just lost another friend. I didn't want to stop feeling the pain of losing Ori, and I didn't want to feel it in front of anyone else.

Except that made me think of lying on my bed, crying in Kairos's arms, and the thought instantly turned to acid in my throat. It was his fault. He told Linnea, and she convinced Ori.

Having so much wealth in a single bag, however, didn't sit well with me, and certainly didn't make for an easy trip to the market, so I called for the boat and waited at the end of the dock. Even so, I felt other people with their eyes on the full leather bag, wondering what was in it, as if money had a scent.

Of course, it was Kairos who was in the rowboat bound for

shore. I stepped in, feeling fury suddenly rushing through and overtaking all the sadness in my bones. "Afternoon, Captain," he said, but he lacked the bright smile. Good. At least he knew I was angry with him.

I didn't respond, instead pushing the boat with my power. I couldn't push too fast away from the shore, but once we were farther away, Kairos took the oars out of the water as I pushed us hard.

"So eager to be alone with me," he drawled, watching me.

If it wouldn't have threatened the jewels, I would have capsized us and let him damn well drown.

"Aspasia, you have to let me—"

"I can literally take the words out of your mouth," I warned him with a glare. "It's incredibly hard to speak without air."

He scowled. "That's unnecessarily harsh."

"Then shut your mouth."

"Aspasia—" he protested.

"Captain," I snapped back.

"You're angry. I see that—"

He flew back as I slammed the bow of the boat into the hull of the *Ancora*. "Coming aboard!" I yelled.

The ropes came down, and I secured one of them while he sputtered and groaned, and I reached over him to do the second. I left him there to start climbing the ladder, and a few heads peered over the rail.

I cleared the railing and jumped onto the deck. "Navya," I shouted.

"Sleeping," Bast said, coming over with arms crossed. "How did it go?"

"Perfect," I told him. "We have fifteen slaves being delivered to the boat by sundown. Be ready to get under way as soon as they're loaded."

"What?" he asked. "How did that happen?"

"I made demands, and the phaedra met them," I told him. The truth was worse—I was a good enough trader and negotiator to get whatever I wanted, and somehow, I was still returning to Sarocca, to Cyrus, with more slaves to keep her rich.

He grinned. "Aspasia, you are the craziest, cockiest trader I've ever met."

"Thanks," I muttered, pushing past him to go belowdecks. Sophy shouted a greeting to me as I slammed my key into the lock for the hold.

"We have fifteen slaves incoming," I told her.

She dropped a pan. "We do?" she cried. Then she shook her head. "Fisk! Copper! Get in here!"

I opened the door and left it open, going down to the treasure hold. We had a few chests bolted down, and one of them was for the crew's money and one was for the ship's money. Hefting the bag of emeralds, I only hesitated a moment before putting it into the crew's chest. I would figure out the rest of it later.

I took the diamond out, putting it into the smaller chest inside that was for my share of the money. I wasn't sure how I felt about keeping that, but it wasn't something that would split so many ways, and I wasn't even sure I could trade it for something that would.

I also knew that gem alone would be worth a whole ship. If I could ever walk away from Cyrus, I could buy my own ship with that.

Pulling out the two small bags, I didn't even bother counting the red. I poured the fifteen remaining pearls into my hand, fifteen more slaves that I would fail to save, and counted out three for Linnea, Thea, and Ori. I put the twelve pearls into the red bag, and the measly three pearls into the black bag.

And yet, Ori was in the black. For now, forever, Ori would be safe.

I slammed the chest so hard the lid bounced open again, and I slammed it once, twice, locking it before I kicked the side of the bolted-down chest as hard and fast as I could until my body ached and my breath was caught between panting and crying.

Shaking my head, I locked the room again. I went down to the lower hold and shouted orders up to Sophy and the team she was assembling—the area needed sweeping and fresh blankets, and I wanted a hot meal for them once they got on board.

Navya woke up with all this commotion, and I told her what was happening. She ordered Kairos and Bast to be ready beside her with weapons and a few of the Elementae up on deck to ensure a smooth delivery.

Kairos kept trying to approach me, but I didn't even have to protest—both Bast and Navya yelled at him that it wasn't the time, especially without Ori on deck.

It was moments like that when I couldn't deny how irredeemable my soul was. I was hurting, and I understood that, but it made me want to hurt someone else instead. It made me want to take a knife and drive it into someone's belly just so they would feel something like I was feeling now.

If he kept pestering me, it was going to be Kairos.

# Bleeding and Bruising

The slaves arrived not long after I did, on two longboats with four armed men delivering them. They kept the slaves' feet shackled when they unchained their wrists, and it made getting them up the ladder slow and difficult. One man fell, and the guard punched him across the face.

"Do not injure my merchandise," I bellowed from the deck.

The guard looked up with a sneer. "Yes, Captain."

In groups of five, they were led down to the hold, shackled to the floor before we returned their chains to the guards. I stayed up on the deck, watching them all brought down. They were valuable choices—mostly men in their midtwenties, brawny and strong, without much show of defiance.

Any other slave trader would have been pleased, but for me, it placed another purple bruise somewhere around my heart.

"Thank the phaedra for me," I called to the guards as their chains were returned.

They bowed to me, and rowed back to shore.

Once out of sight, I turned to the crew. "Anika, get us out of the harbor," I told her. "Copper and Kairos, help me and Sophy belowdecks."

Kairos started to take off his sword belt, but I shook my head. "Keep the sword," I told him.

He obeyed.

Sophy had biscuits and stew ready for the prisoners, and we brought the lot of it downstairs with fresh water. There were a few men who watched us with assessing eyes, and this was the part I watched out for. There was always a moment when slaves, particularly in a hold this size, realized that there might be more of them than there were of us. And we were young. Within a day of being out at sea, I would see it shining in an eye or two—the tempting thought that we could be overpowered, our ship taken, their freedom purchased.

It hadn't happened yet, but people had tried.

Opening up one cage at a time, with Kairos watching, his sword ready, we fed them all and gave them bowls of fresh water to drink. They each had only one ankle chained to the floor, and it was far more motion than most ships allowed. There was a bucket in reach for each of them where they could relieve themselves, and the most dangerous part of the day was when we entered the cells to get the bucket and replace it with a clean one.

No one gave us any trouble, but I could see it brewing. One of the largest slaves was built like a tree, with a shock of blond hair and pale skin that made him look exotic and strange. He watched us, observing too much, calculating everything, testing the weight of his chains with his movements.

When we finished, we brought everything back up to Sophy, and Copper took an armful of dishes and pots up to the deck to clean for her.

"Is that how you're punishing me, then?" Kairos asked, halting me before I could leave the kitchen.

"*Punishing* you," I repeated.

"Making me threaten another man who no more deserves to be a slave than I did?" he asked, crossing his arms. He shook his head. "You said what we do doesn't make the rest of us slavers, but what in the Skies was that supposed to feel like?"

Sophy lifted her eyebrows and turned intently to kneading biscuit dough.

"I wasn't punishing you, you arrogant ass. I needed *help*," I told him.

"Help," he repeated, shaking his head.

"Yes, help." I stepped closer to him so our voices wouldn't echo down the stairs, even through the closed door. "How long, precisely, do you think it will be before those fifteen young, strong men realize they're in a ship manned by children, and that they both outnumber us and could also sail this ship without our aid? What exactly do you think happens then?"

"Nothing good," Sophy added without turning to us.

"You're the best sword we've got right now, so yes, I needed your help. And while I don't think I'll ever ask for your help as a person, as your captain, unless you want off this ship you will damn well assist me whenever and however I demand it. Do you understand?"

"Fine," he allowed. "But you're still punishing me for Ori's decision."

"Oh," I snarled, glaring at him. "I haven't even begun to punish you for that."

Sophy snorted, which sort of undercut the threat I was trying to make, but I whipped away from him anyway, going above deck.

We were out of the harbor as the sun changed the sky to reds and purples as if it were bleeding and bruising. I squeezed Anika's shoulders and thanked her, telling her to go rest for the remainder of the night, and I climbed up to the foremast to sit on the yard, feeling out with my power. It was a calm night—I could feel the rough edge of a storm blowing up, but it was way off south and we were headed north.

It would be a while before we met up with the warm current that would ease our travels back to Sarocca, but it would be smooth sailing up the western Wyvern channel to open water.

I stretched out on the yard, leaning against the mast and crossing my ankles along the yard.

The yard yanked and shuddered, and I looked to the rope ladder off the side and saw Kairos coming up, slow and steady despite the fact that I didn't think he'd ever been up it before.

"Please don't shove me off," he called when he saw me looking.

"Kairos, I want to be alone. How can you not understand that?"

"I'll leave you alone," he promised. "But we need to have a real conversation before I do."

"I assume by real conversation you mean making accusations before stabbing me in the back," I spat at him. "That does seem to be your favorite play."

"Skies," he groaned, cresting the yard and looking at me sitting on it with a rather stricken expression. "How do I do this?"

I scowled deeply at him and didn't respond. Tentatively, he put a leg around the rope and hooked it over the yard, slowly maneuvering around the ladder. At one point, he lost his balance with a gasp, but I pushed wind against him to keep him aloft.

"Thanks," he told me, sitting on the yard and holding tight to the rope. Blowing out a harsh breath, he looked out over the setting sun. "Oh," he said softly. "I see why you like it up here."

"It's usually more for the lack of company," I told him.

He sighed. "She deserved to know."

"Maybe. Why didn't you talk to me about it?" I demanded. "She stormed into my cabin like I had betrayed her."

"Maybe you did."

"I didn't even think of actually handing her over. Not once."

"Because you believed it wasn't what it seemed. You believed she'd be a slave again, and you didn't trust her to make her own decision."

"There are still so many ways they could be taken advantage of," I told him softly. "I wasn't wrong to think that."

"No, but you were wrong to not give her a choice." He sighed. "I didn't realize that it would mean Ori would leave you too."

The dark claws that usually stayed in my stomach were curling around my throat. "Neither did I." I avoided Kairos's knowing, seeing gaze. "He's an earth power," I said. "He never told me."

"You didn't know he had an element?"

"I knew he had the potential. I thought maybe it was something he hadn't realized yet." I shook my head. "I didn't know he could keep something like that from me."

"That explains why he and Linnea bonded so quickly."

I agreed, but stayed silent.

"He was there," Kairos told me. "In my visions, when Cyrus hurt you. He was the one. I think she used him to hurt you."

My chest tightened. "Was?" I asked.

He nodded. "The vision changed. Not for you, but he's no longer there."

I watched as the pinks were quickly tamping out of the sky. It should have been gratitude or happiness or something that splintered through my chest, but instead, I felt like a snake was crawling inside me. Like I was poison, and Ori was only cured by being far away from me.

After all, I had killed his sister.

"Stop," Kairos said, his voice weary. "You're so cruel to yourself, Aspasia."

"What?"

"I don't know what you're thinking, but I can see you punishing yourself."

The sharp whip of anger inside was a welcome relief, and I kicked the yard, making him jump as it shivered. "Don't tell me what to do. Don't tell me not to feel something—you don't have that right."

"So you're the only one who can give orders?"

"That's what being captain entails, yes."

"Captain of a ship that votes on everything."

"*Not* my feelings."

"Ori *loves* you. He wouldn't want you to hurt because he left. He'd feel so damn guilty about that he'd come running back."

"He knows," I muttered, looking at my hands in my lap, remembering how they clutched him.

Kairos huffed. "I'm sure that's why you were so eager to leave. You were worried he would come running right back."

"He won't," I sighed. I lifted one shoulder. "But he would have if I asked him to."

"But you'd never ask," Kairos said softly.

"No," I agreed. A silence fell between us, and I looked up to glare at him. "Part of the vision changed, but not the whole thing, right? I was always going to end up in Sarocca, at her mercy."

He watched me carefully. "If one thing changes, I venture that the whole thing can change, but no, I don't really know that. Did you—" He stopped, considering carefully. "You believe you had an opportunity to change it?"

I tried to swallow back the lump in my throat. "Cyrus wants fifteen women and children. Not fifteen men."

"Which you won't give her."

I looked at him mournfully. "I considered it. I could have asked for anything. The phaedra would have given it to me."

"But you didn't."

"I didn't," I confirmed.

"Why?" he asked softly.

I drew a long, slow breath. "Because I know what will happen to those women and children. While I don't know for sure what will happen to me, I couldn't risk it, even for the chance of getting everything I want."

"What do you want, Aspasia?" he asked me.

"Freedom," I whispered.

He smiled gently at me. "Still a terrible liar. If that's what you wanted more than anything else, you would have chosen differently."

I closed my eyes. He was right, but if that was taken away, I had no idea what I wanted. My siblings, but more than that—a world where we could all be safe together. How foolish could I be, to want more than anything to change the world?

Instead of admitting to this, I narrowed my eyes at Kairos. "Dammit, I'm still mad at you. Don't do . . . this. Whatever you're doing."

His grin returned. "Talking to you?"

"Yes. That's why I didn't want to talk to you." I shook my head. "Besides, it's so much more than Ori. It's Bast, and Navya, and Tanta, and even you. If I'm doing this right, everyone will leave, and find their happy endings somewhere else."

"About Tanta," he said, a lascivious tilt to his grin. "That kiss looked like you'd done that before."

I rolled my eyes. "Yes, *that's* the point of my emotional confession."

"Well?" he asked.

"Well, what are you asking?" I asked, looking at him. "Am I some sweet young virgin?" I said. "No."

"I am," he said easily, his eyes on me, his mouth still hinting at the grin but not quite committing to it.

My eyebrows lifted. "Really?"

His grin returned in force. "You're surprised."

"I am," I admitted. "You're very confident with women."

"I'm confident with everyone," he said.

"You're confident with *me*," I said, my voice a little lower and warmer.

He drew in a deep breath as his eyes lingered on my face. "Why wouldn't I be? I know what I want from you."

This made my breath catch. "What's that?"

"Everything," he said simply. "The little shards of yourself you don't give to other people. I want all of that."

His words made something shiver in me, and I wasn't sure if I liked that. "Still," I said, breaking his gaze for a moment. "You weren't in much of a rush to kiss me. Or move past kissing."

"No," he agreed with a smile. "Maybe that's something to do with seeing the future. When I'm with you, when I'm touching you, I find I don't want to rush a single moment of that. We'll get there when we get there."

I found myself smiling back at him. "You are problematically charming, you know that, right?"

He laughed outright. "And you're harder to leave than you think," he told me, skating easily back to my earlier comment. "But it seems like you've given a lot of people new and better lives. You'll get your reward for that."

I shook my head sadly, thinking of the three lonely pearls in the black bag. "I doubt it. But at least we got the slaves, and some valuable emeralds besides. This turned out to be a good run."

"She'll still be disappointed," he warned.

"Yes," I agreed.

"You may control air, but you have veins of solid steel," he told me, shaking his head. "I have no idea how you turned the loss of three crew members into everything we needed and more."

"Maybe I'm just worried, but I feel uneasy," I admitted to him. "Other ships will have seen those slaves delivered to us, and we've been openly buying goods for days. There were a lot of tough traders there with big crews, and I don't think I'll rest easy until we've offloaded in Sarocca. Especially with Skiver out there somewhere, just *waiting* for us."

"Can they catch us?" he asked.

I blew out a breath. "Sadly, yes. Remember the storm when we left Altia? The way I move air—particularly the faster I go—creates storms behind me. So using my power will also create a wind that they can ride right up behind us. Even if another ship doesn't take an interest in us, those slaves are dangerous all on their own."

"The blond," Kairos agreed. "He's the one to watch."

"I know."

"I'll see what kind of visions I can call," he told me. "What else can we do to be ready?"

"Practice," I told him. "Make sure everyone is ready for a fight."

"I'll step up the training," he said. "Bast's getting pretty good, when he forgets that he hates me."

My shoulders lifted. "That's my fault."

"No," he said. "That's his fault."

I shook my head.

The bell sounded below us, and I saw Sophy and helpers bringing the meal up to the deck. "Hungry?" Kairos asked.

I shrugged. I was hungry, but that was the wrong question. "I don't feel like being with everyone right now."

"It might be good for you," he said. "Just a few minutes, and you can run right back up here."

I pushed out a breath. "Fine. But don't think you can always get me to change my mind."

He laughed. "As you wish, Captain."

He started precariously down the rope ladder, and I called over a loose line to climb down. I got my food from Sophy and went over to the others, sitting on the stairs as people clustered on the deck.

"Ori was the first person I liked on the ship," Copper said, and

I froze. "The first night I slept in the hammocks, he gave me an extra blanket."

"He taught me how to use a knife," Fisk said.

"He always splashed me in the water," Anika said, shaking her head. "I didn't like that."

This made everyone else laugh.

"He always fell asleep on night watch," Navya said, and this earned another chuckle.

"I liked that about him," Arnav defended. "And he was worse with a sword than I was."

"Couldn't hold a conversation worth a damn," Bast teased, and even though it made my heart ache, I laughed at this too.

"Too loyal," Sophy complained with a smile. "I like someone I can distrust. Like the captain!"

This got an uproarious laugh.

"He was awful at braiding my hair," Addy said with a sigh.

"And brushing his own!" someone else shouted.

This went on for a while, turning all Ori's finest traits into half-hearted insults, and stupid Kairos was right. It was good for me, and though it didn't make my heart hurt less, it was good to know I wasn't the only one who had lost a good friend and a loyal crewmate. When Kairos sat beside me, I pressed my shoulder against his, liking the contact as I listened to my crew pay their respects to Ori.

# Child's Play

I used my power to push us up the channel when the wind would have been working against us, and even as I did, it worried me. It was sapping my energy and sucking air into a vortex that another ship from Sayma's harbor could use to catch up to us.

When we hit open water, the weather was good with a crisp breeze and I eased off pushing us so hard, keeping my wary eyes behind us on the horizon.

Once the sun went down, Kairos joined me on the stern deck. I couldn't see out over the water, but my power was still searching, using the threads like a net and clawing fingers over the ocean at my command.

"You're tired," he said, standing close behind me, his chin at the perfect height to rest over my shoulder. His hands joined mine on the railing, his index finger sliding against my small one.

I sighed. "I don't like the way we left the port."

His breath rushed over my neck. "I know."

"Have you had any visions?" I asked.

He shook his head.

I drew a deep breath, and it pushed his chin closer against me. "I should rest," I told him. "I can't feel anything out there right now. But maybe you can try to get a vision?"

"I'll try," he said, pressing a kiss to my neck. "And keep watch."

I lifted my hand to rub my fingers gently over his on the rail. I liked that—he would keep watch when I couldn't, more concerned with the ship's safety than lying in a bed with me. It was what I would have chosen too.

I turned in his arms, kissing him as his hands came around my waist. "Thank you," I whispered between kisses.

He broke off, kissing my cheek, then my temple. "Go rest," he said, smiling at me.

I slid away from him with a sigh, going belowdecks.

I woke up hovering in the air, but instead of falling I was pushed forward by my power, and I scrambled to my feet to catch the momentum. Something was wrong, and this wasn't in my dreams. The net I had cast with my power had something in its web.

I ran up the stairs to the main deck. It was morning, but just barely, and the night shift hadn't been relieved yet. "Kai!" I shouted, glimpsing him in the crow's nest. "Spyglass so' southwest!"

He looked down at me. "I have no idea what that means!" he shouted back.

"Got it," Navya said from the helm, looking out over the water. "Sails, Captain. They're coming faster than we'd like."

"See, I told you there's no point in the lookout," Arnav grumbled, coming up beside his sister.

Navya scowled at him.

"Anika," I said, pointing up at the sails. Her power wasn't strong enough to create backlash, so I'd take the push without aiding our tailwind.

"On it," she told me, rubbing her tired eyes for a moment before raising her hands to the sails.

I jumped down the stairs, bellowing, "Everyone up! All hands on deck! Sophy, we're going to be engaging soon!"

Hammocks swung and deposited half-awake sailors on the floor, and everyone streamed upstairs. Sophy didn't answer me, and as I pushed past some of the little ones, I saw her hammock empty. Was she already cooking?

"Sophy!" I called, ducking into the galley. Sophy didn't answer me. I went to the kitchen and saw the door open to the hold, and the second I saw it, I knew we had a problem.

"Bast," I said more quietly, catching his shoulder before he went up. "Get Kairos and get down here immediately."

He looked past me to the door and immediately turned to obey.

Without hesitating, I went through the door and down the stairs, using my power to help quiet my footfalls.

"Unlock the rest of them, or I'll break his little neck," I heard.

All the damn, bleeding, pus-filled, shit brick hells. One of the slaves was loose, and I could guarantee that it was the blond. I felt around the door with my power as shadows appeared at the top of the stairs. I saw Kairos and Bast with swords, and I motioned them forward and floated my key up to them to lock the door behind them.

The sound clicked, and I felt the reaction inside the room.

"They're coming for you," Sophy warned. "If there's one person you don't want to tangle with, it's my captain."

"That girl couldn't be more than seventeen," he said. "I'll snap her like a twig. Now unlock them."

A pained squeak came out of his captive, and my guess was that it was Fisk. Arnav and Copper were both above deck.

I waved Kairos and Bast forward as I shoved the door open with my power. Sophy hurled her iron pan at Fisk's assailant as soon as she saw the door open, and I yanked Fisk down with my power, out of the man's hands, and shoved Fisk into the hall.

But the man caught the pan and took a vicious swing at me with it. I stopped it with my power, but he followed it up with a fist straight into my face before I knew what was happening. I reeled back, dazed, as Bast pushed past me. Another man was also free, and he was going for Sophy.

Bast tossed his sword to Sophy so she could stop the blond in his tracks, and Bast threw the other man back against the cages. I tried to clear my head, watching as Kairos flicked the pan from the blond's hands in seconds before dropping his sword and beating the man back in sharp, neat moves.

With a deep breath, I yelled, "Enough!" and slammed both of the slaves down to the ground, pinning them with my power as they gasped, confused.

"Sophy, get Fisk and get upstairs," I snapped at her.

She dashed past me, kicking the blond as she went past. "Kairos, help Bast with him first," I said, jerking my chin toward the second assailant. The blond was struggling against my hold, but I had them both securely.

Kairos went over to Bast, and they picked him up, dragging him to an unused cage at the end. "Shackle both his feet," I said, looking at the broken chains in the cage they'd been in before.

We had one cage left, so I figured it was worth separating them. Once Bast and Kairos finished with their charge, I used my power to lift the blond and fly him over the hold to the open cage. "Make sure you chain his hands too," I told them. "Though I hope you've thought better of trying to escape," I said, looking at him.

"No," he told me. "I'll gut you, and I'll hang every member of your crew from the yard just to watch them dance."

"Idle threats when you're chained up," I scoffed, shaking my head though his words raised the hairs on the back of my neck. My face was throbbing, and every heartbeat made my cheekbone feel like it was blooming larger.

Not just his words though—the warning call on my neck was so sharp it felt like glass shards. "Captain!" I heard distantly.

Kairos finished with the slave and locked him into his cage as Bast and I charged up the stairs. I had the key in the door when something slammed into the side of my damned ship, knocking me into a wall even as my power cushioned the blow.

Bast yelped as he almost fell down the stairs, but I caught him, pushing him back up as I opened the door and rushed through, hurrying the boys as I waited for them to slam it shut and lock it again. They ran ahead of me, and I unleashed my power to feel out as I ran the deck to the stairs and climbed up the stairs behind them.

There was another ship lashed to ours, and my people were fighting hard. The Elementae were aloft, raining elements down on the attackers, and the rest of my people were on the deck, swords on swords, and Osmost was wheeling through the lot of it, clawing at the eyes of someone.

Blood. Metal. Contact.

I took a deep breath, feeling the threads crackle, working fast to churn a storm down from the heavens. Even before I crested the deck, I could see the darkening sky and feel the wind rising up, delivering raw power to Anika and me, giving Addy and Fisk some rain to use. The only one it would hinder was Arnav, but he was making the best of the whipping wind, and even Copper was manipulating smoke into distracting, confusing shapes.

I wrapped a line around a man's raised arm and dragged him back to his own boat, clearing the way for me to step out on deck. I cast around, taking stock as the wind lashed at my face like a brutal kiss.

Arnav. He wasn't up on the yards or in the crow's nest like he was damn well supposed to be. He was on deck. He was on his *back*. And some man twice his size was bearing down on him. *Arnav was bleeding.*

A feral cry snarled from my throat, and I ripped the man away from Arnav so violently he landed in the water a hundred feet from the boat. I knew the moment he hit the water, from the angle he landed and the force with which I'd thrown him, I'd snapped his neck.

Casting around, I slashed my power out like vines, whipping against the enemy as they attacked. Four crossbow bolts at my belt rose up and found their marks, burying in the throats of the attackers without a second thought.

I jolted, the deck beneath me rocking hard. The wind was getting high, smashing our two boats together, filling our sails and dragging us awkwardly. With a growl, I turned my attention to disengaging.

Kairos was in the middle of disarming a sailor, but I dispatched his attacker into the water and grabbed his hand, looking him in the eye as I took hold of his power.

From the first time we touched, I felt this ability under the surface, his connection to the roiling force that lined the bellies of the storms I called. I wanted to make him throw lightning, to force it out of him like the visions.

As soon as I touched him, I felt the electricity crackle, my awareness of the pieces of sky that held lightning high above me. Holding my breath, I used our connection and my call of the wind to summon his lightning like it was my own.

He scowled at me and tugged my hand, yelling my name over the rising wind, but I didn't care.

Lightning cracked down on the other ship, snapping their main mast, and struck twice more around us before I let him go. One of the men on our ship abandoned his attack of Navya to run forward to the rail, and it was he who I grabbed with my power, forcing him down to the deck as I stood over him. I stole the air from his lungs and looked down at him, stepping on his chest as he struggled to breathe.

"Cast them off," I ordered Navya.

"You must be the captain," I shouted at my captive, kneeling closer so he could hear me over the wind that made my hair fly out like snakes. "What are you doing on my ship?"

I let him breathe, and he greedily sucked in air, clawing at his throat. Thoughtfully, I took a knife from his waist. "Gems," he said. "And slaves. We all saw."

"Who is we?" I demanded.

"Traders in Sayma," he gasped. "We were in the same port as you."

"You thought you could steal from *me*?" I growled.

"You're a child," he snapped back.

I held the knife up. "And this is child's play," I said, raising my hand.

"Aspasia, don't!" Kairos shouted.

My hand stopped as I jerked to look at him, and my attention diverted, I must have let my control of the captain's body slip, because a moment later his knife bit into my flesh, pushed away by my power before it could do real damage.

Furious, I turned back and buried the knife in the captain's throat, using my power to hurl his body back to the other ship as we came apart. With one mast broken, they wouldn't be able to follow us, but I shoved loose their anchor and let it drop anyway.

It was raining hard now, and I drove the wind harder, cresting us high over waves and letting us crash down, the violent rhythm doing something to assuage my anger.

I wasn't calling the storm anymore; it was here in truth, answering my rage with anger of its own, and I simply guided the ship through the storm. I didn't even turn around to see how my crew was faring, I just focused on getting us far away.

I could feel the edges of the storm, and it didn't take us long to sail out of it. When the wind began to lighten and the rain gentled on us, I finally turned around, heaving with breath.

My crew were desperately holding on to whatever was solid, and as the wild motion eased, Kairos ran to the edge and vomited. Guilt twisted somewhere inside of me, and I went to Arnav, who was clutching a rope and looking a little green. His face was outrageously swollen, a lump on his cheekbone broken open and bleeding. He looked pale beneath it, and his eyes were wide and nervous, watching me as I looked at the cut.

"What were you doing?" I demanded. "You're supposed to be off the deck."

"I'm not a baby anymore, Aspasia," he told me. "I can fight. I can fight with fire and with swords."

"Sophy?" I called, looking around for her.

She was already bundling up to me, her arms full of supplies for such occasions.

"Addy," I called, and she came down from the crow's nest. She had started to develop the ability to heal; like my ability to call a storm, it seemed to be a higher echelon of her elemental power.

"Who else is hurt?" I asked, turning around.

Bast had a cut on his side; Copper had fallen on the deck and scraped and bruised an arm. All in all, our toll wasn't terrible, and slowly my heart returned to normal.

I was kneeling beside Copper still when Addy came over to us. "It's okay," Copper told Addy, shaking his head. "I don't need it. I'm fine, really."

She frowned. "I know," she said, then she looked at me. "Captain," she said, looking at me expectantly.

"What is it, Addy?" I asked her.

"Kairos wants me to help you," she said.

"No, thanks," I told her, touching my nose to see if it was bleeding again. It wasn't, but between the pain and the giant lump forming on it, I was pretty sure it was broken.

Addy looked over to where Kairos was leaning against the rail, watching us with a hard stare. She shrugged at him, and he made an exasperated huff. "Come on!" he shouted. "She needs to heal you."

I stood, feeling pain burn in the cut on my side. "She does not," I yelled back.

"You're damn stubborn," he said, coming over to me.

"Shut up," I snapped as he came closer. With a deep breath, I put my fingers on either side of my nose. I started to press it, but white hot pain seared behind my eyes. "Dammit," I growled, blood starting to drool out of my nose again. "Look, you're going to have to do it."

He grimaced. "Do what?"

"Addy can't heal a bone if it's not reset properly. You have to put my nose straight."

He stared at me for a long moment.

"Oh, come on," I said, narrowing my eyes at him. "Do it and be done with it."

He huffed out a breath and met my eyes as he gripped my nose and wrenched.

My sight flashed in and out, and it took me a long moment to see straight as pain just seemed to pummel my face in waves. I hit the railing, not even realizing I had stumbled back.

But Kairos followed me, and he tugged my shirt out of my pants to look at the cut on my side. Even considering the circumstances, I wasn't immune to the touch of his hands on my bare stomach, and my breath hollowed out.

"It looked like he stabbed you," Kairos said, touching the long but mostly shallow cut.

"He tried," I said. "But as soon as I feel pain, the wind protects me if it can. It's like a reflex," I told him. I huffed out a few breaths before looking down. The cut was long, curling over my hip, but it was bleeding only a little.

"That is so much more useful than visions," he muttered.

Addy looked at me, but I shook my head at her. "I'm fine," I told her. "You should go rest."

Sophy came over to us, crossing her arms. "I think *you* should rest, Captain."

I shook my head. "No. I have to get us more than a day away from them and anyone else who could have followed us from the Sayma port. Then I'll rest."

"Captain—"

"None of us, myself included, could sustain another engagement right now. This is the only option."

"Fine," Bast said from the wheel. "Go to the stern deck. I want you sitting down and resting as best you can. Sophy, if you could get a meal going, I think everyone could use it. Navya and the night crew, get some rest." With a sigh, he looked at me and Kairos. "Duster, stick with the captain. Your power—she can get some kind of energy off it, can't she? Like with Anika?"

Kairos looked to me. "Something like that. But I think I better check on the prisoners first."

"Fine," Bast said. "Take Copper and Sophy with you. Then come and stay with the captain."

I nodded to Bast, grateful for his leadership, and went to the back of the ship. We were still getting good wind from the storm, so it wasn't taking much energy to guide it where we needed to go. Despite the effort, I sent my power snaking down into the bottom of the hold, hovering around making sure that the slaves were behaving themselves.

Anytime I got close to Kairos with my power, I felt him twitching, swatting me away like a physical presence. When I followed my crew back up from the hold, Kairos stayed down, helping Sophy with the meal even though he said he'd come to me.

I pulled back then with a sting of rejection. I could feel the energy drain along my spine, and the more I rested, the more I felt the pain of my injuries. So I obeyed Bast, sitting on the stern deck and watching the sails, driving us as far north as I could without using enough power to help our enemies while the sun began to set.

Several men had died that day because of me. Because of my power. I killed them. Strangely, I knew Kairos was delaying coming to sit with me because of that. That's why he called out to me, asking me to stop, asking me to spare a man I didn't need to kill.

I didn't need to kill any of them. I was more powerful than they were; the man who was after Arnav, I could have just shot him off the deck and let him swim merrily back to his ship. I could have knocked the attackers off their feet and given my crew the advantage, but I chose to kill them. As many as I could.

A part of me rose up at the idea—they were bad people. They were pirates, marauders, and they would have killed us if they had the chance. I prevented them from having that chance.

But a bigger part of me sighed, losing the argument. Like it or not, when I was frightened, I became the scared girl I had been before. I lashed out using every weapon I had, and I aimed to kill.

So when Kairos came to me, slow and reluctant, holding fresh biscuits and hot soup, I had tears in my eyes, and I felt like I'd already had this whole conversation with him.

With a sigh, he sat beside me, putting down the food to touch my hand. Immediately I felt a surge of energy, and it made me realize just how much of my power I'd used.

I curled my fingers around his, and he tossed me a biscuit with a small smile. "How are you doing?" he asked.

"Sore," I answered, which was both the truth and not all the truth. "So now you know what happens when I'm scared."

"You get very, very angry?" he asked, and even as I looked up at the sails I could hear the smirk in his voice.

"It's not an excuse," I said softly. "But I don't always know how powerful I am. I haven't been powerful for very long."

His fingers rubbed gently on mine. "You think I'm mad at you?"

"Not as such," I said. "But you didn't want me to kill that captain. And I did anyway."

"Why?"

My fingers tightened on his, some part of me afraid that saying these things would make me lose him, and I didn't want that. "I'm afraid that I'm always going to be defined by that hurt, frightened girl chained down in the hold of a ship," I whispered to him. "When I'm scared, I forget what a responsibility this power is. What a gift. How I will never be that helpless again."

His hand gripped mine back. "Neither of us is helpless," he said, his voice soft. "We're both haunted by the moments when we felt that way."

I looked at him, surprised, and he drew a breath, not looking at me. "He could have killed you. It would have been my fault, because I distracted you." He tugged my hand and then pulled his fingers free. "You need to eat. I can feel how weak you are when we touch."

He handed me my bowl and I took it, eating slowly and quietly, as the ship rocked with an easy, hypnotic rhythm.

"Is it like this with Anika?" he asked.

I turned to him, raising my eyebrows with a sly smile. "Absolutely not," I told him.

He grinned back. "I meant with our powers. You didn't just help me with the visions—it felt like our power was bound together."

I smiled. "They were. That was . . . intense."

"You didn't expect that?"

I shook my head. "No. I had no idea I would be able to throw lightning through you."

"So was the lightning me or you?" he asked.

I drew back, surprised. "You didn't know you could control lightning?" I asked.

"No," he said. "When would I have learned that?"

"You figured out visions just fine."

He chuckled. "Visions have a way of forcing themselves upon you."

"I liked borrowing the lightning," I told him.

"How were you able to do that?"

I shrugged. "It must be part of that binding. It works a little with other elements—for example, I can kind of call up Addy's healing when she's struggling with it. But with someone aligned with wind, well—you saw."

"It was intense," he said. "It felt like it was ripping out of me. Like I could throw lightning."

I smirked. "You can," I reminded him.

With a belated warning shriek, Osmost swooped down and stole my biscuit, and I yelped, snatching for him as he swooped out of my range, only to land on the deck and gobble it down in front of me, making a *cah-cah-cah* noise that sounded distinctly like he was taunting me.

"I'm going to stuff your bird," I told Kairos, who chuckled and handed me his biscuit.

"I'd really like to see you try," Kairos said.

"Well," I said, tearing the biscuit in half and giving the rest back to Kairos. "I suppose he earned it. You're a fearsome warrior hawk," I said fondly.

Osmost fluffed himself up and made a *kik! kik!* noise before leaping into the air again.

"So," Kairos ventured, looking at me askance. "Is it uncouth to ask if you want company in your cabin tonight?"

My nose wrinkled with a laugh. "*Uncouth*? Really?"

He smiled. "Rude. Uncivilized."

"I know what it means," I said. "I don't have any desire for civilization in my cabin tonight. You, however, are welcome."

He laughed and rubbed his fingers along mine again, and it felt like a balm for the jagged edges of the day.

Later, long after the night crew had come on duty and Navya finally convinced me to let Anika take over, Kairos kept his warm hands on me as I nearly fell into my cabin. When I collapsed into my bed, he just arranged himself around me, holding me, keeping our bodies connected as I dropped immediately into sleep.

# The Unsung Hero

I pushed myself hard for the next two days, speeding our return to Sarocca. With each nautical mile we sailed closer to Diadem, I felt the warning growing stronger on my neck. I knew I shouldn't go back.

I also knew I was going to anyway.

After two days, I started with Navya.

"There's no telling what Cyrus is going to do when I return," I told her. "My current plan is to sail to Altia and leave everyone who I can spare there. I think I'll need one or two people to help with the ship and the cargo, but that's it. I'd like you to be one of them, so when I don't come back, you're captain."

She stared at me for a long time, drawing slow breaths over crossed arms. "No," she said, shaking her head. "Arnav and Anika won't let me leave them behind. I can't bring them with me, if the danger is as you anticipate."

My chest tightened around my heart. "So you don't want to come?"

"I didn't say that," she said, frowning. "I just don't know how to play this." She thought a moment more and looked at me. "You're not asking Bast to be captain."

"You're my second in command."

"He's older than me. More experienced. I'm your second in command because I'm better at taking orders."

My lips pressed tight for a long moment; then I just said, "Yes, I'm asking you to be captain."

"Not him."

"Not him."

"Setting that aside for a moment, it's more than my siblings," she told me. "If we tell the crew we're leaving them behind while you go off to die, no one will agree. They'll fight to the death for you."

I shook my head, lighting a candle as the afternoon light grew dim in the cabin. "It's not just that," I told her. "I know Cyrus, and to hurt me, she wouldn't hesitate to hurt anyone on this ship. That means every person with me is a liability. They could actually get me killed."

There was another long pause as she considered me, having untold conversations within her own mind. "You're wrong," she said firmly. "Your assumptions here are wrong. You believe that you can possibly be considered alone and separate from the crew. But you aren't. This is a family, so whether we're there with you or not, we all have a lot to lose. We can all be used against one another. But we can all defend one another too."

Stepping back, I looked at her, shifting my hands to my hips. "You want to fight back."

"No," she said. "I want all of us to be safe and free. But we made a mistake with Dara."

This fell between us.

"I know you think so too," she said. "None of us are leaving someone behind again."

"There's a difference between leaving and being left," I told her.

"Not really," she said. "You can't leave the ship and escape this. Can you?"

"No," I agreed.

"Then leaving isn't an option here."

I kicked at my cot. "What do you suggest?" I demanded. "Would you all like to come die with me? I can't let you assume that risk."

"No, but you want *me* to assume it?" she asked, and I blinked back. "You want me to go with you and risk abandoning my brother and sister all so I can be captain. I know you trust me, and I will do what you ask of me, but I don't need to be captain. I don't want it more than I want my family."

I stared at her, the words sinking deep in my stomach. She was right—despite knowing it was a risk, I hadn't really thought that something would happen to her, and she would be separated from her siblings. They all would.

Even Kairos, who I was quickly learning to depend on in a fight. He couldn't be risked.

There was only Bast, and I wasn't sure he could be trusted as captain.

"Besides," Navya continued. "Even say we do leave everyone on island. We can't get to them without you. Maybe Anika can do it, but not easily."

I waved this away. "It would take a few days, but we both know there are ways to climb up."

"If you die, it's still Cyrus's ship," she continued. "I couldn't captain it without her permission."

"As soon as you sail out of that harbor, you knock the name off the back and call it something else. Then it's your ship, and no one can say different."

"Captain—" she started with another point, but I shook my head.

"Very well," I told her. "You've convinced me. We stand together or not at all."

She straightened. "I can't really think of another way."

*I could.*

But I just sighed, like I was disappointed. "Thank you," I told her. "For talking it out with me."

"Of course, Captain," she said.

"You should get Kairos and go check on the prisoners," I told her. "Make sure they're fed and comfortable."

"We'll make a plan to stand against her later," she told me.

"Yes," I agreed. "When we get to Altia. Charly's always good with a plan."

She walked out of the cabin, and I followed her, going to the deck where Bast was at the wheel. Navya called for Kairos, and Osmost answered, screaming overhead as Kairos followed her belowdecks. I waited until she was well out of earshot, and I turned to Bast.

"I need your help," I told him softly. "And I need you to keep it a secret from everyone else."

No matter what had happened between us, he glanced around, then met my eyes and nodded.

When night fell, I went to my cabin, exhausted. I lay on the cot, letting the ocean rock me, screwing my eyes shut against the building pain in my temples. Bast agreed to my plan—we'd leave the crew in Altia, then steal the ship and head on to Diadem Port. He would jump ship, and I would return to Cyrus with the slaves and face her consequences.

My mind felt fractured and broken. All day long, I had turned over the situation, questioning and doubting.

Why didn't I just ask for women and children? Why couldn't I, just this once, do something that was truly evil to serve the greater good? I was a goddamn fool.

I could see it in my mind's eye—Cyrus's cool, smug anger. This final blow—maybe it had been her plan all along. Let me stretch my wings and fly so close to freedom, only to smack me down like an insect.

She was going to hurt me. But at least this way she wouldn't hurt anyone I cared about.

Right? They would be on Altia, but they'd be stuck on Altia. They could certainly climb down, but it was difficult and long. What if Anika never grew in strength, and never learned to fly a ship to that height?

At least they'd be alive. That was the most important thing, wasn't it?

Admittedly, I hadn't thought much about my crew being stranded on Altia when I'd asked for the slaves. Like with Linnea, I barreled forward without thinking about anyone else and just concerned with my own damn morals.

"You should probably stop thinking now," Kairos told me.

I opened my eyes and turned. He was in the doorway, arms crossed, leaning against the frame and watching me. "I think you can read minds," I accused him.

He grinned. "I don't need to. You're remarkably easy to read. I'm guessing this is about Cyrus."

It was important that he get back to his family, and if I talked to him about this, about my worry and fears, he would come with me. He was good and strong and loyal, and he wouldn't let me face my demons alone.

"It's about a lot of things," I told him, waving one hand and closing my eyes to rub my forehead with the other. "But I don't really want company tonight."

His warm hand filled mine, and I gasped, pulling away. He held my hand tight. "Why would you want to lie to me more than you want the help I can offer?" he asked.

I jerked my hand out of his grasp. "I'm not discussing this with you."

His damn smile was maddening. "Aspasia. Really. So let me see if I can work through this from your perspective. You think if you don't talk to me about this, I won't be inclined to help you when you go face Cyrus. Or maybe I won't have the option." I didn't look at him, and he chuckled. "I'll take that as a yes. Which means you're assuming you can ditch me—and most of the crew?—somewhere. So probably the island."

"God*damn* it, Kairos, this isn't your business!" I roared, jumping up from the bed. "You need to go back to your family, not die in a Saroccan slave cell."

"So do you, Captain," he returned, not even slightly offended by my outburst.

"If I go in there with you or anyone else, she'll use you against me," I told him, crossing my arms. "And I will let her. So the only chance I have of not dying is if you're not there."

"Or you could help me look into the future so that we know what will happen," he snapped.

I stopped.

He drew a slow breath and came closer to me, his eyes, his body filling my vision and blocking out the rest. "Don't ask me to sit by as someone else I care for gets hurt. Don't do that to me. Please."

"Don't make this about you," I told him flatly.

His arms touched my elbows. "Use me, Aspasia. Use my gift for something good so we know how to defeat her. How to take your freedom and your life out of her hands."

I looked at him, his gorgeous, soft eyes, his strong body, his gentle heart. "What if you see something you can't stop, Kairos? What if I make you feel just as helpless as your family?"

To his credit, he thought this over, his jaw working as he remembered whatever pain and heartache he'd had to face in that aftermath. "I still believe there's a reason I have this power, Aspasia. I believe there's something good we can do with it."

*We.*

Slowly, I held up my palms to him.

He took one hand, but interlaced his fingers through it. "Here," he said, tugging me back toward the cot. He let go of me to get in, arranging himself against the wall and lying on his side. I mirrored his position, looking at him. He clasped our fingers so they were tucked between our chests, and my breath caught as his sword-calloused hand cupped my cheek, the thumb brushing over the top of the scar, chafing the top of my cheekbone in a hypnotic, soft way.

I felt a tug this time on the threads that connected us as the vision came to him. His eyes shut, his eyeballs moving erratically.

"It's not Ori anymore," he said. "But there's someone there with you. You're in the middle of a huge warehouse. She has someone, a boy. Someone else—looks like a guard—is holding a knife to his throat."

I watched his face. "What does he look like?"

He swallowed. "Terrified. Dark hair, tan skin—he could be from the Trifectate maybe?"

It was rare for me to leave crew in Sarocca, for obvious reasons. I could think of one—maybe two—boys who I'd known who matched that description, but it was also vague enough that it could be my brother.

*What happens if I find it before you do?*

My heart kicked up a notch, but it wasn't possible. She didn't have my brother—how would she even know it was him? She couldn't. I didn't even know if *I* could.

"Ah," he muttered, flinching. His eyes opened, blinking fast. "I lost it. Let me try again. That boy . . . it's important. There's something important about him."

I felt him draw hard on my energy when he went back into the vision, and I let him, breathing deeply, trying to balance the energy for him. "Skies," he murmured, his breathing hitching. "Aspasia, she has you chained to a post. She's going to sell you."

A wild, uncontrollable flare of panic lashed through my stomach, gripping my muscles. His eyes opened, feeling the reaction in my body, his gaze steady and warm, holding me more than his hands could do. "You have a choice," he told me softly. "I can't control the future. I can't see enough to see it unfold moment by moment. I can't see why she puts you in chains again. But you have a choice to trust that together, we can do something about it. That if you fall, I'll still be there with you to fight like hell by your side."

With a heavy sigh, I rolled onto my back, looking up. "What about the others?" I asked.

"You're right that she's going to use someone against you. That's remained constant. We have to leave them behind."

"We have to take Bast. It will be hard enough to sail the ship with three of us, and he's the only one without ties."

He didn't object, and I felt a yawning ache in my chest.

"I should have just asked for women and children," I whispered. "I chose wrong."

His hand captured my fingers a moment before his lips brushed my temple. "I never saw it differently, Asp," he reminded me. "Which either means that you couldn't possibly have chosen otherwise, or it means that no matter your choice, she would have punished you. It was always inevitable."

I thought of the seven years that had passed since the day I fell to my knees before Cyrus, my hands soaked and slick with blood. *My blood.* I thought of the days and the people I'd lost and saved, the count in my small bags downstairs.

It was always inevitable.

I sighed into his arms until I could sleep.


It was two more days before we reached our island again. Usually when we stopped here before going to port, it was to free all the women and children and hide our money, but this time there were no people to set free. Still, I knew I had to return, more for Charly's peace of mind than anything else—and it was also the only way my plan could be set in motion. I spent the days trying to be as present as I could with my crew, trying to say good-bye without them ever knowing.

When I brought the ship up to our cliff-top dock, I watched as my crew ran happily from the ship in the afternoon sun. I went down to the hold, checking on the prisoners again before getting my small chest from our treasury. The crew had already taken their money, and the only coin that stayed on board was our operating fund.

Then I followed the rest of the crew, fleeing the boat and going to the house. I saw Charly, and she waved at me over Anika's and Arnav's heads, who were trying to steal some kind of food from her hearth. My chest tightened, knowing I couldn't say good-bye to her. More than anyone, I knew she was prepared.

I didn't go to my room. I brought the chest to Charly's, leaving it on her bed. I was nervous—she wouldn't think it strange if she saw money from me; I usually left some. But if she opened it and saw the amount of money, saw my coin bags with my soul's account, she might guess. She might stop me.

But she also might not.

There were only a few hours until dark, and I walked down the hill to where the forest started and the land began to slope sharply downward. The water from the basin fell off a huge cliff, splattering down a narrow gorge, and it was treacherous but possible to climb down around it. Easier down than up, but still—possible. It was the only way someone without my powers could ever threaten my village.

Part of me wanted to call up the wind, scour the plants and the rocks and the roots that made the steep cliff passable. I wanted to protect my village from anyone else having an easy way in.

But it would also mean there was no easy way out if I didn't return, if Anika's powers never grew strong enough to carry a boat down. It meant Bast couldn't get back here.

I turned away from the gorge and went back to the village proper. It was nearly sundown, and I had only a little while left.

I heard the noise from the main hall, everyone eating and laughing and enjoying themselves. I swayed forward, wanting to join them, wanting to say a real good-bye, the kind of good-bye we all had earned together.

But they would never let me go. And they couldn't be risked.

"Are you coming in?" Navya asked, coming up behind me with a basket of bread.

I stepped back. "No," I said, meeting her eyes. "I need to go check on the prisoners."

She watched my face warily. "Be careful, Captain. You're needed here."

I bent my head. She knew. Maybe she didn't, but I liked the thought that she knew, and understood, and would take care of everyone in my stead.

I kept my eyes on the ground. "I'll see you in a bit."

She sighed and moved forward, wedging her way into the main hall with the bread.

I left. Even as I walked into the night, I could hear their laughter in my mind.

When I got to the ship, Bast was there, standing by the wheel though the ship was on dry land. I went to him, hugging him tight, really needing someone to hold on to for that moment. He hugged back. "Are you sure you want to do this?" he asked.

I nodded against his shoulder. "Yes. I don't have a choice, not really."

"She's not going to hurt you," he assured. "You're too valuable to her."

"Maybe," I said, pulling back. "You know what to do?"

"As soon as you're off the ship, I'll jump and find a new boat for us."

I sucked in a breath. This was the risk—when we reached the harbor, I was going to give Bast the diamond to buy us a new ship. Our own ship that she couldn't command, and if I didn't return, it would have to be a ship he could sail himself. But I knew Bast, and I knew his greedy heart, and if he was ever going to betray me, that was the time.

If he hadn't already cooked up some plan with Cyrus.

"Are you ready?" he asked.

"Permission to come aboard?" Kairos asked, swinging his leg over the rail.

"Granted," I called. I looked at Bast—his jaw was set and tense, and I waited for his swearing, ranting outburst.

But instead he pushed his shoulders back and lifted his chin in Kairos's direction. "You'll stay with her while I get a ship?" he asked.

Kairos shrugged. "Not where Cyrus can see me. But yes, I'll be nearby."

Bast strode forward and extended a hand to Kairos, pulling him forward over the rail. "Good," he said.

Kairos gave him a solemn nod, and they both set to the work of getting us free of the cliff.

I reached out and starting to pull up the anchors. Bast and Kairos climbed the shrouds, unfurling the sails while I got the anchors up. When I was done, I untied the others as they climbed down.

"Hey!" I heard a shout. I didn't look, working faster. "Someone's on the ship! Someone's stealing the ship!"

The voice was closer. It was Arnav, and I didn't look at him, pushing hard with my power. The ship moaned and slid forward on the grass, and I pushed again, my arms shaking with the desperate need to go.

The ship heaved off into the air, sinking a few feet before I curled us around Altia's peak, landing us in the water by the other island. This time there was no clapping, and my heart felt heavy and sore.

"You know you're not going to be able to rest much, right?" Bast asked, taking the wheel. "I can't sail this ship alone."

I knew. "I'll get us there fast."

"But your power—"

Lifting my shoulders, I waved Kairos to the lower deck. "Go check on the prisoners. Be careful."

He obeyed, and I looked up, watching my island disappear in the moonlight. It had gone off so smoothly, and now, stupidly, it hurt that no one tried to stop me. No one paid enough attention to me to notice, and even Navya—who might have known—didn't care.

I was going off to my death, and my family didn't mind.

I tried to sleep for a while, but Bast woke me when he needed help, and I pushed the sails as much as I could. What normally would have been a day or more got us to port by midmorning. It was overcast and gray, and there was a good northern wind like the world was giving me something to work with.

Diadem Port came into view, and I bowed my head to Kamaria, the statue's brave shape unchanged on the horizon. She wasn't a god and I wasn't the type to pray, but as we passed, I just asked her, *please. Let it end today.*

I wasn't sure I knew what I meant by "it." Hopefully my slavery. Maybe my life.

That seemed the cruelest thought of all—that I had fought for so long, only to make it back to the same damn harbor, the same damn room, facing the same damn situation all over again.

Trembling, I focused on the task as we sailed into the harbor, trimming then furling the sails to ease into port. Even as we anchored, I saw Tommaso's ship readying to come on the shore.

"Asp," Bast said softly. I turned to him, and he kissed me. I hesitated, wondering if rejecting him now would make him more likely to betray me shortly.

But still, I pulled away, not meeting his eyes. I could feel Kairos watching us, but he didn't intervene like Bast would have. Bast's hand stayed on my waist.

"Don't die in there," he told me. I pulled out of his arms. I couldn't promise that; that was the whole damn point.

He caught my hand with a sigh. "Asp, I mean don't give up in there. You are so damn powerful—make her see that. Remember that you're only her slave if you let her enslave you."

"I don't know what the alternative is. Why would she ever free me?"

"Money," he said, his eyes gleaming. "You are worth more of it than any of her captains. She knows that."

"Permission to come aboard?" Tommaso called.

"Granted," I shouted back, stepping away from Bast. I waited for Tommaso's men to come on board, and let them escort the prisoners up. Tommaso's eyes shifted around, but he didn't comment on the lack of crew.

"After you," Tommaso told me, gesturing to the ladder.

Sitting in Tommaso's boat, my thoughts were a sick loop of all the things Kairos had warned me about, and wondering what was waiting for me at the warehouse. Who was this boy who was waiting for me? Was it worth hoping it was my brother to simultaneously wish him into this situation?

Was there some other plan that I hadn't seen? Was I just barreling forward, always eager to be a martyr?

The boat nudged the dock, and my thoughts ended. I stepped out, my legs trembling below me. Damn this woman. Damn this city.

Tommaso led the captive men to the slave posts, and Abla came down, raising her eyebrows, checking them over, taking notes while other men unloaded the chests full of shiny things we'd picked up in the south.

I heard her jewelry, slinking and shivering, before I saw her at the top of the steps. Cyrus smiled brightly at me, descending like a queen. I put my hands behind my back, trying not to shake.

"My sweet girl," she said. "Look at what you've brought me. Fine, fine specimens. And so many. Where are the rest?"

"This is it," Abla said. She raised her eyes at Tommaso, who nodded.

Cyrus was still smiling. "No, that cannot be. I remember asking for women and children."

"I couldn't pass up these men. We don't have that much room on the ship, you know."

"You have more space than this," she told me, coming closer. The wind scratched at my neck, burned in my fingers, warning me. "You defied me, Aspasia. Deliberately."

I raised my chin. "Yes."

To my surprise, she looked genuinely hurt. She shook her head. "Why?" she asked. "I told you—I would free you after this. We would be partners. You would be free and rich and powerful. You could have everything you've wanted, and I just wanted you to prove your loyalty to me. But you'd rather be a defiant little girl? Why?"

My heart was pounding. "Because I won't commit more women and children to slavery."

She tilted her head like she was confused. "Yet you don't mind putting men in chains?"

I looked to them, tied to the posts, and the fierce blond met my eyes. "No."

"How does that make any sense?" she asked.

"Maybe it doesn't," I replied.

"Why wouldn't you just have told me this before?" she asked me.

My tongue pressed against the bunch of scar tissue in my cheek. "Would it have mattered?" I asked.

"Yes," she said. "I probably would have killed you a long time ago."

I jerked back.

She laughed. "I said probably. Who knows? But the question remains—why do you do it? You with your morals and your scar and your disdain for the life I have given you, why wouldn't you just run? Hm?"

"You would find me," I said, but the words sounded false in my teeth.

She narrowed her eyes. "Yes, I would, with that pretty face. I'd make you regret stealing from me, for sure. But that wouldn't stop you. No, not someone like you—you have no concern for your own safety. You never have. I've always known you were looking for something else, Aspasia, and using my ships and the access they grant you to do it. I assumed it had to be other slaves. It would only make sense if it was your family."

I couldn't breathe. My eyes tracked her every movement, and my hands trembled with the wind's need to break free.

"I looked, but I couldn't find out who you were before. I couldn't find them."

She stepped closer to me, stroking my cheek, tracing her fingers over the scar. I pulled away, but she gripped my arm, continuing to touch my cheek with the other hand.

"I thought for so long you were defined by your scar," she murmured. "I thought of your face and that's what I would see. My fierce little slave. But weeks ago—just before you last set out—a master came to see my girls. He had a boy with him, just on the edge of being a man. His servant. His slave, actually. With his feet in chains because he tries to run away so much."

Her fingers stroked down to my neck, feeling my pulse hammer beneath my skin. She chuckled.

"You should meet him. I think you'll see what I did the moment you do."

She let me go, and I noticed two of Tommaso's big bruisers come closer to me, their hands on their weapons. My power curled, but they stopped, waiting. Cyrus signaled to someone else, and I heard noise rattling in the back cages where they kept the slaves for auction.

Another guard came forward, knife drawn, holding a sour-faced boy in front of him. I choked out a breath that sounded like a sob as I fell to my knees, helpless.

Gryphon turned to me, and the surly twist on his face faded.

His eyes went wide, and he appeared younger, desperate, eager. Immediately he started struggling, but the guard held the knife tight to his neck.

"Don't fight," I told him, taking a deep breath. *Keep that knife away from your neck so I can rip his hand off*, I wanted to tell my brother.

"When I saw him, I knew. This was fate. This moment was meant to happen. You were always mine to possess, Aspasia, and now I will keep you motivated forever. I mean, look at him. Can you believe such luck? He looks just like you," Cyrus said. "Isn't it uncanny?"

"Tell me what you want," I told her. "*Right now.*" My hands were shaking, the need to release my power, to tear this whole building to the ground and get my brother out of here too strong to fight back.

"You need to be punished, Aspasia," she told me. "This seems like—"

She didn't get another word out. I reached forward, pressing the wind against the guard's arm. The knife still nicked Gryphon, but he shoved the guard and ran for me as my power unleashed. I ripped a hole in the roof and dragged the wind from outside in, tearing at the walls, the roof, the cages.

Gryphon yelled, ducking as something flew past his head.

Wood, iron, the damn scarves I had brought from the Wyverns—my power and my rage gathered into a storm, a vicious, wailing tornado inside the warehouse. My clothes flapped around me in a wild frenzy and I focused solely on my brother. On getting him to *me*.

I churned the tornado around us, opening a calmer eye that was slowly widening so that he could come to me. My outstretched arms shook with the force of the power I was calling, and I screamed, barely aware of anything but the protective space I was casting around Gryph.

Unsure, he raised his head, gawking at the wall of wind. It was still strong enough that it whipped my hair like snakes around my face, and he stared at me in wonder.

Like I was a monster. Or a goddess. Or both.

He lunged forward, taking two more hard steps to wrap his arms around me, holding me like an anchor to this world.

My power reacted as I held my brother for the first time in almost a decade, like a pulse snapping over the cyclone of wind, spitting objects out to the walls.

Gryph turned his neck, and the drops of blood on his skin touched mine, and a hot new rage filled me at the thought that they made my brother bleed.

But my rage—and my power—failed me. It wasn't that it faltered. It was that suddenly, everything stopped, like my power had shattered, had ceased to be. Most of the guards were on the ground, unconscious or dead, but Abla, Cyrus, and Tommaso were hidden behind a table.

"Asp, I'm sorry!" Gryphon told me wildly. "I'm so sorry, I didn't mean to!"

"Get her!" Cyrus roared, and Tommaso leaped up.

Frantic, I called for the wind, but nothing happened. I stepped back, but there was debris everywhere. I stumbled, and Tommaso grabbed me, slamming a punch into my face. Two more and I fell to the ground, feeling like my head and mind and vision had splintered. Tommaso left me there and grabbed Gryphon, and I struggled to sit up.

There was a bright arc of light overhead, and I wasn't sure if it was because of the pain or if it was Kairos, outside, worried about me, fighting to get here. I tried to get to my feet as Tommaso held my brother, searching around for the knife, but my feet wouldn't hold me. I managed to roll over just in time to vomit.

"Asp!" I heard him screaming my name.

"Tommaso, really," Cyrus said, her voice light and amused. Shuddering, I looked up at her, stepping gingerly over the wreckage to come to me. "Can't you see that this situation just changed rather drastically? Put him in his own cell. Put some of his blood in a bowl—but don't kill him. Just enough to be . . . useful."

My head dropped as nausea seized me again, but I saw Cyrus's feet in front of me. Slowly, she lowered down, casting me in shadow as two fingers tipped my head up. "My sweet girl," she said. There was a bleeding cut on her forehead, and for all my rage, it was damned little damage. "My best girl. You brought me the rarest commodity of all. Thank you."

"I will kill you," I tried to snarl, but it came out depressingly like a whimper. Like a plea.

"No, my sweet," she said, stroking over the bursting, jagged, angry parts of my bleeding face. "You didn't win this one. You never won a damn thing in your whole life. You played the only card you had, and fate has protected me yet again. Now that I know what you are, I'm going to sell you off. Once I do, you will never know what happens to your brother. You will never see him again."

She pulled my chin up higher so I saw stars, and I wasn't sure if they were real or imagined.

"You think you're the hero in all this. I know you do, I've known it from the day you cut your face. I saw it again today, with this silly rule you have to protect women and children. With your attempts to save your brother. You think you're good. But that would make me your villain, my sweet, and I'm not. Because at every turn, the gods smile on me. They bless me and love me. I am the unsung hero of this story. You? You are the horse I ride on. You are the stone that builds my castle. You are an object, and nothing more."

Every part of me hurt. As she let me go and my eyes shut, I couldn't consider her words. I couldn't build arguments against her in my mind or heart. I just had a single thought—*no*.

# Count the Hours

I woke up to more pain. There was pain thundering in my head, every pound feeling like it was splintering my skull. I took a breath and new, sharp pain lanced at my throat.

I jerked back from it, only to be met with an unyielding beam at my back. I swallowed, desperately trying to draw in shallow breaths. There was something around my neck—some kind of collar, with spikes pointed at my flesh so I could barely breathe in without impaling my own throat.

My breath shuddered out of me as I looked around carefully, trying to get my bearings. I was on my feet. Tied. Daylight. The room looked familiar, but strange somehow.

Cyrus. I was in Cyrus's palace, in one of the rooms I'd only seen covered in sycophants and sweets. Now it was cleared, and I was tied to a stand.

I had to get out of here. We hadn't planned for this—nothing involved me losing my power, losing my ability to call the wind. Nothing would prepare Kairos to help me now.

I tried rocking the stand to knock it over, but it didn't budge. I only succeeded in piercing my neck, and I spat out a curse.

"Don't," said a forlorn voice behind me. "I really don't want to watch you bleed to death."

"Gryph?" I called. "Are you hurt?" I couldn't get to him. I couldn't even turn to look at him. This all-gods-damned woman was keeping my brother from me, even in chains.

"Fine," he muttered. "Asp, I'm sorry. I should have realized I was bleeding, what it would do to you . . . I didn't. I'm so sorry."

"Stop," I told him. "None of this is your fault. We're together now. That's all that matters."

"It is my fault," he said. "You can't use your power. Because of me."

I frowned. "What do you mean?"

"They put my blood on you," he said. "Usually I can control it a little, but when I bleed, I don't have a choice. My blood takes powers away from people."

I drew a breath deep enough to hurt against the spikes. "That's possible?"

He didn't answer.

"Gryph, this isn't your fault. Don't let her trick you into thinking it is."

"We're going to be sold again."

*Again.* I shut my eyes—worse than the pain was the idea that of all the kids I'd found and helped and rescued, of all the stories I'd heard and all the fear I'd seen in their eyes, my own brother had been feeling the same thing. Somewhere out there without me. "There's not a damn place she can take you that I won't find you. Do you understand me? I will find you."

There was a long silence, and I strained against the spikes to turn, to get a glimpse of him. "Stop moving," he said. "Your throat's already bleeding."

"I will impale myself if it means seeing you're okay."

"I'm not," he said bitterly. "I'm not. None of us were okay since the day they stuck Papa in the communes. Then you left."

"I didn't leave," I said, facing forward against a new burn of tears in my eyes.

"I know," he said softly. "Well, I figured it out."

"You thought I just abandoned you?" I whispered.

"No," he said. "I thought you ran away. To go make a new life where we'd be safe. Like you always said you would."

My eyes burned. I'd been so close. If I just could have found them first, brought them to the island, they would have been safe.

"There were rumors, about children being taken, and I didn't want to believe they'd taken you," he said. "Then they took me."

"Pera?" I asked softly.

"I don't know," he said. "I haven't seen her for years. Not for—"

The doors opened and stopped his words, and Cyrus was there in all her splendor, dressed in silks and gold. Behind her, about fifteen people entered the room.

Cyrus smiled at me, and panic curled in my stomach as I saw Skiver beside her, malice bright in his eyes as he walked toward me. "So is it true?" he asked as they stopped in front of me.

"Oh, it's true," Cyrus said. "You can see the damage she did to my warehouse as proof."

"Hmm," he said, and it sounded like the growl of a dog. "Then what's stopping her from doing the same here?"

"The blood," she said, touching my X, which felt crustier than usual. "Her brother can take away powers."

"Then I want them both," he said.

"You can't afford him," she told him. "But I will give you a vial of his blood to control this purchase."

"She's worthless if she can't control the wind," he said.

"You know her temper," Cyrus warned. "You'll need a fail-safe that doesn't involve killing her."

I glared at her, but said nothing. They were both damn fools. The second they took this blood off me—especially on a ship—they would never get close enough to put it on again.

"Did I hear that correctly?" came a smooth, oily voice. My breath caught as Favo, a man I once had chained in my brig, was now before me, wearing a jacket of tufted velvet and gold thread. His hair was slicked back and shining, and he looked, if possible, more devious than ever.

His mouth quirked as his eyes met mine, but he looked to Cyrus. "Are you saying she's an Elementa?"

Cyrus smiled at him, a new wealthier suitor for her prize. "She is. She can control a whole fleet of ships if you need her to."

His hands settled behind his back as he looked at me, and back to Cyrus. "How does one keep her motivated, I wonder? She looks like she's . . . willful."

Cyrus waved her hand. "That collar? Oh don't worry. She and I just have history."

"I'm aware," he said. "Wasn't she one of your captains?"

Cyrus smiled. "And yet, always one of my slaves as well. But that is a clear example—she can be quite motivated."

"Now wait a minute," Skiver growled. "Don't go cozying up to him. I'm buying her."

Cyrus beamed. "Then you'll pay for her, won't you? My only allegiance is to profit." Smiling at Favo again, she said, "You certainly look like you can pay."

"I can," he affirmed.

His eyes flicked back to me, and I struggled for a deep breath. He'd wanted me to meet his employer before, and I hadn't gone. Now it seemed I wasn't going to have a choice—and I didn't know what lay at the end of that road.

"I promise I will bring every ship I'm placed on to a standstill unless my brother is with me," I swore.

Favo's eyes shot to Gryph, but Cyrus snapped her fingers. A second later blinding, searing pain shot into my side, and a gargled cry escaped my mouth. Someone—probably Tommaso—grabbed my head from the spikes, holding me back and stuffing something dry in my mouth.

"Please do not go stabbing my merchandise," Favo snapped.

"Property isn't supposed to speak," Cyrus said, glaring at me as my eyes refocused on her. I felt like the cloth in my mouth was in my throat, and pain was pouring out of my side. Or maybe that was blood. "She knows better. We don't stab anything vital, don't worry."

"Then name your price so I can be done with this," Favo said.

Cyrus laughed. "We're still waiting for another guest," she said. "Come, you both should look at my other treasure."

Cyrus led Favo and Skiver away, and more people came over to me. A woman stepped up close to me and examined my face, her own features granite and emotionless. A man put his hands on me like he was squeezing fruit at the market.

Then the doors opened again, and I saw a man in a long black coat that touched the floor come into the room. My blood went cold. *A quaesitor.*

He went straight to my brother.

"This is the one?" I heard him ask.

I strained and tried to yell, or fight, but no sound came out behind my gag. I couldn't move except to hurt myself. What in all the hells was the point of my ever-damned power if I couldn't use it to stop this from happening? How was it possible that I had once felt so powerful, so safe, only to end up in a cage once more?

"This is the one," she told him. "That girl was tearing my warehouse to shreds and one touch of his blood made it stop."

"I've been fooled before," he told her. "I need a demonstration."

"No," Cyrus said. "I don't sell faulty merchandise, and I do not offer trials. If you don't want it, someone else will pay handsomely for it."

He made some sort of grunting noise.

Cyrus clapped her hands and came forward to where I could just see her. "Now that we are all here, we will start the bidding with the girl first. She is still young, very healthy. She is a seasoned sailor and has the ability to control the wind. She will be a tremendous asset to any maritime venture you may be engaged in and could be adapted for any number of purposes. Bidding starts at one thousand kings."

Skiver raised his hand.

"Good," Cyrus said. "Eleven hundred?"

Favo raised his hand.

"Fifteen hundred?"

"Twelve hundred," Skiver said, raising his hand.

Favo smirked. "Fifteen," he said.

282 | A. C. Gaughen

"Sixteen?" Cyrus asked, looking to Skiver.

"Sixteen," said the stone-faced woman.

"Seventeen," Favo said.

"Eighteen," Skiver said, but he looked uncomfortable. I was a better pirate than he was, and eighteen hundred kings was nearly the sum of my life's savings.

"Two thousand," Favo said, looking smug.

Cyrus pointed to the woman. "Twenty-one hundred?" she asked. The woman shook her head. Cyrus pointed to Skiver.

Skiver was practically snarling. "No," he growled. Unfairly, his anger seemed to be directed at me, and he took a step closer, glaring.

"Excellent," Favo said, stepping in front of Skiver to shake Cyrus's hand, then coming to stand by me, like he was protecting me.

Maybe he was.

Cyrus and her wide smile moved out of my range of vision. "Now," she said. "Our prize. Doubtless you all know of the tremendous powers of the Elementae, and perhaps you have heard the rumors that have persisted for years—our world is not governed by four elements, but *five*."

There was a hush in the room, and my skin prickled with sweat and fear. A fifth element? Is that what Gryphon was? Not *between* the elements, like Kairos or Copper, but a whole different kind.

For years, I believed that these powers were the counterbalance to all the injustice in the world—a way to give power back into the hands of the powerless, the hurt, the ignored. Was nature laughing at me? All the while, was there a counterbalance to *us*?

"To my knowledge," Cyrus continued, "this is the only living person who possesses the coveted fifth element, the void to negate all the other powers. This young slave is the only known person able to take away the powers of the Elementae. Powerful protection for anyone looking to defend against the supernatural. Bidding will begin at ten thousand kings."

*Ten thousand?*

Favo stepped around me, close enough that I could still see him, but he was paying attention to the bidding.

I couldn't see what was happening, but within seconds the bidding rose to twelve thousand, and I didn't hear voices other than Cyrus. Favo raised his hand a few times, and each time, it made my heart pound. Bidding slowed, and that's when I heard the quaesitor's voice offer fifteen thousand.

Favo drew a breath, looking to me with sad eyes before he raised his hand again. The quaesitor immediately countered. Favo's eyes shut, and he shook his head.

"Eighteen thousand?" Cyrus questioned. "Anyone?" There was silence for several seconds.

"Seventeen thousand it is. Gentlemen, you have one day to produce your funds, at which point, your merchandise will be released to you."

They were generous rules for payment, but it would take several carts full of gold to produce seventeen thousand gold kings. I supposed people didn't often carry that with them.

Favo went to confer with Cyrus, and he pulled out a small purse, pouring something out into his hand. They seemed to be haggling over something, and he poured a little more, and she nodded. He held out the handful, and Cyrus looked toward me.

Hands seized mine, untying them from around the pole. Metallic clinks and thunks released the collar at my neck, and someone bent to untie my feet.

My knees went soft, and I grabbed the pole, staying standing as I turned to Gryphon. He didn't have the same collar I did, but he was tied to the beam like every other slave I'd ever seen, and I ran to him, grabbing his arm even as guards stepped forward to separate us.

"Let her be," Favo said, his voice more authoritative than I expected.

"Just go, Asp," Gryphon whispered, not looking at me.

I dug my fingers into his arm. "Count the hours," I told him. "Because there will not be many that separate us."

"You don't know that," he said.

"Look at me," I told him. I felt half-feral, with blood on my face, alongside bruises, alongside the most terrible resolve I'd ever felt. His eyes met mine, and the brokenness in them made the jackal inside me claw to the surface. "I *do* know that."

He sniffed and gave the smallest nod. He mouthed *love you* like he didn't want to say it out loud.

"I love you," I told him, aloud, fearlessly, recklessly.

Favo touched my arm, telling me to follow him, but it took me seconds longer to let go of Gryph's arm.

"Come on," Favo said to me.

I looked once more at my brother. It would damn well not be the last time.

Raising my chin, I could easily ignore the pain for the first few steps, when Cyrus was watching me with a smug pleasure and Skiver had a dark sneer on his face. No matter what hell I was walking into, I was still grateful that Skiver didn't own me.

But the room was longer than I remembered, and by the time I got to the door I was walking slower, my breath huffing out of my chest. I pressed a hand to my side that was still oozing blood, but the wound wasn't deep.

Outside of the room, I stopped, and Favo put his arm on me. "I'll help," he said.

"Get your hands off me," I snarled.

"I have a carriage out front. Go slow; you can make it that far," he told me.

One leg was starting to lag a little, but I took slower steps. My eyes swam, and I sucked in deep, slow breaths as I kept stepping forward. When we reached the big doorway, the weight of the sun stopped me again. My bloody hand caught me on the doorway, and I stared at it, a little confused. I needed to sit. I needed my power. I needed a damn knife to go back in and saw Cyrus's heart out.

I took a step off the stone stair, and my knees went weak again. I almost hit the ground, but arms caught me, pulling me up. Pain seared up from the wound, bringing my awareness sharply back around.

"I've got you," Kairos said.

Relief broke over me, and I dragged my arms around his neck, hugging him with a shuddering breath. He hugged me tight, giving me a moment when I didn't have to fight quite so hard to stay on my feet.

"What happened?" Kairos demanded, but he wasn't talking to me. I pulled back, seeing the carriage maybe thirty feet beyond. "What did they do to her?" He held me tight, dragging me the few more steps to the carriage. My legs tangled a little, but I managed to wedge myself inside.

Sitting down was such intense relief that I felt like I nearly passed out for a moment, but I sucked in a breath and raised my head. Kairos was tugging up my filthy shirt to see the wound, and I struggled against him. "Why are you here?" I demanded.

He stopped pulling my shirt. "Because you are terrible at self-preservation. Can I look?" he asked, gesturing to my belly. I nodded, and he raised the shirt up with a low groan. "How did they do this to you?" he asked, looking up, examining my cheek and neck next. "I saw the warehouse. I tried to get to you."

I drew in a breath, but even now, I couldn't answer. Not when I had spent so long hiding my family, just to have my one chance destroyed before my eyes.

"The blood," Favo said, gesturing at my face. "Apparently her brother has the ability to cancel out Elementae powers."

Kairos's eyes shut, and I hated him a little. I wanted to see his reaction to hearing I had a brother, the secret I wouldn't ever tell him. I wanted to know what he thought about being powerless, when I had so stupidly shown off with my power and said I didn't need to know how to use a sword. I didn't want him to keep whatever he was feeling right then away from me.

Mostly, I wanted to deserve it. I wanted to be the person he shared that with.

But then his eyes opened, and he sighed, and he stroked my hair back gently. "Your brother," he said softly.

His soft voice was almost my undoing. Tears burned in my eyes, and my fingers curled into his, digging and scratching until I could hurt a little less.

Kairos leaned forward until his forehead touched mine. "We'll get him back."

"I just need to be patched up and get this blood off me," I told him. "Then I will go back there and blow that place into the sea.

The quaesitor will take a little while to get the funds together. We have to get back there before he takes Gryph away."

"Quaesitor," Kairos repeated, looking starkly to Favo. "You let the *Trifectate* buy him?"

"It was one or the other. I didn't have the funds or the authorization for both."

"Do you have any idea what the Tri King will do to him?" Kairos snapped. "With him?"

"They've got to sail him over," Favo argued. "And she can't be beat in a ship."

The carriage jostled, and I whined with pain. "Is this when you tell me how a slave I transported weeks ago now has enough money to pay thousands of gold kings for me at auction?" I raised my head to look at Favo, and then regretted it, and lowered it again.

"I'm not a slave," he said. "You'll remember I volunteered for your little excursion."

"Why was that?" I asked.

"Well," he said, taking a breath, "I was there on purpose, finding information. My employer is looking for something very specific. As it turns out, I think you're the only one who can do what needs to be done."

"Who is your employer?" I asked.

He didn't say anything, and I glared at him, uneasy. Favo lifted a shoulder, but it was Kairos who answered. "That would be the king of Sarocca," he told me.

I felt nausea shoving its way into my throat. "Fantastic," I grunted. "So what is it he wants from his brand-new purchase?"

"Rest," Favo told me. "We'll be there soon, and he can explain everything to you."

Reluctantly, I nodded, trying to figure this out. How long

could I wait? I did need rest—and food and a significant amount of bandaging, preferably—but as soon as his blood was off me, I was going after my brother. If I could get away from them, I could go to the docks and find Bast.

Of course, Bast might not be there. He might have taken my money and run.

Despite the fact that a huge part of me wanted to curl up and lick my wounds and have Kairos keep petting my hair, I couldn't put that first. I needed to put my brother first. I wouldn't get another chance.

Not to mention that if they weren't lying, I'd be a fugitive from the king of Sarocca. I wondered what he did to punish "unruly property."

Far too soon for my liking, the carriage slowed, and Favo said, "We're here."

They helped me get out of the carriage, and my body felt like I had seven anchors strapped to me. Without him forcing the issue, I put my arm around Kairos's neck, and he held my waist, careful and close.

"We should clean you up before you see the king," Favo said, raising his eyebrow.

"Not if he can send a small army to get her brother," Kairos told him.

I nodded.

Favo sighed, striding ahead.

We were at the entrance to a very old military castle that thrust out on a promontory to look over the harbor. Kamaria's statue loomed huge from here, and I looked up at her, wondering if she would care if I lived or died. Wondering if there was even a point to praying anymore.

"This way," Favo said, and we stepped into the stone-dark halls of the castle. He spoke quietly to one of the guards before leading us farther into darkness.

This castle was not the pretty thing of the Wyverni phaedra, or even the white terror of the Tri Castles. It was just functional, a place owned by royalty but inhabited by soldiers.

Favo led us left, away from the ocean, to a room where three men and two women stood around a table, arguing over a map, but halted as soon as Favo's shadow appeared.

They all looked up. I knew the king at once; he was older, the only one not in Sarocca's blue and gold military colors. He wasn't wearing a crown or anything fancy, but there was a set to his shoulders, a weight to his eyes. "Good," he said, looking to Favo. Then his eyes skirted over to me, and he frowned. "Get her a chair," he ordered.

One of the men strode to the side of the room to fetch one, but the prospect of sitting while all these large people loomed over me sounded terrible. "No, thank you," I said, and nudged Kairos forward to help me into the room.

The man brought the chair anyway, but I didn't sit. They all stared at me, and I kept my eyes on the king, defiant, unwilling to back down.

"Gods above, Favo, what happened?" the king asked, taking in my appearance.

"What is it you bought me for?" I demanded. At this, the unfamiliar eyes in the room turned to their king.

He drew a breath that made him taller. "I didn't buy you. Slavery isn't legal here; I couldn't have possibly purchased you."

"My purchase price would suggest otherwise," I returned. "You just paid the most notorious Saroccan slaver handsomely for my skin. So what is it you want with it?"

"Skies," Kairos grunted, glaring at me. "You really are rude, you know."

"You're not Saroccan, are you?" the king asked, and he probably meant me.

I raised my chin, not answering. It wasn't the simplest question—it implied I had things like "home" or "belonging" or something else that would define my nationality. Or was I meant to be defined by my birth for all time?

But he was waiting for an answer, so I said, "No."

"Where were you in the last war?"

"Not here," I snarled.

"Do not speak to my father in such a manner," one of the women said, her hand tightening on an absurdly large sword for her small frame.

The king waved a hand at her, leaning forward on the table. "You were alive for it. I'm sure you felt it—whether you were in the Trifectate or the islands and knew it deeply, or in Sarocca or abroad and you heard of it. For most people, the war ended seven years ago. But for me, it rages on."

I tried to concentrate on his self-important speech, but it was hard. Pain was a beating drum in my chest.

"The boy king got lucky," he told me. "He took down the islands by some miracle or magic, and he overextended himself to do so. I came with the greatest naval power on earth, and I nearly had the whole of the Trifectate as a Saroccan colony, until our enemies to the east invaded our borders. We were forced to cease our attacks."

I dug my fingers into Kairos, feeling like I was swaying even though my eyes weren't confirming that. I didn't know this piece of Saroccan history, but I couldn't say I really gave a damn. "Fascinating," I told him. "I still cannot see what this has to do with me, and I'm quite literally running out of my ability to care."

The princess growled at me, but the king chuckled. "I suppose you are. The Trifectate should be mine, Captain. I want it back. After the war, the boy king spurned my daughter for a desert princess. We could have been allies, but now I will take his country away."

"You sent a ship full of gold to aid them," I accused.

"The *Tri Queen*," he said, lifting his eyebrows. "The Trifectate sent a ship to us for aid, and yes, it left this harbor. But on a very dark night, it vanished, and no one has seen it since."

I studied his face for long moments. "You hid the ship. You never wanted to send the gold."

"But not sending the gold would be perceived as an act of war," he explained.

"Then let there be war," I insisted. "That king is fighting against a resistance within his walls; he can't survive a fight on two fronts."

"He couldn't possibly have won the war against the islanders. He couldn't possibly have killed them like he did. I won't send an army to find out what new tricks he's concocted. Not when his navy now rivals my own. It will take everything I have to repel him, and I still cannot guarantee victory. I want to even the odds while he still believes we are allies."

My breath rasped a little harder in my lungs, and Kairos looked at me in worry.

"Moreover," the king continued, moving his finger down the

map to the Trifectate's communes. "He has the ability to build new ships faster than any other country I've seen because of his labor camps, and particularly the shipbuilding holds. It would be deeply in my interest for someone to destroy those, and disable as many seaworthy ships as possible. You are not my slave; you're free at the end of this conversation no matter what you decide. But if you choose to do this, I will give you a ship, a crew, and ample payment and provisions."

My head swam, but I wasn't sure if it was from this request or the injuries. "What the hell makes you think I can do that? What am I supposed to do, smash the ship to smithereens to break down a wall? There is no way to get out of that alive."

"That's where I come in," said the princess with the big sword. "We can arm you, with things you've never seen before. Explosives that, particularly with your gifts, could be incredibly well used."

"I'm not taking explosives of any kind across the ocean in my ship. That's madness."

"They're really very effect—"

"I'm not harming a single person in the communes. None of those people are there because they want to be. They are slaves, whether the Tri King calls them that or not. You'd have me explode the world in front of them." I shook my head, stepping back and leaning more heavily on Kairos, who grunted. "You'd need an army to do what you're asking, and it seems you're unwilling to send yours. You just want my people to die."

"There is an army," he said. "Desperately waiting for aid. An army that, according to this letter, does not have a chance without foreign assistance. I'm hoping to send them you," he said, releasing a paper to drift down on the table. Kairos jerked when he saw it, and I looked to him, not understanding.

But I shook my head. "It's not enough. I don't see a way to get my crew out of that alive, and I'd never put them in such reckless danger."

One of the men beside him crossed his arms. "Do you need incentive or resources?"

"Both?" I said, flinging my hand over the table. "Maybe—maybe—with three more ships and the people I need to fly them and crew them. Maybe. Maybe with enough earth Elementae to help me collapse the stone without hurting people. You can't go in there like a battering ram—it's the source of their military power. Or you can, I suppose, but you need a bigger ram than I can devise."

The king looked to Favo. "We'd been led to believe you'd gotten into the communes before."

"Many times. *Without anyone knowing*, not to collapse half the valley."

Kairos shifted a little, and it made me sway uneasily. "This will have to wait," he said, looking at me. "She needs rest, and she has wounds that need to be tended. Cyrus still has her brother, and I think it's fair to say that if you could retrieve him, that would go a very long way for the incentive part." Kairos met my eyes, looking for agreement, and I nodded. "Good. Now where can she lie down?"

The king gestured to Favo, and Favo turned. "This way, my friends."

"Stop," I grunted, feeling my stomach twist at the same time my ankles turned weak. My fingers dug into Kairos's shoulder vengefully, but he didn't protest.

Instead, he leaned his head on mine. "Come on," he told me, soft and low in my ear. "You haven't fought like hell to quit on me now." Sucking in a harsh breath, I straightened up and put one foot doggedly in front of the other.

The room wasn't far—it had a single cot, no windows, and a chest full of frightening things that a short woman was rustling through, little gray hairs unplucked from a bun to give the look of a strange halo hovering around her face.

I lay on the cot with a tortured sigh of relief, and Kairos stuffed a pillow under my head and shoulders. I looked down to where my hand was sticky with drying blood—the wound wasn't bleeding too badly now, but my clothes were stuck to it and my skin.

The woman shot me a glance and turned back to the chest. "Take the shirt off," she said.

"I believe I hear the king calling," Favo said, dipping his head to me and leaving.

I grunted, peeling the shirt up to the wound, but I whined when I tried to pull it off. Kairos looked worried, but the woman sighed and turned around, pointing to him. "Hot water," she said, snapping her fingers to the little fireplace.

Kairos leaped up to do her bidding, and I twisted as she yanked the fabric free from the wound, screwing my eyes shut. A second later hot, wet cloth was scraping at it, and I moaned miserably. "For a girl with half her face covered in scar tissue, I'd expect you to handle this a little better," the woman told me.

"It hardly matters if you yell from the pain," Kairos said, bringing the water to her side. "It just matters what you do with the pain. She's been fighting through it for hours."

"It matters to *me* if they yell," the woman grunted, shaking her hand. "All that bellyaching."

I grabbed at Kairos's hand when he was back in range of me and looked at him. "Bast?" I asked.

He shook his head. "He left the ship before I did. I haven't seen him since then."

"Will you go to Gryphon?" I asked, gripping his hand. "I can't . . . I need . . ."

He swallowed. "If you want me to. I don't think I can get him out though."

"I know," I said, looking at him.

"First," he said, reaching up to stroke my hair back, "I need to talk to you."

"To tell me how you sold me to the king of Sarocca?"

He swallowed. "When I couldn't get you, I tried to summon a vision. All it would show me was a fountain in the center of town, and Favo was waiting there. I found him in the morning, and given that the king of Sarocca was looking for someone to fly a ship, it was sort of easy from there. But more importantly, I need to talk to you about the communes. About that letter."

My eyes opened, focusing on him though my body desperately wanted to drift away. "The letter."

"It was from my sister," he said, looking down. "She reached out for aid to the Saroccans, it seems. On behalf of the Resistance."

I had heard of the Resistance for years, in dark whispers and back rooms, the ghost of a savior for the children I'd taken from the Trifectate. "She's with them?"

"She and my brother Rian both. If the king is to be believed, they're going to attack the communes. They don't have the numbers, but they do have incredibly powerful Elementae. If we could get close enough for Osmost to fly in, we could coordinate an attack. We could take back the communes. Free everyone. And the Resistance would actually stand a chance against the Tri King."

I opened my mouth to protest—the odds still seemed terrible to me, and I couldn't put my crew in that kind of danger—but he released my hand and wouldn't meet my eyes.

"If they try this attack and fail, he'll torture her, and kill her. And her unborn child. And my last brother. I told you I thought I was with you on that ship for a reason—this is it. This is the only chance my family has to survive. You are the only chance my family has to survive."

"Kairos . . . ," I said, but I had no idea what else to say. I couldn't stake the lives of everyone I cared about. I couldn't tell him to give up on his family.

"Please don't say no," he said. "Not right now. Just think about it, and give me time. I can't hear you tell me no right now." I nodded, and he leaned forward, kissing me, touching his forehead to mine. "Rest. I'll be back when I know something about your brother."

I watched him go, and the gray woman clucked at me. I scowled at her.

She lifted her shoulders, wrapping bandaging around my middle. "There's less kissing when your entire family is murdered, that's all I'll tell you." She dipped her hands back in the hot water. "Now, let's see about that face."

# Kamaria Save Us All

I slept like the dead. I passed out in the old woman's hands and woke alone in the room, the fire stoked high, furs piled on me, the room oppressively hot. I couldn't tell if it was day or night.

I felt him before I saw him. There was just something about Kairos, there always had been. Some kind of link between the two of us, and I could feel my power curling around his.

My power. I drew in a deep breath, sending air to flicker over the flames. My power. I was whole again.

But Kairos sighed. "He's gone," he told me. I looked to where he sat beside me. "The quaesitor came and got him before I even arrived. I searched the docks for word of him and Bast both. Your brother is on a ship bound for the Trifectate, and no one's seen Bast."

A dull burn curled through my throat and down to my stomach, like swallowing fire. He betrayed me. But then I took a breath, thinking. "No one?" I asked.

His eyes met mine. "Not even any number of places he could have fenced that jewel or purchased a boat."

Slowly, I sat up. I still felt miserable and sore, but it was better having my power. My strength was back, my shield, my sword. I grunted, heaving the blankets off me and throwing my legs over the side. "That's not good."

He shook his head. "No. I don't have enough contacts here, but people know Bast. He couldn't just disappear."

I nodded. "I know a few people to ask. When did Gryph set sail?"

"Last night," he said.

I cast around, but remembered there were no windows. "How long have I been out?"

"About a day," he said. "Though it's been a raging storm that entire time, so they won't have gotten far yet."

I cursed, rubbing my fingers over the bandaging on my stomach. "As soon as the storm eases, they'll have good strong wind to take them. It will take a normal ship eight days to sail to the Trifectate. We've already lost one."

He wasn't looking at me now, his elbows braced on his knees, his fingers braced against one another, waiting. Tense. Not wanting to ask.

"It's not my decision," I told him softly. "We have to get the crew, and they have to vote."

He shook his head. "Not about this. You could tell them what to do, and they'd obey. You could do it if you wanted to." He looked up, his eyes accusing me, and I met the challenge.

"I don't want to," I told him. The depth of the wound was immediate and sharp on his face. "It's risking everyone's life. It's risking everything I've ever fought for. But I'm still going to ask them. I'll make a case for it."

The wound softened, only a little, but he peered at me like he had when he first heard what I did on Altia, not understanding me. Not understanding me when I so desperately wanted him to.

"We need to go," I said, heaving up to stand. "We'll talk to the king, we'll find Bast, and we'll get the crew. We've already wasted too much time."

He stood, and I flinched a little as I stepped, but I straightened up, shoving a sigh out of my lungs. "I'll get Favo," he told me.

The door opened, and the suspiciously canny man was standing there. "This way, Captain."

Favo led us back to the room, but it had changed. The maps were gone, and in their place were a small banquet of food and two big hounds filling the floor with their bodies and paws. It was only the king and his daughter now, talking in serious tones.

The king stood at the sight of me—they all did, except the dogs—and he gestured to two empty seats with empty plates. "Eat, please," he said.

Kairos looked to me, and I sat, slowly. I felt something tugging at my power, and curiously, I tested the threads, looking at the king and then at his daughter.

She was an Elementa.

I took some of the food, and my stomach lurched with need. Kairos sat beside me, and one of the dogs lifted his head. With a long sigh, he pushed up to his paws and came to sit at attention beside Kairos, who stroked his ear. The big hound put his head on Kairos's leg.

The princess stared at the dog, her eyebrows halfway to her hairline, but she didn't say anything. "So," I said.

The king leaned back, tilting his head, waiting.

"You have a ship for me to take?"

He nodded. "The *Serobini*."

I had a large chunk of spiced meat in my mouth, but I smiled.

"Named for the Wyverni goddess of chaos," he said. "This pleases you?"

I swallowed. "Very much so."

"It's crewed and full of provisions, waiting in the harbor," he told me.

"We don't need the crew," I said. He opened his mouth, but I continued. "Furthermore, I haven't fully agreed yet."

"Oh?"

"No. In addition to my freedom, I'd like my purchase price refunded to me. Additionally, I would like to form an arrangement with you."

The woman coughed on her meal, but the king ignored her. "What kind of arrangement would that be?"

"Go after the slavers," I told him. "Wyverns be damned. Slavery is illegal here and yet your new road has opened up a whole new level of trade. You want to cut the Trifectate off at the knees, but they are buying Elementae from Sarocca to experiment on and use, to make them strong. Cyrus displays her wealth and fears no retribution because even you buy from her."

"I have never purchased a slave before this!" he roared.

"No? Then why didn't you march in there with the army and free my brother and me? Why pay her? Why give her money?"

"Why do you trade in men?" he demanded, leaning forward. "You think I can just stomp my foot and tamp slavery out? You think it's that simple? I will have revolution on my hands. I will destabilize the realm as war threatens."

"I think you're willing to let people like me die so that you don't have to face this. I think you're only worried about the Trifectate now that it is coming to your house." I looked pointedly at his daughter, and she gasped.

The king turned scarlet, leaping to his feet, but I didn't back down. "Keep your mouth shut," he growled.

I let a moment pass. "Cyrus is selling Elementae in private auctions. Slaves are being purchased and used for their powers. Children. Does that mean nothing to you?"

The princess put her hand on her father's, and he looked at her, an unspoken conversation going on between them. She shook her head a little, and he bellowed out a sigh before sitting down. He filled his cup with wine, swallowed it, and filled it again.

"I cannot risk my relationship with the Wyverns. Not right now."

"They worship the Elementae. It's an easy platform to say that you are cutting off slavery to defend their kind."

He scowled. "I promise that I will consider it. It's not as simple as you claim, but I will speak to my advisers. Tell me what you need today to agree to what I've asked."

"Protection," I told him. "And finances. You will keep my crew fed and safe, and after this mission, I will use my crew to free as many people from slavery as I can. You will make that happen."

He knit his fingers together, considering me. "When I need your skills, you will make yourself available to me."

"We can discuss it," I told him, shaking my head. "But I will not be a slave again."

"You will destroy the communes."

"I will *attack* the communes. I will do my best to destroy their dry docks and their ability to make new ships. This is if, and only if, my crew agrees. If they refuse, I will come back here and return the funds."

He straightened up, looking first to Kairos and then to me. "That's unacceptable."

"I can't do it without them, and I'm not risking their lives without their agreement," I told him. "It is not up to me."

"Yet you reap all the benefits."

I looked down, considering this. "You could choose to look at it like that, yes."

He drew a slow breath, watching me. I saw something thoughtful in his eyes, so many hidden things that he was sifting through. "I cannot imagine this will be the end of the Trifectate," he said. "War is coming."

"It seems that way, yes."

"This is a blow, but it won't be a killing blow. They still have ships, and they have a zealotry that's hard to counter."

I waited to hear how this involved me.

"I will most likely need your skills for a while before you can single-handedly take on slavery."

A grim feeling settled in my stomach, and I wondered if I would ever truly get away from being a slave, from being chained, by money or iron or circumstance. "As I said, it will always be a discussion. Consider me another mercenary in your stable."

His mouth fell into a line that matched the leaden weight in my stomach. "I want your loyalty," he said. "I want to know you won't turn away and help another sovereign when I need you."

"No," I said, pushing back and shaking my head. "You want a slave. You want something you purchased to always come running back to you." I looked at the dog taking meat from Kairos's hand. "Do you know why dogs are loyal? Because they trust you. Because they see how you treat them over and over and they devote themselves to you. I am loyal to those I love, but my trust cannot be demanded. No slave will ever trust a master."

A muscle in his jaw flared. "You're free. I own no other slaves."

I nodded slowly. "And now we can begin the long business of trusting each other."

He sighed, leaning back, rapping his knuckles on the table. "Very well. My men will take you to the ship."

"We need the letter," I said rashly. I hadn't planned on that, but I felt the awareness run through Kairos's body. "That the rebels sent. It will help us coordinate our efforts."

The king motioned to one of the men, and he stood, leaving the room. The king looked back to me, his mouth tilting up as he examined me. "How old are you?" he asked.

"Eighteen," I said, and immediately frowned. That was right, wasn't it? Honestly, it had been a long time since I'd marked a birthday.

He smiled. "Kamaria save us all," he said, and raised his glass to me.


The king's men led us on horses down to the dock, but as we approached the city square, I couldn't follow them. I nudged my horse in the other direction, and she obeyed my command—which was a little impressive because I wasn't exactly an adept rider.

"Asp," Kairos said, his tone warning. Osmost dove in front of me with a shriek, and my horse halted.

"Hey," I snapped, turning to Kairos. "Do not get your bird to do your dirty work."

"Please. You use the wind. And Osmost does what he wants."

"Sure he does," I grunted, and spurred my horse. Osmost tried the move again, but I pushed forward as the horse tossed his head.

"Asp, you can't do this. Not now, not when we have to go."

"I assure you, I have plenty of time for this."

"Think of your brother."

It was the wrong thing to say. Any doubt filtered out of my veins, and in its place was ice and fire, rage and fury. I spurred the horse and heard Kairos sigh behind me as I rode straight to the door of Cyrus's palace, letting my power feel ahead for me as I swung off the horse.

She was in there. There were at least two others, but they were of little concern. I shoved the doors so hard with my power that one banged off its hinge, hanging off-kilter as I passed through.

Guards came for me, and I threw them back, slamming them into a room across the hall and shutting the door, barricading it in seconds. I pushed into the room with her in it, and she stood there, unafraid, with Abla and Tommaso by her side.

She grinned at me. "My sweet girl. Back already?"

"You knew it wouldn't be long," I said, and my power lifted every small object in the room, flying them in a lazy loop over their heads, paperweights and bowls and small oranges that were bright dots of color in the swirling band. Cyrus faltered at this, looking up at them, watching with dread as a bowl full of flashing silverware rose up. "Like I cared if you ever hurt me. Like it even mattered. But you came for my brother. You kept him from me. You bled him," I growled, and my rage was such a living thing that I trembled with it, and the objects responded, crashing into one another unevenly in the air. An orange got knocked out of the loop and hit Tommaso in the face, and larger objects were rising, pulling to me. A table leaped up, a stool, a bench.

"You can't hurt me," she said, tugging at her dress to show dried blood on her neck like a weak echo of the wound I wanted to leave there. "I have his blood on me."

It was true—my power seemed to break around her. I would have a hard time choking her to death. But that was fine—I could propel anything at her from a distance.

"Does it look like you're safe from me?" I asked, whipping a knife around them so they jumped closer together. "What will save you now, Cyrus? What god will protect you?"

Her lip curled back. "Try it. We'll see who lives, slave."

I felt Kairos's power behind me, warning me away from this. Begging for me to keep control and forget this vengeance. "Not yet," I assured them both. "Tell me where Bast is, Cyrus. It's the only thing that will save your sister's life right now."

Abla looked stubbornly strong, but Cyrus had known to use that particular bait against me for a reason. Abla was the one thing in the world she loved, and her eyes looked from her sister to me. "You wouldn't dare," she snarled.

I sent a knife whipping to Abla, stinging a cut over the side of her neck. She yelped, covering it, but it was a shallow graze. "I'll do it piece by piece if I must."

"You wouldn't hurt my sister," she spat back at me. "Not when you spend so much of your life protecting siblings. I don't believe you, little slave. What about your code?"

Another knife nicked Abla, this time on her hand. "You clearly don't know what my code says about vengeance. You bled my brother, and I'll bleed your sister."

The next slice was deeper, and Cyrus tried to huddle Abla between her and Tommaso, but my strikes were deadly and precise. I stabbed a fork deep into her arm, and Abla wailed.

"Skiver has him!" Cyrus shouted, stepping in front of her sister to block her from me. "Skiver wants to see your whole crew burn. Do you think he's found them yet? Do you think he's peeling the skin off that little girl? Do you—"

Her words ended in a scream as I sent two forks arcing with sickening accuracy into her eyeballs. She dropped with bellowed howls, and I let everything else in the room fall. Abla and Tommaso huddled on the floor to cover themselves.

I stepped closer as Abla cradled her screaming sister and even Tommaso shrank away from me. "You get to live," I snapped at her. "For now. Because if I kill you, three more will step up in your place, and I have better things to do than murder every foul, filthy shit that feels like they can own or beat or sell another human. Because now, you will be afraid of me for the rest of your life. When it is your time to die, you will never see me coming."

I turned, seeing Kairos standing beside me, a sword drawn and ready that I didn't remember him having before.

Even though I hadn't killed her, it wasn't the same thing as forgiving her, or letting this go, or going out to face the much bigger problems. I had chosen revenge, petty and swift, and I saw the judgment of that in his eyes.

He sheathed the sword, reaching for my hand. My power ached to connect to his, but I moved out of his reach, storming back to the horses and the Saroccan guards, who were watching us with impassive, unconcerned faces. "Finished?" one asked.

"For now," I told him, swinging up onto my horse. "Let's go. We're wasting time."

# Little Shards

Kairos hadn't even unfurled the sails before I guided us out of the harbor, new fear raking claws up and down my spine. Skiver had Bast for days. If he was torturing Bast, would Bast have told him where the crew was? Would Skiver have been able to get there by now, and climb up the steep cliff?

When the sails were unfurled, my power rushed into them and took us even faster out of Sarocca. Osmost flew in the updraft of my power, looking happy and proud of himself, but his owner came to me with a sigh, leaning his hip against the railing in front of the ship's wheel.

"You need to think this through," he told me.

"We need to get to the island, save our crew, and save Bast. Then we go after *both* our families. That's all I need to do."

"You're weak and hurt and you must have just used a ton of energy taking down Cyrus. If you push yourself like this you won't be able to fly us up to the island."

"Have you had any visions about the island? The crew?" I asked.

"Yes. Nothing worrisome—I can see Navya and her siblings in their house. I see others finishing a new house, and Charly cooking. Nothing bad." He reached for me, but I avoided his touch. "Why are you pulling away from me, Asp?" he asked, but the way he said it, he knew the answer.

"Because you're trying to see where my energy is, and it's not your business. I'll get us there."

"Then what?" he said. "Say you fly us up, save the day, everything's fine. We're going to have to leave straight off to have any hope of catching your brother, and that's including your power at full tilt. You don't have unlimited power."

"My power is strong," I told him. "It's just me that's sore."

"Aspasia—"

"What is the alternative, Kairos?" I yelled at him. "Skiver could be there already. You didn't see him at Cyrus's. You didn't see the hate in his eyes."

"He'll still have to climb up. He only has a day on us, and you said it would take three times that to climb up the cliff."

"And lose another day with Gryph?" I snapped. "No. Never." My mouth fell into a hard line. "You should rest," I told him. "You're tired too, and we both know your power can surge mine."

"I'm rested," he told me, coming closer again. "Maybe instead of just using my energy, you can take it," he said. His brow was tight and wrinkled, but his eyes were on my mouth.

This time, I didn't back away. "I'm not going to take your energy from you."

He was close enough that he skimmed a hand over my knotted hair, and my skin crackled in response. His eyes drifted shut, and his nose touched mine. "Skies," he murmured. "You're weak, Asp."

My lips pressed his for a chaste, brief kiss. "I don't feel weak."

"That's not true," he said, opening his eyes to look into mine. "I can feel it aching all over you."

I rubbed his cheek, feeling our connection dance over my skin. "You make me feel stronger," I said, kissing him again, light and soft.

His forehead leaned on mine. "My heart stopped," he whispered. "When I saw this hurricane you had called just *disappear*, and I couldn't get to you. I called down lightning without knowing what I was doing. I burned a boat."

I knew what helpless felt like, and I hated that I made him feel that way. "I should have let you stay with me."

His lips were damp when they touched mine, for a longer and deeper kiss. When it broke, he whispered, "You're the captain, Aspasia. But between us, I want to be partners. Equals. When I'm afraid for you, I want that to matter."

I wrapped my arms tighter around him, bringing us as close as we could be. "It does. You matter to me."

"What you said to the king—I know that's about me too. I know it's not easy to trust me."

"I trust you," I told him honestly. "But there's more than that. I want you to be happy. I want you to be back with your family. I don't want you to hurt anymore, Kairos. I won't be the person who brings more hurt to you." I dug my fingers into him.

"Losing you would hurt," he told me. "Watching you in pain hurts. Even the idea of what you'll suffer if we don't get to the island or Gryphon in time hurts. It all burns through my heart."

He kissed me, and this time I felt the push, his energy against mine, trying to break through and slide into me. I pulled back, shaking my head. "Stop," I told him. "I don't want to steal something like that from you."

"Then what about a storm?" he said. "You can use me to call one down, and there would be more natural wind for you to manipulate, right?"

"Yes," I said. "But we've already given them enough natural wind to work with. What if this just pushes them faster?"

"You'll push yourself into oblivion before we even engage."

I heaved a ragged sigh. "All right."

He stroked my skin slowly. "We're getting your brother back, Asp."

I leaned forward to kiss him, feeling my power strengthen as I sent it out high and wide, collecting the hot air hovering above the surface of the water and pushing it upward against the cold air higher above us. The warm air was lighter, eager to push up against the cold and displace it, and the cold air rumbled and crackled at being so disturbed, churning against the warm air as it fell. I felt the changes in the atmosphere singing through the world around me as clouds began to gather and form.

Kairos's warm hands stayed on my skin—my back, my hips, my belly—as the rain started to fall, heavy drops that struck our bodies.

I kept kissing him. I tangled my hands in his hair, digging into his scalp, his neck, his shoulders. The ship began to keel as the wind picked up, the deck tilting sideways even as Kairos's kiss made it tilt back again. His hands stroked under my shirt, up my sides, along my stomach, and I felt the first crack of lightning strike down around us as his hand cupped around my breast.

All he had said was that he was a virgin, not that he'd never touched another girl, but suddenly the thought that this might be his first time touching a girl like this made me feel drunk, and powerful, and possessive, and protective.

*I know what I want from you*, he'd told me. *Everything. The little shards of yourself you don't give to other people. I want all of that.*

It was dangerous and stupid and foolish, but I wanted to give him what he wanted. I wanted him to give me his shards, his pieces. I wanted his heart. I wanted him.

The thought sent power pulsing out from us like a wave, and we rocked against each other, my rump hitting against something—the wheel, maybe, or the rail?—and I used the leverage to tug him closer to me, my hands fists against his sides as lightning slammed down around us.

One bolt struck close to the ship, and I gasped, pulling away from his mouth. The storm was in full tilt, and the hull crested high over a wave. Kairos caught me tight again, leaning into me as we slammed down again. "Skies," he said, holding me and looking around us at the chaos we'd caused.

"I know," I said, blinking against the rain as it got heavier, striking and sliding over my skin, slicking new waterways on my body. The wind pitched and Kairos lurched, but I caught his arm, drawing him to me as the ship surfed up a swell and down the slope on the other side, my knees finding the rhythm of it as he stood behind me, holding tight.

"Come on," I said, tugging his hand. He wasn't good on the rough seas, and I knew that, but when I beckoned, he gripped my hand and moved forward. Maybe it was our connection, or maybe he was finally getting his sea legs, but he managed to follow me without falling, sharing in my love of storms, of the violence and chaos that made me feel like a king.

I led him to the bow, climbing up and out onto the bowsprit. I felt his fear at going so far out, and he clutched at the stays around us while still keeping our hands locked tight together. I went out farther, the few steps beyond the reach of the ropes. Below us was the gutter for the anchor to run out, and the iron weight hung just beneath my feet, swaying in the wind.

I shut my eyes. The wind pushed around me, filling my clothes like sails and rubbing my skin, my hair, my lungs. This was home—teetering on the edge of the brink, flying over the violent sea like I was impervious to harm. The boat pitched dangerously, but I never lost my balance.

Kairos tugged on my fingers, and I turned, looking into his eyes. I saw how he looked at me, without anger or reproach. He stared at me in awe. Fully looked at me, like he was finally understanding all the little pieces I was so desperate to press into his hands.

He let go of the stays, and instead his arms came around me. His forehead touched mine and moved, rain-slick and pebbled with water. His nose touched mine, and this moved too, skating over my cheek as his warm hands pressed to my cold skin. Our lips met, and our mouths opened, and we might as well have been flying. Only my toes touched the ship, and that was bucking and writhing like a wild thing beneath us.

The only thing that mattered was holding onto him and pushing us forward into the chaos.

# Betrayed

We stayed on deck together all night. Kairos drifted off eventually, sitting under an overhang on the deck behind the wheel, his knees spread and bent up so he could hold me tight to him between his legs, letting me listen to his heart beat beneath my ear and trace designs on his skin. Part of me wanted my finger to be a knife, cut him and cut myself and stake my claim in blood. More of me wanted to take every scar I could find off his skin and kill the person who put it there.

I was bone cold from a night in the rain, and yet my skin fizzled and burned like jellyfish were tickling along it. I knew I was tired, but something felt so awake and alive inside me, and I believed it had to do with Kairos. Something had changed in the storm. Maybe it had changed long before that, but by the time a red sunrise was peeking murderously through the dark storm, I knew I was never saying good-bye to Kairos like I had to Tanta, or Ori, or countless others before them.

How would that work? He'd never choose the sea over his

family. He'd never leave them again as soon as I got him back to them. Could I leave the sea? This was the one place I'd ever mattered. The one place I was powerful.

"We're close," he murmured, stirring a little as his hand rubbed up and down my wet shirt. The storm pushed us hard to the island; we'd be there very soon.

He tugged my knots so my head tilted up to his for a kiss, a sweet, gentle kiss that stirred up all the things I had just been thinking of never leaving. It was the kind of kiss that didn't know a thing about good-byes.

Then it was over, and he helped me up and groaned as he took my hand and let me pull him to his feet. "Remind me not to sleep like that again," he grunted.

My fingers traced the trail of a raindrop on his neck. "It wasn't all bad," I told him.

His mouth tilted up, and he shook his head. "No, it wasn't." He tugged me closer to him, kissing my cheek, my temple, and my forehead. "I'm going to make us something to eat. You need your strength."

I took the ship's wheel even though my power guided us. In the distance I could see a white smudge that must have been the water sanctuary on Arix, and I drew a deep breath. Not long now.

Kairos came up with biscuits, dried meat, and cheese, and we tucked together under the overhang to eat with relatively little interference from the rain. He looked out, his eyes on the bowsprit as his mouth cocked up.

"What?" I asked, not tearing my gaze from his mouth.

"I feel like I have this sudden clarity about you," he said. "I like it."

"Oh?" I asked, feeling a little open and caught.

He scratched his chin. "When Tanta was talking about Serobini—"

I frowned. "When was Tanta talking about Serobini?"

He grinned. "When you clearly weren't listening. She said that the goddess of chaos isn't called that because she causes chaos, likes it, or even encourages it. She's called that because there is an inescapable amount of chaos in the world, and she stands between it and her faithful. She fights the chaos back, because she's the only one who can." He touched my chin. "That's what you are. Chaos, violence, slavery—you stand between these things and the people who would be hurt by them. You don't do it because you like it or because you want to, but because you know how, and others don't."

I took a breath, but it seemed to sting my eyes so I tried another breath. He watched me, eating his food, taking in my reaction.

"It's a good thing," he said gently.

I knew that. Some part of me was outrageously pleased by this, but another part of me felt cut open to the bone.

One arm snuck around my waist, tugging us closer. "I was always meant for darkness," he said, his face alongside mine so I couldn't look in his eyes. I tensed a little at this, ready to deny it—he was everything good and light in the world—but he just shook his head a little. "Always," he continued. "I was supposed to be my father's Shadow. It's a sort of spy. An assassin if need be. A gatherer of information and a deliverer of punishment."

There was something in his words that called to me, made me feel like we had that in common. "What happens now that he's gone?"

He sighed. "I don't know what the future of our clan looks like—or if we are even a clan still. I'm sure a leader has emerged for those in the desert, but if that letter is to be believed, my brother and sister have a lot of clansmen with them in the communes."

"How are they in the communes?"

"Hiding," he said, shrugging. "There are tunnels in the mountains, they said. I had heard rumors about tunnels that no one could find before; I imagine my sister manipulated them to her will quite easily."

"She's powerful."

"Very," he agreed. "She hasn't had her gift as long as you, but the strength of it—it feels the same. And she has Kata with her, who is a whole other force unto herself."

"Kata?"

"The only remaining child of the last Vis priestess. She's . . . her power is the strongest I've ever felt. Water element." He sighed. "But my point, about the Shadow—violence has a place and a purpose. I don't judge you for recognizing that."

"But you still think that deaths get charged to your soul somehow, like ballast."

He tucked closer on my shoulder. "I do. I think there is a reckoning for the lives we take. I think there's also a reckoning for those we save. In the desert, everything is about balance."

"On a ship too," I said. "I keep count."

"Of people?" he asked.

"Of the people I enslave, and the people I free. For every person I enslave, a pearl gets taken from those that I've freed."

"Where is the count now?" he asked me.

"Three," I told him. "I'm only up by three."

He squeezed me. "Why is it that you only free the women and children?" he asked. "Why commit the men to slavery?"

My eyes shut, and I lifted a shoulder. "I had to draw the line somewhere. It was the most I could do while still operating."

"Is that all?" he asked.

I opened my eyes, easing out of his arms as I turned to look at him. "I was a child slave. I don't think it's unusual for me to have a certain sympathy for the women and children. I know what happens to them."

There was a softness in his eyes that I wanted to curl into. "I just . . . sometimes, when I'm with you—usually right before we fall asleep—I see flashes. Memories of a man I think is your father. You never mention him."

I pulled away from him completely, rain trickling down my back outside the protection of the eave. "You think—what, you think I commit men to slavery because my father was awful?" I asked, leaping to my feet. I felt an absurd need to fish out my wooden horse, the one thing in this world that could prove my father loved me. That my father was a great man.

"No," he said, staying on the deck and watching me. "It doesn't feel like that at all. But you've never spoken of him."

"So?" I asked, crossing my arms.

He pulled his knees up, bracing his elbows on them. "So do you want to tell me about him? Or your mother?"

I huffed out a breath. "My mother died before I even remember her. She died having my little sister." I looked at him, but he was just watching me, waiting. "It's the same story everyone in the communes has. They said they'd pay my father a great sum for his craftsmanship, and they did. Until one day they didn't let him leave, and we were supposed to be brought to him, but the children were kept separate. It wasn't long after that I was taken from the communes to be sold." My scar burned with the need to be scratched.

"The last time I saw my father, he told me to not let Shalia out of my sight," Kairos told me. "He told me I was responsible for keeping her safe." His voice grew rough on the last word, and the ball in his throat moved up and down. "When her husband hit her—when I didn't stop it—I dreaded going home. I didn't want my father to see I'd failed. And then . . ." His shoulder lifted, and he shook his head.

I uncrossed my arms and crossed them again, tighter, squeezing around myself. "He told me to watch out for Pera and Gryph," I admitted. "I told him I wanted to watch out for him—come help him, actually—because he was so tired. He looked broken already. He told me the children needed me the most. Even if they didn't know it, they needed me more than he did." I dug my fingers into my skin. "The next day soldiers came instead of him to take us to the communes. I never saw him again."

I met Kairos's eyes, and they were shining and wet. "He'd be so proud of you, Asp."

I moved over to him slowly, kneeling between his bent-up legs and pushing his arms open gently. I brushed his hair back, and he looked up at me. "You kept her safe, Kai. Her and her child both. Your father knows that."

A tear zipped out of the side of his eye, hiding in his hair. He closed his eyes, and I leaned forward and kissed him. His hands rubbed along my sides, keeping me close, dragging power and comfort over my skin.

I understood what he meant, why his words made me feel exposed and open and vulnerable. *We are the same.*

His hand crept into mine, and I held it tightly. I knew the island—and fate—were creeping closer, but I sighed, my cheek pressed to his, enjoying the protection of a moment when I couldn't see his eyes. "Kairos," I whispered.

He made a soft *mmm* noise.

"I think I love you."

He went still, and I squeezed his hand experimentally. "You think," he repeated, his voice even, betraying nothing to me.

I wanted to pull away then. "Yes," I said. "I don't really know what it's supposed to feel like, when it's not family love. But I know when it's not love."

"So this is not *not* love?" he asked, and the amusement was clear.

Slowly—more than a little nervous to see the expression on his face—I pulled back, our damp cheeks protesting the movement. "Bast and I—and even Tanta, and some other people too—we were together because it was easy. Because we were crew, and touching each other seemed thrilling and interesting and exciting. Bast always wanted me to feel something more than that, and I never did." I drew in a breath and swallowed. "This is more than that."

He smiled at me, and it made the nervous feeling shiver off. "Good," he said.

I blinked. "Good?"

He nodded. "Yeah. I feel more than that for you too, so it's good that you feel the same."

My heart sped up a little, and not because the islands were clearly visible now, racing ever closer. "You do?" I said.

His hand touched my cheek, a slow, gentle touch that avoided my scar, and his smile was bright and unusually guileless. "Yeah. I love you," he said, so very simply.

My breath stopped, and he glanced over toward the islands, ignoring my stunned silence.

"So try not to get killed," he told me, tugging me forward for a quick kiss before releasing me, and headed out toward the foredeck.

Probably because of his easy confession, I took a moment longer to follow him. I smelled it before I saw it, a strange, bitter thread on the wind that was darting between the rain.

Then the claws of warning sunk into my neck like a physical blow, and I finally noticed the dark smoke blending with thunderclouds on top of our island.

We were just nearing the water temples on Arix, almost a mile before I usually started the ascent to Altia's peak, but I couldn't wait any longer.

"Hold on!" I yelled at Kairos.

The *Serobini* arced hard out of the water, riding the stormy wind high and fast, heading straight for the island. We turned at the last moment to curl into the grassy platform where we'd always put the *Ancora*. I could see fire burning and smoke pouring off our village, but I wasn't sure where it was coming from yet.

The ship landed haphazardly—it was larger than the *Ancora*—and I threw off two of the normal four anchors and grabbed Kairos's hand. "Jump!" I told him, tugging him toward the railing.

To his credit, he just legged it to the railing with me, leaped up, and jumped right off. I used the wind to guide us down to the ground, and we took off running through the slick grass. I saw the big hall—that was not on fire—and ran past it. Down by the lake, I saw people and the fire, and ran for them.

"Navya!" I screamed, seeing her familiar shape with a sword in her hand.

She turned sharply, and Arnav beside her turned, dragging a line of fire with him that he rapidly put out. "Nice of you to stop by!" Navya yelled at me as I slammed into her for a hug.

Arnav and Copper were standing shoulder to shoulder, guiding the fire and thick, impenetrable smoke together. Arnav had lit the tree line around our village on fire, and Copper was keeping the smoke low and coiled, both a barrier against whatever—or *who*ever, more likely—had come up from the base of the island. The villagers weren't there, but every member of my crew stood ready with their power or a weapon. Or both.

Except Bast.

"It's Skiver," Arnav told me over the crackle of the flames. "Bast told him where we are!"

"I figured. Do we know if he's still alive?"

Navya shook her head. "Skiver said Bast sent him to get us for Bast's crew because you were dead. But Bast isn't with him."

"It's all a lie," I said. "Skiver had to have tortured Bast to give us up."

Navya didn't look sure. "Not that I hope he's been tortured, but . . . I hope that's what happened."

I scowled. "What else would it be?"

"He sold us out to be captain of his own ship."

No. Even with everything I knew—and feared—about Bast, he wouldn't cross this line. I shook my head fiercely. "Not possible." I looked to Arnav. "Is Skiver's whole crew here?"

"If not, seems pretty close," Navya told me. "Thankfully I was out here with Arnav and Anika when they first showed up—Arnav just lit the whole tree line up to keep them back."

"You did?" I asked, looking at Arnav.

"Copper helped," he allowed. He and Copper grinned at each other.

"How long have you two kept this burning?"

"A few hours," Copper said with a shrug.

My face twitched into a smile. "Nice to see you working together."

Arnav glared at me, but it didn't have nearly as much venom as usual.

"You did great work," I said. "But now we're going to end this. Do you agree?"

Arnav's glare turned mercenary. He nodded.

"Anika," I called. "Stay by me. Fisk and Addy, I want you closer to the lake—we're going to need you in a moment. Arnav, when they're in position, stop feeding the fire. Copper, keep the smoke low and on Skiver's crew."

"Are we going to let them through?" Navya asked.

"Yes," I said. "We're going to get Bast back."

"And then?" Navya asked. "Skiver knows where our families are."

I glanced at Kairos, who had a sword out and ready. "He also has a serious grudge against me at the moment."

"That's not an answer."

"I know," I told her. "But Arnav can't keep the fire burning forever."

"Very well." She looked at her brother and nodded.

"Ready?" Copper asked everyone.

"Ready," we all called back.

They put their hands down, and the fire relaxed, but it was still feeding on the wood and burning in ways that weren't just supernatural, even under a light mist of rain. I called to our water elements to cool a path wide enough for one person at a time.

As soon as it was doused, Skiver came right through, two swords out, and Kairos smiled as he stretched his wrist, twisting his blade.

When Skiver saw me, he faltered a little, but then a menacing gleam came into his eyes and he started laughing. "Your new master has lost track of you already?" he snarled. "Looks like I'll walk out of here with all kinds of toys."

"Where's Bast?" I demanded.

"I'm sorry I wasn't rich enough to buy you," he told me. "But I have been enjoying the thought of some new master breaking you. Just like I enjoyed seeing you powerless and helpless."

I saw Arnav's face curl at this, and even Kairos and Navya looked tense. Skiver wasn't riling me, but he was getting to my crew. Making them angry, which could make them sloppy. Arnav's hands were sparking, and I stepped forward.

"You have nothing, Skiver. You have no hope of winning here. No chance of stealing or selling or hurting my people. You're going to lose a significant number of your crew. You should walk away now before that happens."

He chuckled, a wet, ugly sound. "You don't have it, slave. If the situation were reversed, I'd have killed you already. You haven't killed me, so you're not going to. You don't have the instinct a pirate needs to survive. So you won't."

"I can kill you," I offered. "If that's what you want. But being powerful means I don't have to. Something you wouldn't know much about."

"Enough," he said. "It's time to fight."

Before he finished the last word, he hurled the smaller of his swords toward Anika, and I sent it skittering away as Kairos rushed forward, disarming him in a few short moves. Other men tried to come in the narrow gap behind him, but I pulled Skiver up with my power, letting Kairos hold a sword against his throat.

"Give us Bast," I shouted. "And some of you get to live."

Skiver started laughing, and Kairos pressed his sword hard enough to draw blood. "You are such a fool!" he laughed. "You always thought that boy was a puppy, and he's a street dog. He'll do anything to survive, and he'll take what he can. I didn't capture him. He's my partner now."

"Bast would never!" Anika shouted. "Liar!"

I blinked at her, surprised to see her brother's fury in her too.

"Then where is your partner?" I demanded.

"Off getting the one thing that would make him wealthy and respected and feared. The rarest commodity I've ever heard of."

My crew looked to me at this, and thankfully Kairos had a firm hold on Skiver because my power faltered. Bast was going after Gryphon? But . . . to save him, surely. If he knew he was my brother, Bast would have done anything—buy a ship, partner with Skiver—to get him back for me.

Wouldn't he?

"Good," I told him. "Then we don't need you. Or your crew."

My power was getting weak, but I still had enough energy to snap Skiver's neck. I sent my power curling along his chin so I could wrench it hard to the side, but as I did, a horrible gurgle came out of his mouth. Kairos stepped back, his sword wet with red as Skiver fell to his knees, his throat cut wide open.

For long moments, nothing happened. Kairos looked up at me, and I looked away. "Fisk, Addy," I said. "What do you say you see these men to the bottom of the island?"

They smiled at each other, and the fire abruptly went out as they pulled water from the lake and sent it rushing over the edge, catching every one of the enemy crew and slamming them through the dense, steep forest.

Arnav stepped forward and shot his power on Skiver's lifeless body. Copper stepped up beside him and pulled the smoke away, vanishing it before the scent of burned flesh settled over us, and in moments, Skiver's body was charred ash, smoking up into the mist.

Kairos cleaned his sword and came to me, his arm around my waist, and there was something in the embrace that was questioning, like we didn't know if what just happened would change anything.

"What was he talking about?" Sophy asked. All the crew closed in around me and Kairos. "What commodity?"

I opened my mouth, and closed it again, looking down. Kairos's fingers rubbed gently on my lower back. "She found her brother," he said softly. "And he has the ability to take away elemental powers."

"Then Bast went to save him," Arnav said. "Crew is family. Family is crew."

"Or he didn't," Sophy said. Navya met my eyes, and I knew she was thinking the same.

"This is why you stranded us?" Arnav asked.

I drew my chin up. "No," I said. "I knew Cyrus wanted me dead. I refused to put you all in harm's way."

Arnav rocked back, anger on his face. "That's not how crew works!" he snapped.

"I told her to," Navya said, crossing her arms. I looked at her, shaking my head, but she shrugged. "I might as well have, and we both know it. I had no right telling you to take it on your own."

"Why did he get to go?" Copper asked, looking at Kairos.

"Because he saved her," Arnav said. "Didn't you?"

Kairos laughed. "I'm glad to see I'm back in your good graces. But the captain has a funny way of saving herself."

"I shouldn't have left without talking to you all," I said. "Without voting."

Everyone nodded, and some people murmured things I couldn't hear. Navya met my eyes. "Don't do it again."

Releasing a deep sigh, I pulled her to me and hugged her. There was lots of hugging after this—Sophy examined my bruised face, Arnav asked Kairos thirty-seven questions—but quickly I asked about everyone else.

"The village gathered in the hall," Copper told me. "We thought it would be easier to defend one place than all the houses."

I hugged his shoulders. "That was an excellent plan. Let's go see if they're all safe."

"I'm going to stand watch for a bit," Kairos told me, kissing my cheek. "Just to be sure."

Arnav stepped beside him, crossing his arms. "I'll stay too," he said. "You don't even have an active power. What will you do if they come back?"

Kairos touched his sword, but smiled. "You're right. I can throw lightning now though."

"Really?" Arnav asked as we started to walk away.

I laughed, feeling my heart swell as we headed into the hall.

Charly and Sophy started cooking immediately, and I waited until everyone was settled, warm, and fed before I pulled my crew aside again, calling Kairos and Arnav in. I told them what I knew—about Gryphon, about the Trifectate, about our new ship and shaky alliance. When Navya asked, I even told them how I knew these things, how I had been sold and theoretically freed. The fact that I had been Cyrus's slave wasn't often discussed, and I saw the confusion on some of the younger faces. A little disappointment, even, like me going through the same things they had made me less.

It made me feel like I was less.

"So there are two things to vote on," I told them. "Whether or not to help my brother, and whether or not to help Kairos's sister."

"I don't understand why a queen needs our help," Navya said, not unkindly, looking to Kairos.

He cleared his throat, and I put my hand in his, threading our fingers together. "Her husband found out she had powers, like us. He tortured her, even though she was with child. His child. She's in hiding from him. She's working with the Resistance to make sure he stops killing people like her. People like us."

His hand trembled a little, and I gripped it tight. "It's the same thing," I told them. "It's the same thing as my brother. We go for both of them . . ." I hesitated. They would go for Gryphon; it was low risk, and it was the core of who we were. Everything I had ever done to protect them had earned this for me. They didn't owe Kairos the same loyalty, and it was a much harder prospect. "Or we shouldn't go for either," I finished, my voice gravelly.

"Going up against the Trifectate is dangerous," Navya said softly.

"Not fighting for family is dangerous too," Sophy said, and Charly squeezed her shoulder.

"It seems like too much risk," Navya said. She looked sadly at Kairos. "Please know I don't say that lightly."

He swallowed. "I know."

I gripped Kairos's hand. "The Trifectate king also killed the rest of Kairos's family," I told the others. "Three brothers and another sister, his mother and father." He tried to pull his hand away from me, but I held it tight. "If there's something we can do, I want to do it."

"We don't have the numbers or the powers."

"The Resistance has more Elementae," Kairos said. "Very powerful ones."

"It's very risky," I told them. "There's no way to deny that. And I don't know how to choose between possibly losing some of us or definitely hurting his family. But I do know that very few people are in a position to help, and we are. But we still vote, and we still abide by the vote."

Kairos pulled his hand away from me. "Vote," he said. "I just can't be here to watch it. I can't know who voted against it." He stood, and I watched him walk away from us.

"Are you voting?" Navya said.

"I'm still the captain," I said miserably. I wanted to vote for Kairos.

She stood. "Very well."

I found Kairos pacing down by the burned-out tree line, peering into the darkness, Osmost fluffed into the grass, watching him. When I came close, Osmost flapped without rising, making a harsh noise at me, warning me away.

I bent down, scratching his head. "I know, friend."

Osmost clicked at me, tucking his wings down again.

I stood, going over to Kairos. He saw me, stopped, blew out a harsh breath and kept pacing. "Do you want to know?" I asked.

He shook his head. "No."

I crossed my arms as he paced past me. "No?"

"Not even a little bit. I don't want to hear that my sister and brother won't get the aid they need—that this crazy journey wasn't about faith, or fate, it was just about punishing me and taking me from them when I could have helped. I don't want to hear that we're going to their aid, and I might be responsible for hurting one of those impossibly brave kids. I can't even think about your brother, and you hurting, and what you would be feeling if they voted against saving him."

He switched back, pacing faster now.

He glared at me when I didn't say anything. "I really want to kiss you and protect you and talk with you about my killing Skiver and whether you hate me for it. I want to tell you the things I saw when I touched him, and I never, ever want you to know what I saw when I touched him. And I can't stand to touch you, because

I can feel you're weak and you need so much strength in the days to come, no matter what they voted."

He huffed and shook his head, and Osmost made a noise that sounded surprisingly close to a sigh.

"Don't forget Bast and whether or not he betrayed you. Or betrayed you yet."

I looked at Osmost, who shut his eyes. "You're unraveling," I told Kairos, raising my eyebrows.

"Yes, I am."

"We leave at dawn," I said. "We're getting Gryph, and we're heading for the Trifectate."

He froze, turning to me, his chest heaving. His eyes met mine, full of light and hope, a dangerous mixture that was like a drug to see. He swallowed, his mouth tight. "You're sure?" he asked. "You're sure?"

I came closer to him, sliding my hands over his impossibly tense shoulders and curling my fingers around his neck. I leaned up to meet his mouth, tugging his head down a little, but he gripped my waist and picked me up to kiss me, letting my legs swing. I hooked my legs around his waist, and he groaned into my mouth. "Come on," I told him, easing away from his mouth just enough to speak, my lips still grazing his. "I want to show you some things."

"What things?" he asked, his fingers digging into my thighs.

My lips pressed against his lightly. "Shards," I told him.

His mouth curled against mine, and his nose rubbed my nose in a slow, gentle touch. "I don't want to leave this unguarded."

"Some of the others are gathering logs and mud to start building a wall," I told him. "We should have done it long ago. They're going to start work tonight. So even if those sailors come right back up, we'll have defenses."

"Very well," he said, kissing me again and starting to walk forward.

I laughed. "You're not carrying me there."

"Try to stop me," he said.

My mouth pursed. Of course I could stop him—I could trip him or choke him, probably even hit him hard enough to drop me. But instead I buried my face in his neck and let him carry me back to the main hall, laughter bubbling up inside me.

He put me down inside the main hall with a cough, and I laughed out loud when I saw Charly with her hands on her hips, glaring at him. "More flouncing," she grunted, waving a cloth at us as she turned around to the fire.

He grinned at me, and I took his hand, leading him upstairs. I pulled out my keys from my belt and opened the door across the hall from mine. I pushed it open, chewing my lip as I motioned him inside.

I stood in the door frame as he went in, looking over the two beds, the little figurines covered in dust. He caught my hand, tugging me into the room with him, into his arms. He hugged me tight.

"There's another sibling," he whispered.

I shook my head. "Gryph hasn't seen her in a long while either. I probably won't ever find her, if she's even still alive."

He pressed another kiss to my temple. "We'll find her."

The dangerous hope of that shivered inside my body, and he held me tighter. It felt impossible, to be standing in this room and for the first time in years feel something other than hopelessness.

To know that in the morning, I would set out and I would return with my brother. He would see this room. He would see this place.

I would get him back.

Still tight in Kairos's arms, he awkwardly walked me out into the hall, tipping my head back to look at me. "Is that your room?" he asked, looking at the other door.

I pressed a kiss to the side of his mouth. He reached around me to open the door, and I fisted my hands in his shirt, bringing him into the room. As soon as we cleared it, he shut the door behind me and leaned me against the wall, kissing me soundly as all these hypnotic ideas ran through my mind, of love and hope and future and *maybe*. So much more than I had ever felt with someone else's hands on my body.

Grabbing the hem of his shirt, I tugged it up and over his head, and it broke the kiss for a moment so I could see the confident, easy smile on his face. He watched me, thoughtful and appreciative, as he did the same for me, drawing the laces of my shirt open and pulling it up over my head, letting the knotted ropes of my hair hit my shoulders one by one like heavy rain.

He looked at me for many long moments before he leaned forward, kissing me as skin pressed to skin. His fingers hooked into my thick leather belt, and he used that to pull our hips together. We twisted so he was pushed up against the wall, and I put my hands on his shoulders, leaning away from him even as our hips stayed pressed together. "I don't want to just kiss you," I told him honestly.

He grinned at me. "As you wish, Captain."

"I know you're not in any rush—and I know you haven't done

this before. I just want to know if that's what we're going for here. Or if I need to prepare myself to stop."

He chuckled. "I like the idea that you find me irresistible, Aspasia."

I frowned, and he trailed his thumb over the expression on my mouth. "I didn't say irresistible."

"The implication was there," he told me, still maddeningly confident.

"My first time I was nervous as three hells," I snapped at him. "How are you still *you* right now?"

He laughed, stroking his fingers down my neck. "Because it's with you. How could I be nervous with you?"

I caught his wandering fingers and laced mine through his. "Tell me," I said. "Tell me that you want this."

The laugh was gone, and in its place an intense, warm stare. He drew a breath. "I want this," he told me, bringing our joined hands close so he could bite my knuckle gently. "I want you."

Heat sizzled over my body, and I felt myself flushing. "Okay."

He stood from the wall, backing me up toward the bed as his hands returned to my hips, and the belt there. "And I am nervous. I want you to enjoy everything we do together, and I'm not entirely sure if I know how to do that for you."

My hands moved along his chest as I shivered. "I'm sure you'll figure it out."

He leaned over me. "I will be exceptionally interested in any orders you'd like to issue, Captain."

His arm caught me around my waist at the same moment my knees hit the bed, and he tipped me backward as a giggle escaped me. He lowered me down, and I pulled his sweet smile closer. "I'll get you shipshape yet," I teased. "Kiss me."

"Yes, Captain," he murmured, letting his grin meet my own.

There was no Bast or Tanta or the three others who had touched my body in the dark. He may have been the virgin in the room, but I quickly felt like the more naive one—I didn't have any idea how this act would change when I felt the way I did about Kairos. I didn't know how different I would feel, so completely open and cared for and loved, especially when he was awkward and nervous and instead of those feelings being contagious, it was easy to just kiss him and show him how to do it better. I didn't know you could laugh while your skin burned for the touch of another person.

But by the time we fell asleep, exhausted and close in each other's arms, it was easy to be certain I was thoroughly in love with him.

# Everything That Matters

It was hard to acknowledge I wasn't at full strength when I felt like my body was bursting every time I looked at Kairos, but I wasn't. I was pretty weak, actually—it wasn't as if we'd slept much, and the day before had been incredibly draining while I was still recovering.

When we boarded the ship, I saw Sophy smiling like an idiot, and I followed her eyes to Mihal and three of the other older boys from the village. "What is this?" I called as Sophy came rushing over to me.

Mihal put his hand on his sword hilt. "You need more crew," Mihal said. "You can teach us, can't you?"

"We really do need more crew," Sophy said.

"Pipe down," I told her. "You boys are needed at the village. What if someone comes back?"

"The wall is well under way; the village is strong and protected," he said. "You're down four sailors."

He wasn't wrong about that. Glaring at Sophy, I swung around.

"Navya!" I shouted. "They need to be voted on before we can leave!"

She came forward, shouting out orders to the crew to vote fast. The sky was beginning to shed its light blue in favor of pink, and it was time to go. When the vote was done, we welcomed the boys in by assigning tasks to get us on our way.

"Anika, Kairos," I called. They both came over as the sails were dropping. "I think I'm going to need both of you to get us down. Anika, can you push us for a while so I can rest?"

"Yes," she said enthusiastically. "I've been practicing too."

"Good," I told her. "Riggers down, weigh anchor, and let's get under way!" I shouted out. The riggers started scrambling down the rope ladders as Kairos and Anika both reached for my skin while leaving my hands free.

I pushed air against the sails, luffing them out, and I felt my power falter weakly before the surge of Anika and Kairos kicked in, threading around me, strengthening me. With a deep breath, I pushed, and we skidded forward on the grass.

The ship was definitely heavier than the *Ancora* when fully loaded, and I drew another breath, pushing hard and launching us over the edge. My hands shook as I guided us smoothly around the island. It felt like the trembling started there and ran up my arms, through my legs, shivering some internal source where my power pooled, desperate to hold on long enough to get all my people to safety. The boat keeled in the air and Kairos stepped closer, one arm holding me without breaking our skin contact.

A few feet from the water I couldn't hold it anymore, and my power gave out as my knees went boneless and weak. My heart was pounding and my head hurt—I couldn't make my muscles obey me, even to hold my head up.

"I have you," Kairos told me, letting me pull on his power and his body both. "Anika, are you good?"

She must have said yes, because he steered me straight down into the hold, leading me to the cabin. He half dragged me with his arm around my waist. He didn't say anything, just pulled me down to the bed and as soon as his heartbeat settled under my ear, I was asleep.

I woke after a few hours, Kairos's heart still beating steadily beneath my ear. My body felt like I'd ridden the anchor to the ocean floor and back. "Ugh," I grunted, lifting my head and regretting it.

The heartbeat beneath my ear sped up a little, and Kairos's arms closed around me. "Go back to sleep," he told me. "You need more rest."

"We have five days before they make the Trifectate," I murmured, pushing up off his chest. "I'll just use my power for a few hours and we can sleep again."

He sat up as I did. "I'm not sure that's fair to Anika—or me, possibly."

"None of it's fair," I told him, wincing as I stood and several parts of my body popped in protest. He caught my hips, tugging me back to the bed and rubbing my shoulders.

"I don't know if you can feel it," he said, his voice low and rumbling in my ear as his fingers dug deeply into my shoulders. "But the moment you wake up, your power starts moving. You can't even help it, can you?"

"I don't want to," I admitted softly. I drew a breath, taking advantage of his being behind me where I couldn't see his face. "You can feel my power; you must have known I was about to kill Skiver. Why didn't you let me?"

He sighed raggedly over my shoulder, kissing the lowest part of my neck and then biting it gently. "Because I didn't want one more death on your soul. And he needed to die."

"You're not a killer," I said softly.

"I am," he returned. "I've killed before, and there will be many more deaths on my soul before I'm done. I don't kill when I don't have to, if that's what you mean."

"But I do."

"Do you?" he asked, and his hands stopped kneading, coming around me, rubbing my arms. "You didn't kill Cyrus."

"I could have walked away. I didn't have to hurt her like that."

He kissed my neck again. "There are trade-offs. Power and violence and mercy—they're all bound up together. I can't deny you gained yourself a powerful bargaining chip. She fears you now." His chin rested on my shoulder. "She took your power away many times. I don't think anyone gets to judge you for how you took it back."

I didn't really believe him.

"You live in a violent world, Asp. The goddess of chaos."

His arms wrapped around my middle, holding me tight to him. I rubbed my hands over his arms. "I don't want to be the goddess of chaos. I just want fewer people to be hurt."

"Then we may need violence to stop the people who are doing the hurting," he allowed.

I shut my eyes, holding him as he held me for a long while.

*We.* We, we, we . . . the word spun out into an eternity in my mind. A gorgeous, tempting, dangerous promise.

He kissed me with a sigh. "The natural world calls for balance," he told me softly. "And we answer."

Pulling out of his arms and taking his hands with me, I pulled him up off the cot. "So let's go answer."

He stretched, groaning and twisting in protest, finishing in a long yawn. "Skies," he muttered, rubbing his face. "I'll get a practice going while you speed us along."

We went on deck, and I told Anika to rest, watching Kairos as he worked with the crew and the new villagers in particular. As soon as he had shifted in my heart, the shift in his place on the ship was clear too—people respected him, listened to him, and he was confident in his easy power by my side.

Of course, this also had to do with Bast being gone. No one was challenging him; he never tried to overpower Navya or belittle her, and she in turn seemed to support his knowledge and expertise. Arnav had suddenly decided he worshiped him, and that changed Kairos's standing with the littler ones significantly.

I watched them practice until dark, and Sophy brought a meal on deck as we all tried to relax under the stars. It wasn't a celebration—weapons were polished and sharpened, and those with powers were constantly training and stretching their gifts. There was a tension running through each of us on board like a string, slowly pulling us closer to our fate.

Anika slept through the night, and I stayed up, Kairos by my side, hiding in the crow's nest so I could push out with my power even as we touched and kissed. When Anika woke, we went to my cabin, and it felt like every time I welcomed him into my body we were fusing, some barrier between us collapsing and bringing us closer, tighter, inseparable.

Three days passed quickly, and I balanced the need for sleep and rest with the ferocious desire to push my power harder, faster. We got lucky (or perhaps the natural world didn't dare defy me), and a brisk wind was clipping at our sails, propelling us faster and letting my power work a little more efficiently to trim the sails and keep us speeding along our way.

Of course, it also meant Gryph's captors and Bast would also have a similar advantage.

I was sleeping, curled in Kairos's arms, when the warning struck me a full moment before I heard the shouting, and several moments before someone pounded on my door to wake me. I was already up and dressed as Kairos groggily blinked before he seemed to realize the situation and immediately got to his feet. "What is it?" he asked.

"Sails," I told him. My power was running out ahead of me, flicking over the distant ship. "I think it's Bast. I don't think he's made it to Gryph yet."

Kairos reached for his sword and followed me as we darted out of the cabin. Up on deck, everyone was pressed to one side, looking at the ship. I didn't recognize it, but looking through a spyglass, I spotted Bast easily enough, doing the same. And it was even easier to see his fairly shocked expression before he began shouting orders to his crew.

A moment later he raised a white flag off his stern, readying his dinghy to come over to us. I brought us up alongside him, a hundred yards away or so, far enough that we couldn't be boarded easily and we could take the wind if we needed to.

"Captain," Navya said at my elbow. "Is this a good idea?"

I watched the small boat deploy. "He's coming with two people," I told her. "Peacefully. We'll see what he has to say."

"He's captaining a ship," she grunted, crossing her arms. "And chasing your brother. What else is there to say?"

"He's crew," I told her sternly. "We give him the benefit of the doubt. If Arnav or Anika was taken, I would have partnered with Skiver too to get them back."

"You wouldn't have needed to," she reminded me.

"Since when are you this distrusting of Bast?" I asked her. "He deserves our loyalty."

"Does he?" she asked. "I don't think he partnered with Skiver out of the goodness of his heart. I think he thought you were sold or dead, and he took advantage of the situation and sold out our home. He let Skiver attack our *home*. I know he's been angling for a captaincy from Cyrus. He told me he wanted me with him because we both don't need powers to sail."

I felt a little dizzy. "He said that?"

She nodded grimly. I'd known he wanted a captaincy, but to steal crew from me?

Shaking my head, I said, "We have to hear him out."

I had barely shouted permission to come aboard when Bast scrambled over the railing, coming at me with a fierce hug. "Ow," I said, pushing him away. "Bast, get off me!"

"I can't believe you're alive," he said, gripping my shoulders, running his hands down my arms.

I pulled away. He was totally unharmed, and I looked to

Navya, who was watching him grimly. The rest of the crew was silent, staring at him. The two bruisers he came with hung back, staying by the railing as Kairos kept his hand on his sword hilt, watching them.

"You thought I was dead?"

"I saw you start to bring the warehouse down, and you stopped, and I tried to get in, but Skiver stopped me, and he said he'd find out what happened. He came back the next day and said you were dead."

"So you joined his crew?" I demanded, crossing my arms. "You just believed him?"

He suddenly seemed to understand how everyone was look-ing at him, and he turned this way and that, looking back to me. "No," he said, frowning. "I did what you said. I bought a boat. I was going to go to the island and get the crew, but Skiver said there was a priceless commodity. Some slave whose blood can can-cel out powers. I have the faster ship, so he said he'd get our crew and I went for the slave."

The word "slave" hit me like a slap each time he said it. I cringed away from him, and he stepped closer to me, but Mihal and Arnav stopped him. "Not a good idea," Mihal said softly to him.

"I don't understand, Asp," he said. "I don't understand any of this."

"That commodity?" I spat. "That slave? That's my brother. Skiver knew that, and I can't imagine he didn't tell you."

Thunder gathered between Bast's brows. "You can't imagine that? Why would I *ever* knowingly go after your brother? I didn't even know you had a damn brother, Aspasia!" he roared at me. "You are always so willing to assume the worst about me. Eager, even."

"She's been defending you," Navya said, cutting between us. "When Skiver came to our *secret* home and tried to kill us and enslave us, she said you couldn't have possibly known. You must have been tortured to give up that kind of information. You don't look tortured," she told him, her voice icy and hard.

"He *had* to keep you safe because otherwise he wouldn't get his portion of the prize," Bast said, glaring at Navya. "I'm aware Skiver isn't trustworthy, but the one thing I believe in is his greed. Without Asp, you were all *stranded* up there. I had to keep you all safe, and Skiver was a means to an end."

Navya shook her head. "You're such a fool, Bast."

His face flattened. "Now wait a damn minute. I did what I thought was best, for all of us!"

"You did what you thought would get you a captaincy," Navya returned.

"Why is my ambition a crime?" he demanded. "Why shouldn't I want to be captain? There was no mutiny; I'd never take Asp's seat away. What did I do wrong here?"

"Nothing," I said. Navya opened her mouth, and I raised my hand. "Unless you still want to capture my brother."

Everyone went silent to hear his answer, and I noticed Bast's new crewmates who Kairos was guarding lean in a little at this.

Bast crossed his arms. "I'll help you get him back, Asp. That's what I always envisioned, the two of us having our own fleet. This is about family."

"So Skiver just gave you a ship and a crew and doesn't expect anything back?" I demanded. "If you're not going to sell this rare commodity, your crew might not be too pleased."

One of the foreign crew tightened his grip on his sword, and I saw Kairos shifting, ready to strike.

Bast didn't seem to sense the weight of this. "I'm captain. They'll follow me—there are other scores."

I stepped closer to him. "Bast, don't underestimate these men. If they know how valuable my brother is, they're going to want him. They don't owe you any loyalty," I whispered to him. "Take your ship and get out of here."

He shook his head. "No. I'm just as good of a captain as you are, Asp. My men will obey me, and I will help you get your brother back. I promise."

"Be careful. You can't trust them. Take your own advice."

His eyes narrowed at this, and he looked over to Kairos, who raised his eyebrows. "Yeah, I'm sure you took that to heart," he told me, shaking his head.

"Don't be an ass."

"Don't use what you know of my past to make me do what you want," he snapped. He stepped away from me, muscles in his jaw working and making him look grumpier than usual. "What happened with Cyrus?"

My face was still swollen and discolored from Tommaso's fists, and if Bast had been the one presumed dead, I would have been imagining all sorts of horrible things happening to him. I already had, just thinking he was at Skiver's mercy. But neither of us had started with those questions, and it just proved how broken our friendship really was.

"Don't worry about it," I told him, waving it off. It didn't change anything. It didn't matter. It didn't fix things. "We don't have time. If you're going to help with Gryphon, then get back to your ship and let's get going."

He met my eyes. "I still want to hear about it. Later."

"Sure," I agreed, but I didn't want to tell him about it. Whatever we were right now, it didn't feel like friends, family, or anything more than that. He hadn't earned the right to hear about the pain I'd been through.

"All right. Let's get your brother back."

I tried to smile at his bravado, but I watched him go back to his crew and I knew he was being naive. Navya stood beside me, crossing her arms. "We can't trust his crew with your brother," she said. "Not if they think he's that valuable."

"I know. But the only other option is to use the wind to drive him off course, and at this close a distance, it will be a struggle to send us on ahead and them away. I don't have the power reserve to keep it up. And besides, Bast would never forgive me for it."

Her stern face watched him row back over the water. "I'll never forgive him for sending men to our home. Ever."

"This is not going to turn out well," Kairos warned, standing with us.

"No, it isn't," I agreed.

"Interestingly, I was just thinking to myself before he arrived, 'You know what we need? Another problem. This seems too easy all of a sudden.'"

I glared at him and he grinned at me, ducking forward to kiss my cheek before calling the others to practice.

I pushed us hard for the next few hours. I knew Gryph couldn't be that far ahead of Bast, given their limited time to each have embarked from the port, and for all Bast's failings, he was an excellent sailor. Sure enough, by the time the sky was burning violet and red, we spotted sails on the horizon. I halted us there, waiting for the sun to go down and calling for every visible light on our vessels to be doused. Bast came across and he looked wary, but I got him to agree to let us board first and secure Gryph, and then he was free to get whatever other prizes there were to be had on the Trifectate ship. We planned that I would reach out and ring his bell once we were ready.

The night grew dark, the moon clouding over and hiding our approach as I used the wind to calm the water, breaking any lapping noise that might come from our ships moving through the night.

I brought a half barrel of grain to the deck, and Arnav lit a small flame, heating the grain inside carefully, burning it to the point of gray smoke curling up but not open flame. Copper gathered the smoke, moving and shaping it around us and the ship that was now a hundred yards off our bow as we took to the rowboats.

Kairos put his fingers around my wrist as we settled into the boats, two swords on his hips and a ready calm in his eyes. As the smoke hovered and stung my eyes, I shifted our hands so I could curl my fingers around his, our hands clasped tight together.

My power was rushing out ahead of me, searching through the Trifectate ship. Damn, they were well armed. And seemingly ready for a fight—they knew the value of what they had, and they were ready to defend their "cargo."

Trying to avoid killing blows, I held on to Kairos and used his energy to make crude, quick work of them, shoving some into walls, knocking them against whatever I could sense with my power. I started with those guarding the brig where Gryph was chained and worked my way up, not wanting to risk finding a sword at Gryph's throat.

The main deck was the worst. They had seen the smoke and though that distraction allowed me to pick a few off, they saw their fellows going down and shouts rose up, the whole place going into full alarm.

Looking over to the other rowboat, I brushed enough smoke away so that Arnav and Copper could see me nod. Fisk and Addy were in the boat with them, and they had orders to get nowhere close to the enemy ship.

Fire burst onto the deck of the Trifectate ship as our small rowboat knocked into the side. I grabbed for the ladder, keeping my eyes up as Kairos, Mihal, and one of his friends followed me. Someone leaned over the rail with a crossbow, and I knocked it into his face before tossing it in the ocean.

I leaped over the edge and into pandemonium. They were rushing to put out the fires on the deck, and as soon as they doused one, another flared up. The sails were starting to smoke, and the sailors were panicking.

"Go," Kairos told me. "We'll take care of this; you get him back."

I didn't like the idea of leaving Kairos—or having him leave me—but this was the plan we had agreed on. So with one last drag of our fingers, our connection broke and his sword met foreign steel as I ran for the hold.

I was barely inside the doorway that led down when someone grabbed my belt, throwing me down the stairs. My power cushioned the blow, but I still slammed down, stunned for a second as someone kicked my stomach and sent pain arcing through my body.

He wound up to kick again and my power shoved him back

against the stairs, his head bouncing against the wooden step before he lay still.

I coughed, shaking my head as I got up to my feet. Two more men were rushing toward me, and I shoved one into a hammock, twisting until he was tied there, and I slammed the other against the wall. He reeled back, fell, and went still.

The ship wasn't built like mine, and it required my power to find the door that led to the lower levels. It was by the stern cabin, and I ran for it, jumping over the bodies I had left. I sent my power ahead of me as I burst through the door, running down the stairs. There were three different compartments—one that could load grain from above, one that was probably their treasure hold, and a final one, the largest of the three.

My skin felt clammy and cold as I walked toward it. The guards that I had already knocked out were slumped in front of the door, but it wasn't the danger of the present moment that was shivering my skin.

The ship was just like the one I had been brought over on, the one where I had spent so many days huddled against other people, the filth and the scent so powerful and debilitating it became a thing, a monster that could kill, striking at random.

I could smell it. I could taste it. Every inch of my body remembered what it was like to be on that ship; the memory of it was carved into the scar on my cheek, dragged up every time I smiled or laughed or spoke. Haunting every moment I lived in this world.

My hand on the door shook, and the only thing that gave me the strength to turn it was the soft sound from inside. My brother was in there, and if I could stop his fear, maybe it would be enough for both of us.

I opened the door, and the room looked smaller without so many people in it. Maybe it was smaller; it wasn't the same ship. But the shackles were still there, lining the floor, so many it looked physically impossible. Sitting, hugging his knees, was Gryph.

I broke the chains on him and pushed him up with my power. "Are you hurt?" I asked, searching for any sign of blood.

He shook his head as I ran to him, wrapping my arms around him the second I got to him, and to my shock, I burst into tears, gripping him so hard I was probably hurting him. But he hugged me back too, stronger than I thought he was.

"You came," he shuddered into my ear. "You're here, you came, you said you would."

"I came," I told him, not even trying to stop the tears. "I'm here. I'm here. Never again. You're never leaving me again."

"I thought someone bought you," he said.

"We are *not* slaves," I growled in his ear. "We will not be chained."

I heard a bell ringing, and I jerked my head up. I hadn't rung that—it was too soon for Bast's crew. I didn't want them anywhere near my brother.

"We have to go," I told him, reluctantly pulling back. I took his hand, holding it tight as I looked at him. "Are you strong enough to walk?"

He nodded. "I'm fine." He chafed his thumb over my hand. "You're not though, are you?" He looked at our hands. "You feel . . . weak."

"Strong enough to get you out of here," I promised him. "Just don't get cut this time."

We ran through the decks, and even when our hands broke

apart, my power still swirled around him, tugging at him, holding him close to me. It felt different than it had with anyone else—almost like feeling someone's pulse, I could feel something beating beneath the surface of his ability, a tremendous, contained power that was humming with life.

As I reached ahead with my power, I felt the deck crawling with new problems—Bast and his crew were on board, and the fight was ending quickly.

I halted before running up the final staircase; we had only seconds. I looked around wildly. "Here," I said, running to the captain's cabin. I broke through the door, remembering a fancy thing I'd seen on our approach that wasn't common on many ships—a little balcony for the stern cabin. I ran out onto it. "Don't move too much," I told him. "When you get there, get straight on the ship. They'll protect you."

"What?" he yelped, but I already had him in the air, flying up and over to the rowboat with the kids on it. He landed a little hard—and from the sound of it, a little on top of Fisk—because I couldn't see well without Kairos's power to boost me, but he was in the other rowboat. I shoved them toward the *Serobini* and climbed up on the railing, jumping and climbing onto the stern deck.

Bast's crew was running down below, looking for me and Gryph, and I stalked forward in the smoke and shadow to see Bast, two of his crew, and my people, all with swords drawn. The remaining Trifectate crew who were conscious and alive were on their knees, their hands behind their heads.

Bast and his people not only outnumbered mine, but surrounded them. But they weren't disarmed yet—and Kairos with a sword in his hand was certainly a dangerous thing.

"What are you doing, Bast?" Kairos asked him.

Bast looked guilty at least. He shook his head. "What I have to."

"They're gone," one of the crew shouted up.

Before Kairos could even look surprised, I sent my power ruffling through his hair, and he grinned. "You should just go, Bast."

"We've got you," he said. "She's not going to let you get hurt, is she? Do you think she'd trade you for her brother?"

"Do you have me?" Kairos asked, smiling at Bast. "Most people are very uncomfortable while I still have a sword in my hands."

"You're not doing much with it," Bast scoffed.

"I don't want to hurt you," Kairos said, his head cocked lightly to the side. "Because that would hurt her."

"We need his blood. They won't kill him—I won't let them. We just need enough of his blood to sell so they can still get their money and I can keep her brother safe."

Kairos shook his head slowly. "She deserves better than this from you, Bast."

"Really?" he spat. "We are *only* in this situation because she never trusted me with the truth. She did this, not me."

There was still a little fire burning on one of the sails, and I sent wind to it, flaming it up, carrying it over to the other sails and sending sparks to Bast's boat. I fed the little fire with wind, letting it flare.

Bast turned as someone shouted, and I ran forward, pushing Kairos, Mihal, and the other boy—whose name I really had to learn—with me over the railing. Mihal shouted, but I guided everyone safely down into the waiting rowboat, shoving away from the edge.

As soon as we piled into the rowboat, Kairos shouted, "Asp!"

and grabbed me, dragging me underneath him. He grunted as I pushed the boat hard toward the *Serobini*, and I looked up to see a bolt in his arm and Bast glaring at me from the railing of the ship with a crossbow in his hands.

I curled Kairos in my arms, unable to look away from Bast. I understood that Bast had been in a bad position—I'd known before he did that his crew wouldn't let that score through their hands. I didn't fault him for that—maybe for his stupidity, but not for the actions of others.

But that arrow was meant for me. He had gone from loving me to trying to kill me, and I could almost see the final thread of my loyalty to him severed.

"I'm enjoying this treatment," Kairos murmured in my ear, "but I'm well enough."

I turned my head a little, petting his cheek before I kissed him full on the mouth. I heard one of the other boys snicker, but I didn't give a damn. "You jumped in front of an arrow for me," I whispered when our mouths parted.

He grunted with a grimace. "I happen to like you alive."

I kissed him until our boat bumped into the *Serobini*, and we pulled apart so the others could climb up the ladder. My crew tossed ropes down, and Kairos and I stayed in the boat as it was hauled up.

"Addy?" I called. They all had scrapes and cuts, but the bolt was the worst of it.

Kairos squeezed my side. "Go on," he told me. "I'll be a good boy and get fixed."

I kissed him once more and took a deep breath. "Arnav?" I called. He appeared with Copper beside him, and I pointed to

Bast's ship. "Do what you can to burn it to the ocean floor," I told him.

Arnav looked delighted, but Copper looked concerned. "They'll be stranded. The other boat doesn't have sails."

"That's exactly the idea," I told him.

He shrugged, and Arnav went to work. Anika jumped in, holding her brother's hand and helping shape the flames.

Like fierce warriors, Navya and Sophy stood to either side of my brother. He was sitting on the stairs, already eating some soup and bread, and Sophy had her hand on his shoulder, mothering him. They both looked at me, and I felt a rush of love run through me. This was family—they would protect mine as I protected theirs. I came forward, putting my hand on Sophy's neck and touching our foreheads together, and she tugged Navya closer to do the same.

"Thank you," I murmured into the safety of the space their bodies created.

Navya squeezed my arm, and Sophy just nodded with a sigh. I sat down beside Gryph, shoulder to shoulder, and I felt tears rising up again.

"Tell me everything," I whispered to him.

"I missed you," he said, pushing against my shoulder a little.

"That's not everything," I told him, smiling softly.

"It's everything that matters," he said.

I leaned into him. "I missed you too."

# Pray to Whatever Gods You Believe In

We went down to my cabin and stayed up most of the night, talking and telling stories—some of them painful, some of them happy. He told me about his power and how strange it had been to realize what he could do, something that was defined more by the people he was around than his own innate abilities. From what he said, it seemed like his power either started after or around the same time as the earth powers began to emerge, a final balance to all the elements.

I didn't know if that meant that, like a flotilla joining the same course on the seas, the Elementae were finally complete, a full force that would be impossible for the Tri King to eradicate completely—or if it meant that with something that could harm us, the threat to the existence of the Elementae was never greater.

I couldn't believe that having my brother by my side would make me anything but stronger.

He was so curious about my power, and I could see his

jealousy at how active it was. I could use mine to protect me, and his could only hurt others.

Now I would use our powers to protect us both.

He asked about Bast and what he meant to me, but he was much more curious to hear about Kairos. He seemed to like the idea of me having someone like that, and when I asked whether he'd found anyone for himself, he said that chains kept the bad people close and the good people far.

"No more chains," I reminded him.

He linked his fingers through mine, a very different kind of bond. "No more chains," he agreed.

Sometime around dawn, Kairos came down to the cabin, knocking on the door and carrying a trayful of breakfast in one hand.

"I'm going to get some fresh air," Gryph told me. I caught his hand, shaking my head, but he pulled away with a slow smile. "We've got all the time in the world. Don't we?"

My heart cracked a little. It wasn't something I could promise, it was barely something I could even hope for, but I still said, "Yeah, we do."

"I didn't mean to interrupt," Kairos protested. "I just wanted to make sure you two were fed."

Gryphon stood in front of Kairos. They were almost the same height, and Gryph stared at him for a long moment. "Thank you," he said.

Kairos wasn't smiling as he nodded once, almost like he was bowing his head rather than agreeing. "You're welcome," he replied.

Gryph moved past Kairos, stealing some food from the tray, and Kairos came in. I took the tray from him, pulling his sleeve up to check his arm even as his free hand came around my back, tugging me closer to him. There was a bandage on it, but it was free of blood. "Addy didn't heal you completely?" I worried.

"It's a little sore, but that's it," he said, ducking his head to kiss my neck. He rose up, looking at me as I covered the wound with my hand. "Something tells me you got no sleep last night, even without me to bother you."

"I don't feel tired," I told him. "I feel like my heart is going to burst. I feel whole. It seems like the most dangerous time to possibly feel like that, right as we're about to go into battle. But I want you to feel this too," I said, stroking his cheek. "I want to see your happiness when you're with your sister and brother again. When you become an uncle."

His eyes closed as a happy smile blessed his face. "An uncle. Can you imagine?"

Hope, that old enemy of mine, danced in my chest. "I can imagine. It scares me a little, imagining these things."

He turned so he could press a kiss to my palm on his cheek. "Because you haven't had enough good things happen to you, Asp. It's time for that to change."

I shivered. "Let's save this kind of talk for after the battle. We must be coming close to the Trifectate shores; we have to make a plan. Have you sent Osmost out?"

"Yes," he said. "It should take him a few hours to return at best. He should be able to find Rian or Shalia fairly quickly if they're not underground. If they are, it will be longer."

"He can find them underground?"

He lifted his shoulder. "Osmost has done more shocking things. And he's always been very attuned to my family."

"Then we're in the eye of the storm," I murmured, and he

nipped my hand. I laughed, pushing back to wrap it around his neck, tugging us closer together. "What shall we do for a few hours?"

"Rest," he said emphatically, kissing my nose. "You can't seduce me. I am unseducible when your safety and health are involved."

I chased his lips, but he kept them away from me, and I laughed. "I'm sensing a challenge here," I told him, tugging his body so that he started to walk me back toward the bed.

"No. No challenge. Just sleeping."

"Maybe a little kissing," I told him, trying to kiss his mouth and getting his cheek.

"No kissing," he said, catching my arms as my hands started to wander. "I will restrain you if necessary."

"Just a kiss," I insisted.

He narrowed his eyes, but his mouth was smiling as it met mine, and I pulled him, knocking us onto the bed. I rubbed my leg along his, and he chuckled, catching me and twisting me so a moment later, he was curled behind me, his arms trapping mine in a bear hug. I struggled, but he held me tight. "You couldn't behave," he told me, kissing my cheek again. "Now sleep."

"By the way," I said, giving up struggling and instead sinking into the only time I'd really ever enjoyed being restrained. "I love you."

He laughed, a low rumble against my back. "I know. I love you too."

We'd slept for a few hours, furled the sails, and kept the ship out of sight of the main channel into the communes, keeping eyes out all around to make sure no other ships were coming.

Osmost returned at the end of the day. He came shrieking up, dropping a paper into Kairos's hands before wheeling and diving at the water for a snack. Kairos unfolded it with a sharp *whoosh* of breath, frowning as he read it.

I didn't wait to see his reaction. "Navya, Kairos, Mihal," I called. "My quarters."

He hadn't been called, but Gryph looked at me, and I nodded. We all went down below, and Kairos met my eyes. "What does it say?" I asked.

"It's from my sister," he said, and the words tangled in his throat a little. He shut his eyes for a long moment, and I wondered if it felt anything like seeing Gryphon again when he was still out of reach.

"And?" I asked softly.

"The Resistance has an army," he confirmed. "Nearly fifty Elementae, and some soldiers besides. Galen believes that more of his soldiers will either join them or refuse to fight, but we can't count on that."

"Who is Galen?" I asked.

His jaw shifted. "The brother of the king," he said, and at my sharp intake of breath, his eyebrow lifted. "Also the founder and leader of the Resistance."

"Quite a family," I said, crossing my arms. I had sketched out a map of the communes—they were built on flat land in the arms of a mountain range, and they had an incredibly well-fortified harbor because of two massive jetties that would let only one ship pass at a time.

"The trouble will be coordination," he said. "The army is deep in the mountains above the palace"—he tapped the left edge of the map—"and they'll have trouble getting too far into the communes without notice. We'll have to start the attack before they can join. Shalia said they'll be able to get some people down into the town here," he said, his finger moving to the left side closer to the jetty, "but she can't risk being seen."

I looked at Gryph. "We can tell her some places in the town to hide," I offered. "There's a cave that she could probably find fairly easily where all the local kids go swimming."

Gryph was looking at Kairos though. "Do you know that's our home?" he asked. "That's where we grew up. Before the communes even existed, we were there."

Kairos looked at me, sighing. "I had my guesses."

"What if Pera is still there?" Gryph asked me.

"No one in the town gets hurt if I can prevent it," I told him. "If she's there, we'll find her as soon as the dust settles." I tapped one of the stone buildings closest to the dry docks. "Our best bet is to use water from the harbor and flood the whole thing. Each commune is essentially a giant stone cell laid out on a massive grid."

"So if we flood the pathways between the cells," Kairos agreed, "we can effectively halt their movements without hurting anyone. Will the cells start flooding too, though?"

I lifted my shoulder. "Very slowly. Maybe a few inches over the course of hours. However, if we break the doors to the dry docks, they'll fill with water. That is going to take water out of the bay. We'll need a lot of water—more than we naturally have here—to stand a chance."

"I think Kata can handle that," Kairos told me.

"What then?" I asked. "What does the Resistance need? There are thousands of soldiers in the communes. Even if we flood the communes, they'll get out eventually. How do we save the slaves and detain the soldiers?"

"They have a third of their fleet inside those jetties," Navya pointed out. "If we can flood things, we can load people onto ships and get them out of there."

"Get the slaves out," Mihal said. "The soldiers can rot."

"They're doing their job," I returned. "We don't kill people if we can help it."

"The Resistance wants to take the communes," Kairos said. "Not just break them. If they can make a stronghold in Trifectate land, they'll have a real chance against the king. Tactically, having the communes and the desert would put them in a powerful position to take over."

"So we get the soldiers on the ships and send them out to sea," I said. "That means if your friend floods it, she has to keep a few of the ships safe at a minimum."

Kairos nodded.

"What kind of defenses do they have?" Navya asked.

"We know about the Oculus," Kairos said, tapping the watchtower in the center. "The Trifectate has been full tilt in rebuilding it last I heard. The jetties are a serious issue. And, of course, there are the regular weapons and a lot of soldiers as well."

"Elementae," I said. "They had some working for them last time we hit the communes. I imagine they have more."

Kairos sighed, a forceful push of air through teeth. "It would make sense for Calix to defend against the Elementae however he could."

"Is Calix the god-king?" I asked him.

"Yes," he said, crossing his arms.

"Very well," I said. "Tell your people to do their best to move into the town under the cover of darkness, and watch for our sails at first light."

"That's it?" Navya asked.

"At all costs, the Trifectate cannot get their hands on Gryphon," Kairos said. My brother's eyes darted around the room, but he said nothing.

"No one gets their hands on Gryphon. Or any of us. We're not losing any more people to the thrice-damned Trifectate," I growled. "So pray to whatever gods you believe in, because dawn is going to bring chaos with it."

We shared the plan with the rest of the crew, and Sophy grumbled and set off to make the meal of her life. Mihal went down to help her with a blush and a shy smile, and I let them. I hoped there would be time enough for them to do everything her older sister would disapprove of.

Fisk and Addy got their instruments, and to my surprise, Gryphon found something he could drum on and chimed in with them. The easy way they made space for him shattered me.

We didn't dance. We clapped and shouted, beating away the impending sense of danger and disaster with the violent slap of our hands and the pitch of our voices, but dancing seemed like it was too much, as if instead of defiance it would just invite a devil onto our deck.

Sophy and Mihal brought the food to the deck and sat together, his arm wrapped around her, and I saw Kairos sitting by Gryphon. I brought them food, sitting one step below Kairos and wedged between his legs, Gryph beside me. My heart was so full.

That, more than anything else, scared the hell out of me. It seemed like the worst possible time to be happy.

I wasn't the only one lost in my own thoughts. Kairos was holding me, touching me, but his eyes were distant, and I pinched his leg. He looked down at me. "Yes?" he asked.

"You're worried."

He nodded. "I can't call any visions about tomorrow. Nothing about it is clear to me."

"Now you know how the rest of us feel."

"It makes me wonder," he said. "I don't think anything about tomorrow is settled. Nothing is meant to be, meant to happen. It feels like the whole world is hinging on this battle."

I leaned my head against his propped-up knee. "Better than bad visions, right?"

He didn't answer, and I looked up at him. His face was drawn and tight. "I'm going to try to call something," he said, leaning down to kiss my head.

I frowned in worry, but he stood and walked to darkness on the stern. Gryphon watched him go. "He can see the future?" he asked.

"Sometimes. It's difficult to control." I looked at him thoughtfully. "Can you take away powers without bleeding?" I asked.

"Usually," he said.

"Can you focus it? Like I can point my power—if you were using it to disable someone, would everyone around feel its effect?"

"I don't think so," he said. "I'm not sure."

I wondered if that would be useful for tomorrow. Wondered if it was worth the risks.

"Do you mind if I go with him?" Gryph asked. "I haven't really seen many people using their powers."

I smiled. "You're free now, Gryph. Do what you'd like."

My brother bumped my shoulder and stood, going to follow Kairos to the stern deck.

I leaned back on the stairs, watching my crew, and Navya quickly replaced my brother at my side. "I'm sorry about Bast," she said.

I glanced at her. "We're both sorry about Bast." I sighed. "Whatever happens tomorrow, I want your eyes on the kids," I told her. "Not me. Don't feel bad about that for a second. If you're protecting them, I have less to worry about."

She met my eyes. We both knew she would protect her siblings with her life—that wasn't really what I was saying. I was trying to give her permission not to be distracted by anything else. "We've had a damn good run," she told me.

I laughed. "Don't tell me it's over."

She turned, looking toward the rear deck. "It's fine if you want it to be. We'll manage. The king will find a new secret weapon. Cyrus will find someone else to hate. You can just walk away."

"Not yet," I told her honestly. "I'm not ready to leave the sea. But I am beginning to understand there might be things worth leaving for."

"This is why I don't gamble," Navya said, shaking her head. "I never would have guessed those words would come out of your mouth. Certainly not on account of a duster. But it's good. This isn't a life you were supposed to stay in forever."

"It's the devil's bargain," I said, lifting my shoulders. "All over again. I could free so many people with the king's protection. But it means more death. More risk. More pain."

"More good-byes," Navya said, craning her head back to look at the stars. "Always, more good-byes."

I followed her gaze as the weight of that settled into my chest. "I don't want—" I started, but I stopped as I heard a grunt and a thud from the stern deck. Navya and I both jumped up, scrambling up one short staircase and the next to the stern deck. Gryph was sitting with his head braced between his knees, and Kairos was standing, leaning over him, breathing hard.

"Gryphon, look at me," Kairos said, his hand on his shoulder.

"Gryph?" I asked, my voice much higher and more full of fear than I thought I was capable of when no one was bleeding. I slid to my knees beside him, and Navya held back. "Kai, what happened?" I asked.

Kairos straightened as I rubbed Gryph's back. He was holding his head, breathing hard. "I don't know. He . . . I think there's more to his power than we know, Asp."

"What do you mean?" I demanded.

"He touched me, and it felt . . . it felt like touching you, but tenfold. I think he can magnify powers *and* take them away."

"What?" Navya and I both demanded.

"Ugh," Gryph said, raising his head and blinking. "Three hells, does it always hurt like that?"

"Does what always hurt?" I asked.

He rubbed his temples. "His visions."

"You saw his visions?" I asked.

Gryph nodded. "A piece, I think. But really. Is that pain normal?"

Kairos shrugged. "Common, if not normal."

Gryph moved, then froze, gripping his stomach. Then he relaxed, breathing deeply and slower. "You saw visions?" I asked.

"Yeah," he grunted. "That's never happened before. Sometimes

I can really feel someone using their power—that happened with you and the wind—but this was different. Did I see the same thing as you?" he asked, looking to Kairos.

"I don't know," Kairos said, frowning. Then they both looked to me.

Navya sighed. "This sounds like a longer conversation, so if no one's bleeding I'm going back to the wheel."

She left and I stood, taking Kairos's offered hand and helping Gryph slowly to his feet. "What did you two see?"

Kairos's eyes shifted to Gryph, a thread of worry sliding through them that I didn't like, but Gryph smiled. "I think I'll leave that one to Kairos."

I flushed, turning to Kairos, but he shook his head. "Nothing . . . shocking," he said, but his eyes shifted away from me.

"What the hell did you two see?" I demanded.

"I think his power shot me into the distant future," Kairos said. "Very distant."

Gryph grinned. "Not that distant." He chuckled.

"So you *magnified* him? Did you know you could do that?" I asked of my brother.

Gryphon shook his head, wincing and heaving out a breath. "No. Honestly, I've never been in a situation where I wanted to *help* an Elementa—and where I wasn't bleeding. Most of the time my mas-master just used my blood on other people," he said quietly. "I haven't even known I had *any* power for very long."

"It was intense," Kairos admitted, looking at his hands. "Much more than a flash. It was like a whole life, in a minute."

I crossed my arms and looked between them. "Which brings me back to what exactly you saw that you're being so cagey about."

"I'm going to . . . go," Kairos said, frowning as he ducked past me.

"What did you see?" I demanded again, pushing my brother.

"Nothing," he said, a small smile on his face. "Just that you're happy. And still with him."

I couldn't help being pleased by that, but I tried to scowl and pushed him again. "Well, the future changes," I told him.

His smile faded. "It does?"

"Yeah," I said. "I mean, it can. It doesn't mean we won't all be happy. It means it just might not be the way he saw it just now."

He looked down, and I wished I knew what he had seen. I wished we hadn't been apart for seven years and he would know how to trust me with whatever he was feeling.

His eyes followed into the darkness where Kairos had gone. "You should take it easy on him. These visions hurt."

I brushed his hair back. "I'm sorry."

He shook his head. "You didn't do anything. You don't get to think you're responsible for all the suffering in the world, Asp. Please remember that."

I gave him a rueful smile. "Please keep reminding me of that?" I asked.

He looked at me for a long time, the worry in his gaze making me uneasy. "As long as I'm able." He shook his head. "Give me your hand," he said.

I put mine in his, and I felt his power roiling right below the surface. The power shifted and moved, but it didn't break out.

He sighed. "I don't know how to do it again. With Kairos, it just pulled right out of me."

I took a deep breath, remembering how I could pull on

Kairos's power. Reaching into him, my power breached his walls and suddenly started drinking him in, gulping in a feeling like liquid sunlight.

My crew yelped as the sails filled so hard we keeled portside and my hands broke from Gryphon, the force of my boosted power leaving as fast as it had come.

I jerked back, my skin tingling and burning where we'd touched. He was staring at his hand, stunned. "Oh," he breathed.

My heart was beating too fast as the feeling rushed through my veins like a thousand-proof liquor. I sucked in a breath, putting my hand to my chest. "Gryphon," I gasped.

"I can help," he said. "If you can pull this from me—I can help tomorrow."

I couldn't feel the weakness that had been plaguing me anymore. I knew the value of that, but I still shook my head. "You have to be safe. More than anything, you have to be kept safe, Gryph. I can't lose you and they can't get you."

He nodded. "But I'll still help."

I wanted to argue further, but he put his arm around my neck and tugged me toward the deck. "Come, Captain. Your public needs to hear from you."

I frowned, resisting him. "We don't do speeches on this boat," I told him.

"You should start," he said. "I barely know these people, and I know they're scared. They're doing this because they love you."

He pushed me toward the ship's wheel, and Fisk and Addy stopped playing. Everyone turned to me, and I frowned at Gryph, crossing my arms. "Oh, hells," I growled at him.

He grinned.

I looked for Kairos and found him sitting on the stairs. He got up, his eyes heavy and sad. What had he seen? A future with me? If that were true, why did it make Gryph so delighted and Kairos so hurt?

"Look," I said, stepping closer to the rail. "Tomorrow is going to be terrible. Really bad." Someone coughed, and I looked for Navya, who shook her head. "Hells," I grunted. "I guess—I guess what I should really be saying is thank you. I haven't always been the best crewmate or captain, and you all threw in your lot with me. You've followed me this far, and I will do everything I can to keep us all safe tomorrow. But today and every day, it's been a privilege to serve with you."

"I'm the one who should be saying thank you," Kairos said. "You all saved me and freed me, and now you're rushing into danger to help my family. I know what I've asked of you, and I am honored and humbled that you all chose to risk your lives for this. For me."

"This is family," I told him. I looked over all of them, and saw faces nodding back at me. "We are family."

Copper was near Kairos, and he patted his shoulder. Kairos gave him a small, hesitant smile.

"Enough of this, now," I told them. "Night shift, to your posts; the rest of you, get some damn rest."

There were chuckles, and I turned to see Gryph smiling at me. "Do you want to stay in the cabin?" I asked him.

He shook his head. "No. I found the hammocks, and they're very comfortable. You need your rest too."

I gripped him in a tight hug with a sigh. "I don't really like letting you out of my sight."

He hugged me tight. "Just rest, big sister."

I didn't let him go. *Big sister.* I savored those words. How long had it been since someone could call me that? Years. I squeezed him tight and reluctantly let him out of my arms. "Good night," he told me.

I let him go and saw Kairos a few steps away. I walked over, touching his hand. "I'm going to batten down the ship," I told him quietly. "I'll go belowdecks in a few minutes."

He still looked sad and distant. "Very well," he told me.

I moved past him, checking in with the crew and making sure everyone had their orders for the night, and I saw Kairos and Gryph talking for a few minutes before they both went downstairs.

By the time I got to the cabin, Kairos was already lying in the cot, facing away from me. I got into the bed behind him, curling my hands around his shoulders and kissing his neck. "What did you see?" I asked softly.

He covered my hand and issued a heavy sigh. "A lot," he said. "And there were things I didn't see too."

"You're being cryptic," I accused.

"I know," he said. "I'm sorry. I just . . . I don't know what I'm supposed to tell you and what I'm not."

"Tell me whatever's bothering you."

"You're not supposed to know the future," he said. "It changes things. Especially knowing that it's not really set in stone."

"You're not meant to keep this pain to yourself," I told him.

"It's not all pain," he said, his fingers warm on mine. "Apparently there is a version of the future in which you and I have an awful lot of babies."

I nearly pulled away, but he held my hand, chuckling. "I think that's a little presumptuous of the future," I told him.

"It is," he agreed. "That's what Gryph saw, you know, that he liked so much." He heaved another sigh, shifting to lie on his back and pull me into his side, my cheek over his heartbeat. "I think I have to tell you something."

I looked up. "Something worse than a ship full of babies?"

He smiled gently at me. "That's not a bad thing."

"Says the man who won't have to shove them through his hips."

"You create family wherever you go, Aspasia. Whether you give birth to them or not, we will always have children around us, I think."

I dug my fingers into his skin, irrationally pleased by that idea.

"The vision—it was like I was running through the years, so many images and scenes that I thought I was going to die," he told me, and I listened to his chest rumble. "I saw many things, but I didn't see Gryph."

I sat up immediately. "What do you mean? You mean he dies?" I demanded.

He sat up too, catching my hands. "I don't know. I didn't see him die. I tried to read him again, but I couldn't see anything. I don't know what that means, but you're the one who said that maybe I get these visions to help prepare for them. Maybe I don't get to change them; maybe I just get to tell you to get you ready."

"No," I said, pulling my hands away. "The future isn't set. You saw Ori bleed and that went away. We make choices, and things change. Right?"

He caught my arms. "Yes."

"Right. Right, then it just means I'll save him. Something was supposed to happen, but I'll save him from it."

"Aspasia, what if you can't save—"

"No," I told him, breaking his hold on me. "No. We have these powers for a reason. My brother is not going to die within hours of me finding him again."

"Okay," he said, capturing me in his arms and pulling me against his chest. I was shuddering, and I let him, hugging tight into his chest and letting him pull me down to the bed.

I rubbed my head into his neck. "I'm sorry," I whispered. "It can't be easy to tell me things like that. To even suspect things like that."

He didn't answer, just stroked my back and held me tight.

"I know how much the visions hurt. Are you in pain?"

He nodded. "I'm well enough. I just want to hold on to you, and everything will be fine."

Those weren't quite the same thing, but I held him as tight as he held me, and let us fall asleep.

# Worst Possible Time

We woke up before the dawn. I stayed in his arms as long as I could bear, but my power was already out and racing ahead, searching for the sentry ships in the harbor. We'd be able to get around them and get in place by first light.

"Hey," he said, pulling my attention back to him. "I love you. Remember that."

Closing my eyes, I pressed my lips to his, twining my body around him and hoping it wouldn't be the last time we kissed. "Tough to forget, landlegs."

He held me tight, kissing me again.

"And I love you too," I told him when we parted. "Let's go save the world."

He laced his fingers through mine. "Thank you, Aspasia. For this. For fighting."

One more kiss. And another. "Don't thank me," I told him. "In here we're equals, remember? This isn't a favor. This is just what we have to do."

Another sweet, precious kiss, and we stood, dressing and fully kitting out for battle. I had a second belt of bolts wrapped over my usual belt, and Kairos had two swords and a spare on his back, and knives besides. I looked at him appreciatively, and he grinned. "What?" he asked.

"You're even better looking when you're armed," I told him, and he laughed.

I started pushing the ship into position even before we crested the deck. Tension crackled in the air, and the crew was waking up fast without anyone forcing them awake. Navya was on deck; she and a few of the others who didn't have powers had taken the night shift, and she looked tired but resolute.

Closing my eyes, I stretched my power out, rolling my shoulders as I shook it out like a blanket. There was a good wind, but I needed more. I needed raw power. I needed chaos.

I sent my power climbing like a vine over the threads, winding higher and higher until the air was thin and light. With a yell, I wrenched, twisting the air, pushing cool against warm, high against low, and I felt the answering shift around me.

By the time we were close enough to see the signal fires on the jetties, it was just on the edge of dawn, and the morning was coming in to illuminate dark thunderheads. My heart was beating fast and wild, and Kairos stood to one side of me, Gryph to the other. With a deep, steadying breath, I sent my power out to the fires, pulling the air away from them. The signal fires flickered and died, leaving plumes of smoke where flames once were.

Immediately, we heard soldiers rushing down the jetties, yelling and shouting about alarms and the fires. The wind picked up, my feral pet, my vicious friend, lashing at my face.

My ship passed through the jetties, and as we cleared them, I sent my power out, pushing every soldier I could off the structures and into the water.

It wouldn't buy much time, but it got us through the jetties without a flurry of arrows in our hides or hull. I glanced over to the town—my home, a place that felt as foreign to me as everything else here—and wondered how long it would be before the Resistance came to our aid.

If they were coming at all.

The rain started to splatter on the deck, and I measured the distances. We were at the farthest point from our target, the giant, stone dry docks where the Trifectate built their ships, the source of their naval power. We had to destroy all three of them to satisfy Sarocca, but if the Resistance wasn't here—wasn't ready to aid us—we were going to die.

Soldiers were streaming onto the ships at the long piers to our left. They were smaller boats, designed to move quickly, with sails and rows of oars jutting out of the sides to maneuver. If the other Elementae didn't appear, we had no chance. My power wouldn't break down those hulls, and my power wouldn't get us out of here alive. The storm would run its course, and we would be stranded.

"Addy," I called, and she came and took my hand. I sent my power turning in a circle above the water, and her power started lifting the water up, the two working together to create a water funnel that swirled like a shimmering tornado along the surface of the water, churning with the force of the storm. It was like the water and the gathering, bruise purple clouds connected through this unnatural funnel.

The twister bent and curved, launching toward the other

ships as we rushed forward. It scuttled one ship, throwing it off course, but as our water funnel blocked one, two ships tacked around the twister, the men on them yelling to coordinate efforts to move.

"Anika, take the sails," I ordered. She stepped up as I went to the railing. Bolts of lightning shot down from the sky, and Kairos smiled at me, but both bolts missed the ships.

Addy and I worked together, kicking up blasts of cold spray to slow the ships, keeping wind against them, but they weren't scrambling to avoid us anymore. Instead, one ship lined up a row of long-range bowmen, and I couldn't tell what the other was doing.

"Archers!" Navya shouted.

"I think they're out of range," I told her grimly. I couldn't be certain—every moment the distance between us shifted as we moved forward and they rushed to intercept us. "Arnav! Keep your eyes on the bow—they might have archers as we come into the shipbuilders' hold."

"Aye, Captain!" he yelled back.

A volley of arrows shot out, but they were thirty feet short of us. I huffed out a breath.

"Asp!" Kairos called, and I turned to see the other ship launching something at me. I pushed it behind us with the wind, but before it hit the water, it exploded, rocking a crater in the water.

We all reeled back. "What is that?" Navya yelled.

"Damn kings dabbling in explosives," I growled. "Sarocca has something like that, and of course they think they're the only ones." To everyone, I commanded, "Those cannot come near this ship! Kairos, keep your eyes on that ship and that ship only."

"Yes, Captain," he agreed, but he looked over to the town too.

"The Resistance better be here any damn moment," I growled at him. "Or we're not getting anywhere *near* those dry docks. And furthermore, we're dead."

"Another shot," he warned me, but Addy spouted water up to catch the shot. It lessened the explosion, but didn't cancel it out entirely.

"Archers off the bow!" Arnav reported.

It wasn't even claws at the back of my neck. Now I felt the wind curling around my throat, warning me that if things didn't change in the next moment, we were going to die here.

"Light them up!" I shouted back at him. "Everyone hold on. I'm going to buy us some time."

"Asp, it's too early," Kairos warned me. "You won't be able to sustain it if you take us off the water now."

But Gryph threaded his hand into mine and the wind howled. Pure, unadulterated power rushed through me, spurring our ship on faster as I sucked in a breath. "She'll be fine," Gryph said with a smile.

I heard the Trifectate archers screaming as their weapons lit on fire. I interlocked my fingers through Gryph's, meeting his eyes as the wind whipped my hair from my face, pulling at my clothing, demanding my attention.

"You have to let me know if I'm taking too much," I told him. "If it hurts, or it's weakening you."

"I promise. For now, I feel . . . powerful," he said, and I saw the heady, confident gleam in his eye that I recognized deep in my soul.

I pressed my forehead to his, and I barely felt the tug on my power as the bow tipped up. The deck leaned, everyone holding on, Arnav whooping in triumph as we rose up.

I let my brother go. The water rushed fast away from us, and we were mounting high toward the roiling clouds.

*Untouchable.* Up here, I was the master. I was the captain, the commander, I was the keeper of the skies. Up here, my brother and my crew beside me, I was powerful.

"Stay away from the Oculus," Kairos warned. "They've rebuilt it enough to hurt us."

I looked over at the spindly watchtower that I'd crumbled last time I'd been here and nodded. I keeled the boat, turning us high and to the left, circling back over the piers and army encampments.

"Arrows!" Kairos called.

"Get back!" I yelled, and he pulled away from the edge.

A volley of arrows thudded into the wood of our hull. "It's fine," I said. "As long as they're not hitting us."

"You can't stay up here forever," Kairos told me. "There's no damn point."

"How long until your sister shows up?" I demanded. "All I can do is buy us time. We're not going to be able to crack open those dry docks without a lot of explosives or an earth element."

Kairos craned up, looking down at the ship that had thrown explosives at us, which was starting to turn before it crashed into the massive stone gates of the dry dock.

"Well," he said, lifting a shoulder.

I huffed out a breath. "All three hells. Gryph, tell me if I'm taking too much of your energy," I told him, reaching for his hand.

"I don't think that's how it works," he said, lacing our fingers together. "It's like my ability to shut it off—it doesn't diminish my power, it *is* my power."

I felt the surge immediately, and shutting my eyes to focus, I thought of keeping our ship aloft with one hand, and with the other, I reached out to the turning ship.

It was like trying to capture a fish in a pond, and I couldn't do it with my eyes closed. Gritting my teeth, I opened my eyes, focusing harder. Our ship faltered in the air, and gasps and shrieks rang out around me before I righted us.

"*Hells*," I growled.

"Just like you told me," Kairos said softly, standing closer to me. "Focus on the threads. Focus on what makes you strong."

*Hope.* It was easy to call up, looking down on the small, sleeping town that I had grown up in, the last place I'd seen my father, the last place I'd seen my little sister.

My eyes fluttered shut again, and I tracked the movements of the enemy ship down below. They had turned, but I pushed a gust of wind at them, turning the enemy ship around again, straight at the massive wall that blocked off the hold.

The wind whistled greedily as it swept through my clothing and sails, and I could feel it down below, driving the ship irrepressibly forward.

Keeping my eyes closed, I used the screams of the men on board as guidance that I was doing the right thing. I smashed the ship against the gates, holding it there to give the men a moment to jump clear. I didn't want any death that I didn't need.

The ship faltered and fell a little as I shoved the Trifectate ship over the gate, smashing the thing into the empty hull of the shipbuilding dry dock.

With a frustrated growl, I opened my eyes. Nothing had exploded.

"Hold on," Kairos said, and he grimaced, focusing on the ship.

Three lightning bolts smashed out of the sky, and the first two left black marks on white stone, but the third struck home.

The force of the explosion was so strong it knocked us hard over to the side. "Anika!" I yelled, and I felt the buoy of her power underneath mine as I tried to hold on. Then Gryphon's rushed up to me, and Kairos's.

I drew in a shaky breath as we righted ourselves. The exploded ship was pluming black smoke over orange flames, and we all stood rapt, watching it burn.

"I can't hold us much longer," I told them, shutting my eyes for a moment.

"Asp," Kairos said at the same time Gryphon tugged my hand and said, "Aspasia!"

I looked to where they pointed. The water was pulling away from the shore, and the muck-filled harbor was exposed, lobsters and crabs skittering for cover as their homes were lost.

I turned to see the ships in the harbor keeling over as the water pulled out, coiling out past the jetties.

"Asp, do you see that!" Sophy yelled behind me.

We watched as the water grew, mounting into a massive wave that towered high over the jetties. It seemed to hold for a moment, impossibly aloft, before it broke like an egg and snapped through the jetties, swamping the grounded ships in the bay. It rushed through the broken dry dock's gates to flood the burning ship and hit hard against the other two.

It was incredible to watch from above as the water crashed through the communes, never breaching the stone structures but keeping them isolated, using their own design against them.

"Aspasia!" Anika yelped.

"I have it," I told her, trembling to hold the ship with my power. She dropped her hands, and Arnav put his arm around her neck as she breathed hard.

"Kairos, hold on to me," I ordered. I put my hands out, using them to focus my power as I attempted two different tasks at once with both Kairos and Gryphon coursing through me. I lowered the ship to the rough water and started breaking any of the undamaged, unmanned ships free from their docks or moorings and sending them into the communes behind us.

I held my breath as we sailed over what used to be the land, between two of the dry docks. They were all filled with water; one was shattered, one was mostly whole, and one had a broken gate but solid walls.

Finally, I let every rope of power I was using drop, and my knees went weak. I went down to the deck, and Kairos and Gryphon were both beside me, guarding me as I breathed.

"The doors in each cell are going to let in some water, so we have to work quickly," I yelled. "We'll go cell by cell and subdue the soldiers and get the slaves out." I looked at Kairos. "Your sister and her people can sort through the soldiers, right?"

Kairos nodded.

"Good," I said. "We do not get caught, and we do not get hurt!" I yelled at the rest of them. "Prepare to jump."

We sailed to the side of the first commune cell, and I slowed our ship down as Kairos, Sophy, Navya, and Mihal and his boys and I all leaped onto the wall of the commune. The others threw ropes over as I looked into the cell. Soldiers were running out, pushing the slaves back into the buildings as the soldiers raised weapons to us. I slammed them all into the wall and held them there. "Go!" I yelled to my people.

Mihal and his boys jumped into the cell, bringing people out and helping them climb to the edge of the wall. Once they were all up on the wall, I let the soldiers go and brought another ship knocked loose from its mooring into position behind us, then slammed the soldiers back again as my people helped the slaves load in to the other ship.

After maybe ten minutes we were out of the cell, but there were hundreds more, and this was a serious strain to my power.

But there was nothing to be done. We got back onto the ship, and I pushed the two ships together over to the next cell. This time the slaves got out to help too, and the loading in took less of my power. Every time a girl younger than sixteen or so appeared, I searched her face. I couldn't help it. I would never give up hope that I would find my sister one day too.

We had finished four of the cells when I saw another boat coming down the new waterways and immediately bristled. The sails were furled, and one of the masts was broken—this was definitely powered by Elementae.

When I heard a woman scream, "Kairos!" I knew they weren't here to hurt us.

Kairos jumped from the ship onto the closest wall and just took off running. He leaped with no hope of clearing the ocean, and I sent him flying to the next wall over. He didn't even look back to thank me, and he just kept running. I helped him leap twice more, and then he was at his sister's ship.

I watched him still, hungry for it, desperate to see that moment when he was reunited with his family. They were far away, but I saw him hug her, and another man join their embrace, and possibly two others, I wasn't sure.

"Asp!" Gryphon called, and I turned back to the task at hand.

Part of me kept looking back to Kairos, feeling like he was half of my heart and he had just gone someplace I wasn't welcome.

We cleared another cell before Kairos started running back along the commune walls to us, and I helped him leap over one. He was halfway along the next one when suddenly he just fell, plunging into the water.

I jumped onto the wall, confused. I ran over to the edge closest to him and flew myself over to the next.

Power slapped against me. It was a wind power, and the wind immediately felt tense and conflicted, unsure which master to obey. I shoved back against it as I saw Kairos's head bob up and gasp a breath before he was shoved down again, and I ran fast, leaping off the edge and diving into the water.

The water itself was dangerous. I kept my eyes open, swimming past broken wood, stone, even a sad pair of shoes floating in the water. I saw him, and it almost looked like he was fighting against something on the surface keeping him trapped below. His movements were slowing down, and I swam hard. I had been born by the sea, and I didn't need a damn bit of power to be a strong swimmer.

I surfaced for one breath before diving low, coiling on the ground before shoving up and catching him from the side, bringing us both to the surface. I felt power surge through the water like a hand, scooping us up and putting us on the commune wall as I pushed on his chest. "Kairos!" I shouted, rolling him on his side so the water in his mouth could pour out.

He coughed and almost fell off, and I felt the foreign wind power push at me again.

"Bitch," I growled to whoever owned it. I stood up, guarding his body. The commune cell beneath me had soldiers in it, but no one who seemed to have powers. I cast around, but I couldn't see anyone.

"There!" a woman from the other ship yelled, pointing to the Summer Palace, built into the hills of the communes and currently above the flood of water.

Damn.

Looking back at my ship, I grabbed at our dinghy with my power, pulling it off and throwing it in the water. I looked around for Gryphon as even that made my power feel like a sore, over-used muscle, and I saw him and Mihal running down the commune walls to me.

Was it safer to leave Gryph behind? He didn't have much power without me, which would expose him, but I didn't have much power left without him.

Swearing, I steered the dinghy over to his wall, and Gryph jumped in. "Mihal!" I shouted as he started to as well. "Get back to the others!"

He nodded, and I drew the boat close to me and helped Kairos in as he breathed long breaths, shaking his head. "I like swimming even less," he told me.

"That was a bad example," I told him, squeezing his hand as we all took our seats.

"Get Kata," he said, nodding to his family's ship.

I didn't question him, just sent the dinghy zipping through the water to his family's ship. "Which one is Kata?" I shouted, and a pale-skinned, white-blonde girl appeared, climbing down the ladder. Kairos's pregnancy-swollen sister appeared too, but Kata halted.

"Shalia, stay here!" she shouted. "We'll head to the Summer Palace, and you and the boys figure out the soldiers."

"You need Elementae," Shalia returned, following right down behind as Kata jumped into our boat. Once they were both in, I started to push us, and Kata glared at me. "It's much easier to move the water than to push the boat with wind," she told me.

I glared back, but my power needed the reprieve. "Fine," I allowed.

"What does he do?" she asked, nodding at my brother as we shoved forward.

But I felt the incoming push of wind and turned forward, standing in the boat as I spread my hands, rejecting this other person's power. The air trembled with the force of our conflicting powers, and I grabbed at it, using the threads that connected us to rush back along the strands.

"They've got a wind power in that palace," I confirmed, feeling the source of the power up on the wall we were headed for.

With a heave, the wind relented to me, pushing whatever art the foreign Elementa was working away and letting us pass. The wind was mine and it would always obey me.

The walls of the commune began to crack as we passed by them, and I caught my breath. If a wall broke, not only would it kill many people like animals trapped in a cage, but it would throw us into the mix and take a tremendous amount of Kata's power to avoid it.

"I see it," Shalia confirmed, holding her hands out as the cracks stopped spreading.

A few of the communes sprang leaks, but it didn't seem like this person had the ability to harness the pressure of the water on the stone. As we drew closer, I could see at least four people up on the ramparts of the Summer Palace, and I shoved my power against the walls, hard enough to shake them. They all ducked down and started scrambling off the wall.

"Look," Kata said to me. "If you and I combine our powers, we can create a very pressurized blast of water to break the gates." We were much closer, and I saw soldiers replacing the Elementae.

"I can take any metals away from the gates," Shalia promised, frowning at the massive gates ahead.

"They have explosives," I warned. "We have to get in there quick or they will make a mess of the communes."

"And our ability to float," Kairos agreed.

"They're lighting something," Gryph reported.

I grabbed the pale girl's hand. "Now!" I said, and the boat slowed as I grabbed Gryph's hand too. I wrapped my power around hers like a rope, blasting air through the water as she aimed it at the gates.

A charge exploded right as it hit the water beside us, and people started screaming in confusion in the nearest commune. The palace gates ahead of us blasted open, and the last few hundred feet were over the dry land to the palace.

"Hold on," I snapped, and used my power to lift us up and fly us forward.

"Why are we going into the heavily fortified palace?" Kairos yelled.

"Because those are our people," Kata said. "Whether they know it or not."

"Skies!" he growled, placing his sister between his body and the plank seat as we all ducked while the boat rushed through the open gates. We slammed down into a garden, skidding over grass and into a bush as I leaped up.

"Gryph, stop anything you can that isn't us," I told him.

"I can't do both," he responded. "I think it's a better idea to boost you."

Kata's bright eyes flared at this knowledge, looking at my brother, but I shouted, "Behind you!" as soldiers fired arrows at us.

Shalia held up a hand, and the arrows, with their metal tips, fell like someone slapped them out of the air.

I sent up a volley of crossbow bolts, killing the first round of guards who attacked us. I felt the wind power again. The wind was a physical thing to me, and I grabbed it, wrapping my power around it and pulling the Elementae out.

A young man was dragged into the courtyard and looked at me, shocked. He put his hands up as my power let go of him. "Don't hurt me!" he cried.

Another flight of guards came to the courtyard, and Kairos slammed a lightning bolt in front of them. "Stop there," he commanded. "Shalia?"

She nodded and pulled the swords out of their hands, sending a river of flashing silver deep into the courtyard.

There was only the slightest hint of smoke before the boat suddenly caught fire. I couldn't pull the air out of it without choking us, so I used the wind and shoved us all out of the boat.

It wasn't the only fire. The long line of bushes that marked the edge of the garden had caught fire, creating a barrier between us and the guards. Interesting.

A thin girl with a cruel look to her face stepped forward. There were at least four others—and the boy—with her, the others back in the shadows, pressed against the stone wall.

"Shalia," she called, and I turned sharply.

"Danae," she said, nodding.

*Danae?* Oh, excellent. The Third Face of God was an Elementa?

Danae looked down, and the cruel look of her faded a little. "How is he?" she asked, and I didn't know who she was asking about.

Shalia's breath was ragged—she was looking at this girl with genuine pain. "He misses you. So much. You have to know that."

Oh—the man with Shalia was Danae's brother, wasn't he? Shalia was her sister by marriage.

"And I can go to him now, can't I?" Danae asked. "That's what you would do, right? You'd move heaven and earth to get back to your siblings."

Shalia sighed, swaying forward, and Kairos took a step closer to her. Even Kata seemed tense and ready. "My siblings don't make me choose between them," she allowed.

Danae nodded. "But I chose," she said. "And I picked Calix, not Galen."

"Because you thought you had to," Shalia said. "Because you loved him while very few other people do. I understand that kind of loyalty."

Danae shook her head. "Just go, Shalia. I don't want to kill you, but I won't let you hurt these guards or the others."

"You're fighting for the wrong side," Kata told her. "Your brother kills people with our powers. He *tortured* her. When he doesn't need you anymore he will kill you."

Danae's cruel glare was back, and her hands burst into flame, turning her sleeves to ash. "Don't you think I know that?" she snarled. "He made me like this. He made me into a monster!"

"We are not monsters," I told her.

"What are you staying for?" Kairos continued, and her flames went out. "We're taking the communes. You won't be able to stop us now. Join us."

"Even if you take the communes, he will keep coming, and he will have Elementae fight for him until he can eradicate them once and for all." She shook her head sadly. "He won't stop until you're dead, Shalia. Until we're all dead. You know that."

Shalia stepped back, forming a line with the rest of us. "There's another way, Danae. We're going to fight him, and whenever you realize how poorly he's treated you—how little he deserves your love—I will welcome you at my side. I promise you that."

Danae screamed. She raised her hands, fire rushing over them again and arcing toward us. I pushed at it with the wind, but it caught into a larger flame. I ducked, and Gryph leaped in front of me. The fire went out abruptly, and I gasped.

No, he hadn't just exposed his incredibly rare and valuable power for something so trivial as my skin not being a little crisper, had he?

I stood, shoving him behind me, but Danae was looking wondrously at her hands. "By the grace of the Three-Faced God," she breathed. She looked up, tilting her head at me. "Calix said it looked like blood. It *was* blood," she said. "You are the magical thing he's been looking for all this time. You can take this power away."

This time she drew a knife and started running at me, and I

shoved her away, but it seemed to be a signal to the others, and at least eight Elementae rushed out into the garden.

Serobini, goddess of chaos, would have been very proud of the melee that ensued as all the elements and some other powers, like Kairos's lightning and someone who seemed to be able to control shadows and make mist, combined into one swirling battlefield of color. Danae was coming straight for my brother and me, and with or without her fire, she was shockingly fast. Gryph couldn't stop her power while he was boosting mine, and I needed everything I had to repel her as she came at me again and again, a knife flashing in her hand while she fought with fire and steel.

Even though her fire fed on my power, I was stronger than she was as an Elementa, and I kept repelling her, making her dodge anything I could find before she burned it away. She burned the bolts I flung at her, she got up when I knocked her down. I had the advantage, but not by much.

That was until I heard, "Aspasia!" screamed out in a girl's voice.

I couldn't help but look as one of the Elementae, a short, round girl, started running for us. "Gryph!" she screamed.

*Pera.* Now, at the very worst possible time, my sister was here—and she was fighting for the other side.

Fire flashed out before I could even call out to Pera, burning over my face and side, and I fell. Other voices started screaming my name, and I leaped to my feet as Pera slammed into me. "Pera!" I cried at the same moment as she screamed Gryph's name. I turned and saw Danae drag him up by the hair. There was a burn on his hand and his shirt was still smoldering, and his eyes met mine.

I pushed Pera behind me as Kairos touched my arm. He swung his sword. "Danae, please. That's her brother."

Danae had a knife to his throat. "Get that boat into the water," she ordered.

"You really don't want to take me on while we're on the open ocean," I growled at her.

"The boat isn't for us," Danae said. "All of you can go. You can take whoever you want with you. Whoever wants to go. But I keep him. That's all I want."

"You can't have him!" I snapped. "The last people who tried to take him from me lived just long enough to regret it."

"I believe that," she said. "But you should get in the boat." She turned and looked at the line of hedges, and the fire went out. The soldiers had fallen back, but she yelled, "Kill them!" and they immediately rushed forward.

She slipped behind their lines and into the palace, holding my brother.

I went wild. My power was hanging on by a thread, but this was not happening to me again. Pera's hand slid into mine, and I felt her power against my skin. She screamed like a banshee beside me, and gravel and dirt started flying around, spurred by my wind, whipping through their ranks. Kairos dove into it, his swords flashing, and I just trusted my power to know enough not to hurt him. All I had left was instinct, and heart, and hope.

Goddamned hope.

When we were down to the last few men, Kairos shouted at me to go after him.

"I'm coming with you!" Pera yelled as I tried to pull away from her. I looked at her—another sibling I didn't know except for the same stubborn tilt to her chin we all seemed to share, another sibling I could lose in a heartbeat—and I kept her hand as we ran forward.

I smelled it first, before I saw the red trail on the floor. Blood. Our brother's blood.

"Pera," I said. "Please wait out here? I won't have powers. You won't have powers."

She looked at the floor and looked back to me. "Then you'll need me twice as much," she said.

I squeezed her hand, walking down the hallway as I felt swamped. Even without the blood touching me, it dampened my powers. Maybe because there was so much of it, or maybe something within him was making it more powerful.

Like fear.

I followed the trail into a large room that looked like it had once been used for parties and now was filled with strange equipment. I had heard of the brutal art the trivatii liked to practice—there was more than a little blood staining the items scattered around.

Danae had drawn a circle around him in blood, and he was sitting in a chair, his skin pale and sweaty as she arranged things around him, a knife and a bowl that was collecting his blood from where she'd cut his wrist.

"I will end you," I told her.

Her eyes narrowed at me. "I knew how to kill powerful people even before I had this power," she said. "Did you? Do you think you can best me without it? My guess is you've spent so much time with your power to defend you, you wouldn't know the first thing about doing it for yourself."

"He hasn't done anything to you."

She had the decency to look hurt by this. "I'm sorry. But he will fix everything. He will protect my brother. He will heal me."

"It doesn't last," I said, starting to move slowly in a circle, drawing her away from my brother. She'd left a knife close to him—if he could get it, we could all get out of here. Alive.

Pera started circling the other way, but staying farther back than I did. "What do you mean?" Danae asked, looking askance at Gryph.

"His blood only lasts as long as it's on you," I told her. "Which means you need him alive."

She turned, looking at Gryph, and I took my chance, jumping and slamming her to the ground. "Run!" I screamed at them. She flipped me over, trying to buck me off, but I caught her, flipping her over again and hitting her across the face.

Her response was fast and debilitating. She slammed her fist into my throat and her knee into my stomach in blinding succession, and before I even tried—and failed—to suck in a breath, she was off me and running. My siblings and the bowl of blood were gone.

It took me long seconds to get up again, and I stumbled into the hall, weak and reeling. I slipped on my brother's blood. I slammed into the wall, shoved off, and kept going.

Someone was screaming. It was like I couldn't see everything at first, not really, and all I could understand was that someone was screaming.

Only pieces made sense. Kairos, down by the water. Kneeling. Holding. Pera was close—maybe she was the one screaming. Danae was standing between them and me.

And the blood. All the blood. All over Kairos, bleeding into the water.

Blood that was coming out of my brother.

My limp, pale brother, half in the water, half in Kairos's arms.

I was closer to them. I didn't remember moving. Then I was

beside them, and then I was in the water. The bowl was empty, and the water was red in an ever-growing circle. But it wasn't just that. The blood wasn't coming from the cut on his wrist.

It was coming from his neck.

"I didn't do this," Danae was saying. "I didn't! I didn't want him to die."

"He ran out here," Kairos said. "He could barely hold the bowl. He said—he said—"

"I wouldn't have killed him. He didn't have to do this. I'm not my brother."

"Get the hell out of here, Danae!" Kairos roared at her. "I swear I will kill you myself."

He was so heavy. Maybe I was weak—I wasn't sure if there was a difference. But that was the only thing I could feel—just the weight. I knew I was wet, but I couldn't feel it. I saw my hands stroking through his hair, but it was like I wasn't moving them myself.

"She's a water power, isn't she?" I asked. I raised my head, looking for the girl with the pale hair. "Where is she? She can heal him. She needs to heal him."

Kata appeared, looking confused. She looked to Kairos, to Shalia whom I hadn't seen before, and Shalia's hand covered mine. "She can't. Even without the blood, she can't heal someone who's dead."

Why would that matter? Why was that important? It wasn't.

"Heal him!" I yelled.

"He didn't want to be used against you," Kairos said. "Or anyone. I don't know if he was even strong enough to survive before he cut himself."

"He didn't cut himself!" I screamed.

It was Kairos's eyes that reached me. He sunk right into the core of me, and the truth along with him. There was a reason Gryph wasn't moving, a reason Pera was by my side and crying. There was a reason the pale-haired water Elementa couldn't heal him.

My brother was dead.

My brother was dead.

My brother was dead.

# The Magnitude of Grief

Hope was ash. The worst part was that I knew my sister was there, somewhere, hurting as much as I was. And I couldn't comfort her. I couldn't see past my own grief to even acknowledge hers.

Someone was touching my face. With water. Cool water. And a cloth. I opened my eyes, and Shalia was there. "I remember you," I said softly.

She gave me a sad smile, and it was a ghost of another smile I loved. Just the thought of that—of loving someone, anyone—made my body hurt. Or my heart. Or everything.

"I'm Shalia," she said. "You saved my life, once." She looked around and the smile grew. "Maybe twice, now. Both times we didn't have much opportunity for introductions."

Her smile hurt. The idea that someone could smile hurt. I shut my eyes, but she kept stroking my face with the cool cloth.

"This is the worst part," she whispered. "The first time you wake up. It takes you a second to remember—maybe even longer—but you do. And it happens all over again."

I didn't open my eyes, but I felt a tear slide out and onto the bridge of my nose, then off my skin entirely. I wanted it back. It made no sense, but I didn't want anything else stripped from me, and certainly not my grief for my brother.

"Living will hurt for a long while," she continued. "Breathing. Moving. Being any kind of happy is the most painful thing you've ever felt, because they can't feel that anymore. That's why I wanted to be here, not Kairos. But he's waiting for you. Sick and worried."

I opened my eyes, and it felt like my whole face was full of salt water, like I'd nearly drowned. Maybe I had—or maybe I'd been crying so much it was the same thing. She knew how this felt because she had lost more than I had—so many siblings and her parents, all at once. Time had taken them from me one by one, but it was different for her.

For them. Kairos was sick because he knew what this felt like. He didn't want it for me.

"You've lost so much," she whispered. "It's so unfair that you had more taken away from you."

More? She didn't mean—

"Your sister is here, and safe," she said quickly.

"Where is here?" I asked, finally.

"Your ship," she said. "We're tied to ours, still in the harbor. It will take a while for the effects of—well, for the effects to wear off before Kata can drain the communes again. There will be more fighting, probably, and a lot of other things to do. But everyone seems to think we'll hold the territory."

"You and your damn war," I spat.

"There are bodies," she said, and she moved the cloth along

my arm. "In the water. Hundreds of them, mostly soldiers. Mostly soldiers—I say it like that makes it better. Did they know what they were getting into? No, I don't think they did. I think they were grateful not to be the ones inside the communes, and it was only an accident of fate that spared them from that life. And another accident of fate to take that life away—I wonder, if they knew, if they would have chosen the communes."

*If they knew.* There had been so much sadness in my brother's eyes when he asked if fate would change—I thought he was talking about me. Maybe he was, but maybe he knew what he had seen, knew he was going to die. I should have seen it.

Another tear was stripped away from me, and I wished I could light it—or something—on fire.

"Even as the child that my husband thought he killed kicks in my womb, I wonder if I would have chosen differently. If someone told me how many people would die today, if I would have chosen the same."

"And?" I couldn't help but ask, bitterness turning my throat to acid.

"If it had just been me," she said with a sigh. "Maybe I would have laid down my life. Maybe it would have cost just as many in another way, but I think, faced with the true cost, I would have done it. But when I found out my baby was alive, and every moment since then—I can't. I could never choose to do anything but fight to protect her."

"We came here for you," I snarled, but it sounded piteous. "For your damn baby, for *his* damn broken heart. I knew—I never would have done this. I knew I was making a mistake, and I did it for him. You cost me my brother."

Her soft hand was cool on my face, and I lost more precious tears. "I know, dear one. I know."

"You had your brothers," I accused. "For years, you had them and you were happy and whole. I just got him. I just got him, and you stole him from me."

"Sit up," she told me, frowning and her eyes bright with tears. "I can't hug you properly while you're lying down and I'll hurt myself if I lift you, so Skies Above, sit up."

To my horror and humiliation, I obeyed her. She came onto the cot with her swelling belly and hugged me tight, and everything I had shattered. I sobbed until I felt empty, and full, and broken, and drowning. I sobbed until my head pounded and the burn on my neck and face seared and I could hardly open my eyes.

The tears ended. Even though I tried, it wasn't possible to drown myself like that, and eventually, I was so sore and tired I didn't have anything left to cry, so I left the cabin.

Kairos was right by my door, his eyes heavy and full and sad, and to my horror, I shied away from his gaze. I couldn't—I didn't even know. I just couldn't.

The hallway was narrow enough that I had to brush by him, but he just let me go. I think I hated that even more than I hated the idea of seeing him, or talking to him, or touching him.

I found Pera up on the stern deck, like she knew it was the last place I'd really spoken with Gryph. She was leaning on the railing, gazing out at the Summer Palace.

She glanced at me as I came close, a guarded fear in her eyes.

"Hey," I said softly.

She leaned harder on the railing, ignoring me.

"Are you hurt?" I asked.

She shook her head. "No. I'll get out of your way as soon as the water's gone."

I frowned. She thought she was leaving me? Hells, I didn't have to give her the option to leave me, did I? I wasn't *that* fair of a captain. "You're not in my way."

She huffed out a breath. "Sure I am. I show up, try to kill you, and ruin your happily ever after with Gryph. You did notice that I got him killed, right?"

The words burst in my chest like one of the explosions. How many times had I dealt with this—she was hurting, and I knew that, and she was using it to lash out at me, but damn, just hearing his name burned. "He killed himself, Pera," I whispered.

"Right. After Danae—who taught me how to use my power, by the way, and I even spent considerable time thinking I had her to replace losing you—cut him and made him think he had to. After I attacked you, not knowing—not knowing *anything*," she snapped.

"And I attacked you right back," I told her. "You weren't the only one who didn't know."

"I'm not staying here," she said, turning to face me with tears in her eyes. "What, you and Gryph have been living out your perfect lives without me and now you think, well, one sibling's dead, guess I might as well replace him?"

"Pera," I started, but I reached my hand for her and she jerked back.

"I'm not even sad!" she screamed at me. "I just lost my brother and I'm not sad because I didn't even know him. You both abandoned me so I don't get to be sad about him!"

"Stop!" I heard, and I sighed as Arnav stormed right up to her. She pushed him away, but he kept yelling at her. "Don't be a child and yell at her because you don't know how to talk about what you're really feeling," he said. "Your sister takes on a lot of hurt for other people. And she just found your brother. And they were both slaves. No one abandoned you by choice. Your sister would never do that."

I blinked, a little stunned to hear that come out of his mouth. "Um, thank you, Arnav."

He scowled, but shrugged at me. Then he looked back to Pera. "And you get to be sad about anything you want," he told her. "Even if it doesn't make sense."

She didn't respond, just crossed her arms. Then she loosed one to swipe a tear away and crossed them again.

Arnav ducked his head, glancing at me again before leaving us alone.

"You were a slave?" she asked, and her mouth twisted and shook.

I touched my scar, but it was partially covered by bandaging because of the burn. "That's how I got this," I told her. Then I looked around and added, "Really that's how I've gotten all of this. Good and bad."

"Who . . . owns you?" she asked, and slapped at another tear.

"No one, now," I told her. "I'm the captain of this ship. Everyone who crews it has been a freed slave too."

Her eyes followed to where Arnav stood on the steps with his back to us. "Him too?"

I leaned on the railing, and the stretch reminded me that just about every part of me was sore. "You don't have to stay with us, but no matter where you go, you're not getting rid of me. I've been searching for you for a very long time."

She looked at me, her arms still crossed, but tears were rolling down her cheeks and she was trying so hard to fight them back she was nearly purple. "You have?" she asked.

It was important that she could see my eyes, my face, and I turned to her fully before I promised her, "Yes."

She covered her face then, sobbing freely like I had done not long before, and I slowly pulled her into my arms. She didn't hug me back, but she leaned against me, and for now, that was more than enough.

She went to sleep for a while, and I told her to sleep in my cabin while I sat on the stern deck, my back against the rail, just trying to breathe and feel the ocean beneath me. I didn't try to reach out with my power just then. I didn't want it. I didn't think I'd ever want it again.

Navya came and sat beside me. She didn't say anything, just mimicked my position and sat beside me. Silent. I knew why—it had always been this way between us. We would never have the perfect words or anything that could fix the horrible things we faced together, but we showed up. We stuck together, and we showed up.

Slowly, the rest of the crew filtered in. Sophy sniffed and sat on my other side, looking at Navya. "Did you tell her yet?" she asked.

Navya shook her head slowly.

I looked to Sophy.

"We lost Addy and Kamil," she said. I only had to find Mihal's ashen face beside her to know Kamil was one of the people I hadn't bothered to learn the names of. Now in death, I'd never forget it.

"How?" I asked, my throat hoarse.

"One of the cells," Mihal offered. "It didn't have any slaves, just more soldiers. We weren't expecting that."

I nodded, closing my eyes. I reached over to Sophy and Navya both, and took their hands, and just held still as this new pain shoved its way down my throat, circling my heart and curling along my ribs. Staying there, where it would always stay.

I knew before I opened my eyes when Kairos arrived. He sat down between Arnav and Copper, and I felt the electric pulse of his energy when he connected their hands. It took me a long moment to realize that everyone, every member of the crew, had joined hands together, like we still knew how to pray.

Maybe it was more like the power, and we didn't know how to grieve, or give grief up. We just knew how to share it with those around us.

My eyes fell on his, and I kept breathing. He looked so tired and ragged and hurt. I felt my own cruelty again, of not letting him in, of not touching him and kissing him and doing all the things I wanted to do. Things I couldn't imagine doing, not when my heart felt like this. Things I had to do, when I could see the pain in his face.

He just gave me a tiny smile and a gentle nod.

Other people drifted up the stairs in front of him. A tall, handsome man with green eyes was helping Shalia up the stairs protectively, like she might tumble down them and shatter like glass. I frowned and wondered if that happened to women in her state.

Behind them, the pale girl and a man who had to be another desert sibling. He looked the worst of all of them, and I recognized something in him. He was taking on all their hurt, just like I was. He felt responsible for it.

I wondered if he was always the oldest sibling, or if he had come into it after the tragedy of their family.

To my surprise, my crew shifted, making space for them in the circle. We dropped hands to slide and move, and we didn't pick them up again, but the energy stayed the same. Shalia leaned against her brother, and I saw sadness as she did so. I wondered if he told them what he'd been through without them. Even the most basic details—hearing your brother had been a slave was enough to break your heart.

Finally, Pera came slowly up and sat on the very edge of our strange group, dragging her knees up and putting her head on them.

"What happens now?" I asked softly, looking to Kairos.

He rubbed his sister's arm, but it was the pale girl who answered. "The Resistance has taken the communes," she said, and the words fizzled over my skin. My home was free. It wasn't much, it wasn't everything, but this part of the Trifectate that had been responsible for so much pain was now beyond the reach of its cruel king.

"Now we need to hold it, and secure allies for the war to come. It will be a while before we can make the water go back—my power is faulty at best until the blood completely disappears, and the jetty is broken and I can't get a good current in from the sea. Shalia's working on that. But there are people on the ships and still stranded in the communes who need food and supplies."

"And the soldiers," the green-eyed man said. Then I remembered—*she* was his sister. The bitch who hurt my brother.

I looked at Pera and Kairos and Shalia and Navya and all the others. Sisters were sisters. Family was inalienable. "Did she get away?" I asked roughly, looking at him. "Your sister."

His eyes lingered on me for a long time, and Shalia reached out to touch him. He nodded slowly. "I think she swam past the jetty. We haven't been able to find her." His throat worked. "I am so sorry for what she did to you."

There would be another day, when I could acknowledge the pain I'd seen in her, but not yet. I nodded to him. "So we need to get back through the communes—without powers."

Kata shook her head. "When you're feeling up to it, the wind shouldn't be affected by the blood. The water contained it."

*Up to it.* Not likely. "What else?" I asked. "What do we do *now?*"

"We need to feed everyone," Sophy said with a heavy sigh.

"The Summer Palace is large enough," Shalia offered. "Once it's . . . once we clean it a little."

The green-eyed man scrubbed his face with his hands. "Clean it a lot," he corrected.

"We need to burn the dead," Kairos said, his voice low.

"Bury them," the green-eyed man countered. "Here, burning is a disrespectful death. Not like the desert."

Kairos nodded, and I nodded too, looking around. "Then we should get to work," I said.

I stood first, and everyone slowly got to their feet as I started to assign tasks. We lowered dinghies into the water and sent crews out to row through the passageways with food and supplies, but I hesitated when I thought of sending anyone out to the Summer Palace.

"I'll go to the palace," Sophy told me, reading my mind. "We'll get food and cook it and start sending it out to the rowboats. Our supplies will only take them so far."

"Sophy, the blood—" I told her, and my whole body hurt.

She met my eyes. "I can clean a little blood, Captain. Don't worry." She started calling out a crew to come with her, and Navya called out names for another boat to go over to the floating ships of freed slaves, including picking someone who looked like the ill-begotten son of an ox and a god who had been on Shalia's ship.

"Is that a khopesh?" I asked when he turned around and showed a massive blade strapped to his back, but he was too far away to hear me.

"That is Zeph," Kairos told me, standing a foot or two away and putting his hands behind his back. I didn't like that. "He is the self-appointed and slightly overprotective defender of my unborn niece."

"How does he wield a khopesh with one arm?" I marveled. "Those are massive. I've only ever seen them in the Wyverns."

"Arrogantly," he assured me. "But the one-arm part is new."

He was still keeping his hands away from me, so I stepped closer, closing my eyes and letting our foreheads touch. He issued a low, soft grunt, and I let my nose drag over the tip of his. "You're hurting," I told him.

"You're hurting worse," he said, and his hands touched my hips. It felt like I could breathe again when he touched me. "And you're hurting because I couldn't stop him. I didn't get to him in time."

"You would have given your life to stop him if you could," I breathed. I knew that. I believed in that more than any gods or fate or destiny. That was real. That was true.

He nodded a little. "Shalia said I should let her patch you up. Then you couldn't look at me."

I nodded. I couldn't even explain or mitigate that feeling for him.

"I know this particular kind of hurt," he whispered. "I'm sorry I couldn't save you from it. I'm sorry I failed again."

I pushed forward, wrapping my body around his. "I failed too," I whispered. "We all failed."

He hugged me tight, and shivers that started in me ended in him. "You told your family what happened to you?" I asked, soft in his ear.

He nodded, rubbing my back, his grip hard and still loving. He squeezed the muscles in the back of my neck, and even though it was too close to the burn, it felt good. "It felt so wrong. They hear slavery, and they think I went through things like everyone else on this ship. But it wasn't the same."

"Don't compare your pain to others'," I told him. "Your experience scarred you the same way it did for all of us."

He shook his head. "I never lost hope. I never stopped believing I would be free. I put so much faith in fate, and I don't know why. I don't know why, Asp."

"Because you are hope," I whispered. "The same way I am chaos. We see all the dark places in the world, and we still stand up. We still fight." I shuddered. "He knew, didn't he? Was that what you two spoke about?"

"Me and Gryphon?" he asked.

I nodded. "He knew what the vision meant."

Kairos kissed my cheek, my ear. "Yes, he knew."

The shaking went deeper inside me. "And he still went. And he still fought."

"Chaos and hope," he breathed. "Just like his sisters."

"Chaos and hope," I repeated, and this time, when I cried, the tears ran off onto Kairos's skin, and it felt like they never really left me at all.

We cleaned up. There was more fighting—skirmishes here and there once the water receded—but the vast majority of soldiers donned the green dragon that those loyal to Shalia's lover—Galen, apparently—sported. Those who didn't were sent away on the road to the capital, a decision that shocked me. Kairos tried to explain that these men once all followed Galen, and that I had done the same thing with Bast. Chances were, he would come back to resist me again, but that didn't mean I could kill him outright.

It almost made sense to me then. Almost.

Shalia broke the road after they'd left, and there was no way a non-Elementae army was getting back through to the communes.

The slaves we freed wanted to leave. Some wanted to stay— this was the only home they'd ever known—but most wanted to leave, never trusting that a new regime didn't mean new chains. I didn't blame them, and I volunteered to take them to Sarocca and get amnesty from the king. I was fairly certain I could talk him into it, and if I couldn't I'd find them somewhere safe.

On the fourth day, Kairos and I and the rest of the crew left the ship. I held tightly to Kairos's hand as we walked up the muddy path to the Summer Palace. On the green hillside beside it, there were more than a hundred black holes marring the earth.

Graves. So many graves.

We started with the smallest wrapped bodies—Gryphon, Addy, and Kamil. We gathered near the places they would be laid in the earth, and I gripped Kairos tighter than could have possibly been comfortable.

Everyone shifted to look at me. I had never actually seen someone buried before—I didn't know what to do.

"She doesn't have to say anything," Navya said. "We all know how brave he was. He stopped the Trifectate from using him against us all. His sacrifice was incredible."

Pera came and stood beside me, meeting my gaze fiercely.

"He was definitely brave," I agreed softly. "But let's not pretend these were good deaths. These were not honorable or right or good. They were horrible, and senseless, like so many other things in this damn world. Addy was even younger than him," I said, pain bashing around inside my chest again. "And the fact that Kamil was a year or two older doesn't make his death any better. There are so many things in this world that are just designed to inflict pain on others. That's just how it works."

I shut my eyes, and I saw Gryphon smiling at me, even when Kairos's vision had shown him there was no place for him in the future and he knew what that meant. "But all three of them were brave. And they were full of hope and happiness, and more than anything else, knowing all the awful things we face, that seems like the most radical act. They were the most courageous rebels among us. Their deaths had nothing to do with anger and retribution, and everything about love and hope."

I shut my eyes, and Kairos's arms were around me, sheltering me. I looked at his sister, and she was crying as she lowered them into the graves with her power and covered them over, and Galen comforted her as she cried.

"She never got this," Kairos whispered. "She never got to say good-bye to our family."

I sighed against his head, shaking mine. "You can never say good-bye to family," I told him.

I clung to Kairos as Galen walked forward, going to the grave of every soldier and murmuring three times over every grave some prayer I probably should have recognized. It seemed like he knew all the soldiers, but that couldn't have been possible, and I wasn't ready to wonder whether the magnitude of grief was measured in the number of lives you lost or how much they meant to you.

# Rewrite a Path in the Stars

The communes had changed. After the burial, everyone went to the large soldiers' section of the communes, and there was a heavy sort of celebration that was victory and mourning in one. Fisk played his instrument, and he kept Addy's on a chair beside him, silent and still. I watched Galen and Shalia dance—they looked so very sad, so tired, and yet they stared into each other's eyes, and she'd give a soft smile, and he'd smile back, and I could see it. It was so clear how much they loved each other. How solid and unquestioned that was.

My gaze drifted, and I saw Kairos watching them. He loved them both—in different ways, for sure, but he loved them. His brother Rian was beside him, and they spoke, and they both smiled, sharing a grin. Kata came, her pale hair looking like silver, and she smiled at Kairos's brother and took his hands, drawing him out near his sister. His smile changed as he looked at her, hot and smug, pulling her back against him and kissing her.

Kairos met my eyes, and his grin wasn't as cocky as usual,

but it was on its way there. He came past people slowly to get to me, leaning against the same wall I was leaning against, facing me.

I smiled up at him. "I leave in the morning," I told him softly.

"We leave in the morning," he corrected.

Sighing, I looked over to his family and shook my head. "No, Kairos. I'm leaving alone. You can't leave them. Not when they just got you back. Not after what's happened. I can't do that."

He caught my hand, bringing my fingers to his mouth and pressing his smile to my knuckles. "Oh, my sweet. The only one I'm not leaving—ever, if I can help it—is you."

"I can't stay here," I told him, even as my heart thrilled at that. "I have to get those people settled. We have to get back to the village. And Pera—I don't know what I'll do about Pera."

"I wasn't asking you to stay here," he said, and having kissed every knuckle, switched to my fingertips. "I'm coming with you. Salt in our blood, all that."

"But your sister—"

"Needs foreign allies right now. And to know these people are safe. Do you believe in marriage?" he asked.

"What?"

"Do you believe in marriage?"

I frowned. "No, not particularly. Mostly I think it's done for religious or political reasons, and I don't have many of those."

"Well, I guess I won't ask you to marry me then. What about all those children I saw?" he asked.

My skin flushed, and maddeningly, he kept kissing my hand, moving to the wrist now. "Well, I don't think a war is a good time to start a family, but I'm not opposed to the general idea."

"Fantastic," he said, kissing his way up my arm and using it to pull me closer.

I closed the gap, pressing against him as his arms clasped around me, and I stroked his cheeks with both my hands. "Kairos. I can't take you away from them."

"You can leave me behind," he said. "But I will always come for you. I will always find you. You can sail over every ocean you can find, but my heart will always want yours. You move the heaven and stars when I'm with you, Aspasia. I won't ever want to leave my family in an unsafe situation, and I will always try to go to their aid when needed, but so will you. No matter where that takes us. We will go there together, and rewrite a path in the stars."

I drew a long, shaky, nervous breath, looking into his eyes. I knew what it was now to look at someone's face like you could stare at them for hours, always seeing more, never tiring of the view. Of the love in his eyes. He loved me. I loved him.

"And Gryph told me to."

I wrinkled my nose. "What?"

"He told me to always stay by your side. He told me we belonged together. I don't intend to dishonor his memory."

I frowned hard at him. "Did he really say that? Or are you just invoking my dead brother's memory to get me to do what you want?"

"What we both want," he said, smiling. "And I will never tell, about the rest."

"Kairos, that is really cruel if he didn't say that to—" I started, but he laughed and kissed me. I pulled back. "I am serious." He kissed me again.

And what a kiss. A deep, soft kiss that somehow made it

possible for me to feel sad and hurt and also very much in love with the man on the other end of it.

Kairos stopped abruptly but didn't move far from my mouth. "He definitely said it," he whispered against my lips. He kissed the corner of my jaw, right by my ear, and paused, breathing gently against me so I felt his breath warm my neck.

I curled my hands into his shirt, leaning against him, resting my head against his neck. He hugged me, the moment turning from lust to comfort in a blink, and I felt my power taking his warm breath and threading it around me.

It was still there. I wasn't ready to use it, but I knew there would be a day when I was. Just like there would be a day when I wanted Kairos's lust more than his comfort—my power was just another part of me, and I was free to use them all. I was free to love, and grow, and maybe start a family without fearing that my children would be slaves.

That wasn't true yet. That fear would always be there, because I had known too much of how the world worked. But I wasn't afraid anymore. I was going to stand by Kairos's side and fight to change that world, not just desperately try to clean up the messes that protected, pampered monarchs created.

Maybe not in my lifetime, but I would make sure my children—our children—inherited a world without slavery.

"Look," he told me softly.

I followed his hand to the wall. We were near the very corner of it, and there, in the dark, were little drawings on the stone, maybe made with something burned rather than ink. I ran my fingers over it reverently. "Apparently even soldiers need to create something joyful," I said.

Kairos kissed my temple. "Art is the language of hope," he agreed.

"Damned hope," I whispered sadly.

"Damned, difficult, joyful, beautiful hope," he said.

"Damned, difficult, joyful, beautiful hope," I whispered back.

# Acknowledgments

I have to admit, writing this book's acknowledgments feels a little anticlimactic after revealing a debilitating disease in the last book.

Fortunately, I don't have any news to report on that front—my eyes are very stable, my diabetes is doing great, and I have not needed Herculean efforts to support and protect me and my heart recently.

So it may make these acknowledgments sound less dramatic, but the support, love, help, and friendship I've received have been no less powerful.

So let's talk about the various crews that made this book possible, shall we?

To Mary Kate, captain of the stalwart vessel Editorial in the Bloomsbury fleet, thank you for your love and support, and the way that you always push me to consider deeper, think harder, and become a better writer with everything I write. I am so lucky and proud to continue working with you! To Claire, Lizzy, Emily,

Erica, Courtney, Cristina, Cindy, Beth, Brittany, Oona, Melissa, Donna—thank you for making both this book and my career shipshape (weighing anchors, filling sails, swabbing decks, calls to ports, and so forth). I so appreciate that you stand with me and this book!

To my agent and first mate in my career, Minju—thank you for always keeping a weather eye on the horizon and steering us away from coming storms. I love sailing this ocean with you!

To those vicious pirates on board the feared ship Jolly Writers, including First Mates Tara Sullivan, Katie Slivensky, Allison Pottern Hoch, and Annie Cardi, and my beloved crew Tiffany Schmidt, Diana Renn, all the Erins (Bowman, Cashman, Dionne), Gina Rosati, Sarah Aronson, Elly Swartz, Emery Lord, Trish Doller, Cristin Bishara, Zoraida Cordova, the marauding collectives known only as the Apocalypsies and Class of 2k12, I will always have some rum (tea) to raise in your direction and drink with you when we meet. Thank you for all the adventures!

To all those bloggers, readers, and fans with the proverbial knife in your teeth and bookish flag snapping in the breeze, thank you for sailing all around the internet to share your love for me and this series. Thank you to the #Elementae as a group, and in particular What Sarah Read, Andi's ABCs, Miss Melissa Lee, and Irisheyz77. And to all independent bookstores, but especially Buttonwood Books, thank you so much for your love and support.

To my Girl Scouts flotilla, including but in no way limited to Amy, Jennifer L, Liz, Lori, Danielle, Pi, Heather, Kim, Kelly, Padma, Eleni, KT, CW, Shelly, Molly, Olivia, Joanna, Jennifer T, Cristina, Evalyn, Daniel—I mean literally all of you, you redefine

Go-Getter, Innovator, Risk-Taker, and Leader for me every day. You are constant inspirations and I am so grateful to be sister to all of you.

To the crew that I have stashed all around the world and in every corner of my heart, including my St Andrews battalion Ashley, Iggy, Alex; HGSE blackguards Caitlin, Jenna, Tyme, Holly, Leigh, Jo, Aysha, Juliet, Scott, and of course, of course, Steve—thank you so much for pushing my thinking and my heart; high school swashbucklers Jenna, Courtney, Beth, Nora, Robin, and Andrea; and to my favorite villains of all time: Leah, Renee, and Nacie, I am stronger, smarter, happier, and full of joy for having you in my life. Thank you and love you!

There is crew, and then there is family. Alisa, I mean, I've only been through this once so far but a) I'm pretty sure I lucked out, and b) I think there's a big difference between being My Brother's Wife and being My Sister, and you are absolutely the latter. I am so grateful for you and love this beautiful family that you have created and invited the rest of us to participate in. I love you! Kevin and Michael, you are the best brothers—I love how you show up on my tour stops and every event you possibly can, get copies of audio books or foreign editions before I even know they are out there, and generally keep a better eye on my career than I do. Your support reminds me that I can do this, and that this whole career is still kind of a miracle. I love you.

Alison—God I hope this isn't a spoiler, but welcome to the family (can the Gaughen Girls officially be the A Team now?!)! Love you!

To Papa, there is a significant part of this book that was born the first time you took me out on the water. Somewhere in an alternate universe I'm still there, hanging on the railing of the *Indomitable Spark*'s bowsprit, pretending I'm a pirate and a mermaid and a god as we plunge down over the crest of a wave. Thank you for giving me that incredible sense of vast wonder and those beautiful memories. I love you.

To Mumma, thank you for showing me that family is everything—and when you open your heart and love people *like* family, you'll have a richness in your life beyond compare. Thank you for making me feel like everything I accomplish is special—I always strive to be the woman that you see when you look at me. I love you.

To Little C, I wonder daily what the world will look like through your eyes as you grow up. I want to fill it with art, and hope, and family, and freedom, and love so that you can have all of those things without having to fight for them. From here on out, this one, and every one, is for you. I love you.

KAITLYN LITCHFIELD

**A. C. GAUGHEN** is the author of the Elementae series and of *Scarlet*, *Lady Thief*, and *Lion Heart*. She serves as a learning specialist for the Girl Scouts of Eastern Massachusetts and on the board of the nonprofit Boston GLOW, creating opportunities to encourage and engage teen girls in the Greater Boston area. She has a master's in creative writing from St. Andrews University in Scotland and a master's in education from Harvard University.

www.acgaughen.com
@acgaughen